FUTURE EARTH

Copyright © 2023 Mark Alan Lindsley.

All rights reserved. No part of this book may be used or reproduced by any means, graphic, electronic, or mechanical, including photocopying, recording, taping or by any information storage retrieval system without the written permission of the author except in the case of brief quotations embodied in critical articles and reviews.

This is a work of fiction. All of the characters, names, incidents, organizations, and dialogue in this novel are either the products of the author's imagination or are used fictitiously.

Archway Publishing books may be ordered through booksellers or by contacting:

Archway Publishing
1663 Liberty Drive
Bloomington, IN 47403
www.archwaypublishing.com
844-669-3957

Because of the dynamic nature of the Internet, any web addresses or links contained in this book may have changed since publication and may no longer be valid. The views expressed in this work are solely those of the author and do not necessarily reflect the views of the publisher, and the publisher hereby disclaims any responsibility for them.

Any people depicted in stock imagery provided by Getty Images are models, and such images are being used for illustrative purposes only. Certain stock imagery © Getty Images.

ISBN: 978-1-6657-4793-6 (sc)
ISBN: 978-1-6657-4795-0 (hc)
ISBN: 978-1-6657-4794-3 (e)

Library of Congress Control Number: 2023914607

Print information available on the last page.

Archway Publishing rev. date: 11/02/2023

FUTURE EARTH

A POST-APOCALYPTIC WORLD AT THE END OF TIME

MARK ALAN LINDSLEY

Dedicated to all those who believe.

The inability of the mind to correlate all the world's contents is a most merciful thing. Living on a calm island of ignorance amid the raging seas of infinity, we were never meant to venture far. Old Earth science has hitherto harmed us little, yet someday the piecing together of that ancient knowledge will unlock such terrifying vistas of reality, and of our own frightful position therein, that we shall either go mad from the revelation or flee from the deadly awakening of enlightenment into the peace and security of a new dark age.

—Kiel, First Commander,
Imperial Intelligence Service

ONE

a VIEW FROM THE NORTH

> I am falling. Blackness covers my face.
> —Ignotum pro Magna,
> Terminus 8:62—63

Kiel looked down through the transparency of his personal keep, absently watching an Eligor army column slowly rumble toward the northern battlements of Opal. What could be seen of the sky above had darkened to slate as great billowing clouds piled over the city threateningly, causing the growing gloom of the approaching twilight to deepen.

"Ah, how apropos. A storm approaches."

Lightning flickered in the distance, followed by an angry peal of thunder that rumbled over the city and through the darkened room. Several chance raindrops thumped noisily against the diamond-paned transparency, momentarily distorting the view with rivulets of liquid crystal.

"And soon it breaks."

A cold shudder ran through Kiel's heavily muscled shoulders as he stood, lost in a kind of instinctive listening. The sounds of booted feet, of clanking armor, and of the endless trundling supply wagons all faded as the last of the soldiers were lost in the dusty haze of an autumn afternoon—vanishing, it seemed, as were the empire's days of glory.

Although Kiel was not a superstitious man, a particularly grim verse from the Ignotum pro Magna ghosted through his mind concerning the end days, as foretold in the last chapters of Terminus.

"I am falling."

Kiel's troubled thoughts were suddenly interrupted as the communication terminal crackled to life behind him.

"Commander? Commander Kiel?" a static-interspersed voice called.

After a moment's hesitation, Kiel turned and walked purposefully to the terminal, depressing the response stud with a weighty claw. "Yes, what is it, Lieutenant Thorn?"

"Commander, the package from Kirsk has arrived," came Thorn's tense response.

"The body of the Ikonian?" Kiel asked sharply, feeling the scales on his neck rise in anticipation. At long last! He'd been waiting for this news.

"Yes, sir. It is being readied by the bioweapons personnel on sublevel six. You wished to oversee the autopsy?"

"I'm on my way."

"Understood, Commander."

The crackling of the grid faded as lightning again painted the rock walls of the room and thunder boomed, closer this time. Releasing the response stud, Kiel set his jaw.

"I will see this invader—this mythic Ikonian devil. Other matters can wait."

Kiel exited his chambers, swiftly navigating the timeworn corridors and spiral stone staircases. Guards, manning entrances and checkpoints, snapped to attention with drill-trained impenetrable eyes. Red circles—symbols of the Imperial Intelligence Service—glinted against black leather uniforms. Kiel glided through grand halls and connecting passageways strewn with the debris of neglected cracked masonry, torn tapestries, and broken, meticulously designed stained glass windows where dust motes danced in dim multicolored shafts of fading daylight at his passing.

Entering a transit tube, he turned to take in the gallery he had just traversed. The tube's door slowly slid shut, erasing the scene of decay.

Perhaps these truly are the apocalyptic end days as prophesied in the Ignotum pro Magna, Kiel thought as shadow enveloped him.

As the tube began its silent descent, the cryptic verse from Terminus came again to Kiel's mind, the words seeming to foretell current events: "I am falling. Blackness covers my face."

Six levels beneath the ancient city of Opal, Kiel exited the transit tube. The pervasive smell of mildew, intermingled with something less pleasant, assaulted his senses.

Thorn, dutifully waiting, saluted smartly, touching the ground and then his forehead in the Eligor fashion. Stepping in beside Kiel, he motioned.

"If you will please follow me, sir."

"Lead on, Lieutenant, and be quick."

Kiel followed the soldier as he hurried through the cold, cobweb-bedecked catacombs with a growing sense of anticipation. *Finally, a bit of luck!* Finally, the army had retrieved a specimen of their foe, a member of that enigmatic race that had suddenly and inexplicably sacked the northern city of Kirsk, killing all in their path, unmerciful, unstoppable. Admittedly, a live capture would have been better, but even a corpse could be made to reveal secrets.

At the end of the winding passage, a creaking iron door automatically trundled into a wall recess, revealing a vaulted amphitheater filled with watchful soldiers and bioweapons personnel, all of whom stood silent, waiting. Leather uniforms creaked and boots shuffled as Kiel surveyed the chamber. A collection of knives, saws, hooks, and other, less identifiable implements glinted on a linen-covered table, mere props in the melodrama about to be acted out. Yet it was the center of this gothic arena that inevitably drew Kiel's attention, for there, lying on a wheeled gurney was the lifeless body of an Ikonian.

"Macabre," Kiel muttered, closing on the corpse.

"Black devils," Thorn hissed, involuntarily slowing, while his golden eyes widened in disbelief. With a warning glance from Kiel, the lieutenant quickly reverted to his severe posture.

Kiel returned his gaze to the inert body before him; wisps of vapor rose, swirling in serpentine tendrils about the corpse, adding another surreal dimension to the scene. It was not difficult to see why Thorn had momentarily forgotten his military etiquette. The Ikonian, lying stiffly, its sharply angular head arced back at an unnatural angle, was totally alien in appearance. Even the brutish, shambling apelike humans seemed more acceptable by comparison.

There was no questioning why some within the empire had begun referring to Ikonians as "insect men"; certainly, the creature stretched before Kiel resembled a two-meter tall bipedal arthropod. Six legs, or rather, two legs and four arms, branched away from a streamlined chitinous thorax pigmented with a polychromatic blend of browns, greens, and yellows.

"Natural camouflage," Kiel muttered. "Impressive."

Kiel's limited knowledge of Ikonians had come from his studies at the Eligor Military Academy. He recalled those dusty parchments filled with strange illustrations cobbled from rumor, legend, and myth, scowling even more as his memories returned. There were disturbing differences between those ancient sketches and the body that now rested before him—principally among them, this specimen was clothed.

The insect resting before Kiel wore a tight dark green garment, seeming to be military by way of its cut. A peculiar slumbering face, its forehead engraved with a seven-sided glyph, adorned the front of a protective formfitting helmet. Two oversized compound eyes glinted from under the rim of the helmet as Kiel stared back in meditative thought. Something about this creature smelled of the Old Earth, and he found the aroma most distressing.

The sound of approaching footsteps brought Kiel out of his momentary funk. He lifted his uneasy gaze from the lifeless creature and focused on an old, spindly Eligor who stood regally before him, inwardly wincing as he did so.

"Sar, it's been an age and thrice again," Kiel said, greeting the Bioweapons Division's senior officer coolly.

"Ah, Kiel," Sar returned in a derisive tone, eyeing the commander of Imperial Intelligence as if he were looking at an inferior. "You recall my name? Your memory has certainly improved over time. A pity it was not so reliable in your days at the academy."

Kiel smiled a mirthless smile. "Charming to the last as always. Yet as I recall, I was one of your most promising students—a student who is now, technically speaking, your superior."

"Most promising, you say?" Sar chuckled mockingly, ignoring Kiel's implied warning. "I retract my previous statement regarding your improved memory."

Kiel's golden eyes narrowed. "You may begin the autopsy," he ordered in a measured tone.

Sar, grinning imperiously, turned to the task at hand, impatiently gesturing to three junior bioweapons scientists, who began cutting the outer garments away from the Ikonian. *Not with ease,* Kiel noted, forgetting his anger toward Sar. Unlike ordinary cloth, the fabric of this creature's uniform could not be easily cut; rather, it had to be forced open with metal shears.

"The garment is obviously some kind of advanced armor, possibly Old Earth in make," Sar began lecturing, then scratching his observations in a notebook. "This would explain why our soldiers did not fare well at the Battle of Kirsk."

Did not fare well? It was a ridiculous statement. It had been a massacre, and the old scientist well knew it. But concerning the uniform, Sar seemed to be correct. Kiel's scales crawled. To see authentic Old Earth technology, with its ancient, near-magical aura, worn by a primitive Ikonian was most distressing.

Sar continued to spout more theories and to conjecture while the fabric was slowly ripped and peeled back, exposing more and more of the variegated body beneath. "The fabric is quite possibly an advanced form of fibrous polymerized protein, something akin to the high-tensile-strength, high-elasticity material used in Old Earth body armor. Just imagine, for a moment, if you could synthesize spider silk. Then it would be possible to—"

Kiel rubbed his scaled forehead with a weary hand while Sar droned. Obviously, it had been some time since the decrepit old lizard had cornered an audience. *Let him make the most of it—for now.*

"And look." Sar set aside his notebook, grabbed one of the creature's arms, and carefully folded it. A sharp-edged bladelike growth, fused to the elbow, swiveled away from a recess in the upper member. Sar touched the appendage gingerly. "Clearly a biological defense. Note the elongated ulnar spur. We are probably looking at an insect that has been bred specifically for soldiering. Ikonians might be split into castes like, say, ants or termites: workers, soldiers, farmers." Sar prattled for a time. "Further, I would not be surprised to find that these spurs are poisonous."

"Poisonous?" Kiel looked up with new interest.

"Certainly poisonous," Sar stated confidently. "An insect of this type would have the ability to biosynthesize organic compounds of a neurotoxic and/or histolytic nature—alkaloids, piperidines, formic acid ..." Sar continued to gingerly test the blade weapon as he lectured.

"Is it sharp?" To Kiel, the strange appendage seemed to glisten like the blade of an Eligor triple-fold steel sword.

"Biological weapons of this nature can be, and usually are, sharper than steel edges," Sar explained. "The composition of this blade—polysaccharides and matrix proteins—would allow a creature of this sort to—"

Tan Ru, a junior scientist, mercifully interrupted what promised to be another agonizing discourse before it began. "We've found something, Sar," he called in a reedy voice. "Look here."

Both Sar and Kiel edged closer to the examination table. Others in the chamber muttered nervously. The Ikonian's uniform was stretched back, revealing a metallic blister fused directly onto the shell of the creature's upper right forearm.

Kiel elbowed Sar aside and eyed the device. Yes, his foreshadowing had been correct. This was, had to be, Old Earth technology—and of a previously unknown type.

Sar peered over Kiel's shoulder, equally mystified. He turned to the junior scientist. "Tan Ru, open that device immediately."

With some effort, Tan Ru pried open a protective cover, revealing approximately twenty translucent vials, each containing a liquid in varying hues of ocher. The mechanism was elegant in its complexity, but to Kiel, its purpose was an utter mystery.

Sar edged closer. "Look here," he piped, pushing Tan Ru aside once again. Tan Ru glanced at Kiel, who returned the look with a knowing gaze. Kiel watched while Sar peeled back muscle tissue and veins with yellowed claws.

"These vials are attached to tubes that feed directly into what I assume to be the circulatory system of the creature. And here"—he peered at a tubelike wire and traced its darkened shadow under the exoskeleton until it exited at the neck—"the arm device appears to be connected to the headgear by a cable running under the carapace."

Kiel stared uncomprehendingly. "Connected to the headgear? What is it about the headgear that would require a connection of this type?"

At Kiel's gesturing, Sar attempted to remove the creature's helmet, but it resisted his efforts. Kiel peered below the rim as Sar continued to tug at the covering.

"Correction," Kiel said grimly, restraining Sar's effort. "The blister is connected to the *head*, not the headgear."

Sar peeked under the helmet. It was true. The cable split into seven smaller wires that disappeared directly into the creature's cranium.

"Ghoulish and deliberate," Kiel remarked. "But again, I pose the question, why?"

Sar harrumphed. "Evidently it gives the wearer mental command over the device." His haughty voice carried a hint of the professor he used to be not tolerating ridiculous questions from an impudent student, even if the former student was a commander in the Intelligence Service and even if the question was relevant.

"Mental command? Is that possible?" Kiel asked, disbelieving.

Sar confidently continued. "I would hypothesize that the liquid in the vials can be pumped directly into the circulatory system of the Ikonian upon receiving a signal from its brain. Yes, quite obviously."

"If you are correct, then the liquids must have a function, but what function? And why would such a device happen to be implanted in this curious fashion?" Kiel leaned forward in growing wonder.

Sar stood grandly. "Any second-rate bioweapons scientist would venture, based on the fact that the vials are connected to the circulatory system, that they modify the creature's abilities in some way."

Kiel frowned but remained silent. It was a reach, but a logical reach.

Sar, now seemingly bent on proving his theory, shouldered his technicians back and began tugging at one of the vials in an attempt to dislodge it.

"Take caution, sir," Tan Ru said, as if it was often his role to protect his impulsive superior.

"Mind yourself!" Shooting an imperious look at Tan Ru, Sar grabbed a metal probing tool from the junior scientist's coat pocket and continued working. The metal tool immediately encountered a wire. A shower of sparks flew from the device.

"Black devils! Be careful with that thing!" Kiel growled as he and several of the junior scientists instinctively backed away. The guards in the back of the amphitheater began murmuring and shuffling uneasily.

As the last of the sparks faded, Sar looked over his shoulder. "It appears to be electrical," he turned back. "What's this?"

With a slow hissing sound, one of the vials automatically emptied itself into the Ikonian's lifeless body. Suddenly and without warning, the body jerked and began to move with deliberate life. The flat and lifeless glaze covering the eyes vanished, replaced by the shimmering intelligence of a now living being.

"Black devils! Get away from that thing!" Kiel barked, stumbling backward.

It was too late.

In a blur of movement, the scythe-like weapons protruding from the Ikonian's arm darted upward, impaling Sar, lifting the astonished scientist in the air, his boots crazily pattering and scraping on the ground beneath. Screaming scientists reeled back, escaping through the door, as wild-eyed guards moved quickly forward, not fully comprehending the chaos erupting around them.

The insect thing flung Sar's dying body aside, slid to the floor, and stood, moving its head to take in the room and its terror-stricken occupants. The arm device hissed again. The creature seemed to swell in size, and then it attacked.

One, two, and then three of the soldiers died within moments of the assault, expressions of confusion and disbelief contorting their dying faces. Thorn, mortally wounded, reeled back, colliding into Kiel, as the remaining guards screamed desperately for help.

Recovering from his momentary shock, Kiel quickly pulled helmet and sword from his dying lieutenant while the last of the guards, unprepared, unable to understand the nature of the horror that faced them, slid lifeless from the creature's arm blades.

The guards had unwittingly purchased Kiel a few extra seconds to analyze the threat. He hoped it would be enough. Unsheathing his sword, he cautiously approached the insect.

The Ikonian, turning to the new threat, eagerly accepted the challenge. In a flurry of action, the first commander of Imperial Intelligence collided with the lightning-quick Ikonian. It was a blinding sally of swordplay.

Within moments, the singing arm blades of the insect crashed into Kiel's helmeted head, causing a spray of blue sparks. Kiel staggered. His vision clouded momentarily.

By the All-father, what strength! This was going to be a thorny fight.

The Ikonian moved in closer, its slashing arm blades a blur of movement to Kiel, who barely sidestepped the agile, near-invisible attacker. The Ikonian pressed the fight harder, its chitinous daggers nearly slicing Kiel's middle, before he jumped backward in a leveraged spring, avoiding being disemboweled by a scale's breadth. Kiel returned the attack and managed to connect, wounding the insect's abdomen, but the Ikonian hardly noticed as its arm device hissed. The lesion flickered weirdly, and in an instant, the injury healed itself before Kiel's astonished eyes.

"Black gods of the Old Earth!" Kiel panted in fearful awe.

Like rapacious phantoms materializing from the mists of time, the two uncanny opponents circled each other in an age-old ballet of death, feeling for stable footing amid the bodies and equipment that now lay strewn like flotsam throughout the chamber.

Again, the arm device issued forth its familiar hiss, and in an instant the battle began anew. Kiel parried desperately and riposted, his arm thrusting wide. *By the eight hells, I am tired,* he thought. The Ikonian seemed to know it, appearing to be careful in making sure that Kiel's tremulous near-exhaustion was no sham. Now that the insect thing had measured Kiel's reach and something of his style, it began to push the fight harder and harder, until even it began to show signs of exertion.

A klaxon finally sounded somewhere in the outer hall. *Damn the*

Bioweapons Division for their secrecy! Kiel knew the labyrinth of winding passageways that branched and twisted under the complex; it would be an eternity before help arrived. Again came the frightful hiss, the whisper of Old Earth sorcery, and again the creature swelled in response with renewed strength.

Kiel gave ground steadily as they circled. Sheer desperation kept him going now. The Ikonian's arm blade came flicking in faster than before. Kiel saw the danger, but his weary, late-acting arm could not make the parry. He felt the hot bite of the wound along his side.

Yet with the hurt came rage, and the rage was fuel. Kiel let his fury drive him forward. He struck hard and fast, stroke after stroke, and then he staggered, halting, feigning total exhaustion before his reserve of energy was truly gone.

Reeling forward, he suddenly thrust, putting all the power in his shoulders behind the blade. The sharp point tore through the Ikonian's head and into its brain. Greenish hemolymph spurted from the wound. The remaining arm vials emptied into the creature's blood; the head wound flickered with ghostly foxfire; but at last, the injury was too severe. The hellish creature shuddered, the death tremor rattling the steel blade that connected the Ikonian and Kiel. The Ikonian stumbled forward a few faltering steps, crumpled to the floor, and lay still.

Everyone in the room stood hushed. Kiel's leather uniform hung in tatters. He looked at the red-stained chamber and at the helmeted heads tilted grimly upward as if in a last invocation for help. Kiel found the strength to set a foot upon the ruined face of the Ikonian and wrench the sword blade free, throwing it to the ground with a clatter. He staggered back against the wall and leaned there for a moment while the world grew gray and dim with the throbbing of his heart, as if it were his own blood that pooled upon the floor. But he was not bleeding much. His searching claws told him that the cut along his side had parted little more than leather and scale. Slowly, his strength returned to him.

A stampede of booted feet exploded into the chamber as a squad of armed soldiers entered. Stumbling to a stop, they stared at the bloody carnage before them in awed and confused silence.

"Ah, you have come, but you come too late," Kiel said blandly as the soldiers looked on helplessly. "The orchestra has completed its last set and the dance is done."

"Orders, sir?" the lead soldier asked in a bewildered tone.

"A mop and bucket would seem in order," Kiel responded, gazing grimly at the crimson-streaked room.

The soldier saluted and began barking instructions to his subordinates, while the surviving bioweapons scientists timidly reentered the chamber.

"Black devils, but it seems he's proved his theory," swore Tan Ru, who stared at the grotesquely twisted form of Sar's riven corpse that was now being dragged away by the heels.

Kiel removed his dented helmet and tossed it to the blood-smeared floor as Sar's body disappeared from view. It seemed he would not need to reprimand the old lizard after all. He turned to Tan Ru. "Congratulations on your unexpected promotion. May your theorizing be less difficult to demonstrate."

Tan Ru grunted in grim acknowledgment, focusing on the inert form of the Ikonian. "After the room is back in order, we can begin."

Kiel raised his hand. "I have seen enough. You may complete your examination in my absence."

Tan Ru nodded in understanding.

"After you finish stripping the Ikonian of its technology, lock up the remains." Kiel suspected he would not sleep well with a zombie thing lying free within the walls of Opal. "I will require a full report as soon as possible.

"Oh, one more notation," Kiel added before leaving the room. "In the future, if we receive any more Ikonian corpses for study, remove the head before you begin the examination."

Kiel stepped into the transit tube, spellbound. The tragedy that had just occurred held dire consequences for the imperium. Ikonians must have exhumed a terrifying and previously unknown technology from an Old Earth necropolis and employed it against the Eligor. There could be no doubt that it was Old Earth in nature. Kiel was too familiar with the telltale signs to suspect otherwise—the exotic materials, the exquisite, near-magical melding of design and function.

"Ikonians with Old Earth technology," he muttered in disbelief.

But why should that be surprising? Ikonians were not alone in their apparent fascination with Old Earth artifacts. Eligor scientists also dabbled in the recovered sorcery-like technology of the Others like ants toying with a slumbering colossus.

"The Others." Kiel muttered the second word like a curse. The Others were godlike beings who had passed into oblivion at the end of the Fourth Age, countless millennia ago—passed in a war that had nearly shattered the earth. But their technology remained buried, waiting.

By the time Kiel returned to his quarters, a raging storm had broken over Opal. Torrents of rain beat against the window's transparency, while jagged forks of lightning flickered and stroked from the sky above. Kiel eased his muscled frame into a creaking chair, lit a candle, and eyed the latest Imperial Intelligence report, entitled "Battle of Kirsk—Damage Assessment."

"Battle? More like the *Sack* of Kirsk," Kiel whispered as a long, shaking blast of thunder tore the sky like brittle parchment.

During the past quarter cycle, the Ikonian host had swept, like a tidal wave of fury, over the Eligor northern border. Reinforcements from every major city-state throughout the imperium had moved north to repel the invasion. From Ozareth, Ixxis Roi, Helikontha, Sub Korra, Ozgarthe, Heidrun, and Opal they had come, but it had been too late: Kirsk had been laid to waste and, with it, most of the imperial government, including the emperor himself. Now, it seemed, the army merely fought a delaying action, falling steadily back toward the more southerly military complex at Sub Korra, just north of Ixxis Roi. And if Ixxis Roi fell, Opal would be next.

Those of the Grand Union of Opal, the largest remaining governing body within the empire, were desperate for a way out, screaming for the Imperial Intelligence Service, and screaming for Kiel, to hatch a plan.

Kiel began leafing through the cheerless report again, momentarily pausing to eye several crude sketches of the Ikonians. The drawings seemed to shift and waver with sentient life as he slid the candle closer to the parchment. The artist had overlooked the arm device that Kiel now knew to be there.

"Ikonians with Old Earth technology." Kiel's thoughts would not focus. The Ikonians had never been aggressive and had never shown interest in Old Earth artifacts as far as anyone knew. Even humans shunned the ancient technology—mostly.

As midnight passed and Kiel began to nod off in exhaustion, the light panels above his head suddenly flickered to life.

"At long last," Kiel growled as he wearily rose, walking deliberately across the cold room to the heating coil, which was now coming to life with warmth.

The army corps of engineers had been working feverishly, repairing the primary hydrogen-cracking tower and its resident generator. Long maintenance lapses had finally caught up with the resurrected Old Earth device, adding electricity to the growing list of critical shortages within the city.

"Five short years since its introduction, and we find ourselves enslaved to electricity—enslaved to yet another Old Earth technology," Kiel whispered sadly.

A flickering ghostly shadow at the far end of the room caught Kiel's golden eyes as he stood warming his outstretched hands. Apparently, the Memory Sphere had also come to life when power was restored.

Kiel, ignoring his stiffened hands, walked over to the Old Earth creation and stood before it, meditative. The Memory Sphere was a nearly transparent orb of crystal-like material approximately one meter in diameter that sat squatly on a featureless iron-gray cube. The object's near-magical power instantly branded it as Old Earth, and although Eligor scientists had pompously taken credit for the device when it was handed over to the Imperial Intelligence Service, Kiel would have known blindfolded that the technology was immeasurably beyond the abilities of Eligor science. There was other, less obvious evidence of the Memory Sphere's ancient origins: its memory could not be completely altered to suit its new Eligor masters. As verification of his conviction, Kiel asked a question, the answer to which he already knew.

"Where were you constructed?"

The interior of the sphere clouded as if in thought. Swirling mists began to part in bursts of multicolored light to reveal a coalescing three-dimensional picture. The picture moved fantastically as if Kiel were gazing at a miniature world entrapped within the device. There, flickering and shifting before him, were humans, or rather the prehumans of old—the Others.

Kiel's scales rose at the silent admission. Not so long ago, in the days of the old empire, it would have been a death sentence to even suggest the Others were human. Indisputably, contemporary humans bore no resemblance to these godlike beings of precataclysmic earth, at least in technical ability. But the naked fact, deeply suppressed as it was, remained.

Kiel refocused his attention on the Memory Sphere. The Others gestured at a colossal building that loomed over them, sterile-looking in its angular perfection.

"Tuli suuri tuulen puuska iästä vihainen ilma meren kuohuille kohotti lainehille laikahutti tuuli neittä tuuitteli aalto impeä ajeli." The unknown liquid words flowed from the Memory Sphere.

The scene quickly drifted to a pennant-looking glyph etched on an upper wall, probably identifying the structure. The Memory Sphere flashed, and in the next instant, Kiel was whisked through the wall. Strange fantastic machines moved and flickered with bursts light, and below them, Memory Spheres marched endlessly on a gliding belt-like track. The scene settled to the floor level, where another prehuman Other pointed and boasted in the same unknown language.

"Ympäri selän sinisen lakkipäien lainehein tuuli, tuuli kohtuiseksi meri paksuksi panevi!"

Then leering proudly, the human faded and the picture returned to the same glyph that had decorated the front of the building. The glyph hovered in space for a moment, then vanished in the swirling mists of the device. The sphere darkened and its animate movement slowed as if it were preparing to slumber, when Kiel, frowning in thought, asked another question.

"Show me the image of an Ikonian."

Again, the clouded interior of the Old Earth creation roiled and quickened in bizarre imitation of conscious thought. Materializing before Kiel inside the crystalline sphere was a very simple drawing of an Ikonian, complete with spidery Eligor lettering below it. "Ikonian," it read simply.

Eligor scientists had inserted this new information after long, haphazard efforts to master the machine. The drawing and the accompanying letters were so pathetically crude that Kiel felt a pang of embarrassment. Surely, even this pitiful achievement was a credit to Eligor science, a striking victory amid sightless dabbling to have done this much, yet the outcome was shockingly childish in comparison to the original information.

"Prehumans, Others. *Humans*," Kiel whispered. "Humans created this device." The admission, though accurate, was still difficult to acknowledge. True, contemporary humans had only just climbed back out of the trees and had scarcely progressed beyond flint knives and animal skins in their engineering and technical abilities, but once, an age ago …

His thoughts suddenly coalesced, and the beginnings of a fantastic idea sprang to life. Was it possible? Could the humans have retained this gift of resourcefulness, of near-magic? To look at them now, in their crude rock-pile cities, to reflect on their barely sentient grasp of science, one could hardly identify them with the transcendent creators of the Memory Sphere, the inventors of the myriad technological achievements of the Others, yet they had the same brains. The ability was—had to be—still there, hidden, latent. With the resolve of the desperate, Kiel left the now slumbering Memory Sphere and walked to his desk, where he stabbed a clawed finger down on the communication terminal.

"Yes, Commander?" a drowsy aide shortly answered.

"Make an appointment for me within the Grand Union tomorrow at first light."

"As you wish, Commander.

"Commander?" the voice continued.

"Yes?"

"An intelligence report has just arrived from Sub Korra—"

"It can wait," Kiel answered, interrupting.

"As you wish, Commander."

Kiel released the response stud, put his desk in order as best he could, and retired to his bed. The storm had passed, and the moon appeared behind tearing clouds. Leafless autumn branches scratched at the transparency, casting the room with skeletal shadows. The storm had indeed passed, but there was a larger tempest on the horizon. Kiel settled into fitful slumber. Yes, tomorrow he would reveal his anarchic plan to the government of Opal before it was too late.

"You are quite mad, Kiel. Yes, quite mad. Do you honestly believe the humans would enter into any cooperative agreement with the Eligor Empire after what our late emperor attempted? I am sure the humans wish nothing less than to see Eligor genocide, even if it means dealing with the Ikonians at some future point in time!"

Seth, who now glowered down at Kiel from the audience dais of the Grand Union of Opal, looked almost comical as he sat, attempting as best he could to look regal and important. He was an old and skeletal Eligor who, in his day, held power second only to the Imperial Grand Union of Kirsk itself. Now, as was the case with so many others within the crumbling empire, Seth had been reduced to a mere shadow of his past glory. The other five members of the Grand Union seated around him had fared no better. While their golden robes were clean and obviously well cared for, underneath, their bodies appeared bony and shrunken, not unusual considering the recent rash of food shortages.

There had been a time, not so long ago it seemed, when this august body would have caused such dread to well up within Kiel as to cause his stomach to knot in sour queasiness. Now these haggling and bickering Eligor were barely able to keep order within the walls of the Grand Union. *Paradoxical,* Kiel mused. *The Grand Union are now quite probably as wary of me as I had once been of them.*

Seth's eyes narrowed to red-rimmed slits of yellow fire as he continued. "Let me refresh your faltering memory concerning our recent conflict with the humans. Not quite two cycles ago, our late emperor sent the Eligor army south to crush the Protectorate of Merja Soria and subjugate their race as is ordained in the Ignotum pro Magna. Because of this, the humans could not possibly harbor a shred of benevolence toward the Eligor Empire, even considering that it was our army that was repulsed and subsequently destroyed."

Seth's statement was true. The humans had fought passionately, defending their homeland tooth and nail. Eligor military tacticians had simply not predicted their barbaric ferocity and cunning—proof again of their potential, Kiel reflected. The humans had first halted, then destroyed the bulk of the Eligor invasion force at the Battle of Koth—nearly sixteen battle-hardened divisions. Of the original force that swept through the breached Gondakar Barrier and into the pastoral northlands of Merja Soria, only one in five had returned. Of the Eligor soldiers who had survived the rout, half again had died from injuries incurred, not by the humans, but rather by the Eligor army's own malfunctioning Old Earth weapons—biomechanicals that had been suddenly released from their electronic shackles. Humans, primitive as they were, had employed their own resurrected Old Earth technology, an electrical disruptor of some unknown type, or so the Eligor scientists theorized.

One thing was beyond scientific theory: the humans had done nothing to provoke the conflict. So far as Kiel knew, they had never spied, raided, threatened, or blustered, or so much as thrown a stone, in uncounted eons. Simply put, they had never been the threat the Ignotum pro Magna had claimed them to be. Even after the invasion had been crushed and the last Eligor soldier had hobbled back across the border, the humans had not retaliated. They had simply set about rebuilding and fortifying the Great Barrier at Gondakar, leaving the Eligor to lick their wounds—and they were many—in solitude.

Kiel's jaw tightened in silent frustration. Why had the empire blundered so terribly, basing the entire war on a book of religious claptrap? All that effort and material wasted in the south, when the real threat, the Ikonians, lay hidden in the far north, apparently waiting for such a disaster to attack the Eligor nation. And attack they had.

"I share your concern in respect to the probable human response," Kiel replied, "yet I can find no other possible solution to our current dilemma. If we are to believe that the Ikonian attack on Kirsk is merely an isolated move"—he let an indifferent tone enter his voice—"a move designed to push back a perceived threat, and not truly an invasion, then we might attempt to ride this current crisis out."

Several of the Grand Union members murmured and grumbled in apparent agitation at Kiel's statement.

Seth, raising his hand in a demand for silence, spoke again.

"You've made your point, Kiel—as sharply as ever." Seth sighed, scowling more deeply. "A precautionary move it is not. We are compelled at this time to inform you that the army depot at Sub Korra has been attacked. Our army is holding the attacking force at bay, but only just."

His fist slammed down on the podium. "No, we believe—we know—the Ikonians are truly bent on our systemic destruction. They obliterate everything in their path and take no prisoners. There can be no other possible reason behind these attacks. It is genocide! It is extinction!"

Nausea welled up into Kiel's scaled throat at the revelation of the motive for the attack. No need now to wonder at the contents of the intelligence report waiting for him at his command center. Sub Korra, deeper still within the Eligor northern border, ever closer to Opal. The Eligor Empire had not yet stabilized from the Ikonian assault at Kirsk, and Kiel knew better than most what this meant to their already overtaxed army.

Kiel's leather uniform creaked as he straightened his back in feigned resolve. "Well then, what is your response to my plan? Either you accept it as the best I can provide, or you can argue and deliberate while the Ikonians proceed to eviscerate our nation. I fear we have very little else at our immediate disposal."

The Grand Union murmured back and forth among each other for some time. They had tasked Kiel, as first commander of the Imperial

Intelligence Service of Opal, to deliver a working plan beyond what the army was now capable of, which was very little indeed. And Kiel had delivered. But this plan was fantastic, beyond their wildest expectations.

While the members squabbled heatedly over the vexing plan, Kiel's attention was drawn to the Grand Union chamber itself. In its days of glory, the chamber had been a vast hall of splendor. It had corbelled ceilings adorned with colorful murals and mosaic designs supported by tremendous green-veined marble columns. Its floors were inset with gold and silver filigree polished to a mirrorlike finish. Priceless wall tapestries depicting scenes of past glory hung over walls of jade and lapis lazuli.

Now, dust and debris littered these hallowed chambers. Here, a broken piece of masonry, there, a discarded manuscript. Along the far wall, below a gnawed tapestry, a raisin-eyed rat scampered for cover. The detritus revealed clearer than words could ever convey the current urgent state of the empire.

After a seemingly endless debate accentuated by bouts of near-hysterical gestures and bickering, the council before him finally quieted, and all eyes again turned to Kiel.

Seth spoke, his aged voice sounding like dry leaves rustling in a cold autumn wind. "Commander Kiel, we truly wish you had been able to deliver a more, shall we say, sensible plan, rather than the wild one you have given us. Yet, all realize these are difficult and troubling times. The demon has escaped its proverbial prison, and it is too late to recover him. Therefore, we of the Grand Union of Imperial Opal agree to your most exceedingly extraordinary scheme."

The sense of relief that washed through Kiel at Seth's utterance was unexpected in its depth. He truly believed in his heart that his plan was the only possible way out of their current crisis. Anything less would have spelled certain doom for the Eligor Empire, the Eligor race. He suspected those of the Grand Union believed this as well.

"As you might have assumed, Kiel, we must insist that you be the one to carry the plan to fruition," Seth's withered voice continued. "The army, or what is left of it, will be too occupied with the defense of Sub Korra to offer any assistance, even if they could be persuaded to join you. You are hereby granted the authority to amass whatever other provisions you might require for your, ah, adventure. You will immediately contact us if—that is, when—you return from the human Protectorate of Merja Soria. We are rapidly running out of time, as I am sure you are well aware."

Kiel touched the ground and then his forehead in respect, then turned to leave, Seth's voice came again. "Failure is not an option, Kiel. You carry the combined hopes of the Eligor nation on your shoulders."

If you are trying to inspire me, old lizard, you are most assuredly failing, Kiel thought as he left the Grand Union.

Kiel had known he would be the luckless Eligor picked to carry out this plan. But strangely, he would have had it no other way. He had convinced himself the humans were not the malevolent animals that were mentioned endlessly in the psalms and parables within the Ignotum pro Magna. Still, he shivered at the thought of seeking out humans, creatures that not so long ago had crushed the combined might of the Eligor Empire at the pinnacle of its former splendor. Even the Ikonians would have been envious of such work.

TWO

THE MERJA SORIAN

> They lust for treasure in the tomb, where ancient hands were wont to spread the gold and gems of fiery bloom and priceless riches for the dead.
> —Vena Korela,
> Saga of Vainamonen, Runa 10

Great, gnarled oaks loomed about Bishop like spectral phantoms, while a chilled uneasy wind moaned through their ancient branches. Behind him, the sounds of initiates eating, laughing, and gaming could be heard, but he paid them no heed. They seemed but ghosts in this land of the dead, unreal and unwelcome.

What in the eight hells was he doing out here? What series of events had brought him to this dreary land?

It wasn't the first time he had posed these silent questions, nor would it be the last.

Bishop rummaged through his pack for a bit of smoked meat, a slice of goat cheese, and a lump of wayfarer's bread while reflecting on his past.

More than ten years had elapsed since he had left his family's farm and joined the Order. Though he had never been particularly religious, the Order seemed, at the time, infinitely preferable to growing turnips or tending pigs. Certainly, being born a distant and all but forgotten relative within the Great House of Arakiel, he had seen little else in the way of options.

He began gnawing on his tasteless dinner. "Should've stayed on the farm," he muttered. "At least I would have had a warm bed and decent food. This wayfarer's bread is beginning to lodge in my throat."

Bishop wondered if this would be his fate, living in the wilds like an animal with no hope of advancement. He knew of others within the Order who had leapt to the rank of standard-bearer in half the time he had, those with connections, power, good fortune—advantages that he did not possess. It seemed he would remain a standard-bearer for the rest of his miserable life. He had tried to convince himself, his friends, and his family that he was happy and content with his lot in life, that this was all he had ever wanted in respect to a career, but he was only fooling himself. He had wanted more. The excuses were only mental liniment, a way of coping with his own self-perceived laziness, life failings, and missed opportunities. And every year that passed made it harder for him to believe his own wretched excuses. What was worse was this: he was fairly certain his friends and family didn't buy a word of it any more than he did; they were simply too respectful to mention it.

And what of the Riika?

Bishop absently rubbed the device that was permanently locked around his left forearm, noting the dull glint of the strange untarnished Old Earth metal.

Yes, what of the Riika?

The wind moaned, the autumn leaves rustled, and the acceptance ceremony drifted through Bishop's mind as if it had happened yesterday. Knights of the Order had solemnly positioned the strange metallic halves of the Old Earth relic around young Bishop's left wrist in accordance with ancient Merja Sorian tradition. Inert and unresponsive, the Riika had already been offered to twenty-three young men during the village rite of acceptance that day. But unlike what had happened with those before him, indeed, unlike what had happened to any young hopeful in the history of the village, the halves flashed, accepting Bishop, locking permanently around his wrist while shouts of astonishment and elation were heard throughout the town square.

"May the bearer find the key," the knights chanted in unison.

The knights stepped away, their arms folded meditatively within the sleeves of their cloaks, quietly brooding, observing, while the town erupted in celebration with provisions of every description, games of chance; flute, horn, and drum; ale by the barrel; and folk dancing accompanied by laughs, gay shrieks, and applause from onlookers and participants alike, while the runa singers sang their songs of prophecy fulfilled, mostly drowned out by the village tumult. It was all quite overwhelming.

"May the bearer unite the Great Houses and bring Merja Soria again under one rule," the knights intoned in booming voices. The throng erupted with renewed roars of approval.

But the acceptance, heralded throughout the surrounding farms and hamlets as a sign from the ancients, seemed the only magic the Riika bestowed upon its bearer. Soon, the excitement faded. The townsfolk went back to their dull, monotonous lives, and Bishop, immediately hauled off to a chapter house to begin his initiation and training, found he was no better off than he had been before the Riika—possibly worse off.

What of the Riika, indeed!

Bishop eyed the contrivance, turning his wrist in the moonlight. There it rested, a seamless, near-perfect wristband, supple like leather but possessing strength far beyond that of thrice-forged steel—beyond anything known in the present age. True, the Riika had allowed him begrudging entrance into the Order in accordance with the Rule. Whether that was a blessing or a curse, time would tell.

"Blessings and curses," he muttered, forcefully biting another mouthful of food, food that seemed to have lost even more of its meager taste.

He absently brushed the crumbs from his travel-stained clothing. Blessings and curses undeniably!

When Bishop had returned from his first foreign assignment, he and Hunter, his companion on the mission, were raised from attendants to standard-bearers. But while Hunter had been blessed with a coveted post at the principal chapter house at Troyes, Bishop was cursed with another tedious mission beyond the Gondakar Barrier. A cloud of doubt moved across his face at the thought. Perhaps the Riika brought disaster upon the bearer instead of luck? Was that its ancient gift? Bishop considered the current assignment as the obvious paradigm to his growing suspicion.

Thirteen days ago, Quain, the commander of Bishop's chapter house, entrusted him with a letter of treaty to Tong Ren, executive officer of the corporate sphere of Baikonur, an ancient city of the Old Earth located beyond the northwesternmost frontier of the protectorate.

"Foragers!" Bishop spat the word as the wind moaned around the fire. "Scavengers and grave robbers to everyone else, digging up their evil Old Earth magic to trade and sell, usually to the accursed Eligor."

Bishop pondered the scavengers, creatures that had once been human before the titanic wars that ended the Fourth Age had changed them. "Better to leave them to their Old Earth necromancy."

Bishop and the ten attendants under his command traversed hundreds of kilometers of thick forest, penetrating the foothills of the towering Arus Kor Cordillera, a dark and evil land that figured into many a grim fable. Then, threading their way north through the windy passes and swampy forests bordering the dreaded Eligor Empire, they followed the coastal lands and salt marshes of the Western Sea that led to the forager city.

Arriving in Baikonur at last, Bishop had found the venerable and philosophical Tong Ren a splendid host—for a forager, anyway. Tong Ren's underlings had plied Bishop and his companions with exotic food and drink, and for their part, Bishop and his men were politely careful not to show their distaste for the gray-skinned mutants, each man keeping one hand on his coin pouch just the same. In short order, Tong Ren and his advisers had decided to accept the protectorate's treaty of friendship and trade. Tong Ren had handed Bishop a signed document of acceptance, inscribed in the writhing ideographs of their language—the formal replies and felicitations of the corporate sphere of Baikonur.

That had occurred five days ago.

"Do I disturb the profound meditations of the nobly born Bishop?" purred a soft, effeminate voice behind him.

Bishop started, grabbing at the hilt of his sword before he recognized Councilman Mawr, wrapped like a monstrous cocoon in a flowing cloak of gray velvet, as he materialized out of the gloom.

Tong Ren had also furnished Bishop and his men with a member of the high council to accompany them through the forager lands and back to the protectorate as an emissary to their government. However, Bishop did not like his guide, this Councilman Mawr.

The councilman before him was a refined and dandified little forager with a soft, lisping voice. He wore a spotless gray suit, inappropriate for rugged travel, and had saturated himself in expensive perfume. He never soiled his soft, manicured hands by doing any of the camp chores, but instead kept his two assistants busy day and night ministering to his comfort and ensuring his dignity.

Bishop looked down on the little forager and his peculiar habits with a hard-bitten contempt. The councilman's dreamy gray eyes and purring voice reminded Bishop of a cat, and Bishop often told himself to watch this sly feline for treachery. Even more, Bishop resented the councilman for his exquisitely cultivated manners and easy charm, because although Bishop's training within the Order had given him some slight polish, he was still at heart a young backwoods soldier not suited to the ways of a diplomat. And was that his fault? No!

"You remain silent, my most excellent travel companion."

Bishop started to growl a contemptuous curse. Then, remembering his ambassadorial duties, he turned the oath into a formal welcome that sounded unconvincing even to his own ears.

"By the, ah … Good, uh, evening, Councilman Mawr."

"Perhaps the princely standard-bearer is unable to sleep?" murmured Mawr, appearing not to notice Bishop's ungraciousness. "I am fortunate to possess a sovereign remedy for sleeplessness. A gifted apothecary concocted it for me from an ancient recipe, a decoction of mandrake, ground and spiced with witch hazel and honey."

"Witch hazel and honey?" Bishop held back a shiver. "Thank you, no. It's not a matter of sleep. It's something about this place that keeps me awake when, after a long day's ride, I should be as tired as an initiate after a night of gaming and swilling ale."

Noting the slight wincing of the councilman's features, Bishop silently cursed his crudity. But Mawr only replied suavely, "I think I understand the misgivings of the excellent and high-born Bishop. Nor are such disquieting emotions unusual in these, ah, legend-fraught northern woods."

"Legend-fraught? What do you mean by that?" Bishop questioned, unable to hide a note of unease in his voice.

The councilman's narrow shoulders twitched beneath the gray cloak, a predatory spark flickering briefly in his dreamy eyes. "By that I mean to say that this spot lies near the tomb of an ancient executive officer of the foragers, Olethros of Baikonur, whose spirit is said to haunt these woods." The soft voice dropped even lower. "Legend also states that a magnificent treasure of gold and precious jewels was buried with him. And this tale I believe to be true."

That statement crystallized Bishop's attention. "Gold and gems? Has it ever been found, this treasure?"

The forager surveyed Bishop for a moment with an oblique, contemplative gaze. Then, as if having reached some private decision, he replied, "No, Master Bishop, for the precise location of the trove is not known except by one soul."

Bishop's interest was complete now. "To whom is it known?" he demanded, suspicious.

Mawr smiled with surreptitious satisfaction. "To my unworthy self, of course."

Bishop's interest wavered. "If you've known where this treasure was hidden, why haven't you assembled a recovery team?"

Mawr smoothed the fabric of his suit indifferently. "Unlike my lowly self, most foragers are haunted by superstitious fears of a curse laid upon the site of the old officer's tomb, a tomb marked by a dolmen of immense stones. Hence, I have never been able to persuade anyone to assist me in seizing the treasure."

Bishop's eyes narrowed as the moths of reason began to eat at the fabric of Mawr's intricately woven tale. "Why haven't you dug it up then?"

Mawr spread his soft, manicured hands. "My dear sir! There are genuine dangers in these woods. I would need a trustworthy assistant to guard my back against any stealthy foe, human or animal, that might approach while I was busily unearthing the plunder. Moreover, a certain amount of digging, lifting, and prying is sure to be required. A statesman like me lacks the musculature for such rude physical labor."

Bishop's eyes narrowed further, but he said nothing.

Mawr continued, saying, "Now listen, my good human: I have led the honorable Bishop through this valley, not by happenstance, but by design. When I heard that the executive officer wished me to accompany the brave standard-bearer southward, I seized upon the proposal with enthusiasm. This commission came as a veritable gift from heaven, for Your Lordship possesses the strength of three foragers. And, being a southern-born foreigner, you naturally do not share the superstitious terrors of my people. Am I correct in my assumption?"

Bishop hesitated as he looked about the darkened oaks with some genuine concern, then he caught the glittering eyes of Mawr, studying him. "Superstitious? Why, no, of course not! Don't be ridiculous."

The forager waited until several soldiers passed and then sidled closer, his voice dropping to a barely audible whisper. "Then here is my plan. I would like to recover the treasure and present a portion to your government as a personal gift, but of course a sizable percentage would belong to the both of us as, shall we say, payment for services rendered?"

A certain caution restrained Bishop, whose interest had rekindled and was quite intense by now, from immediately assenting. Certainly, if the Order were to catch wind of an adventure such as this, it would not bode well for Bishop's future career.

"Why not take a squad of my soldiers to help us?" he grumbled. "Or your assistants? Certainly we'll need help in bringing the plunder back to camp."

Mawr shrugged his shoulders, nonchalantly inspecting his fingernails. "It is not necessary. The treasure is said to consist of two small chests, each packed with exceedingly rare and precious gems. After giving the majority as a gift to your esteemed government, we shall barely carry away the fortune of a small princedom. And why share this paltry treasure with others? Since the secret is mine alone, I am naturally entitled to a fair share. Then, if you are so lavish as to divide your share among your warriors, well, that is for you to decide."

A small princedom?

It took no more urging to persuade Bishop to accept Councilman Mawr's scheme. The pay of a standard-bearer was meager and usually in arrears. Bishop's recompense for his arduous service so far had been many empty words of honor and precious little hard coin. It was not by accident that many within the protectorate referred to those within the Order as "poor knights"—and Bishop was a long way from even becoming a knight.

Bishop's hand inadvertently dropped to his coin pouch; two, maybe three, copper riders rattled a lonely tune of poverty. "A small princedom, eh? All right, fine, I'll do it. But only because most of it will be going to the protectorate, you understand."

"I will go fetch the digging implements," murmured Mawr, his eyes shining like a cat's in the dark. "We should leave the camp separately so as not to arouse suspicion."

"Yes, yes, let's get on with it before I change my mind," Bishop growled.

"Excellent!" Mawr hissed in unbridled delight. "And now we part, to meet again just before moonrise, which should occur about one double hour hence, giving us ample time for our rendezvous."

Two hours later, Bishop silently met up with the forager on the outskirts of camp. His men continued their gaming and drinking. He made a mental note to reprimand them for their careless and inattentive behavior after he returned.

"You will follow me, most noble standard-bearer. It is but a short walk," Mawr whispered, glancing about the wood furtively.

Bishop nudged the forager forward in nervous impatience. "Get on with it before someone sees us or before I come to my senses and quit the whole ill-thought-out adventure!"

The forager bowed reverently, then melted into the night, leading Bishop along the boulder-strewn stream that intersected the camp behind them. Within an hour, the ravine opened on either side of them, revealing a grassy meadow. The stream angled off to the right, curving out of sight between banks clustered with scrub oak and tree ferns.

As they entered the meadow, the crescent moon rode above the early autumn trees, casting an elusive light upon a tumulus that thrust out of the meadow directly before them. Bishop forgot his premonitions, as at its top was the dolmen of which Mawr had spoken. It was made up of six vine-ensnarled, dully glistening shafts of stone, holding a massive circular slab of rock at its top. Here then was the tomb of the long-dead forager executive officer; the treasure must be buried either directly beneath it or below one of the supporting columns.

With Mawr's crowbar and shovel on his shoulder, Bishop pushed forcefully through a clump of tough rhododendrons and started up the hill. He paused to give the puffing forager a hand up. After a brief scramble, they both gained the top of the slope.

Before them, the dolmen rose from the center of the gently convex summit of the tumulus. The mound, Bishop thought, was probably artificial, as sometimes in ancient times such mounds were piled up over the remains of great leaders within the protectorate. But if the treasure were at the bottom of such a pile, it would take more than one night's digging to uncover it—more like several months just to clear the undergrowth away from its base. Bishop turned to question his companion, but he was not given the chance.

With a startled curse, Bishop clutched at the shovel and crowbar as both tools began to slide from his grasp. The vines below his feet had suddenly become animate, seizing upon the tools and pulling them toward the closest supporting column. Bishop held onto the implements with all his strength, his muscles straining. Centimeter by centimeter, however, the force overcame him. When he saw that he would be drawn against the shaft with his tools, he released them. Flying toward the stone, the shovel and crowbar struck it with a loud double clank as more vines wrapped and knotted about them.

Releasing the tools did not free Bishop from the ensnarling tendrils that now wrapped about his legs and body as powerfully as they had the shovel and the crowbar. Staggering and swearing, Bishop too was dragged against the shaft. His back was pinned to the column, as were his upper arms, with the creepers twining about them like living rope.

His head inside the securely strapped-on metal helmet was also pinned to the shaft, as was the sheathed sword at his waist.

Bishop struggled to tear himself free but found that he could not. It was as if green chains of iron held him securely against the column of dark stone.

"What demon's trick is this, scavenger?"

Smiling and imperturbable, Mawr tiptoed carefully over the trailing creepers and strolled up to where Bishop stood pinned against the pillar. "Scavenger, is it?" he purred smugly. "I see I'll have to silence your vulgar tongue."

Tittering softly, the forager took a silken scarf from one of the front pockets of his immaculate gray suit. He waited until Bishop opened his mouth to curse, and then nimbly stuffed in the scarf. While Bishop gagged and chewed on the cloth, the little creature knotted another scarf securely over Bishop's mouth and around his neck. At last, Bishop stood, snorting but silent, glaring venomously down into the smiling face of the diminutive forager.

"Forgive the ruse, O noble savage!" Mawr said, lisping. "It was needful that I concoct some tale to appeal to your primitive lust for gold in order to lure you hither alone."

Bishop's eyes blazed with fury as he hurled all the might of his body against the emerald bonds that held him against the pillar, but it did no good. He was helpless. Sweat trickled down his brow, cooling in the night air. He tried to shout, but only grunts and gurgles came out.

"Since, my dear standard-bearer, your pointless life approaches its predestined end," Mawr said, continuing, "it would be impolite of me not to explain my actions, so that your lowly spirit may journey to whatever hell your barbaric gods have prepared for it in full knowledge of the causes of your downfall. Know that the government of the most amiable but foolish Tong Ren, the executive officer of Baikonur, is divided between two parties. One of these, the plutocratic Black Jaguar, welcomes contact with the humans of the south. The other, that of the populist Red Serpent, forbids all association with your barbarous society. And I, of course, belong to the selfless patriots of the Red Serpent. Willingly would I give my life to bring your embassy to destruction, lest contact with your archaic protectorate contaminate our pure culture and upset our perfect social system."

Mawr paused, allowing his words to etch into Bishop's mind.

"Happily, such an extreme measure seems unnecessary. For I have you, the standard-bearer of this band of foreign devils, and here around your neck hangs the treaty with your uncouth and heathen protectorate."

The dainty little forager, producing a small pearl-handled pocketknife, carefully cut the leather cord securing the documents around Bishop's neck and tucked them into an inner pocket, adding with a malicious smile, "As for the emerald bonds that hold you prisoner, I will not attempt to explain their subtle nature to your childish wits. Suffice it to say that they are a type of carnivorous plant that will consume what remains of you once their symbiotic opposite has satiated its appetite. So fear not, it is no unholy magic that holds you captive."

Bishop had partly guessed as much, but the knowledge served him little as he chewed on the gag.

"And so, my good savage, farewell. You will forgive this humble person for rudely turning his back upon you during your last moments. Your demise is a pity in a way, and I should not enjoy witnessing it. Had you had the advantages of a forager's upbringing, you would have made an admirable servant, say, a chamber boy, or a bodyguard for me, since you are such a handsomely proportioned creature." Mawr eyed Bishop hungrily. "But alas, things are as they are."

After a mocking bow of farewell, the forager withdrew to the lower slope of the hill, being careful not to step on any of the loose creepers. With great difficulty, Bishop looked around him. To his left he sighted the shovel, the crowbar, and the rusty bowl of a helmet, while on the other side, a time-eaten dagger was wrapped against the stone. He tested his strength against the vines that held him crushed against the column. He could move his lower legs and arms and even turn his head somewhat from side to side, but his body was firmly gripped by the living ropes that held him.

The moon, now floating high above the woodland, limned the black shadows in its white glow and patterned the forest floor in grotesque designs. Bishop observed that around his feet and elsewhere around the base of the monument, grisly remains of other victims were scattered. Bones and teeth were heaped like old rubbish. He must have stepped upon them when the vines pulled him up against the shaft.

His attention returned to the task at hand, seeking some means of escape. He wondered if the councilman's plan was to leave him trapped against the shaft until he died of starvation and thirst. At dawn, his men would certainly find him missing and would begin to search for him. Then again, since he had sneaked out of the camp without leaving word of his going, they would not know where to look. But surely they would scour the forest and eventually find him. Then Bishop would make short work of the treacherous two-legged weasel.

Below the mound, Bishop heard an eerie clicking sound. Straining his eyes in the shifting moonlight, he saw that Mawr had not left the scene after all. Instead, the forager was sitting cross-legged on the grass at the bottom of the hill, near its base. He had drawn a curious metallic device from a pocket and was fingering it.

As Bishop watched Mawr manipulate the device, a grating sound filled the chilled air as if an immense door was opening above him. The muscles of Bishop's neck stood out as he twisted his head to look upward; the helmet ground against the stone, and the chinstrap bit into his skin.

Bishop peeked above the rim of his helmet, the blood freezing in his veins. "Gods of the Others," he muttered in dismay.

Very slowly, a hidden panel was sliding outward on the upper side of the pylon. Bishop watched the queer recession of the portal as it gaped wider and wider, finally sliding to a stop, fully open. Amid the night's ghostly distortion, something moved in the hole, and a wisp of steam curled upward and out. The aperture was black, and the darkness was almost material, yet it could not fully hide the movement that shifted within. The blackness, though distressing, seemed to be a positive quality as it obscured the bulk of the animal that now emerged from its place of imprisonment. The odor that met Bishop's nostrils was intolerable, as if the thing had sprung from a hellish charnel house. Bishop could now hear a sound like heavy breathing as the creature lumbered into sight, squeezing its leprous black bulk through the portal and into the outside air. An awful frog head atop a ring of writhing tentacles now broke away from the portal and leered down upon him with distended eyes. Bishop's imagination yielded simultaneous pictures of a frog, a squid, and a human caricature morphed into one single living fiend.

As Bishop watched in growing horror, the monster sent one of its suckered members groping along the shaft toward him. The greasy appendage glided over the surface of the stone like a snake. As the tentacular arm closed, Bishop could hear a hissing, spitting sound like hot iron being slowly immersed in water.

A tittering laughter reached Bishop's ears, and he focused his attention back on Mawr. The forager was now pointing his device toward the slimy tormentor. Bishop looked again at the monster, closer this time.

Black devils! Bishop silently screamed.

There were the telltale signs of some hybrid type of Old Earth biomechanical. Knotted bundles of flexible metallic cables ran over the monster's body like blood vessels, carrying life-nourishing energy to its various artificial parts. And there, barely visible around its bloated neck, was a control collar. Metallic plates slid and moved under the creature's semitransparent skin, and a ghostly light began to phosphoresce within its gut, flickering with a pale greenish color.

Bishop strained anew at his leafy bonds. He had had a near-terminal encounter with one of these Old Earth monsters in the past, but then he'd had full use of his body and an armed contingent of soldiers to back him up.

The wind had changed, and a vagrant downdraft carried more of the sickening stench to Bishop's nostrils. Now he began to understand why the bones at the base of the shaft bore that oddly eaten appearance. The thing probably exuded a digestive fluid by means of which it consumed its prey. Bishop wondered how many men, enemies of the Red Serpent cult, had stood in his place, bound helplessly to the dolmen's supporting pillars, awaiting the searing caress of the Old Earth monster that was now descending toward him.

Then a new thought intruded upon his mind. *The Riika!*

Bishop never before had entertained the slightest consideration that there existed animate power within the Old Earth device, never suspected that it in fact did anything, yet something seemed to be feebly awakening within the Old Earth creation. If there was any protective power to be had from the Riika, it would have to come now and this certainty of imminent destruction appeared to be the key needed to unlock its power. He concentrated on the device sealed round his arm while also creating a mental picture of his green shackles. Nothing. Terror slowly built in his gut and a sense of hopelessness crept over him. He concentrated harder, refusing to give in to his despair. Yes, again there came a sensation of tingling and slight warmth from the Riika, followed by the smell of smoke. Bishop looked down as all but two of the restrictive vines blackened, turning to white ash before his astonished eyes. The Riika had done its work, its power apparently spent, but it was not enough. He was still held firm by the remaining vines.

Despair gave new strength to Bishop's cramped, tired muscles. He threw himself from side to side, striving with the last ounce of his strength to break the grip of the remaining ropes that imprisoned him.

To his surprise, he found that, in one of his lunges, he slid to one side, partway around the column.

So, the Riika had loosened the remaining vines, though Bishop knew that he could not elude the monstrous biomech for long. He lunged again, and this time something scraped against his armored side. Looking down, he saw a rust-eaten dagger lying against the column, held loosely by a half-rotted growth of the imprisoning vine. His movement sideways had brought the hilt of the weapon against his ribs.

His upper arm was clamped against the stone by the vines, but his forearm and hand were free. Could he bend his arm far enough to clasp the haft of the dagger?

He strained, inching his hand along the stone. His body scraped slowly over the surface; sweat trickled into his eyes. Bit by bit, his straining arm moved toward the handle of the dagger.

"Behold, O lord of fools, the surprise that I arranged for you." Mawr giggled, taunting him. "Resurrected from the ashes of the Old Earth, a biomech that has come to lovingly caress you with its tender touch."

Bishop struggled even more at the sound of Mawr's mocking laughter. His arm muscles were strained to the limit, and his hand was touching the dagger. In an instant, he held the hilt fast. However, as he strained it away from the vines, the rust-eaten blade broke with a sharp pinging sound. Rolling his eyes downward, he saw that about two-thirds of the blade, from the tapering point back, had broken off and now lay wrapped in a green grip. The remaining third projected from the hilt. Bishop was able, by a muscle-bulging effort, to move the weapon away from the shaft.

A glance showed him that the remaining length of blade was sharp and double-edged. With his muscles quivering from the effort of holding the implement away from the stone, he brought the stunted knife up against the first of two loops of the vine that gripped his torso. Carefully, he began to saw at the tough creeper with the rusty blade.

Every movement was agony. The torment of suspense became

unbearable. His hand, bent into an uncomfortable twisted position, ached and grew numb. The ancient blade was notched, thin, and brittle; a hasty motion might break it, leaving him helpless. Stroke after stroke, he sawed up and down with exquisite caution. The stench of the creature grew stronger, and the sucking sounds of its progress toward him louder.

Then Bishop felt the first loop snap. Hastily, he began sawing at the next. After what seemed like an eternity, the final vine gave way to his efforts. Now half freed, Bishop became aware of a whispering palpitation upon his head. The stench was now overpowering. He knew the antagonist from above had reached his helmet and was now pushing this way and that, groping over the metal surface, seeking flesh. Any instant, the corrosive tentacle would stretch down over his face.

Frantically, with his free hand, Bishop unbuckled the chinstrap of his helmet and tore himself away from the deadly constriction of the lower vines.

Bishop staggered away from the column and stood for an instant on trembling legs. The moonlit world swam before his exhausted eyes.

Glancing back, he noted that the beast's suckered member had now curled about his now empty helmet. Baffled in its quest for flesh, the monster sent more tentacles down and outward, wavering and searching in the moonlight. Apparently, its rudimentary eyes were of little use, as they missed the fact that Bishop had escaped. On the edge of the mound, Mawr, ignorant of Bishop's breakout, sat cross-legged on the grass, giggling like a schoolboy on a romp.

He reverently replaced the control device back into his suit pocket. "It is done. It is done." He sniggered proudly.

Ripping off his gag, Bishop, avoiding other, seemingly inert vines that lay flaccidly about the ground, pounced. He came down, outstretched hands first, upon the little councilman. The pair rolled through the grass in a tangle of thrashing limbs, accompanied by the strident sound of Mawr's squealing. Bishop quickly pinned the councilman, but Mawr continued to shriek in a paroxysm of terror until Bishop cuffed him on the side of his head, snapping him out of his hysterics.

"Your Lordship, please," Mawr blubbered weakly. "I misjudged you. Let me go. I will show you the treasure. Please!"

Bishop ignored the begging while groping in the forager's suit and tearing out the leather cylinder containing the treaty documents.

He glanced into the tube, making sure the documents were still safely inside it. Below him, Mawr twisted sinuously and violently, the bones of his skinny frame seemingly irrelevant, his body more wriggling snake than forager. Bishop could not steady his grip on the hysterically twisting form. He cursed loudly as Mawr slithered frantically out from under him and darted back up the slope to within a meter of the monolith, all the while stabbing frantically at his control box. Bishop scrambled to his feet and sprinted after the treacherous forager.

In ancient times, when the monster was not so old and sedentary, it might have reacted in some deadly fashion, responding instantly to Mawr's frenzied electronic goading. But now, in its twilight, the thing merely trembled in apparent irritation as flickering phosphorescence rippled over its leprous skin.

The forager shrieked in terror as Bishop again tackled him; the control box hurtled into the night sky and was gone. Mawr, yammering in hysteria and desperate to escape, viciously bit into Bishop's arm. Bishop yelped in surprise, instinctively hurling Mawr away from him. Mawr struck the column with a thud and slid unconscious to the ground at its base as several of the vines instantly curled and knotted about him.

The blow was merciful. The forager never felt the delicate touch of the biomechanical as a glassy, semitranslucent tentacle reached his face and curled about it. The forager's heels began to move silently up and down as Bishop looked on, transfixed with revulsion. Shaking off his paralysis, Bishop moved to free the councilman, but it was too late. Mawr's features blurred, his flesh dissolved, and his skull appeared in a death grin. An instant later, two more tentacles dropped and curled around the councilman's body, the monster flushing pink with nourishment.

With a parting look, Bishop turned from the grisly scene to descend shakily to the meadow below. At the bottom of the mound, he noticed the control device lying on the ground, glinting dully in the moonlight. With a silent curse, he smashed the Old Earth mechanism with the heel of his boot and then, with weary resolve, silently retraced his steps back to camp.

Bishop had barely reentered camp when Mawr's two aides approached out of the gloom. "Where is the councilman?" the slight, aquiline-nosed Fayed asked worriedly. "We have not seen him and are becoming concerned. His bathwater is cooling."

Bishop had hoped Mawr's disappearance would not be noted until dawn, but such was not the case. "The councilman has, ah, been recalled to Baikonur. Some kind of emergency, or so he said. Mawr asked that you, his trusty aides, complete the task of delivering the treaty to the protectorate in his stead."

The two foragers stood silently, first looking startled and then appearing somewhat relieved. "This is most unusual," the somewhat stouter Thaddeus said. "But who are we to question the motives of the most venerable Mawr?"

"Yes, of course, who are we but wretched servants, as the councilman is always so quick to point out?" Fayed added.

Bishop thought fast, then jerked his thumb in the direction of Mawr's belongings. "You needn't worry about dragging that wagonload of rubbish—ah, baggage—along either. The councilman has, uh, instructed me to leave it so as not to encumber our journey. He will undoubtedly send others to retrieve it for him at some later date."

Mawr's aides looked at each other in redoubled relief. "He is truly gone then?" asked Thaddeus.

"Apparently, it was a very important crisis, one requiring his personal attention, overruling his travel to the protectorate."

Thaddeus rubbed his gray chin in thought. "Truly, it is a fact; the esteemed councilman is not fond of traveling. I am of the opinion that any opportunity to excuse himself from this adventure would have warranted his leave."

"Not that we mind administering to his every whim," Fayed noted.

"Not in the least," Thaddeus seconded eagerly.

Fayed smiled broadly. "And what a sin to waste the most excellent Mawr's bathwater, wouldn't you agree, Thaddeus?"

"Most assuredly, I would."

Thaddeus looked at Fayed; Fayed looked at Thaddeus. With a sudden outburst of tittering laughter, they both skipped off toward the tub arm in arm, like two children on a romp.

Bishop stared after them with one eyebrow raised.

After informing his own men of Mawr's "sudden emergency," Bishop rolled himself in his blankets, but sleep did not come easy.

Gripping the now inert Riika, Bishop silently wondered at its lifesaving gift. The normally inanimate Riika had saved his life. Life he had been given, but a diplomat of the forager government lay dead in the woods, and Bishop was left with coming up with an elaborate excuse for his sudden inexplicable absence.

Bishop lay on his back, both thinking and trying not to think. He'd have to relay a very creative report about this incident, but it would take some time to sort out the night's events in his mind. For the moment, he would just welcome sleep.

THREE

A WALK IN THE FOREST

> Crimson kings on battle towers.
> Saints on gothic star-flung spires.
> Hermits on their peaks of snow.
> Heroes on their funeral pyres.
>
> —Vena Korela,
> Saga of Ilmarinen, Runa 49

T'Sa finished stoking the cooking fire as a flurry of sparks swirled into the chilly evening air like fireflies. "Are you ready for your dinner, sir?" he asked politely.

For the entire two-day journey, T'Sa, a young soldier in the Eligor army, had been overly deferential to the commander of the Imperial Intelligence Service, seeming to take pleasure in administering to his every need.

Probably never fraternized with officers before, Kiel thought, sighing. But it was not unpleasant to have such a young, respectful Eligor with him on this grim mission. He traveled with nine other Eligor, handpicked by Kiel himself immediately following his fateful meeting with the Grand Union of Opal. All were superior soldiers, who now settled tiredly in the snow-patched clearing.

"Yes, of course, T'Sa," Kiel answered, taking a drink from his canteen. "A hot meal after a day's march would be splendid."

The detachment from Opal had set up camp at the southern foothills of the Ona Arka mountain range, five days' journey from the human frontier. The setting sun tinged the snows of the higher peaks with red, and a cold autumn wind stirred the upper pines with a mournful sighing sound.

T'Sa saluted smartly and began rummaging in his pack for food. "I'll have something for you in short order, sir."

Kiel stared for a moment and then seated himself on a fallen log as the camp sounds drifted through the air. For the past fifteen days, Kiel had marched with his escort detachment through the upper passes of the range and down into the lower elevations, venturing deeper into the illimitable distances of the south. At the end of their trek, the humans waited. How would the Eligor be greeted?

Kiel accepted the food—typical Eligor travel rations of small game meat—from the dutiful soldier and settled himself on his log, where he began munching absently.

How would they be greeted? Yes, that was the real question. By the tip of a sword, Kiel suspected. But what other choice did he have? What choice did the Eligor Empire have? He looked up at the stars, which were just beginning to appear in the twilit sky. They seemed unalterable, perhaps as unalterable as his course of action seemed to be.

The Eligor Empire and human protectorate had never been close, at least as far back as Eligor histories would allow one to look. The recent war could have only crystallized the humans' hatred toward their age-old antagonists.

"Yes," Kiel muttered. "It will be an interesting reunion indeed." His eyes became distant as he recalled the final days of the last war, a grand invasion that had suddenly turned into the worst defeat in Eligor history.

Working within the Imperial Intelligence, Kiel, of course, had seen the bleak reports as they issued in, reports initially kept from the Eligor masses for fear of widespread panic. He had readied himself for the coming task of investigating the failed invasion, an inquisition that would surely involve the IIS—Imperial Intelligence Service—home guard in a paroxysm of military fratricide. The emperor would not accept failure.

Kiel shook his head at the ludicrous thought. He recalled the maimed and wounded soldiers staggering back to Opal, their once proud uniforms shredded and bloodstained, only to face the wrath and retribution of their own government. Yet the chance for revenge would not be given to the emperor and his home guard. Ikonians had suddenly swarmed out of the north, swallowing Kirsk, the emperor, and his plans of retribution before it could be unleashed upon the failed army.

The humans had not counterattacked. The humans. What was his obsession with the humans?

A sound from the surrounding wood brought Kiel instantly out of his deep thoughts. He slowly lowered his half-eaten food and stood, looking into the growing gloom of the forest. His fellow Eligor followed suit. They both quietly drew their swords, looking at each other in growing dread.

"What ...?" T'Sa began.

"Quiet," Kiel hissed.

No sound broke the stillness of the dark forest that around them, yet something was coming down the shadowy trail. The huge trees shouldered each other like taciturn giants, and their intertwining branches shut out the light, turning the white moonlight gray as it filtered through. The trail that meandered among the trees seemed like a dim road through a deathly quiet spirit world. Even the treading of a soft-booted foot seemed a startling disturbance. Somewhere far out in the murk of the evening, something moved. The sound came again, closer this time.

A dry branch snapped somewhere close. Kiel felt his scales rise as he perceived something massive moving in the gloom of the brooding pines just beyond the firelight. A shadow coalesced and grew distinct, pausing at the edge of the glade like the embodiment of a nightmare.

Kiel froze.

The monster that now stood in the clearing had curiously pale-colored fur, making it seem ghostly and unreal in the dim light. But there was nothing unreal about the low-hanging head of the savage, the corded metal cables, or the ivory teeth that glistened in the firelight. On noiseless padded feet, it stood like a phantom out of the past, a survivor of an older, grimmer age.

"A biomechanical," Kiel whispered.

Others of its kind could now be made out among the trees, gliding silently like monstrous phantoms, encircling the Eligor so as to trap them. For a moment the lead beast stood, its eyes locked on its prey, and then, with an earsplitting roar, it attacked.

Shouting a curse, Kiel ripped his sword from its scabbard and turned with his comrades to meet the howling charge. His blade met the first beast with such force that the head separated from its shaggy shoulders, then dropped and hung by the cables. The corpse fell, twitching, to the scarlet snow beneath it. Kiel twisted to face another attacker; he drove his sword straight into the bestial face, watching as it dissolved in a smear of ruined flesh.

Now the biomechs were upon them in force, assailing the Eligor detachment in a demonic frenzy. Bows twanged, lances were thrust, and swords whirled and slashed. Beyond the ring of attackers, Kiel saw his new lieutenant Kar Cha fighting for his life. The Eligor had lost his helmet, and his leaf armor now hung in tatters, glinting red in the fading light. He retained a lance, and this he used to skewer one of the attackers, but there were too many. Kar Cha disappeared under the assault of three more beasts. After that, Kiel became too busy to notice anything but the battle that swept around him.

The melee swirled like autumn leaves in a storm as soldiers hacked, cursed, and yelled. In a red haze of fury, which was thickening before Kiel's eyes, Kiel swung his sword in desperation, weaving a shimmering web of death about him as ravening teeth ripped away his cloak and opened rents in his leaf mail. Talons slit the leather jerkin beneath, until he was bleeding from a dozen wounds. Under a patch of low pines, he and T'Sa stood back-to-back, fighting for their lives as the battle raged around them.

In a flash, it was over.

The half dozen remaining animals retreated into the wood, leaving a hushed silence across the bloody glade. Bodies lay trampled in the churned mud and snow. Here and there lay the steaming, twitching body of a downed biomech, its ruined Old Earth components hissing and spitting blue sparks into the night air. Kiel turned barely in time to catch T'Sa as the soldier slumped from a mortal wound. Kiel lowered the soldier to the ground.

T'Sa looked through bloodied eyes at Kiel. "I go to the halls of the All-father to the feast everlasting." Then he was gone.

Kiel gently lowered the riven body to the ground. "Go well, T'Sa. I fear we will meet again soon enough."

Resheathing his sword and grabbing a pack, Kiel surveyed the carnage for survivors. Besides himself, three Eligor had outlasted the battle. None were unscathed. Kiel himself was bleeding from multiple wounds. "Gather yourselves," he said sharply, setting his shoulders with resolve.

"Kiel, you are wounded," Ter Ka, the contingent's tracker, said with concern. "Your wounds need tending." Ter Ka was himself freely bleeding from a dozen or more cuts.

"No time for that. There will be no rest for us this night." Off in the distance, a howl floated on the wind. The biomechs would soon be back, and in greater numbers. Kiel straightened his shoulders, and his men hastily prepared their packs.

"Can we at least cover our dead?" Ter Ka asked, looking with melancholy at his lifeless comrades.

"No," said Kiel grimly. "They will serve the empire in death as they did in life. They will hold our enemy's attention while we make good our escape."

As Kiel had foreseen, the biomechs had not followed, content to feast on the fallen. The brief respite had allowed Kiel and his fellow Eligor the opportunity to flee southward. But before long, the biomechs were once again upon their trail. In two days of random attacks, the beasts had killed two of the three remaining soldiers; the third and last died later from his wounds.

Kiel surveyed the gloomy forest. He knew that alone, without his bodyguards, he could not fight off another attack. He ran on half blinded, while all around him, like the silent soldiers of some frightful army, the trunks of thousands of ancient black spruce were upraised. An early snow clung in dim white patches beneath the occasional break in the forest canopy, and the gurgling of hundreds of rills from the melting ice could be heard. This was a dark, silent, gloomy world even in summer, and now as the dim light from the steel-gray sky faded with the approach of an early autumn dusk, it seemed more somber than ever. Kiel looked over his shoulder, noting with futility the loping forms of shadowy gray closing in.

The cold forest air burned within his straining lungs, until every breath was like inhaling the blast from some hellish ice furnace. Devoid of feeling, his leaden legs moved like pistons. With each stride, Kiel's booted feet sank into the water-soaked earth and came out again with a sucking sound that continually revealed his position to the beasts behind him.

He struggled on without pausing, his consciousness his only ally. Kiel's grim Eligor heritage would not let him give up, even in the face of certain defeat. More importantly, if he failed, it would not be his death alone, but quite possibly the destruction of the entire Eligor nation. How he knew this, he could not say, but he did not doubt the truth of it.

The humans were ever in his mind now. It was as if they goaded him as surely as the biomechs behind him.

Snow began to fall, big wet flakes that struck the ground with a faint yet audible hiss, spotting the earth and the towering black spruce with myriad dots of white. Great boulders materialized, shouldering out of the needle-carpeted earth, as the land grew steadily rockier at this lower altitude. Before long, Kiel found himself stumbling up a scree-covered rise. The pebbly upgrade slowed him as he felt his final reserves of energy begin to wane. As Kiel struggled, he imagined he could feel the biomechs growing nearer, their hot, fetid breath falling heavy on his neck.

Kiel staggered to the top of the rise and found he was looking down into a thickly treed valley. The world swam before his eyes. Directly ahead, just visible through the trees, was an encampment. He knew the camp was not Eligor—it couldn't be, this far from Opal—but the growling and slavering of the biomechs behind prevented him from stopping or swerving as he pondered the dangers of the unknown site. With his last ounce of strength, he ran straight toward the half dozen large gray tents and the handful of black-clad figures gathered around the remains of the night's cooking fires. The figures looked up in surprise.

"Humans!" Kiel hissed in wracking pain.

He heard one of the humans call an alarm, but not in time for anyone to block his path before he reached the first tent. Kiel dodged around several more before reaching the far side. He stumbled, fell to his knees, and looked back, his vision fading. The humans, who seconds before had been sprinting after him, abruptly stopped and turned as a more immediate threat made itself known. The biomechs that had been charging after Kiel broke into the clearing, slowing as they saw the humans, who stood frozen in surprise. Kiel could guess what the beasts were thinking: Why pursue one difficult meal when here were a dozen that weren't running?

Indeed, the humans were not running; they were ducking into their tents in search of weapons, seeming to have forgotten about the lone, bedraggled Eligor behind them. The biomechs approached slowly as if they were hoping to avoid frightening their prey away, while the humans began to appear with cocked and loaded crossbows. An officer barked a command, and quarrels flew.

Several darts from the first volley rattled off the biomechs' metallic components. Some found their mark, penetrating mouths, eyes, and muzzles. Kiel's perception dimmed, but through the growing haze he could hear the monsters screaming. He perceived them fleeing back up the hillside. The humans, those who were not reloading their crossbows, were pursuing them, apparently unwilling to leave any wounded biomechs to roam the borderlands. Kiel fell forward into the grass as the sound of hesitant footsteps approached. The humans would surely fill his body with arrows. He lost consciousness before the expected missiles hit.

Kiel drifted on a timeless journey through strange lands, a million life ages away from the earth and all things earthly, yet something reached across the void, something tearing ruthlessly at the separating curtains of his dreams, and intruded into reality. Monstrous eyes burned into his, eyes like pools of yellow fire that seared into his very soul. A ravening biomech was crouching in the shadows, and in the next heartbeat, it would spring upon him!

Kiel jerked into consciousness. Was he still facing the howling, blood-mad biomechs that had chased him mercilessly through the mountains? No. As his mind cleared and focused, he came to realize that he was no longer in the wood at all, but confined within a prison of some type. Yet it was not a cold and filthy prison as one would have expected within the Eligor Empire. This prison was warm, dry, and clean.

There was little doubt that it was in fact a prison, because the two small windows cut high into the back wall were very securely barred. The windows looked out upon a tremendous wall that loomed in the distance—the Gondakar Barrier. Kiel could only assume he was now on the human side of the barrier, having been transported here while unconscious. He reached absently for his sword and found—not to his surprise—that the scabbard was empty.

Kiel stiffly rose, the life pouring back into his aching muscles. He had been lying on a cot that sported a comfortable straw-stuffed mattress covered by clean blankets of a soft material unknown to him. As his consciousness moved another notch toward full recovery, the smell of food caught his attention, and he now became aware of a hollow aching hunger in the pit of his gut. After his first near-fatal encounter with the biomechs, he had been chased for at least two, possibly three days with nothing more than water for nourishment. And who knew how long he had lain unconscious within this strange room?

Kiel quickly discovered that the savory smell originated from a wooden platter piled with several kilos of fresh raw meat. A flask of water completed the offering. The thought of poison briefly entered Kiel's mind but was quickly discredited; if the humans had wanted him dead, they would not need to trick him with poisoned food. The type of the meat was alien to Kiel, yet the flavor was better the best he had tasted in Opal since the last war. It was not rancid and spoiled, as was the normal Eligor fare of late.

Kiel thankfully devoured the food and drink. As his strength returned, he began to make a closer examination of the cell. The rock walls and flooring were crude compared to the Eligor norm, but instead of the dank, moldy catacombs found within Opal, this room was warm. Even a cheerful candle flickered, giving off light.

Kiel eyed the candle. It no doubt represented the primary source of light for this primitive culture. "Yes." He nodded. "The humans do not share our interest in Old Earth technology. So much the better for them."

In the far corner, there was an elevated seat made of rock that, after Kiel had removed the wooden cover, was found to possess a bottom through which there was a constantly moving stream of water, no doubt to carry away any waste so as not to soil the cell. *Very strange*, Kiel thought, *to use such engineering, primitive as it was, for a mere prison cell.*

Approaching footsteps on the other side of the ironbound door interrupted his investigative musings. His jailers had arrived.

FOUR

A VIEW FROM THE SOUTH

> Forget me not around your hearth,
> When cheerily smiles the ruddy blaze,
> For dear hath been its evening mirth
> To me, my friends, in other days.
> —"The Traveler's Song"

The pale haggard autumn moon rode high over the tavern quarter of Anwar Kili, where soldiers from the nearby chapter house were enjoying their weekly furlough. Along the crooked cobblestone streets, swords glinted in the shadows. The shrill laughter of women rose, and the noise of scuffling and fighting sounded in a back alley. Lantern light reflected colorfully from diamond-paned windows and open doors, through which drifted the smell of wine, savory foods, and ale. Some could be heard singing along with the rhythm of the runa singers' song of prophecy.

In the Inn of the Seventh Gate, the merriment thundered, shaking the low smoke-stained roof, while soldiers from every rank within the Order gathered—timid initiates, cool-eyed sergeants, and swaggering knights accompanied by their haughty women. Several well-upholstered lasses called out orders of food and drink in strident voices, which carried over the raucous din. There were men from half a dozen of the Great Houses this night—men sent by the Order to defend the border from the still-perceived threat of the Eligor Empire. A giant Saraknyalian brute, taciturn and dangerous, sat oiling his sword and eyeing the crowd suspiciously. A Narakan recruit with a hooked nose and a curled blue-black mustache haggled with the barman over the price of his ale. A blue-eyed, massively muscled Meresinian sullenly studied a gaming board, muttering a half-heard curse at his opponent's last move.

Bishop sat at the serving board, ignoring everything around him except a slim, young serving woman, Bythunian judging by her long mane of black curls and green eyes. Her whole figure reflected strength without detracting from the femininity of her appearance despite her garments, which were incongruous with her present environment. Instead of a skirt, she wore short, wide-legged silk breeches that ended a hand's breadth above her knees and were held up by a wide silken sash worn as a girdle. Flare-topped boots of soft leather came almost to her knees, and a low-necked, wide-collared silk shirt completed her costume. She should have been posed against a backdrop of sea clouds, painted masts, and wheeling gulls; there was the color of the sea in her wide eyes.

Bishop found her breathtaking.

"Frayja, listen, I know of a meadow where there are deer, flowers, and a small brook. I'll pack a lunch. It would be wonderful. I am nearly sure that after my last assignment I will be going nowhere for a long time." That at least was true enough. The rest, Bishop would work out as he went along. Certainly there must be some place in the wood that met his description.

"You said that the last time, and you took off without so much as a goodbye. You were gone for weeks and weeks. Tell me true, there is another girl, isn't there?" Frayja's darks eyes smoldered.

"No, no, it's this dratted *Order* business. I had to leave, and do you know what? The mission was successful. Why, I believe—I am sure, rather—that I will soon be promoted to master or even commander, with all the privileges and prestige that come with such a grand title."

"They will pay you more, yes?" The frown on her young face had settled into icy, calculating speculation.

"Yes, yes, more money. Why, copper riders will turn to golden riders and cascade from the heavens, like a shower from the gods!" Bishop flung his arms wide for effect.

Her cold, wintry speculation thawed as her face broke into a bright smile. "Oh, Bishop, imagine a big house with the latest fashions and comfort! And children, Bishop, lots and lots of children!"

Children ...

"Well, I was thinking more on the order of spending the money on a barn, a nice horse or two, and maybe even one of those new silver-lined saddles I have seen in the southern cities of Koth and Troyes. Gods of the Others, wouldn't that be something?" A dreamy smile curled on Bishop's mouth as he entertained the wild thought.

Children?

Frayja's smile, on the other hand, had again flattened.

Bishop's dream faded almost as quickly; he was not so dense as to have missed the sudden change. "Of course, once you get your house and all. Certainly you didn't think I meant *before* that?"

Frayja's smile slowly returned, more dazzling than ever, this time accompanied by a sultry stare. "Shall we talk further about this, say, two days hence? Say, in that meadow you know of? It is settled," she said with a note of finality. "Pick me up on the morning of the twelfth of Yellowleaf. I will be waiting. And don't forget, I like earrings."

The beautiful Bythunian woman whirled and was gone before Bishop had time to blink.

"Frayja, no, wait, *earrings?*" *What in the eight hells!* The fading vision of silver-lined saddles and of cavernous barns packed with horses was shattered by the hurtling rock of reality that Frayja had thrown. Bishop barely had enough money for ale, let alone anything that would come even remotely close to what he suspected—no, what he knew—Frayja wanted. Indeed, Frayja fully *expected* it.

"Black gods of the Others, woman!" he cursed, slamming his fists down on the serving board.

Gods and women!

They were both equally as hard to fathom, and both equally as dangerous.

Before Bishop had time to stew any longer over the plight he'd just been duped into, a heated conversation drew his attention.

A stout Semyazan trader from the Deep South had come up to do business among the swollen ranks of the Order. Apparently, the Semyazan's opinions were controversial, with shouts of mirth and anger meeting his every remark. He halted in his conspiratorial ramblings just long enough to thrust his bearded face into a tankard of foamy ale. Then, blowing foam from his lips, he barked to the crowd:

"By the Others, I tell you truly, the protectorate has struck a deal with the Eligor! Why else would we not have attacked after their destruction at the Battle of Koth?"

There was a chorus of argument caused by the remark. The trader sat back and smugly nodded, seeming to enjoy his newfound popularity.

"The Eligor are said to be as thick as flies on a dead mule just beyond the Gondakar Barrier. No doubt they are massing for another assault—and we do nothing to stop it! Even the Order seems ignorant of the looming threat. The all-seeing, all-knowing Order, mind you!"

There were a few nervous chortles at the mention of the Order, but most elected to remain silent. It was never considered wise to implicate the Order in a conspiracy.

A poke on his arm caused the trader to turn his head; he was angry at the interruption. He saw a young man of medium height and build standing beside him, scowling.

"Who in the eight hells are you?" the trader growled.

"Bishop," said the stranger. "Bishop of House Arakiel, and a standard-bearer of the Order."

The trader's eyes flickered with momentary caution at the mention of the Order as he took in the rangy youth with his sandy short-cropped hair and blue eyes.

Quickly recovering his composure, the trader sneered. "House Arakiel? Never heard of it." Swilling his drink and slamming it back down, he added, "And why is it that you interrupt me, standard-bearer?"

"There's no truth to what you say. My men and I have just returned from beyond the northeastern border, and we haven't seen so much as an Eligor's shadow." Bishop was mostly proud of his profession, and this trader's blathering seemed to suggest a broad streak of incompetence. "You have no call to spread such hearsay."

There were shouts of agreement mingled with more speculation.

The trader smiled smugly. "What I spread is my business, and I spread it because it's the truth. Everyone knows there are hundreds, thousands—yes, thousands-of those Eligor dogs snuffling at the border. And what do we do about it? Nothing!" The trader stabbed his finger at Bishop accusingly. "Truly, if anyone is spreading anything, it's the protectorate spreading manure on the field of truth!"

Bishop seethed. He detested the Eligor as much as any man, having been present at the Battle of Koth, when the protectorate was nearly defeated in the last war. He knew better than most what the lizards were capable of. Still, what this trader preached sounded not only ridiculous but also downright treasonous. "I don't believe a word of it. I've never heard such barefaced ribaldry in my life!"

The crowd muttered their agreement with Bishop's statement, but the trader widened his eyes in mock disbelief, then burst into a roar of derisive laughter. "And of course, you would know everything there is to know about the world. Certainly one of nineteen or twenty years would be the master of all worldly wisdom by now, wouldn't he?"

Bishop looked around, embarrassed at the mocking laughter that greeted this remark.

"Come, come!" the trader shouted. "Tell these poor fellows, who have only been in the army since before you were weaned, about the world!"

Bishop ground his teeth in barely suppressed rage. He wanted more than anything to cuff the trader across the face, but no; tomorrow he had an appointment with his chapter house's commander, Heimdul, an appointment that would be touchy enough without a taproom incident to compound matters. Heimdul was likely to bring up the subject of one misplaced forager, namely, Councilman Mawr, the conniving little ferret whose accidental death had haunted Bishop's return from Lop Nor.

No. There would be no fighting tonight.

Biting back a response, Bishop slammed his tankard down, threw the barman a copper rider, and stalked out of the tavern amid a roar of laughter.

As the early morning light filtered through high windows of the Anwar Kili Chapter House, Heimdul laid a parchment neatly on his desk and began reading in silence. After a time, he looked up. "So, you think you're ready for something more challenging than foreign relations, is that it?"

From the outer courtyard, the sounds of an undermarshal's bawling and barking of orders, of men marching, and of practice swords clashing permeated the bowels of the ancient citadel. Bishop recalled his own beginnings within the Order as an initiate and wished he were back in those innocent days with nothing but the wrath of the undermarshal to worry about.

"Sir, I was trained to defend the protectorate against its enemies. I know nothing of international relations; I know nothing of diplomacy.

I am only asking for a decent assignment, something worthy of my training."

More than anything, Bishop wanted to put distance between himself and the circumstances surrounding his last mission, even at the risk of angering his commander. The risk was preferable to waiting around for someone to suddenly wake up, wonder at the odd details of his last mission, and call for explanations he dare not give.

Heimdul didn't bother to look up from his reading. "Worthy of your training? We gave you an assignment—a simple enough one at that. You returned with a treaty, which is to your credit, but in the process, you've misplaced a forager diplomat, specifically, Councilman Mawr, a small detail that is not to your credit."

There it was. Bishop's worst fears suddenly crystallized before him. There were suspicions concerning the doctored report he had tendered regarding his last assignment. But what other option had he had? He simply could not reveal certain truths of the matter, specifically, the unauthorized and self-serving search for treasure and the subsequent, albeit accidental, death of Mawr. No, that would have been his last report. Instead, Bishop had stuck to his original story, that being, Councilman Mawr had suddenly returned to Lop Nor because of important personal reasons, an explanation that proved to be fleeting.

As expected, Lop Nor had sent a query confirming the absence of Mawr, sealing the fact that the councilman was in fact missing and presumed dead. Fortunately, Tong Ren did not pursue the matter. Bishop didn't need to wonder at the executive officer's lack of concern over the disappearance of the conniving little weasel. Tong Ren was too much the politician to have overlooked the traitorous dealings of Mawr.

Heimdul, having finally finished his reading, turned the parchment over and eyed Bishop.

Here it comes, Bishop thought, tensing in his seat.

"As for reassignment, your request is hereby granted. You will be given a new task immediately."

Bishop jerked in surprise. *That was easy,* he thought. *Too easy.*

"The grand master of the Order has requested assistance in a matter of state security." He gestured toward the parchment he'd been reading. "It turns out that the profile he has requested just happens to match up with your experience and training," Heimdul continued. "Do you want the assignment?"

"Well, yes. But the grand master?" Bishop blinked. Perhaps he should not have been so eager for another assignment. It seemed, however, that he had dug a hole and was now constrained to jump in it. "The grand master. What does the grand master want with a common standard-bearer?"

"You'll have the chance to ask that question yourself. There's a master here waiting to talk to you." Heimdul slid the mysterious parchment into an open file labeled "Bishop—House Arakiel." After closing the file, he stood.

"A master is here? On the base? On this base … now?"

"A master is here, and he wants to talk to you." Heimdul looked at Bishop. "You will, of course, have the option to refuse the assignment if you don't think you're up to it."

"Ah. Yes, sir." *Refuse the grand master and anger a master in the process? Of course. And why not?* He could refuse the grand master as long as he didn't mind rotting in his current position for the rest of his natural-born life or, worse, someone taking a closer look at his last assignment.

Heimdul, clutching Bishop's file, walked to the door. "I will inform the master that you are ready to see him."

Ready? Bishop would not have used that word exactly. When was anyone ready to talk to a master?

Heimdul closed the door behind him, leaving Bishop alone in the room to ponder his fate in silence. What had he stepped into here? Maybe the talk about an assignment was a ruse. Maybe they were here to interrogate him. Maybe they did know about the hidden details of his last assignment.

Curse it to the eight hells, I hope not! Bishop thought. It was bad enough killing a worthless forager, but to falsify a report for the Order?

Struggling to take his mind away from that paranoid scenario, Bishop began studying the office he now occupied in silence. He noted the candles drearily flickering in their sconces around the room, casting dark, ominous shadows across the plastered walls, which sported several ancient paintings of unrecognized men in military uniforms, all of whom seemed to be leering at him. A hearth sat gaping like a black maw against a wall, smoldering, the last few embers threatening to die. He noted a spider on a high rain-streaked windowsill that was in the process of busily wrapping a freshly caught fly. Bishop closed his eyes, slumping deeper in the creaking chair.

Moments passed before the door again opened and the master glided in with Bishop's file in hand. Bishop immediately stood at attention, rigid as a post. The master closed the door behind him and walked past Bishop, his black chain mail clinking, as if he didn't see him.

Bishop's stomach growled.

The master was the type of man who commanded attention and something more. His face was long, smooth-shaven, and ashen, which together with the sunken cheeks lent a corpse-like appearance, that is, until one looked into his eyes. The color of ancient ice, the eyes gleamed with cool, calculating purpose. The master wore an austere black sir coat with the oak tree symbol of the Order emblazoned on the left arm and the breast. Well-maintained boots squeaked with the sound of freshly oiled leather as the master moved.

Bishop eyed the man. Yes, this man was a typical master through and through, but it wasn't just his looks and armor that identified him as such. The man exuded arrogance. According to the scuttlebutt in the lower ranks of the Order that Bishop frequented, these masters saw security breaches everywhere and did whatever they pleased to close them. Any persons unfortunate enough to have drawn their suspicion did not fare well. It was said you could have your career smashed, even have your property confiscated—or worse.

Bishop knew the Rule, all seventy-two articles. He suddenly recalled one article that had caused him more than a little consternation since the forager incident:

> We of the Order fight the battles of the protectorate, not fearing to have sinned in neither killing the enemy, nor fearing for our own deaths since dealing out death, nor dying for the Order, which contains anything criminal but rather merits reward. In this way fighting for the Order, the Order is maintained. Truly, he who freely takes the death of his enemy as an act of vengeance will more easily find consolation in his status as a soldier of the Order. The soldier of the Order kills safely and dies safely. Not without cause does he bear the sword. He is the instrument of the Order for the punishment of evildoers and for the defense of the protectorate. Truly, when he kills evildoers, it is not homicide but rather malicide, and he is considered the Order's legal executioner.

The master seated himself at Heimdul's desk and reopened Bishop's file, laying several yellowed parchments neatly in front of him. He then proceeded to study each document in the most maddening and tedious way. Finally, after an age, he looked up and spoke.

"Standard-Bearer Bishop, Bishop of House Arakiel," the man said, seeming to pronounce *Arakiel* as if it were a foreign word to him.

"I am Bishop." Bishop saluted smartly. "Bishop of House Arakiel.

The master ignored the salute as he leveled a disdainful gaze on Bishop.

Bishop had heard these devils were ill mannered and evasive, and this particular representative's behavior was not in any way deviating from the stereotype. Bishop finally let his salute fall to his side, all the while feeling like a complete idiot.

"At ease, Standard-Bearer Bishop of House Arakiel. You will address me as Master Bryn," the master finally responded, returning his attention to the papers laid out before him. "Yes, well, you are a standard-bearer and the possessor of a Riika." This wasn't so much a question as a statement of fact.

"Yes, sir. Ah, yes, Master Bryn." Bishop's heart skipped a beat at the mention of the Riika. That he was in possession of the Old Earth device was not common information, yet knights had been present at his acceptance ceremony, and who knew, maybe there had even been a master present. The thought was troubling because the Riika was now tied to Bishop's ordeal with the forager.

In a practiced tone, Bryn spoke again. "The information I am about to share with you is not to be shared with others. Do you understand the consequences of divulging it?"

"Well, yes, I suppose so."

"Yes or no will do."

"Yes."

"Good," Bryn cut in. "It is disappointing when someone breaches our trust." He removed another parchment from the file and slid it across the table toward Bishop.

"Read and sign on the line at the bottom of the document." Bryn stabbed the lower half of the document with a finger as if it had offended him in some way. "It acknowledges your understanding of the secure nature of the information you will be given."

Masters! Always with their secrets! Still, Bishop read the nearly unintelligible lengthy document, then dipped a quill and signed, and slid the paper back across the desk.

Bryn inspected the document, blotted it, slipped it back into the open file, and again eyed Bishop. "I will begin by asking you a hypothetical question regarding world affairs."

World affairs? Bishop stared uncomprehendingly.

"Suppose I were to tell you that the Imperial Eligor hierarchy, including the emperor himself, has been recently obliterated, an Eligor city-state has been eviscerated, and the Eligor social structure is on the verge of imploding. Simply put, the Eligor Empire, as we have always known it, is hovering on the edge of total collapse. What would you say to that?"

"On the edge of collapse? The Eligor Empire?"

Bryn studied the effect of his words while Bishop's mind absorbed the wild idea. The Eligor Empire that had, a little more than a year ago, sat at the protectorate's northern borderlands, on the verge of collapse? How could that be? Bishop's grandfather's grandfather had lived with the Eligor threat. Was Bishop to imagine that he would live to witness the final collapse, an end to uncounted millennia of unrelenting hostility? But what if it were true! And why would Bryn bring it up if it weren't? Bishop did not feel confident enough to ask any details about Bryn's hypothesis, but the mere possibility of such a development intrigued him.

Bishop squared his shoulders and responded, "I would say excellent!" He took a deep breath and allowed himself a weak smile. "I would say thank the black gods of the Others!"

Bryn sat motionless, stoically staring at Bishop as if he were being scrutinized under a magnifying glass.

Bishop's smile drained from his face like melting ice as Bryn continued to stare. "It would be *good*, wouldn't it?" Bishop asked.

Bryn eyed him a moment longer. "Perhaps yes, perhaps no."

Yes and no. What was this devil getting at?

"The Eligor Empire has been a monstrous threat. In fact, it has posed the single largest threat that our protectorate has ever known. Yet if it were to fail ..." Bryn paused and became introspective. "If it were to fail, it would leave behind a power vacuum—a vacuum that, again, hypothetically, could be filled by a potentially greater threat."

Bishop's forehead furrowed with his incomprehension. "Greater threat? What could be a greater threat than the Eligor Empire?"

"What could be a greater threat than the Eligor Empire indeed?" Bryn repeated the words, nodding absently, his eyes unfocused as his mind was lost in thought.

"You, of course, know of the Vena Korela?" Bryn suddenly asked, his eyes refocusing, holding Bishop's own in a viselike grip.

Bishop's mind shifted to the new, unexpected line of questioning. "The Vena Korela? Well, yes, of course I have heard of it. Its philosophies are taught to all new acolytes. Its values and teachings are the basis of the Order itself."

It was a textbook response.

"I am aware of our training programs, Standard-Bearer Bishop, but have you any idea of its deeper content?" Bryn pressed.

Bishop, his ears flaming, pondered the question. The book was nearly mythical, and there were no copies; copies were considered heresy—a lessening of the original. The book was said to reside within the walls of the principal chapter house at Troyes. Its basic teachings and philosophy were known, but as for the deeper contents, who knew? "Besides my instruction within the Order, I have heard it sung about by the runa singers."

"What do the runa singers sing about the book?"

"They sing of the Vena Korela as a holy book, written by divinely inspired hands after the Old Earth ended, after the end of the Fourth Age, I believe. They sing of its giving us our laws and telling of a time of a reawakening, a return to enlightenment, and a time when the protectorate will be reunited under one rule and again be given dominion over the earth."

Bryn nodded, smiling as a teacher would to an astute child. "The runa singers sing of truth. The Vena Korela is as they describe, but it is much, much more. The keys to the ancient mysteries of the Others are enclosed within the book, keys that will be used to find and unlock their ancient knowledge and bring about enlightenment and the restoration of order by uniting the Great Houses and, as a consequence, Merja Soria itself under one rule. The protectorate would be united again."

Bishop had heard something to this effect at his acceptance ceremony but had understood very little of the ritual. And he certainly had not been let in on the sacred teachings of the Vena Korela beyond what was common knowledge. "Why is it the keys have yet to be discovered?" he asked.

Bryn darkened dangerously. "The text has been interwoven with prophetic verse, making its translation and interpretation difficult. Add to this the bewildering science, or, if you will, the magic, of the Others."

What Bryn was saying was true: in eons past, the earth had been destroyed by a massive war that employed forces so far beyond current understanding that for countless centuries it was more easily explained as magic. Even now, many people within the protectorate were more apt to believe the old mythos rather than embrace the modern explanations of technology and the age of the Others as being anything less than supernatural. Bishop himself was undecided on several points, being torn between the traditionalists, who populated the world with gods and spirits, and the more modern heretical priests of science.

"Why these questions of the Vena Korela? What does it have to do with a greater threat to humans?"

"You make the connection. Good. The Vena Korela devotes whole chapters to the Eligor, yet it also speaks of other postcataclysmic denizens of our planet in addition to that dark and evil race—denizens who have, or so it is said, been perpetually separated from the protectorate by the Eligor Empire."

Bishop's skin prickled as he began putting together the pieces from

Bryn's line of discussion. "Who or what, exactly, is said to reside beyond the Eligor Empire?"

"Those who are mentioned within the Vena Korela: the Ikonians."

Bishop's eyes widened as he started in surprise. *Ikonians!*

Bryn looked on as Bishop struggled to remember the bits and pieces of lore he had picked up over the years about that mythic race. The Ikonians were, according to the runa singers, magical insect beings that resided beyond the Copper Mountains, far to the north, whose roads, hills, caves, fields, rivers, lakes, and forests, or so common stories attested, were infested with these mysterious beings. The Ikonians were said to be possessed of supernatural powers that made them, at best, unpredictable and, at worst, dangerous. Parents warned their children about Ikonians, monsters able to fly from their mountain homes and steal them away if they were disobedient. The superstitious blamed them for storms, earthquakes, famines, and wars. The Ikonians were, in short, akin to chaos.

Common sense told Bishop to stifle his initial urge to share this bit of knowledge with Bryn, as then it would emphasize Bishop's backcountry origins. Anyone confessing to a belief in the superstition surrounding the Ikonians, or so Bishop suspected, would also project the image of one who believed in giants, shape-shifting monsters, genii, demons, trolls, and other folkloric creatures. Yet if there were nothing to such stories, why would Bryn have mentioned the Ikonians?

Bryn seemed to read Bishop's mind. "Previously, nothing was known of the Ikonians except from brief passages within the Vena Korela. We are still not wholly convinced they truly exist and, if they do, whether they are human, insect, or beast. We suspect, if in fact they are real, that they are most certainly of flesh and blood, not magical."

Bishop was thankful he'd stayed silent.

Bryn continued. "As I am sure you are well aware, the Eligor Empire has always been sandwiched between the protectorate and the northern lands beyond, making that domain too remote and isolated to ever allow us to gather evidence concerning the existence of Ikonians—a venture previously seen as being of little strategic importance at any rate."

Bryn locked his intense gray eyes on Bishop. "That venture is no longer seen as unimportant and, I might add, is no longer seen as impossible."

A remote corner of Bishop's mind began to tingle with apprehension.

"We have recently acquired intelligence that suggests the Ikonians actually exist. Further, the intelligence suggests that these creatures are on the move, smashing through the northern Eligor Empire and, ultimately, moving toward our frontier. This information, however sketchy, has us somewhat concerned, as you might have guessed."

Bishop's tingle of foreboding broke like a tidal wave upon his conscious mind. Ikonians! Mythical beings from a childhood fable come to life, smashing their way through the Eligor Empire and moving toward the Gondakar Barrier? The thought was fantastic but terrifying. The Eligor invasion had only just been stopped in the past war, two years previous, and that effort had taxed the protectorate to the very limits, draining it of its collective strength. What could be expected from Ikonians?

Another thought suddenly entered Bishop's reeling mind. "What do you need me for?"

Bryn smiled again and nodded as if he had been expecting the question. "We require reconnaissance. We need to know what is truly going on up north. You will go to Ikonia, investigate these rumors, and in the unlikely event that they are true, attempt to determine the reasons for the attacks. That is your assignment."

Bishop's eyes widened, and his mouth dropped open as if it were on a hinge.

Bryn shrugged indifferently, waving a hand in the air. "Quite probably, there isn't a shred of truth to any of it. In either case, after you are certain of the situation, you will return to the protectorate posthaste and report your findings to the Order."

Bishop began shaking his head as the full weight of Bryn's words seeped in. "You want me to go to Ikonia—*through the Eligor Empire*? You're joking! I wouldn't make it ten kilometers beyond the Gondakar Barrier, let alone circumvent the city-states of Opal and Kirsk."

"Well, if our information is correct, Kirsk won't present a problem. The Ikonians have already obliterated it."

Bishop leaned back in his chair, dumbfounded, yet before he could say anything more, Bryn continued. "You need not worry about the Eligor Empire. The Order will be providing you with a guide. He is waiting for you at Gondakar."

"A guide? What do you mean, a guide?"

"A, ah, an individual who has spent a considerable amount of time behind the Gondakar Barrier. He is an expert on the Eligor Imperium. It is his responsibility to take you safely through their lands and insert you within range of Ikonia. After you have completed your assignment, he will extract you and bring you back safe and sound."

"An individual"? "He"? "Him"?

Apparently Bryn was not going to name this guide. Bishop thought he knew most of the trackers within the Order. There weren't that many of them, and none, to his knowledge, had ever penetrated more than ten kilometers beyond the Gondakar Barrier.

"Begging your pardon, sir, if this guide is first-rate, then why doesn't he collect this information? Why do you want me to go?"

"You are an experienced standard-bearer of the Order and the possessor of a Riika; your travel companion is neither."

The Riika again. What did the Riika have to do with anything?

Bishop chewed on what he had been told and, more importantly, what he had not been told. Something did not sit right.

Bishop chose his words carefully. "The bearer of a Riika I am, but I must ask you, what possible difference could that make? As far as I know—as far as anyone has ever told me—it's useless." This was not true, and Bishop knew it, but what could he say that would not eventually lead back to the missing forager?

Now it was Bryn's turn to grow uncomfortable, as if he had divulged more than intended. But Bishop took no pleasure in the anxious transition, as it suggested that an unknown and frightening element was being kept hidden from him.

Bryn's eyes narrowed in thought, as if he was weighing his reply. "You wish to know the truth? The truth concerning the Riika?"

"I am the bearer of the device. It might make a difference in the outcome of my quest," Bishop responded logically.

"Very well," Bryn replied with a note of finality. "You have a point: it might be of some benefit to enlighten you to certain knowledge concerning your inheritance. We will conclude your mission details in due course. But tell me first, what do you already know about the Riika?"

Bishop glanced at the contrivance that was locked permanently around his left wrist, feeling as if Bryn could read his thoughts; he would have to be very careful. "I know very little about the Riika. I was told that it was created by the Others. I was told it recognized me as its rightful inheritor and that ages ago it was a talisman of great power and a symbol of human sovereignty. But I will concede, after wearing it for these many years, that it has served me not in the slightest." Bishop sat in terror, hoping beyond hope that Bryn could not see through his subterfuge.

Bryn nodded. "Yes, well, its original use, to a degree, is something of a mystery. And as for your limited knowledge on the subject, those with such knowledge are not typically at liberty to give details concerning the device, even to the bearer of said device. It is part of the Rule. You will swear to me and to the Order an oath of silence before I proceed."

Bishop pondered Bryn's words. He was familiar with the Rule but had never seen the Riika, not even hint of the device, mentioned within any of its seventy-two articles. There were riddles within riddles here, but buried deep within them all was also the promise of illumination or, at the very least, a step toward illumination. "I swear an oath to you, by my honor as a standard-bearer of the Order," Bishop said solemnly, lifting his hand to his heart.

"Very well, as long as you fully realize the consequences of any breach in my trust." Bryn began to speak more slowly, seemingly not at all certain that Bishop was honest. "The Saga of Levanah has become so mythologized that interpretation is exceedingly difficult, but I will tell you what I know and what I have come to believe in terms of its interpretation."

"Saga of Levanah?"

Again, a cloud passed over Bryn's eyes as if he were not at all comfortable with discussing the subject with a lowly standard-bearer. An internal struggle was being fought within this grim man, and Bishop wondered at its meaning.

"Yes. Well, our combined knowledge of the Riika comes from the Saga of Levanah, an obscure book within the Vena Korela."

"I have not heard of the Saga of Levanah."

"You would not have until you were initiated as a master. But your situation is unique, so I deem it necessary to enlighten you."

"What of this saga?" Bishop questioned, curiosity momentarily holding sway over his fear of the master before him.

"It is considered a poetic masterpiece, yet it is not read for its lyrical value alone, but rather as a source of historical data. The trouble with the Saga of Levanah, as with all parts of the Vena Korela, comes in the interpretation."

"Interpretation?"

Bryn nodded knowingly. "During the original compiling of the Vena Korela, a runa singer within the Order named Ilmarinen collected the Levanah songs, gathering verses from runa singers scattered throughout the protectorate, and assembled them into one complete saga, a continuous epic narrative pieced together from the scattered pieces of the original song. Regrettably, for untold centuries the original compilation of Ilmarinen was only sung, never written, as it was considered a sacrilege to write things down in those days, a decision that further muddled the original facts. Some four hundred years ago, the grand master Yara realized that a written version was necessary to protect from degradation through word of mouth, so he authorized the one written copy that we now study at the principal chapter house at Troyes. The manuscript, the written Saga of Levanah, is currently separated into ten runa, or groups, that when sung together make up all the known history concerning the Riika."

Bryn studied Bishop's reaction, seeming to realize he knew nothing of what was being said. "I will try to recall the most relevant runa of the saga, as it is my personal specialty. And because of this, among other reasons, I was the one chosen to deliver your orders. It may help you understand the difficulty in its translation. Remember, we are only studying these runa to help us gather information about the past so that we might better understand the future, information that we can glean from no other source."

"I understand," Bishop said.

Bryn eyed Bishop for a moment as if assessing his intelligence. "The first runa relates to the creation of the central hero of the story. The gods of the Others sang into existence the grand wizard Levanah, the original bearer of the device that you now possess.

"Runa five tells of the forging of the first Riika, a magical device or talisman also referred to as the 'Sampo', the terms are synonymous. The wizard Shabbathai, realizing the power of Levanah's magic, urged him to journey to the Copper Mountains to forge a great weapon. Levanah hesitated and ultimately refused, but Shabbathai tricked him by singing into existence an enchanted army that threatened the gods. Levanah believed the gods of the Others were about to be attacked and reluctantly forged the Riika, inseparably melding his spirit to the weapon and locking it permanently to his arm."

Bryn's eyes became distant as he sang a verse in a guttural voice, as follows:

> Levanah struck fire.
> The sun flame flashed
> With a copper tongue.
> In six vaults of flaming colors,
> The wizardsmith Levanah
> Hammered out the Sampo and
> Devised the ciphered cover,
> From the point of a raven's quill,
> From the milk of a farrow cow,
> From a tiny grain of barley
> And the summer fleece of a ewe.

Bishop struggled to understand what was being sung to him. He was certain it was a rare and singular chance for him to understand more about the Riika, but it seemed beyond his ability to comprehend.

Bryn's eyes sharpened. "It is difficult to understand, Bishop. You must attempt to look beyond the words with your mind's eye."

"Yes, of course, I will try."

Bryn eyed him a moment longer, then continued. "Runa six describes the theft of the Riika. Shabbathai demanded Levanah share the Riika, but Levanah refused. Shabbathai vowed to get revenge and left. Levanah was angered by the threat but heeded the warning, retiring to the safety of the Copper Mountains. However, Shabbathai, using a secret passage under the mountains, sang an enchantment onto Levanah, causing a deep sleep to descend upon him. Shabbathai worked free the Riika with a magical chant and escaped. This detail suggests the Riika could be detached at some point in the past without killing the bearer.

"Runa eight describes the final exploits of Levanah and the battle for the Riika. Awaking and realizing the Riika has been stolen, Levanah conjured up a storm and called upon the demon Madim to stop Shabbathai, who was blown overboard and washed up on an island. Levanah attacked Shabbathai and recovered the Riika."

Bishop listened intently, struggling to comprehend what was being said.

Bryn continued the story. "Runa nine involves the death of Levanah and the final disposition of the Riika. Shabbathai, seeking the Riika and revenge, hunted Levanah on this island and, hiding, shot Levanah with a magical poison arrow. Levanah died and was thrown into a pit after being chopped to pieces by Shabbathai, who in the process of trying to regain the Riika, shattered it. The act of shattering the Riika killed Shabbathai and caused the Great Cataclysm. At this point the Riika, or rather a portion of it, was lost."

Bryn sang again, with such emotion that a lump caught in Bishop's throat at hearing it.

> This was Levanah's end,
> Death of the grand wizard,
> Falling into death's black pit,
> Down to the caverns of the dead,
> Down to the eighth hell,
> Awaiting his rebirth.
> The Riika is broken,
> Awaiting its rebirth.

But there must have been more. "What of his descendants?" Bishop pressed.

"I was about to tell you," Bryn said, scowling at the interruption to his tale. "Runa ten describes Levanah's line and the reforging of the Riika. The gods were told what had happened and retrieved a drop of Levanah's blood from the island. From this blood they created Levanah's children, but they passed from the earth before recovering all the pieces of the Riika. Levanah's children began an eon-long search that will only end with the birth of the chosen descendant and his subsequent reforging of the Riika."

Bryn sang again, his voice catching with the same emotion as before:

> Let the rope of time wear out.
> One day go, another come.
> They will be waiting
> To bring back the Riika,
> To bring back Levanah,
> To make whole that which was broken.
> They will set a new moon in the sky and
> Free a new sun in the heavens,
> And there will be gladness on the earth
> After the great darkness.

"What does that mean, exactly?" Bishop wondered aloud.

"The myth, Bishop, the legend, in part, I believe, suggests that at the proper time, at the time of our most desperate need, the Riika will be made whole again, uniting the Great Houses and, in so doing, forging a unified government and bringing about a golden Sixth Age. Sadly, the most desperate time in the protectorate's history came with the Eligor invasion of which you are already well aware. No such restorative miracle occurred; still, it is just possible that the worst has yet to unfold."

Bishop pondered all that he had heard. "Unified? But the Protectorate of Merja Soria is unified," Bishop said.

Bryn's eyebrows rose mockingly. "Oh, it is, is it? Have you never wondered why we refer to Merja Soria as a protectorate?"

Bishop stared, not understanding Bryn's question.

Bryn waved a dismissive hand. "The legends are mostly that: legend. Still, the Order believes there truly is more to the Riika. A key, if you wish, has been lost through the ages, one that if found will unlock knowledge that could be of immense value to our security and to our very existence. They also believe that if such a thing exists, it is most assuredly in the Copper Mountains, a region not too far from where you are seeking to go, if anything of the old maps we have can be believed. It is a fact that is too close to prophecy to ignore."

Bishop pondered the information. It was a bit short of what he had expected, but it was a start. "There is just one thing I don't quite understand."

"That is enough for now. I have told you more than I should have, and I become passionate when talking of the Saga of Levanah and forget myself."

"What of the other descendants?"

"I have told you what you need to know."

"But I must know about—"

Bryn darkened with impatience, and fire leapt into his eyes, seeming to melt through leagues of gray ice in an instant. "Standard-Bearer Bishop, I'll be blunt. You are first in line for this assignment, but certainly there are others we can enlist. We can always send you in search of the lost forager if you so desire. Do you want the assignment or not?"

Gods of the Others, you have me like a rat in a trap and you damned well know it! Bishop had extracted all he was likely ever to get out of this master concerning the Riika, an object that undoubtedly was a key factor in his having been chosen for this assignment.

"Well?" asked Bryn.

Bishop did not need to ponder the question. If he was sure of anything, it was this: refusing an assignment, any assignment, from the Order was not in his best interests. His previous assignment flitted through his mind. The mention of the forager seemed to be the fulcrum they were using to move him in the direction of this mission. They had him caught like a fly in treacle, and they knew it.

"I suppose I will go, but—" Bishop began.

"Now returning to your assignment," Bryn cut in, "I will firstly state that our instructions for your expedition cannot be charged with a narrow or mercenary spirit, but rather, one of careful and studious observation. Your objectives are as follows: link up with the guide that we have provided you at the city of Gondakar, just below the Gondakar Barrier; proceed into and through the Eligor Empire; and finally, penetrate the Ikonian frontier to authenticate or contradict the rumors I have previously told you of. Along the way, you are to acquaint yourself with the natural resources of the country, the character of the land, and any notable precataclysmic ruins you might happen upon. You will bring home a detailed account of all these things, together with such articles as you should obtain in the course of your travels, with the most vigilant care and attention given to any Old Earth technology that you might discover along the way. As no written orders of any sort are to accompany you, is this last point most clear in your mind, Standard-Bearer Bishop?"

Bishop nodded his understanding while pondering the implications of what he'd just heard. The protectorate generally regarded technology as having a worth far beyond that of gold, but most associated it with those things best left alone, such as poisonous snakes, poisonous spiders, or scorpions.

Bryn grew grave as he spoke again. "For the sluggard's brow, the laurel never grows; renown is not the child of indolent repose."

Bishop swallowed hard as he felt a trickle of cold sweat running down his forehead.

"Now, if you don't mind, I have some paperwork to catch up on. If—when—you return, you are to contact me directly. And remember, you are bound by the articles of the Rule to keep all you have heard close to your heart. Do you understand? Is this most clear in your mind?"

Bishop mutely nodded and stood, not knowing what else to do. Bryn deftly dipped his quill in his inkpot and began scratching away at his paperwork as if his subordinate had already left the room. Bishop, mostly from habit, saluted and turned to leave.

As Bishop reached the door, Bryn added, without looking up from his paperwork, "Oh, one more minor detail. You have been assigned a wolf-bird; you may pick him up at the aviary. The both of you will leave at first light for Gondakar on the morrow."

"A wolf-bird? Thank you for the offer, Master Bryn, but I really don't need one." Bishop's heart pounded as he inched closer toward the door. *A wolf-bird! Gods of the Others, anything but that! Better to be handed over to the Eligor for slow roasting over a pit of coals.*

The master looked up from his paperwork and stared blandly. Bishop was about to repeat what he had said when Bryn responded, slower this time as if for emphasis, "You have been assigned a *Corvus corax intelligentus*—a wolf-bird. You will gather him up this afternoon and will leave for the Gondakar Barrier at first light on the morrow."

Bishop's mouth opened, but nothing came out except a dry rattle.

Bryn's eyes became hard as granite. "Pick up your winged companion, gather reconnaissance on the situation up north, determine the reasons for the supposed Ikonian attacks, return to the protectorate posthaste, and report your findings. Any captured or acquired Old Earth technology, any gained knowledge of the Riika, comes directly back to me. Those are your orders.

"Dismissed!"

The Riika again! Bishop silently shrieked.

Returning to his paperwork, Bryn added, "Good luck on your assignment. Oh, and don't forget to close the door on your way out."

The wolf-bird aviary was set in the southwestern corner of the Anwar Kili Chapter House grounds, as far away from human activity as possible. As with all such aviaries of this type, it consisted of roosts, a rookery, and feeding facilities, all of which were connected to several adjoining outbuildings housing the human staff, whose job it was to care for the birds.

"Wolf-birds!" Bishop growled, as he closed reluctantly upon the aviary. "Of all the accursed things that could have happened to me, why did it have to be wolf-birds? If things weren't already bad enough, and they are most assuredly bad enough!"

Bishop had solidly formed his opinion on wolf-birds as a young boy on his family's farm. As he walked, he recollected those first encounters with the winged devils. He had been tormented, teased, and heckled in the planting fields until he was wont to take up a bow and end the avian harassment. But of course, that would have been illegal, and the birds knew it.

The dire memories of his youth sharpened as Bishop warily entered the compound. Glancing up into the trees with their low-hanging branches, he immediately spied a mob of perturbed wolf-birds, all bobbing and flapping in the lower branches, cawing, cackling, and cursing a squirrel that had committed some transgression against them.

Bishop's heart went out to the squirrel. He only hoped it had successfully purloined an egg. One less wolf-bird in the world would be a welcome blessing in Bishop's book.

A twig unexpectedly snapped under Bishop's boot, and he froze, but it was too late. Alerted by the slight noise, the birds abruptly ceased their angered shrieks, then turned and stared. Bishop returned the stare, feeling as if he were back in those fields of his youth, waiting for the tormenting to begin anew. This time, however, there would be a debt to pay with interest—regulations be damned. What else could they possibly do to him?

Bishop's alert paralysis was broken as a wolf-bird warder stepped briskly away from an administration building and approached. The man's oversized black eyes darted over Bishop in an impatient, nervous fashion. "I am Warder Elias. Can I assist you in some way? Is there something you desire?" he asked curtly.

Bishop relaxed a bit, taking in the hawkish man, wondering briefly if close association with the birds had somehow morphed Elias's appearance over the years. "I was sent by Master Bryn to pick up one of those things." Bishop jabbed a thumb at the black mob that was staring motionless above them.

"Ah yes, we have been expecting you. You are late, late!" Warder Elias's arms twitched involuntarily as if he were ruffling unseen feathers. "You would be Bishop? Bishop of House Arakiel?" Elias inquired in a businesslike fashion.

"Word of my recent assignment travels fast, I see," Bishop muttered, his attention returning to the feathered creatures that were crouching vulturelike over his head.

"Why, of course, efficiency is our credo. We finished the paperwork some time ago. It is all in order. Now, if you don't mind, I'll retrieve your travel companion."

Elias looked up and, with a harsh croaking sound that stabbed into Bishop's spine like an ice pick, called to the black throng. A single bird separated from its brethren and glided to a rest on the warder's outstretched, leather-gauntleted arm. Warder Elias seemed finally to relax and regain something of a normal manner.

Bishop and the wolf-bird eyed each other suspiciously.

"This is Storm Singer, son of Gray Mantle, son of Wolf Raven. One of the best, he is," Elias said proudly, eyeing the bird with unconcealed admiration. "Yes, one of the best he is."

Bishop had never seen more admiration in young parents than he now saw in Elias's eyes. It almost caused his stomach to turn.

Storm Singer was a large, jet-black creature, larger in fact than a goshawk or even a red-tailed hawk, with a distinguished high brow protecting a brain far larger than that of a normal bird its size. Obviously, the animal—as with all its kind—was yet another descendant from the age of the Others, in the vein of the Eligor and the foragers, Bishop grimly noted.

"Hey," Bishop muttered to the creature.

The wolf-bird continued to eye Bishop with dark, shiny orbs of jet, but it did not reply—did not, in fact, so much as blink.

"Hey!" Bishop repeated.

The bird, seeming to lose interest in Bishop, began preening its feathers.

Bishop turned back to Elias. "Listen," Bishop began.

"Hey!" the bird suddenly said in a near-perfect imitation of Bishop's voice.

Bishop's attention returned to the bird, but the bird still seemed consumed with its feather care.

Bishop again turned to Elias. "Listen, this bird doesn't seem very bright. I'm no regular army grunt and—"

"Hey," the bird called again. "Hey, grunt."

Bishop stared at the bird in growing anger. "Can that thing talk or not?!"

"Of course, he can talk. You just heard him do so!" Elias said indignantly.

Bishop glowered at the creature. "The name is Bishop."

"Bich-hop," the bird muttered.

Bishop's eyes widened in embarrassed anger as he glared at Elias. "No. No, no, no. I am not going through this again. I don't want this one. How about one of those?" Bishop waved a finger toward the remaining birds perched in the nearby tree, all of which were cackling in what sounded disturbingly like laughter.

"I am sorry, the others have been assigned," Elias replied.

"It only figures that I would get the village idiot," Bishop muttered under his breath.

Elias's eyes bulged as if he had been personally insulted. "I beg your pardon?" he said angrily.

Storm Singer suddenly jumped to Bishop's shoulder, interrupting

Elias's outburst. "I have made a decision," the bird said, now perfectly articulate. "I will keep this human, however dull-witted he appears to be."

Storm Singer began picking at his feathers again as if Bishop were no more animate than a fence post.

Bishop's initial surprise quickly eroded into anger. "Get off me. You'll foul my shirt!" He shook his shoulder, attempting to dislodge the bird, but to no avail. Storm Singer cawed in mild amusement as Bishop twisted, shook, curled, tucked, and wobbled. Finally, his efforts exhausted, he gave up.

The bird cocked his head, bringing his jet eyes close to Bishop's own. "Yes, dull-witted, but with times being as they are …"

Without warning, and before an astonished and infuriated Bishop could respond, Storm Singer spread his wings, jumped into the air, and was gone.

Bishop had reached the limit of his endurance. "Black gods of the Others! Why am I to be saddled with a wolf-bird? Am I being punished for something?"

Elias glowered at Bishop. "Wolf-birds are the most valuable trail companions you could ever wish for. You would be wise to remember that."

Bishop threw his arms into the air in exasperation. "Sure. You have to say that—you're a warder—but I don't buy it. I think they were loosed on the world as yet another plague, like the Eligor!"

Elias gasped in offended astonishment, then whirled around and stomped back into the aviary, leaving Bishop alone with the cackling, which still peppered down through the trees.

After checking the back of his shirt, half expecting a nasty surprise, Bishop eyed the surrounding trees. The mob of wolf-birds still stared back, but Storm Singer had disappeared, hopefully for good. In any case, Bishop would sneak out of the chapter house in the early hours of the morning and leave the dratted flying rat behind.

That would be that.

Long before the eastern sky grew pale, signaling the coming day, Bishop was well on his way to the city of Gondakar. For a short time, he followed a forested lane northward, until it broke out along the hedgerow borders of a farming district. Bishop glided quietly along in the predawn silence. Even the wild things hardly noticed his passing. He crossed a small stream by a narrow plank bridge and stopped on its mossy rock-lined bank to quench his thirst. The stream was no more than a winding black ribbon thickly bordered with leaning alder trees and dew-scented undergrowth. Away to the west, Bishop noted, it fed several farms that twinkled with lighted lanterns in the gently rolling valley below him. The faint smell of woodsmoke and bacon drifted by. Farmers were up milking their cows and tending their chickens, oblivious to Bishop and the quest he had been set upon.

"Just as well for them," Bishop mumbled as he continued north into the approaching forest.

The sun finally crested over the eastern sky, casting cathedral-like streamers under the treed canopy. Bishop walked along the gurgling, stony-sounding stream as the sun rose above the forest, slanting through the thin silver mist. Dampness on the autumn leaves glimmered, and webs of gossamer twinkled on every vine maple and fern like many strands of silvery pearls. Mist rose from the ground, momentarily hanging at waist level and swirling in silent eddies as Bishop passed. Though harvest was well under way, some ripening salmonberries, the last of the season, remained, providing a welcome midmorning breakfast as Bishop walked. Truly, it was a wonderful day to be on the trail, the dangers of the mission seeming to be momentarily distant. Bishop began to softly sing a tune he had learned as a youth: "I think of you, my love so fair, your golden curls of shining hair."

"Hoo, Bissshop!" came a voice from above, followed by a black shadow that flitted across the sun-dappled ground before him.

Bishop, accustomed to forest life as he was, jumped in sudden alarm, half unsheathing his sword before realization dawned on him.

Storm Singer!

The wolf-bird had not flown off after all! Bishop slammed the sword back, feeling like an initiate again. Standard-bearers of the Order weren't supposed to be tracked, and certainly not by a brainless bird. Nevertheless, the thing had found him somehow, flitting silently among the trees, no doubt waiting for Bishop to relax so as to scare the wits out of him.

Storm Singer wheeled, dropped, and lightly settled on Bishop's shoulder as if it was already his time-honored roost. Bishop did not try to dislodge the bird as he had previously. Instead, he continued to stalk down the trail, trying as best he could to ignore the creature that now sat indifferently upon his shoulder. Maybe the thing would catch the hint and leave. But no. The bird ignored Bishop's silence—did not, in fact, seem to give the matter the slightest thought. Storm Singer merely sat preening his feathers without an apparent care in the world, bobbing up and down in rhythm to Bishop's stride as if the bird were some grotesque ornament attached to his shoulder.

Finally, the picking and ruffling sounds of Storm Singer's cleaning unhinged Bishop, causing him to break his vow of silence.

"Foul my uniform just once and I'll have you for dinner—on the end of a skewer!"

Storm Singer looked up, his black eyes shining. "Pardon, the end of a what?"

Bishop eyed the bird narrowly and then sighed. "Never you mind. Probably wouldn't be much of a dinner anyway. Nothing but gristle and bone, I'll wager. I'd spend the day just pulling the feathers out."

Storm Singer shrugged, returning to his grooming. They walked for another hundred yards or so with nothing but the *pick, pick, ruffle* of feather-tending to break the silence.

"Black devils, man! You're infesting me with lice!" Bishop suddenly barked in maddened exasperation. "If you want to sit on my shoulder, fine, sit there for all I care. But no more picking!"

Storm Singer ceased his preening and flared his throat feathers. "I assure you, human, wolf-birds are the cleanest of Mother Sky's children, certainly cleaner than any ground-plodding animals that you are likely to name."

"Ha, that's a laugh!" Bishop barked as he angrily tramped though the wood. "I'll have you know I took a bath last week!"

Storm Singer's eyes narrowed, becoming two glistening shards of obsidian. "Tell me, human, are all standard-bearers so ill-tempered?"

Bishop rubbed his eyes in resigned weariness and slowed his pace. He could go back and forth all day with this flying rat, but what would be the point? He was only reducing himself to the bird's barely evolved mentality.

"All right. Fine. Standard-bearers are not irritable; they just prefer to travel alone."

"Alone? Without a wolf-bird?" Storm Singer shook his ebon head. "That would not be wise, no."

"Oh, it wouldn't, would it?" Bishop growled sarcastically.

The wolf-bird continued to shake his head. "Our two respective species have relied on each other's rather specialized sky–earth attributes since before the end of the Fourth Age. Our nest lore tells us that half a rabbit is not as rewarding as the whole. Also, the egg is both yellow and white, inside and out."

"You don't say?"

"I say."

Storm Singer comfortably folded his wings and directed himself toward Bishop. "Perhaps if I were to tell you something of our nest lore, you could more fully appreciate the bond between wolf-bird and human. It is quite interesting, as you, I am sure, will agree."

"I am sure you mean the bond between human and wolf-bird." Bishop rolled his eyes but mutely listened to the bird as he walked. What choice did he have?

"Wôtan, the first human to bond with our kind, who was also known as 'Earth Fury,' kept two wolf-birds, one on each of his shoulders: Sun-Thought, or Huginn in our language, and Sky-Memory, or Muninn, again in the language of our kind. They accompanied him on the hunt and into battle, acting as an extension of his eyes and ears. Further, they were—"

"Two wolf-birds? The poor wretched devil!" Bishop exclaimed with mock concern.

Storm Singer ignored the remark, croaking out his nest lore until Bishop was fairly sick of the subject. But still Bishop listened. This creature was, after all, going to be his trail companion for the foreseeable future, and who knew, maybe the flying rat would come in useful somehow—maybe as a hat.

Storm Singer told of fern and flower, of the ancient ways of trees, of strange and magical creatures of the deep forest of which few humans knew, of secret things hidden, and of things of special worth to wolf-birds found under leaf litter and bramble. He told of hoarded treasure, of the delight of glittering gewgaws and sparkling trifles, and of the sacred nature of the nest and of nest gods and their central role in the wolf-bird pantheon—things only a bird would hold dear—yet most of Storm Singer's tale centered on human–wolf-bird history.

"Thus, wolf-birds," Storm Singer finally concluded, "for uncounted centuries, successfully aided humans. From the association between humans and wolf-birds came several of your most respected names, such as Wolfraven, Cloudwolf, and Ravensfoot. Isn't that interesting, human?"

"Oh, it is indeed," Bishop replied, yawning in boredom. He had never heard of anyone with such ridiculous names but decided against disputing the bird. *Wolfraven?*

"You will require my assistance," Storm Singer stated with absolute conviction. "Even with your, ah, guide, I will be invaluable in scouting the road ahead for danger. The lands beyond the Barrier are not safe."

Bishop stopped and stared in utter surprise. "Guide? You know of this so-called guide? What else do you know about this mission?"

"I was given a full report by the Order, just as you were," Storm Singer replied with an aloof, rasping voice. "I hold the rank of sky ranger within the Order.

"Sky ranger?"

Bishop reddened with indignation. The wolf-bird had been given a report by the Order? How degrading. He was about to probe the bird for details when Storm Singer suddenly took flight.

"Where in the name of the Others do you think you're going now?" Bishop yelled.

"Your ground-plodding travel is too tedious for me. I will meet you on the other side of the Gondakar Barrier. Hurry along now, human. Hurry," Storm Singer cawed as he faded from sight.

"Hurry along? I'll hurry along and make a hat out of your feathers, that's what I'll do!" Bishop yelled back, but the bird was gone, leaving Bishop to brush off his shoulder in fuming silence.

Two uneventful days of travel through the northernmost lands of Merja Soria brought Bishop to a spot within sight of the Gondakar Barrier, a massive rock wall separating the humans from the Eligor Empire that lay to the north. Below this part of the Barrier stood Gondakar, a city that served but three purposes: to guard, maintain, and patrol the Barrier along the entire length of the Eligor frontier.

As Bishop recalled, the city originally had been constructed as an armed labor camp, and it was here, centuries ago, that the first basalt blocks of the Barrier had been laid in an effort to shut out the threat that lay to the north, a threat that would soon encompass Bishop and the mysterious guide the Order had provided him. Bryn had said this particular individual knew the Eligor Empire better than anyone else within the protectorate. Bishop truly hoped so. The dangers beyond the Barrier were legendary.

As Bishop neared the main gate of Gondakar, a guardsman detached himself from a gatehouse nestled under the arched entry and motioned him to stop.

"What business do you have in Gondakar?" the guard growled, holding out his hand for Bishop's papers.

"I am Standard-Bearer Bishop. I—"

"I didn't ask for your name, you clod. I asked what business do you have in Gondakar!"

"I was sent by Master Bryn," Bishop began hotly, rifling through his tunic for the required papers.

The guard's face blanched and his hand dropped lifelessly to his side. "A master? I ... I'll take you to the base commander at once, sir."

Bishop stared in bemusement. *Sir?* The rudeness of gatehouse guards was legendary throughout the protectorate. They usually took an age to examine identification papers, unless of course a few copper riders were offered to speed the process. Bishop had never gotten through a guard on his word alone and certainly had never had one call him sir.

The guard nervously barked to a subordinate, "Wolfraven, stand in for me!" He quickly ushered Bishop through the gate. "You will follow me, sir."

Sir again? Bishop stared a moment and then mutely followed the guard through the arched entry and into the cobblestone streets of Gondakar. Like all border cities, this one was filled with a mix of human beings from every corner of the protectorate, all coming to serve in the maintenance and defense of the frontier. The drone of a dozen accents assaulted Bishop's ears as the restless pattern of the city wove about him, but the humans paid him no heed. They dickered over the price of vegetables, gambled in side alleys, gossiped, swilled their ale, and busied themselves with the day-to-day necessities of life so common throughout the protectorate. Only the guard, hastily walking ahead of Bishop, seemed to be acting in any way out of the ordinary.

At the far eastern end of the fortified city, built literally against the Barrier, stood the central military compound of the ancient city of Gondakar. A cylindrical turret reached to the top of the wall, probably housing a spiral stairway allowing access to the crenellated battlements above. Two soldiers stood stoically on either side of two great ironbound doors, eyeing Bishop suspiciously as he approached. "The base commander is waiting for you"—his escort pointed nervously—"in there."

The man hastily left, melting back into the populous cityscape, while Bishop, quizzically staring after him for a moment, turned and walked past the guards and into the building's atrium, stepping aside as Gondakar soldiers came and went in a continuous stream. At the back of the atrium, an army clerk sat at a large desk, scribbling busily on a parchment. Not knowing what else to do, Bishop walked to the desk and noisily cleared his throat.

"Yes?" the clerk muttered, not bothering to look up from his scribbling. "What do you want?"

"I am Bishop."

"And?" The clerk returned in a bored tone, still scribbling. "That means what to me, exactly?"

Bishop flushed with anger. "I'm a standard-bearer of the Order. I was sent by Master Bryn to pick up a guide."

The clerk paled just as the guardsman had done at the front gate. Jumping to his feet, causing his chair to fall clatteringly behind him, he quickly saluted Bishop.

Bishop warily saluted back. *What in the eight hells?*

"Wait here, sir." The clerk stumbled away from his chair and hastened into the gloomy corridor behind him.

Sir again. Bishop looked around. His voice had obviously carried. Soldiers were now eyeing him strangely as they passed. Something was up; Bishop had been too long in the Order to overlook the signs.

Soon, the nervous clerk returned. "Commander Kayeri will see you immediately," he said, saluting again nervously.

Bishop shrugged, then followed the soldier through a maze of halls that eventually opened into Commander Kayeri's office, which, Bishop suspected, sat directly against the Barrier itself.

Before him sat Commander Kayeri.

Here at last was someone who did not flinch at the sight of him. Quite the contrary, as Bishop stood saluting smartly, the commander merely sat behind a great oaken desk, scowling back at him in silence. Bishop had been told stories about this veteran fighter from the Battle of Koth but had dismissed many of them as being overblown. Looking at the man now, he believed he just might have been wrong.

Kayeri was a hundred-kilogram hulk with broad shoulders, slate-gray eyes, and dark springy hair atop what was undoubtedly a two-meter-plus frame. A melodramatic sword slash, cutting across the left side of his face from forehead to chin, completed the rather striking look. The man eyed Bishop for a moment longer before abruptly breaking the silence. "I don't like this cloak-and-dagger nonsense."

Bishop blinked at Kayeri. "Cloak-and-dagger …?"

Kayeri cut Bishop off. "I don't give a damn if you are on business for the Order. That impresses me not in the least. My sole concern is getting rid of you and your guide as soon as possible."

Bishop, still confused, mutely nodded.

"Sign this. It is a receipt paper, releasing the guide into your charge," Kayeri growled, thrusting a sheaf of paper to the edge of his desk. Bishop quickly signed, noting the oak tree symbol of the Order emblazoned on the upper right-hand corner before the paper was snatched away and stuffed into an open drawer.

"That will be all for now. You are to report back to me at midnight. Until that time, you are to keep as low a profile as possible. Don't be late. Midnight. I don't want you or your guide to remain here one minute longer than necessary. Is that clear?"

"Yes, sir." Bishop saluted again and was hastily herded back out of Kayeri's office.

"What in the eight hells is going on here?" Bishop demanded of the soldier who had all but chased him out into the streets of Gondakar.

The soldier shrugged weakly as if begging Bishop to drop the subject. "The tavern quarter is away west, if you would care for a drink while you wait, sir."

Bishop eyed the man a moment and then, throwing his hands up in resignation, turned and stalked down the dusty street in disgust.

Bronze lanterns were glittering by the time Bishop reached the western end of the city. He purposefully walked into the first tavern he found.

"The Eligor are crawling all over the protectorate!" a man inside was barking in a gruff, grating voice as Bishop entered. The man glanced boastfully at the other patrons of the tavern and gulped the ale that stood at his elbow. The flames leaped and flickered in the taproom firepit, but no one answered him.

"I tell you, it's a stinking Eligor plot, that's what it is!" another man echoed.

Bishop groaned as he stood in the open door. *Not again*, he thought. He made his way through the smoke-filled taproom, where several soldiers sat drinking and brooding over the mysteries of the world. Several others were wrangling over a game of dice in the corner. Bishop had heard these complaints of nonexistent Eligor intruders many times. In his mind, the stories defamed the protectorate and were all but treasonous.

The first speaker, a short, stocky, evil-faced fellow, opened his mouth as if to reply, then hesitated as he noticed Bishop for the first time.

The barman also noticed Bishop. Leaning forward to secure an ember for his long-stemmed pipe, he eyed Bishop and muttered to the short fellow, "You'd be well advised ta keepin' tha mouth shut."

In turn, the speaker grumbled under his breath, muttered an oath, and turned from Bishop as the latter approached the wine-splashed serving board.

The barman brought ale to the rough-hewn table and then stood back in the shadows. His features, now receding into vagueness, were luridly etched in the firelight as it leapt and flickered, while the two small eyes of the barman stared unblinking at his new guest.

"What do I owe you?" Bishop asked, reaching for his coin pouch.

"No charge for ya, gov'na," the man grated, absently wiping grease down the front of his stained apron.

Bishop glanced up into man's face, wondering at his unexpected generosity. The barman's eyes dropped sullenly before Bishop's stare.

Gulping the ale, Bishop looked around the dimly lit room. Behind him, a pair of gamers had stopped their gaming and were staring at him in cryptic speculation. Others had lowered their eyes uneasily, avoiding one another's glance.

"How've things been on the border these days?" Bishop questioned, turning to the man seated next to him.

"Ah, great, just great." The man swilled down the last of his ale, scrambled out of his chair, bumped into a table, nearly upsetting it in the process, and hastily left.

"Thanks for the conversation," Bishop growled.

The man on the other side of Bishop was too drunk to move. He was crouched there over his ale, trying to focus blurry eyes on him.

"I'm not 'fraid of you," the man slurred.

Bishop stared.

"Everyone here knows who you are. Why d' you try to hide it?"

The barman coughed and scowled at the speaker.

"And just who does everyone think I am?" Bishop asked, darkening in growing anger.

The man smugly chortled, taking another swig from his mug. "A no-good, Eligor-loving devil from the Order, that's who!"

The Order! So that was it! They thought he was a master!

"I'm not a master," Bishop responded. "By the eight hells of the Others, where did you get that wild idea?"

"Sure you're not. Sure you're not. Juz an everyday soldier, I s'pose. Juz an everyday soldier who has come to mollycoddle our guest." The drunken man slobbered, trying again to focus his eyes. "I'll say this though, y' sure small fer a masser—fer a master."

"I told you, I'm not a master! And what's this about a guest?"

The drunken man laughed and belched in chorus. "As if y' don't know."

Getting up, the man staggered out, followed by a steady trickle of the bar's remaining clientele. Finally, the barman scanned the empty room and then scowled at Bishop. "I hope yer goin' to buy a lot o' ale, friend," he grated in barely suppressed anger.

Bishop looked helplessly around the vacant taproom. "I'm really not a master," he said meekly.

After three hours of solitary drinking, Bishop quit the tavern, leaving a stack of empty tankards as testament to his attempt to nullify the barman's anger. It was approaching midnight, and Commander Kayeri did not strike Bishop as the type who would lightly overlook any tardiness. Once Bishop again had made his way past the blurry-eyed guards and entered the candlelit administration building, the waiting clerk again escorted him into Commander Kayeri's office and hurriedly left, closing the door and locking it behind him.

The commander still sat at his desk shuffling papers as if it was his eternal job to do so.

"About bloody time!" Kayeri grumbled. "Let me introduce you to your travel companion." The commander gestured absently with one hand.

Bishop followed the commander's finger to the far end of the room. There in the gloom, flanked by two soldiers, stood a frightfully large, hooded man. Bishop's eyes widened and his jaw dropped as the man pulled back his hood.

Bishop stumbled backward, nearly tripping over a chair in the process. "Gods of the Others, man! That's an Eligor!" Bishop's sword sang from its sheath, and he crouched, ready. "Stand away from that devil!" he barked.

Kayeri jumped from his chair and quickly moved in between Bishop and the Eligor. "Put down your weapon, you damned idiot! That's an order!"

Bishop slowly lowered his sword, not daring to take his eyes away from the monster that loomed behind Kayeri.

The Eligor, a creature considerably larger in size than an average human, wore bronze-colored leaf armor that covered most of its green-scaled body. Its lower arms and legs were bare except for a black leather undershirt exposing massively muscled scaled skin that rippled with power. A brass-colored helmet tinted green with patina covering most of the Eligor's hairless, scaled head bore the winged skull crest of Imperial Eligor. The only other noticeable symbol was a red circle emblazoned upon each of the lower sleeves, which were made of leather. Bishop could only guess at what the red circles represented.

The creature's face was elongated and streamlined, lending a sleek, predatory appearance to its overall countenance. Ivory teeth protruded from the sides of a lipless mouth as if for the sole purpose of ripping and tearing flesh. Yet it was the creature's golden eyes that chilled Bishop to the bone. Being set forward like those of a man, they seemed meshed with a vast, cool, and unsympathetic intelligence that spoke to Bishop of evil deeds and determined purpose.

Though decidedly reptilian in overall demeanor, the Eligor was still something of a macabre human parody. The thing stood upright with a clawed hand resting lightly on the pommel of a massive sawtooth sword.

A crackling sound came from a throat device as an artificial voice filled the room: "My name is Kiel, Kiel of the Eligor Empire."

FIVE

OLD PREJUDICES

> The lizard's bones have gone to dust.
> His evil sword has turned to rust.
> His soul it screams in hell, I trust.
> —From a popular pub song of the protectorate

Bishop glowered at the Eligor, not daring to move, as Commander Kayeri angrily reseated himself.

"You don't like me, do you, human?" the Eligor's odd Old Earth translator crackled over the hissing and clicking sounds of the creature's real voice. "I don't blame you, I suppose."

The Eligor touched the ground and then his forehead in some sort of attempt at a formal greeting. "Yet I believe we can put aside our differences considering the current situation."

Bishop ignored the Eligor and turned to face Kayeri, flushing in undisguised rage. "That thing is an Eligor!" he barked, stabbing a finger in the creature's direction.

"Yes, he's an Eligor," Kayeri returned stoically. "And what of it?"

"But this is not what I—"

Kayeri cut Bishop short. "Standard-Bearer Bishop, did you or did you not accept this assignment?"

Bishop opened his mouth to respond but was interrupted by a knock at the door. "Yes?" the commander called.

"The Eligor's release papers are ready for your signature, sir," a voice returned.

"Very well, you can bring them to me in a few minutes."

The Eligor's release papers? Something tugged at Bishop's mind. "How many people know about this assignment?" Bishop asked, suddenly suspicious.

Kayeri stared back at Bishop. "Your current assignment is highly classified, as you should have well been made aware. We've only informed those with a need to know. The medical staff, the prison staff, the auxiliary security staff…"

Everyone knew about this but me! Bishop silently screamed. *So that explains all the strange looks I've gotten since entering Gondakar.* The whole situation was beginning to coalesce, with a very unpleasant aroma attached.

The Order knew Bishop wouldn't have accepted the assignment if he'd known the truth. An Eligor! Only a year ago these demons had smashed their way through the Gondakar Barrier and poured into the northlands of the protectorate, laying waste to everything in their path. Bishop had watched thousands of his countrypeople die; some of his closest friends had not survived. The humans' ultimate victory at Koth had come at a terrible cost.

Bishop turned and glared at the Eligor, trying to sort his own emotions—anger, disbelief, and mortification. Finally, he felt the most significant of them all, which was the weary, mind-numbing frustration of having been had, like a rat caught in a trap.

Bishop could no longer stay silent. "Commander, let me be frank. I accepted this assignment on the assumption that my guide was at least human. Gods of the Others, man, even a forager would have been better company than that—that beast!"

Kayeri's flaming eyes riveted on Bishop. "Do you question every order you receive, Standard-Bearer Bishop? Is it the nature of the Order to explain every detail of every assignment to those selected to carry them out?"

Bishop was sobered at the mention of the Order. He straightened. "No, sir, it is not, but—"

Kayeri leaned back in his chair, looking more relaxed. "It would be unfortunate to report back to Master Bryn that you had difficulty carrying out your orders." The self-assured expression on his chiseled face transformed into a frown once he detected movement from the other side of the room.

The Eligor, who through most of the conversation had merely stood motionless, now appeared to become agitated.

"Commander Kayeri," the translator crackled. "Forgive me for interrupting, but where are the rest of the Order's soldiers?"

Kayeri closed his eyes in frustration. "Commander Kiel, you were promised professional assistance from the Order. No mention was ever made of numbers."

"There must be an error," Kiel replied slowly. "I will need at least two divisions of regular soldiers. As for specialized personnel, I will require—"

"No mention was ever made of numbers," the commander repeated loudly. "Bishop here—or so I am told—is one of the best. He is a standard-bearer and, so I am told, has other unique abilities that might be useful."

Kiel glanced knowingly at Bishop's Riika and gave a brief nod. "So I see."

Bishop eyed the Eligor. The scaled brute seemed to recognize the Riika. This was disturbing to Bishop since only a few within the Order could properly identify such a device. Bryn's previous fascination with the Riika flitted through Bishop's mind. Bishop wondered again at what he had been told.

Either this Eligor beast had guessed at the Riika's identity or he was privy to information that was supposed to be known only by a select few within the Order.

Kiel continued to shift his weight uneasily. "Forgive me again, Commander, but I believe I have not made my case as urgently as I should have to the Order. The Ikonian threat is vast, on a scale that you cannot begin to imagine. One lone, painfully emaciated human, however impressive his abilities, will simply not be enough. We will require at least twenty or—"

Bishop stepped forward earnestly, interrupting Kiel. "I would agree with the Eligor, ah, thing here. I could not hope for any chance of success. Furthermore, I—"

Commander Kayeri slammed his fist down on the desk. "That is enough! Bishop, you are hereby ordered to complete your assignment, or you will be summarily turned over to your superiors for discipline! Commander Kiel, either you will accept what Merja Soria has to offer in the way of assistance, or you will kindly take leave of it! Now, gentlemen, what is your decision?"

Kiel and Bishop eyed each other in silence for several moments.

"Well," Kiel said, breaking the silence. "Any help is better than none. And I must admit, none is what I expected."

"Very well, Kiel. Bishop, what is your decision?"

Bishop was cornered, and Kayeri knew it. "I'll go as ordered. But that doesn't mean I have to like it. Master Bryn didn't say anything about—"

"Your grievance is noted," Kayeri barked. "Guards, escort these two sullen rapscallions through the exit tunnel. I am sure they are anxious to be on their way. Good luck, gentlemen." He began leafing through his paperwork, signaling to all present that the conversation was most assuredly at an end.

The guards hastily ushered Bishop and Kiel to the back of the labyrinthine administration building, where a set of packs sat ready. Kiel strapped a rather large metallic contrivance onto his back, while Bishop heaved a standard trail pack, bulging with wayfarer's bread, onto his own shoulders.

The guards then directed them to a spiraling stone staircase that wound down into the darkness below the garrison. Lighting a lantern, the forward guard gestured to the opening, and Bishop, closely followed by Kiel, reluctantly began the descent. Reaching the bottom of the flight of steps, they were silently led along a straight rock-lined tunnel for what seemed like an eternity.

Bishop looked up at the massive scaled demon in front of him. What had he blundered into here? To imagine the Order, the Holy Order of Merja Soria, involving itself and the protectorate in Eligor affairs. The Eligor, for the love of the Others! The stories of their treachery were legendary. They were animals, mindless beasts, two-legged demon lizards, creatures who were a mockery of humankind and an enemy of humankind. To think that Bishop had been so easily duped by Master Bryn! Certainly, the wolf-bird was beginning to look like the better part of the arrangement, and that was saying a great deal indeed. Bishop thought again of the Riika and the turn of luck he was beginning to associate with it. If only there was a way of removing the devilish device before it consumed him completely.

Before long, the tunnel terminated at the base of yet another staircase, this one leading back up into the gloom. A guard pointed up into the spider-haunted darkness of the staircase. "You are now on the other side of the Gondakar Barrier. Once you close the outer door, it will lock. Be absolutely sure that it does lock. We don't want any unwanted 'lizards' in our cellar."

"No. No lizards in the cellar," Bishop grumbled as he angrily glanced at Kiel.

Both the guards chortled as they left the two reluctant travelers in the darkness. Bishop, not bothering to look at the Eligor, began to climb. Kiel silently trailed after him.

The two travelers exited at the top of the stairway and found themselves in a treed area several hundred meters beyond the Gondakar Barrier, its gray mass looming above them in the frosty starlit sky. The doorway, concealed in the side of a rock outcropping, swiveled silently back as Bishop pushed it closed.

As the rock door locked behind him, Bishop turned to face the Eligor in the gloom of the night. "Listen, chief, I want to make a few things clear. The only reason I am here is because I was ordered to be here. If you get your scaled hide in a pinch, don't expect me to so much as spit to save you. Got that? As far as I'm concerned, the Ikonians—if such fables even exist, and I doubt they do—can go ahead and have the Eligor Empire. We are well rid of it. I don't care."

Bishop began stomping off toward the looming forest before he heard the Eligor's artificial voice crackling behind him.

"You there, Sha Tar. You're going in the wrong direction, that is, unless you would prefer to wade through the Moeras Kor Depression."

Bishop stopped in midstride. *Moeras Kor Depression?* "I knew that. I was waiting for you to point out the correct trail so we can get on with it."

"Very well, try to keep up, Sha Tar," Kiel muttered, marching off in a northwesterly direction.

"What in the eight hells does *Sha Tar* mean?" Bishop grumbled, reluctant to ask.

"Never mind. It is of no concern."

As the night grew old, Bishop found himself deep within the southern forests of the Eligor Empire. He gazed at the sugar gliders flitting and scratching among the old, strangled branches that were thick with lichen and ivy. He hoped the squirrels were the only fauna that they would encounter on this ill-omened mission, but it wasn't likely. He could hear other noises besides the squirrels scratching. Grunting, scuffling, and thrashing came from the undergrowth in an endless procession of sound. Bishop was wont to inform the Eligor ahead of him of the noises but elected to keep the observations to himself. The lizard could do his own trail work.

As they walked, the wood thickened even more, shutting out the starlit sky above them, creating a tunnel of great trees that leaned into one another and grew together. Through this tunnel wound their narrow path, in and out among the giant trunks. Soon, the night sky behind them was like a small starry hole far to their rear. The quiet became so deep that all Bishop could hear was their boots thumping along. The ancient trees leaned over them, seeming to listen. Some trees lay dead or dying among the dense wood, amid the rotting mold and mushy logs of their fallen brothers, upon which grew strange fungi that shone with dim phosphorescence, giving just enough light to navigate the gloom.

Threading in and out of the oaken aisles between the gigantic phosphorescing boles, the travelers silently passed a tremendous dolmen of mossy stone in what was once a clearing, telling of older and more terrible dwellers of the wood that were long forgotten. Bishop eyed the monolith as they passed, remembering the last mission he had been set upon. He hoped this was not an omen.

Occasionally, a slender beam of moonlight that had the luck of slipping through some opening in the leaves far above, and then even more luck in not being caught in the tangled boughs and matted twigs beneath, stabbed down thin and bright before them. But this was seldom, and soon it ceased altogether.

With a sigh, Bishop drew up his sword belt. The everlasting silence and gloom of the primeval forest was already beginning to depress him. He found himself thinking of the open groves and sun-dappled meadows of Merja Soria, of the ruddy cheer of his family's steep-thatched, diamond-pane-windowed house, of the fat cows browsing through the deep, lush green clover, and of the hearty fellowship of the brawny bare-armed plowmen and herdsmen. How different things were on this side of the Barrier, in the accursed land of the Eligor Empire.

Bishop eyed the lizard ahead of him. The lizard would have stood out in a crowd of Eligor; of this Bishop was certain. It was not so much his unnatural size, his height, and his great shoulders, though these features lent to the general effect. It was more that his face, scaled, dark, and immobile, held one's gaze, and his golden eyes glimmered with icy intelligence and determined purpose. Each movement, no matter how slight, bespoke of spring-steel muscles working in perfect coordination. There was nothing deliberate or measured about his motions; either he was perfectly at rest—still as a bronzed statue—or he was in motion with a catlike wariness. How old the Eligor was, Bishop could not guess, but if pressed, he would have estimated at least twice his own age, which somehow made it all the worse. This was going to be a long assignment.

As the night faded, there came a greenish light around them, and in places Bishop could see some distance into the trees on either side of the path. Yet the light only showed him endless lines of gnarled trucks marching off like monstrous soldiers in some hellish army. Now the silence between him and the Eligor had begun to wear on Bishop; he wished he had not reacted so violently toward Kiel. Like it or not, this was going to be his traveling companion for the foreseeable future, and hating him would only make things worse. Besides, Bishop argued to himself, surely there were a benevolent Eligor. Maybe this creature was one of them.

Kiel was the first to break the silence as his translator crackled to life. "I would suggest that, when possible, we rest during the day. The biomechs are most formidable in the sunlight, and it would not be advisable to catch their attention while they are fully charged."

"Biomechs? Here, during the day? Are you sure?" Bishop frowned, eyeing the surrounding forest with a renewed sense of caution. "I would think that being predatory, they would hunt during the night."

Kiel gave Bishop a peculiar look. "Believe me, I know of what I speak, human. The biomechs are just that, part machine, and thus require sunlight to power their Old Earth components. Certainly, they operate at night, but without their more specialized electronic capabilities—capabilities that you are welcome to test, but not at my expense—they are useless."

Bishop, not understanding a word of what Kiel had just said, was about to make a comment about the biomechs and their similarities to the Eligor when he was startled half out of his wits by a rasping sound above him.

"Ho, Bishoppp. You have picked up your travel companion, I see."

Bishop, his heart pounding, seethed as recognition settled upon him. He had forgotten about Storm Singer. The wolf-bird settled onto Bishop's shoulder, flaring his neck feathers as he took in Kiel for the first time. "By the Great Egg in the Sky! And to think that I considered humans uncomely."

Kiel ignored Storm Singer's insult as he eyed the bird in silent amazement. "What an incredible creature. Is it to accompany us to Ikonia?" he asked, his eyes riveted on the bird.

Bishop nodded. "I'm afraid so. As you can plainly see, there are actually two of us who were befooled into helping your scaled hide."

Kiel raised his left hand to Storm Singer, and to Bishop's surprise, the bird jumped to alight upon it.

Storm Singer puffed his breast feathers in pride. "What precisely did you say? Incredible creature? Well, I can always overlook appearance when it is compensated for by higher intelligence."

Kiel delicately scratched at Storm Singer's neck with a clawed finger.

"Truly, I must say that I was beginning to believe that I had made a fatal decision by asking the protectorate for help."

Bishop rolled his eyes. "Oh, come now, Sir Eligor, it's just a miserable wolf-bird. Don't hang all your hopes on Storm Singer's mite-ridden hide."

Kiel looked up. "I'm sure that you do not understand, human. You behave as if you have no idea what this bird represents from a technological perspective."

Bishop threw his hands up in confused frustration. "Technology? What technology? It's just a bird."

"Just a bird," Kiel said, repeating Bishop's words. "Just a bird. Tell me, human, did the birds—wolf-birds as you so name them—always talk?"

"As long as I've been around, they've talked."

"Forgive my ignorance, but how long does your particular type of human live? How long have you been around?"

"I am nineteen," Bishop growled. "Old enough to know of what I speak."

"Nineteen ... cycles? Years?" Kiel shook his scaled head.

"Nineteen years, yes. And how old are you? Thirty? Thirty-five?"

"Sixty-two times have the yellow leaves fallen on the imperial avenues of Opal since I graduated from the Imperial War Academy at Ixxis Roi. I am sure you don't understand me. How long has this species been known to communicate with humans?"

"Sixty-two." Bishop stared a moment at the Eligor in open amazement before collecting his thoughts again. "Since before the Great Cataclysm. Probably even before the beginning of the Fourth Age, I suppose."

"And before then?" Kiel pressed.

"They were just wretched birds, I guess. More wretched than they are now." Bishop grew more irritated. "You know, I'll be honest, if you have a point to make, Sir Eligor, it's escaping me at the moment."

Kiel grunted. "Have you never wondered at what it must have taken to change them"—Kiel continued to gently scratch Storm Singer's neck—"to alter them in some nameless way so as to allow them to communicate with your kind?"

"No, but I have thought of several ways to rid myself of them." Bishop noted Storm Singer's white eye membranes had closed in rapture from the unexpected preening. It maddened him all the more.

Kiel seemed lost in thought as he studied Storm Singer. "This creature's genetics were changed to suit its human designers untold millennia ago. It was crafted by your human ancestors to an exact specification for an explicit reason. Such awesome power and ability is what brought me to your protectorate. That ability is still there, human, locked up in that tiny head of yours. And I am betting the entire Eligor Empire that it is enough to stop the Ikonian threat."

Bishop frowned. "I still think you're crazy, chief. And by the way, I don't have a tiny head: it's the standard size—for humans, anyway."

The hairs on Bishop's neck unexpectedly prickled. He rapidly scanned the dark wood. Something in the forest was not right. Kiel, too, began scanning the surrounding forest in alert stillness. An anxious silence had unexpectedly washed through the woods, causing the awakening bird and insect life to instantly quieten. Nothing could be heard except the gentle wind moving through the upper branches of the great trees. The weary expression on Kiel's face had become one of alert apprehension. Even Storm Singer had come out of his trance and was now scrutinizing the surrounding gloom.

"Something is wrong," Kiel muttered.

"Gods of the Others, now what?" Bishop grabbed at the hilt of his sword. "Storm Singer, here's your big chance to live up to the lizard's expectations. Go, scout our perimeter."

Storm Singer was too distracted by the unnerving silence to respond to Bishop's gibe. The bird nodded and instantly took to the air, wheeling up into the trees and disappearing.

Moments passed. The silence became ever more oppressive, but nothing stirred; nothing moved.

"What is it?" Bishop hissed, straining his eyes to see through the gloom. "What's wrong?"

Several squirrels, foraging for food, had scrambled to the nearest tree and were now disappearing among the upper branches.

"I fear a biomechanical," Kiel said.

Bishop gaped at Kiel. "Fine guide you turned out to be. You guided us right into a biomechanical. Aren't we supposed to avoid biomechs?" A howl split the forest silence, and a chill swept down Bishop's back.

"No time for your mindless blather, human. We're in trouble."

Bishop didn't need the warning. Biomechanicals were legendary in the protectorate, a relic weapon left over from the Old Earth. A shadow flitted through the forest, causing Bishop to start, but it was only Storm Singer retuning from his aerial patrol.

"Something approaches from there." The bird pointed a feathered wing in the direction from which they had come. "It is big and—"

Before the bird could relate the nature of the threat, a weird inhuman call caused the early morning air to shudder as it rang throughout the silent forest. Somewhere at the edge of Bishop's hearing, a deeper cry answered, and he knew it had not come from the throat of a herbivore.

"What now, Sir Eligor? Run? Build a fire? Sing songs?"

"Too late for that," came the flat response. Kiel raised his sword, ready.

Bishop slid his sword from its sheath and followed the Eligor's stare. Down the path they had but moments before traversed, something moved in the shadows, soon to approach.

Bishop felt the short hairs on his scalp prickle. With some slight shaking of the thick foliage, the bushes parted, and a monstrous form came into view. The dim, ghostly light filtered through the leaves and shone down on the beast's glossy coat, rippling with the play of great muscles and corded metallic cables beneath it. The thing, as Bishop knew, was a survivor of an older, hellish age, an ogre of ancient human legend—a biomechanical.

Storm Singer took flight, settling onto one of the lower branches of an overhanging tree with an enraged cawing and bristling of his feathers, but the monster paid him no heed.

Bishop stood frozen. He had not looked upon one of these primordial brutes since his first assignment. Innumerable myths and legends lent the creature a supernatural quality, induced by its Old Earth origins and its fiendish nature. It was only with the greatest effort that he did not turn and flee.

The beast that glided toward the two travelers was longer and heavier than a common mountain lion and almost as bulky as a bear. Its shoulders and forelegs were so massively muscled as to give it a curious top-heavy look. Its hindquarters, though lower and smaller, were corded in muscle as well. A curious metallic collar ringed the beast's neck, to which steel cables were attached from various parts of its hairy body.

The creature's jaws were enormous, and its head wrapped around them as if ripping and tearing were its only function. The biomech's mental capacity must have been small, as there seemed no room left for a brain. It could have had no instincts other than murderous destruction fed to it by the Old Earth implants. The beast, simply put, was a carnivorous machine run amok, a horror of fang and talon.

The beast stopped, eyeing the two travelers. An awful hunger burned a golden color in its wide, unblinking eyes, a hunger not only of belly emptiness, but also of a lust for death dealing. The gaping jaws slavered in expectant readiness to devour the meal it knew was coming.

There followed a tense silence, during which Bishop felt his heart could be heard pounding kilometers away. The beast lowered its head and snuffed the trail, then lifted it again, its eyes orbs of yellow balefire. A growl came from low within its throat as it gathered itself for the attack. In that instant, Kiel hurled his sword.

With all the weight of shoulder and arm behind the throw, the sword was a streak of silver in the dim light of the forest. Almost before Bishop realized what had happened, he saw the mechanical beast rolling on the ground in its death throes, the blade of the Eligor weapon having split its skull wide open. Blue sparks showered the ground with a spitting sound, and blood pumped and spurted over the leaf-littered earth, while the creature's great paws padded the air in a horrid pantomime of death.

Kiel bounded to the animal, wrenched his sword free, and dragged the limp body off the trail. "Now we run—and we run fast," he hissed, leading the way northward and away from the steaming, twitching corpse. "There will be more, but if we are quick enough, they will have difficulty tracking us."

Now they ran, avoiding clinging briars and low-hanging branches, sprinting between trees without touching them, and always planting their feet in the places calculated to show the least evidence of their passing. Storm Singer glided silently above, dropping occasionally to report on the terrain ahead.

No sound followed them as they ran below the great brooding trees. Bishop gripped his sword uneasily, turning to look at the gloomy arches behind them. His flesh crawled with the momentary expectation of ripping talons and fangs leaping from the shadows.

"I've heard tell that these biomechanicals will continue to track us down regardless of how fast or how long we run," Bishop said, panting.

Kiel shook his head. "Not if we can get beyond their territory. These are border mechs; they will stay close to the Gondakar Barrier. But if we are too slow, we'll be sure to run into more of them. And if that happens, we are done for."

For the remainder of the afternoon, they continued to move rapidly away from the borderlands of the protectorate, Kiel leading the way deeper and deeper into the ancient Eligor wilderness.

Late in the afternoon, Kiel finally grunted with satisfaction. They had reached a spot where the underbrush was more scattered and an outcropping of stone was visible, wandering off northward. Even Bishop felt more secure. Not even a mountain lion could trail them over naked rock.

Kiel pointed. "We will rest one last time before the final push. But keep alert. A wounded hare takes no nap."

A low hill pitched upward, girdled and covered with thick trees and bushes. Near the crest, Kiel slid into a tangle of rocks, crowned by dense bushes. Sitting there, they could watch the forest below without being seen. It was a good place to hide, and they could defend it if necessary.

Storm Singer drifted out of the sky and settled on Bishop's shoulder. "I have spied the area. Nothing but a rabbit or two."

Bishop eyed Kiel. "Fine way to start our trip, wouldn't you agree, bird?"

Storm Singer elected not to respond, picking absently at an offending feather.

"You humans are a whiny lot, there's no doubt of that," Kiel said in a banal tone. "Did you think it would be easy? Just a stroll in the park, is that what you thought?"

The ghostly twilight of dawn spread through dense, moss-covered branches as mist rose from the warming ground. Patches of sky visible to the eye altered in hue, changing from pastel pink to deep cobalt.

Bishop set himself to watch the forest below them, fuming because of Kiel's last remark. "Knows the Eligor Empire like the back of his hand, they said. Knows it backward and forward, they said."

Kiel did not respond. Rather, he sat himself opposite Bishop and scanned the forest silently. The hours passed. Bishop fully expected to see a snarling machine beast thrust its muzzle through the leaves, but as the hours of the day went by, no stealthy footfalls disturbed the ominous silence of the forest.

Once, late in the afternoon, far behind them to the south, a scream drifted to them on the cool forest air, but whether it was from a biomechanical or some other creature of the forest, no one could say.

The sun lowered and set, and the forest grew dim before Kiel deemed that it was dark enough for them to emerge from their hiding place.

"Are we out of the woods yet?" Bishop finally asked Kiel, as they began moving away north.

Kiel turned quizzically. "The woods continue for many a days' trek." He was thoughtful. "But at last, we are beyond the mechs' territory."

Bishop sighed.

A little past midnight Bishop stumbled to a stop, panting. "May I humbly request we stop for nourishment and a bit of rest, before I fall over dead?"

Kiel grunted his assent. "Very well, human," he said, veering off the darkened trail. "We will rest tonight. But don't get used to being coddled like a hatchling. There are areas ahead we dare not stop, day or night."

The Eligor chose a spot where the interlacing branches of the great trees rose in mighty arches, hundreds of meters above the moss-carpeted earth, creating a gothic moonlit cathedral among the giant trunks. Bishop threw some firewood together, grumbling and muttering as he did so.

The twigs that Bishop flung onto his small cooking fire popped and crackled to life. The upleaping flames lighted the countenances of the two travelers. Kiel seemed ancient in the gloom as he stared absently, the red fire glinting off the bronze leaf mail that he wore.

Bishop glanced at the Eligor, dappled in the forest shadows, and not for the first time was struck by the creature. The Eligor was tall and massive, almost monstrous, built with the savage economy of the wolf and being no less the natural killer. Proof of his murderous ability had come with the apparent ease with which he had so casually dispatched the biomech behind them.

Storm Singer descended from the night sky to alight on the ground. "This glade is as safe as any. I will take my leave of you to enjoy my evening rations, if it is all the same to you."

"Keep your little raisin eyes open for danger," Bishop growled. "I'll turn you into the evening rations if we are surprised while we are resting."

Storm Singer, probably as tired and worn out as Bishop, grumbled something as he took flight into the low overhanging branches. As soon as Storm Singer was perched comfortably above the two travelers, Bishop set about unpacking his bedroll and ordering his supplies. The silence between him and Kiel was becoming strained again, causing him to remember that, after all, Kiel was going to be his trail companion for the foreseeable future.

Finally, Bishop could stand it no longer and begrudgingly spoke. "You there, Kiel, do you have any young?"

Kiel was rummaging in his pack. "I wouldn't know, human. I am an Eligor."

That's right, the Eligor didn't raise families. Bishop should have remembered what he had been taught in military school—Eligor young were raised in communal nests. He tried again. "Do you enjoy gaming in the empire? Tenpin? Jousting? Cards?"

Kiel didn't respond for a moment, busying himself with his pack. "Under the current circumstances, I would say that staying alive is sport enough." That was that.

Bishop threw up his hands in resignation and set about to easing his gnawing hunger. Neither one of them had eaten since leaving Gondakar; they had not had the time for anything more nourishing than wild berries washed down with water gathered in haste from several streams they had skirted.

Bishop retrieved a piece of wayfarer's bread and chewed in frustration.

After a moment, he decided to give it one last try. "What's for dinner, Sir Eligor?"

"Rats."

Bishop reddened. "You don't have to be rude about it. Seriously, what's for dinner?"

Kiel pulled a stiffened hairy corpse, complete with beady black eyes and a long, naked tail, out of a metal tube with a *fooomp* sound and bit the head off. He looked mildly at Bishop. "Really." he said over the sound of masticating bones and sinew. "Rats."

Bishop's stomach lurched.

"And what of you? What are you having for dinner, human?" Kiel smacked his lips then ripped off another portion with teeth that were obviously designed for said purpose.

"I think I'll eat later," Bishop muttered, pitching the half-eaten bread back in his pack with a shiver.

Bishop sat for another thirty minutes in silence. Damned if he was going to try to have any more conversation with this repulsive barbarian lizard. The two of them could complete this mission without another word spoken as far as he was concerned.

Bishop began arranging his bedroll with an angry flourish, when Kiel cleared his throat noisily. "So, human, have your superiors mated you yet?" his translator crackled.

Bishop shot a startled look toward Kiel, his ears burning. "I beg your pardon?"

Kiel stared unemotionally. "Excuse me. Perhaps you are not old enough to take part in mating. There is much about your culture we do not know."

"Not old enough? I'm plenty old enough—have been for quite some time. It's just that humans aren't 'mated' like a barnyard animal." Bishop slid into his bedroll and turned his back to the Eligor.

Kiel cleared his throat one more time. "Yes, of course. I've got another rat. You haven't eaten, and the road is long."

"No rat tonight, thank you very much. Just sleep." Bishop shivered again.

Bishop settled himself before sighing in resignation. Obviously the lizard had tried to make small talk, and it would be a long, tedious trip if they couldn't communicate. Bishop slowly turned in his bedroll.

"I have eaten rabbit," he began.

"I, no doubt, have many children," Kiel stated simultaneously.

Bishop laughed awkwardly. "Well, if I haven't got any children, it isn't for lack of practice."

They both chortled this time.

The next day, the conversation became a little easier and less strained, consisting of simple questions and answers concerning trail routes, their corresponding hazards, and the general lay of the land within Eligor Empire. By evening of the third day, Bishop felt comfortable enough to apologize for his behavior at Gondakar, when he had first met the Eligor.

"I am sorry for my outburst at Gondakar, but you must understand that the Eligor are not well loved within the protectorate. I mean, you can't possibly blame me for the reaction, can you?"

"I do not blame you, human. I realize how fortunate I was not to have been killed outright when I approached your frontier."

"Well, all right then. Fair enough. By the way, I don't like being called 'human.' My name is Bishop." Bishop grudgingly held out his hand.

Kiel raised his hand as well, not understanding the complexity of the human gesture, until Bishop grabbed his hand and shook it.

"Ah," Kiel muttered in understanding. "Bishop it is. And you may call me Kiel—Kiel, first commander of the Imperial Intelligence Service of Opal."

Bishop jerked his hand away as if it had been burned, staring in disbelief. "The Imperial Intelligence Service? You mean like the Order of Merja Soria?"

Kiel thought a moment. "I would gather that the two services share some commonality. Why?"

Bishop threw his hands up in disbelief. "That's a peach! Here I am assisting the very devil that, in all probability, orchestrated the last war." Bishop began pacing back and forth in anger. "It just doesn't get any better than this, does it? And for a moment there, just for a moment, I was almost ready to believe that, just possibly, you were an innocent. But no."

Bishop abruptly ceased his pacing and stabbed a finger at Kiel. "Why did you attack us anyway? What did we ever do to you?"

Kiel's expressionless golden eyes seemed to study Bishop momentarily before he responded. "You flatter me, human, but I can assure you that I had nothing to do with the war you speak of. At the time, I was a subcommander with very little in the way of real power. In fact, I didn't even leave Opal during the invasion."

"Well, that's a comfort," Bishop growled as he sat down heavily, still eyeing Kiel with suspicion. "But you must have known why we were attacked. Come on, out with it, Sir Eligor."

Kiel's eyes narrowed. "Surely your Order has informed you of the nature of the conflict?"

"No, they have not—probably because they still don't even know."

Kiel sat silently for a moment, contemplating his response to Bishop's demand. "I do know the reasons for the war, but they are complicated."

"Try me. We humans aren't as dumb as we look."

"You couldn't possibly be," Kiel returned flatly.

"Watch yourself, chief." Bishop bristled.

"Very well." Kiel sighed, holding up his scaled hands in resignation. "I can see that we will not be able to continue until I tell you what I know. But please, let us at least establish a camp for the day. Is that acceptable?"

"Oh, all right." Bishop begrudgingly agreed.

After selecting a campsite, they sat across from each other in a concealed forest glade while multihued avian life gabbled and cackled in raucous abandon overhead. Kiel settled himself, drawing another stiffened rat from his pack. "So, you wish to know the reasons behind the human–Eligor conflict?"

Bishop nodded, rummaging for a bit of cured meat and yellow cheese from his pack as the Eligor began to dine. Kiel's nauseating diet was becoming tolerable so long as Bishop put it out of his mind while he ate his own rations.

Kiel chewed and smacked heartily. "Very well, but I warn you, it is a very complex question you task me with answering. To begin, you will need to know something of Eligor time so you can follow the account."

"Time? What has time got to do with the Eligor invasion?"

"Time has everything to do with the invasion, as I will attempt to explain." Kiel ordered his thoughts. "For the Eligor, the governing of time is fundamental to our culture. The arrangement of time governs every activity of individual life. It also governs the scheduling and execution of all state-organized events as they pass through their various cyclic progressions.

"Cyclic progressions?" Bishop shook his head. "I'm not sure I follow you."

Kiel nodded knowingly. "This does not surprise me. To the Eligor of the old empire, time was circular, and it was believed that events returned to the same place in time by completing a particular cycle, say, as does the orbit of the moon or the planets. At such a time, or so it was believed, the course of certain events might be changed."

Bishop stared blankly as Kiel attempted a more comprehensive explanation. "If, say, you were to return to a point in time and somehow change an event, you could expect the future to change as well. Such was the case with the human–Eligor conflict. I have heard tell that the ancients believed this in regard to the beginning of a new calendar year and the taking of an associated pledge intending somehow to improve upon the fortunes of the previous year."

"Yes, well, cycles and cycles. It's all blather to me," Bishop grumbled. "I asked you to explain why you attacked us, not to bore me with your ridiculous calendar."

"Human," Kiel grated grimly. "For once try to follow what I am saying. It's the only way you are going to understand the question you have asked me. Do you want an explanation or not?"

Bishop raised his hands. "Yes, fine. Go ahead."

"Very well. It is necessary that you understand the importance of our calendar; it was the cultural foundation of the old empire since the Great Cataclysm."

Bishop sighed. "I am trying to understand, but who can say how much time has passed since the Great Cataclysm? You talk as if you truly know the exact date."

"Believe me, we know how much time has elapsed since the Zero Date."

"Zero Date?"

"If you will allow me, I will continue."

Bishop nodded wearily, taking a bite of food.

"Very well," Kiel continued. "Since the first days of the old empire, we have relied on a series of calendars that move in unison, forming one master calendar. The two-hundred-sixty-day cycle is made up of twenty groups of named and numbered days used in a system that records the exact amount of time that has elapsed since the Zero Date, the date of the Great Cataclysm, a very important date in our history." Kiel gave Bishop a knowing look.

Bishop returned the look but remained silent. He was sure no one within the protectorate knew when the Great Cataclysm had occurred, and it was with the greatest restraint that he kept his incredulity to himself. Bishop wished to know about the war, and it seemed the lizard saw some special significance to the Eligor calendar, which he would suffer upon Bishop before he continued.

"Yet, as I have stated, the Eligor system of time involves more than the two-hundred-sixty-day cycle. There is a three-hundred-sixty-five-day solar calendar divided into eighteen months of twenty days each that accompanies the two-hundred-sixty-day calendar. These two counts are in simultaneous operation, and I can only explain them as two engaged, rotating gears in which the beginning day of the larger, three-hundred-sixty-five-day wheel would align with the beginning day of the smaller, two-hundred-sixty-day cycle every fifty-two years, which constitutes one Eligor Great Cycle, so that any day can be identified in both cycles at the same time."

"And all this means what?"

"If you will allow—"

"Yes, yes, of course." Bishop yawned. "It seemed to me like a simple question."

Kiel eyed Bishop narrowly and again gathered his thoughts. "In the days of the old empire, our race, for whom it was important to ascertain the proper day for every act of significance, carefully calculated the parallel and periodically overlapping paths of these measurements, watching for specific celestial alignments that were plotted on an even larger wheel of time that cycles every six thousand years. Most of the alignments were benign and did not overly concern us, yet occasionally one was not benign and did cause us concern. Nearly every aspect of day-to-day life for our race was controlled by our calendars: gathering food, building, and of course, going to war."

Bishop's eyes widened as the import of Kiel's words suddenly coalesced in his mind. "War? You're joking! You invaded our protectorate because of your calendars?"

"Well, partially, but—"

Bishop stared, dumbfounded. "I am beginning to understand why it is so important for me to understand your dratted calendar system, so we can prepare ourselves for the next war and the one after that, and so on and so forth throughout time!"

Kiel stared back at Bishop with flinty eyes and then turned and began unpacking his supplies. "This is pointless. Your brain is just too small to attempt to enlighten it. I see no reason to continue if you are just going to mock me."

Bishop struggled to control his anger. He needed to know more. "All right, all right. It's just that—I lost friends in the war, and it is difficult to believe they died because of an incomprehensible Eligor calendar, or calendars, or whatever."

The sounds of forest life drifted through the still air as Kiel turned to face Bishop. "The calendars dictated when we attacked. Why we attacked, that was something else."

"What else?"

"Fear."

The word hung on the air for a moment before Bishop responded. "Fear? What could you have possibly feared from us?"

"What could the Eligor have feared from the humans?" Kiel muttered knowingly. "Tell me, Bishop, have you ever heard of the Ignotum pro Magna?"

"No. Should I have?"

Kiel's eyes narrowed dangerously. "Yes, you should have. Because if you had heard of it, you wouldn't be plaguing me with your nonstop questions."

Bishop glowered but elected to remain silent as Kiel continued. "The Ignotum pro Magna is an oracle, a chronicle of events, a scripture. It was compiled shortly after the Zero Date and is tied to the calendar system that I have just struggled to explain to your simple wit."

Kiel opened a panel on his metal pack and produced a small black leather-bound book whose cover sported a graven cluster of thunderbolts gripped in a gauntleted Eligor hand.

"How convenient, you just happened to have a copy," Bishop remarked sarcastically.

"It was the law, Sha Tar," Kiel's translator crackled with anger. "Every Eligor was required to keep a copy close; failure to do so was considered a crime punishable by death. Our packs are designed with the book included." He then held out the book. "This is why the Eligor invaded your lands."

Bishop sobered, eyeing the tome that rested lightly in Kiel's hand. "What is it about the book that would provoke an attack on our protectorate?"

Kiel smiled thinly as if having expected the question. "I will read the first chapter for you, if you would like."

Bishop silently nodded his assent, settling himself on his sleeping blanket.

Kiel opened the book and settled himself. "I will read from the book of Vinaya or in the human tongue *'Foundation'*, chapter one verses 1 through I believe 43, as it is there that you will find the final answer to your question."

Kiel leafed through a few front pages and read aloud as follows:

> [1] Before the Zero Date, there were the Others. [2] And the Others were gods, and they lived in golden cities on the land and in the sky. Good and evil, light and dark, night and day they were. [3] And in their likeness, the Others of Daylight created the Eligor in order to serve and worship them, and in return for their pious servitude, the Eligor were given the lands beyond the great cities to tend and care for as they saw fit.

> The Others taught the Eligor to hunt and to cultivate the soil. They learned how to spin and to weave and to build huts. And they became skilled in the working of pelts and in the making of pottery and the forging of iron.
>
> 4 Now the Others of Darkness were wroth at the Others of Daylight, for they wished the lands beyond the golden cities for their own evil purpose, and greed and malice consumed them utterly.
>
> 5 The Others, both of the light and of the dark, were forbidden by the All-father to interfere in mortal events once they had been set in motion. As a result of this cosmic law, the Others of Darkness brought forth the Sha Tar in their image, and the Others of Darkness filled them with a terrible destructive lust.

"Just a minute," Bishop said, interrupting, absently waving a hand. "That phrase again, *Sha Tar*. Tell me, what does *Sha Tar* mean?"

Kiel coughed. "Warrior. It means *human* warrior."

Bishop's eyes narrowed in incredulity as Kiel hastily continued, reciting as follows:

> 6 Now this abomination did not go unnoticed by the Others of Daylight, and they warned the Eligor of the danger. But the Eligor did not believe and thus were not prepared when the Sha Tar came to them, for they were far craftier than any of the beasts the Eligor had known. 7 From the darkness the Sha Tar came to the borderlands of the Eligor, begging to enter, and they used many honeyed words and false promises, and the Eligor were deceived.
>
> 8 And so it came to pass that the Sha Tar were allowed to inhabit in the lands of the Eligor.
>
> 9 Many cycles passed, and while the Eligor were righteous and upheld the Law, the Sha Tar spread like a plague and brought sin into the lands beyond the golden cities of the Others.

[10] In Fourteen Reed of the Second Grand Cycle of Kala, the Sha Tar rose up and cast the Eligor into cruel bondage and forced poverty, and for seven times seven cycles and three, the Eligor ate the bitter fruits of hopeless oppression and despaired, for the Sha Tar held sway over everything."

[11] Now the First Eligor, whose name was Sol, cried out to the Others of Daylight, but they would not listen, for they were wroth with the Eligor for ignoring their warning. [12] Yet the Others of Daylight had not forgotten their beloved children and at last heeded Sol's plea. They gave to Sol the secret girdle of the Iron Thunderbolt, and he went forth to do battle, for he was bitter and filled with fury over the broken covenant with the Sha Tar.

[13] Now, unbeknown to Sol, the Others of Darkness were lurking nearby and saw what had been done. They touched the wrists of the Sha Tar and gave them the Key of Power. [14] The Sha Tar took up the Key of Power, and there was war in the lands beyond the golden cities. The corpses of the dead were piled seven high throughout the land. Plague and pestilence were visited upon the living, and foodstuffs were poisoned. To escape destruction, Sol and the remaining Eligor threw themselves into rivers to cleanse and conceal themselves.

[15] Now righteousness was on the side of Sol, and now he flew swift and powerful against the Sha Tar, who believed them to be dead. Sol took up the girdle of the Iron Thunderbolt and cast it at their hated enemy. Incandescent columns as brilliant as a hundred suns rose from the land, killing countless Sha Tar and reducing their villages to cinders. [16] Sol was victorious and drove the few remaining Sha Tar from the lands of the Eligor. He found the Key of Power and broke it into many pieces, throwing them from the land, and was victorious. But Sol was saddened at the destruction he had wrought. And

so it came to pass that Sol buried the girdle of the Iron Thunderbolt in the Copper Mountains and hid its terrible secret from the earth.
[17] Sol and his followers built a great wall to keep out those remaining Sha Tar who still survived, and for a time there was peace again in the land.
[18] Now the Others of Darkness were enraged at the Others of Daylight over the fall of the Sha Tar, and there was a war in the golden cities and a great din in the sky. The sky held a hundred moons and blossomed with the light of a thousand new suns and a hundred thousand stars, and the passing of the days could not be told. Dense arrows of flame, like a great shower, issued forth upon creation, surrounding the land. A thick gloom at once settled upon the earth, and all points of the compass were lost in darkness. [19] Fierce winds began to blow, and the clouds roared upward, and the oceans were shaken. The sun wavered in the heavens, the earth shook, and the Others, both good and evil, burst into flame and crumpled to the ground. And all that remained of them were broken bits of their once great magic, now scattered everywhere.
[20] The war was great, and many things changed and they were not as they had once been.

Kiel looked up from the Ignotum pro Magna. "This continues through twenty books, each with its own name associated with it. It ends with the last book, called Terminus, which is an archaic Eligor word for 'divination' or 'prediction.' There is no exact human translation. But my mind wanders. I will finish what I have started." Kiel leafed through the last few pages of the book of Vinaya. He began reading again, as follows:

[42] Now Sol gave the Eligor and all their descendants the First Law.
[43] When the Grand Cycle of Kala closes, seek out the remaining Sha Tar and cut them down. Heed this

warning, for otherwise they rise again from the ashes of their old dominion, find the scattered pieces of the Key of Power, and employ its evil power. Do as instructed and you will be a great nation. Your name will be great, and you shall rule all the land with an iron scepter until the end of days. [44] Disobey this command and the Sha Tar will come for you like a wolf in the night. Oblivion will be your destiny, and the Eligor Nation will be no more.

"There are a multitude of other laws we need not bother with." Kiel closed the Ignotum pro Magna and looked at Bishop. "The Grand Cycle of Kala mentioned in verse three of Foundation closed on the opening day of the invasion—one Grand Cycle after Fourteen Reed, of the Seventh Cycle of Kala, mentioned in verse ten."

Bishop sat stupefied. "You act as if you believe every word of that book. It isn't even close to being correct. For one thing, the Others were prehuman, not gods. At least I think they were human."

"Yes, well, some of us knew the truth, but only a very few. That particular detail was kept from the masses. Yet, as with all ancient texts, there are a few grains of truth within them and more than a few bits of chaff. The trick is to winnow fact from fiction. Tell me, Bishop, do you know where the Eligor came from?"

With an effort, Bishop pulled his mind away from the fantastic Ignotum pro Magna. "Well, I think that the Others created them, like the wolf-birds, but—"

"Good." Kiel's eyes shone with a fiery light. "But why? For what purpose?"

"As some sort of weapon, I think."

"A weapon against whom?" Kiel pressed.

Realization seeped into Bishop's eyes. "Against an already existing threat." He glanced at his Riika. "Touched them on the wrists," he whispered. "Pawns in a war that started so long ago that no one can remember the original reasons behind it."

"Very good, Bishop," Kiel responded. "But there is a greater mystery afoot. Where did the Ikonians come from, and why are they attacking now? There is no mention of them in the Ignotum pro Magna. They do not fit the puzzle. The Ikonians have lain dormant for untold eons. Now, suddenly they produce an advanced technology and attack with a fury that is beyond imagination, seemingly just as bent on our destruction as we once were with that of the humans. It is as if they have been set in motion by some outside agency, a force that we have yet to understand."

"Well, let me be very blunt," Bishop replied. "I don't believe that the protectorate truly cares what happens to the Eligor after the last war. And after listening to your explanation of the Ignotum pro Magna, I am compelled to wonder when your calendar will again call upon the Eligor to kill the Sha Tar."

Kiel looked at Bishop. "The humans don't need to worry about that any longer. The Ignotum pro Magna and the old calendar died with the last war. Oracles don't last long after they are proven to be inaccurate. They would have been abandoned long ago if it hadn't meant death to do so."

Bishop didn't look convinced. "Well, I hope so. And the Eligor Empire aside, I can certainly understand why the protectorate wants to know what's going on up north anyway, even if only half of what I've heard is correct."

"I am sure that you have not heard the worst. The Ikonians attack like biomechs in their ferocity, but there is a difference in that those fiends are nothing but mindless Old Earth automatons. There is purpose behind the Ikonian attacks, of that I am sure. It is ultimately up to you to discover that purpose if our two respective governments have any hope of devising some type of defense against them."

"Up to me, is it?" Bishop grumbled. "That's another question that has been nagging me from the back of my mind. Tell me, exactly why aren't you going with me? Is it that you more fully realize the dangers than I do? More so than you have let on?"

"That is not the reason, human. All of twenty years does not give you the right to show such utter absence of thought," Kiel's translator grated.

"Then what is the reason?" Bishop demanded.

"The empire has sent scouts into Ikonia for centuries, with extremely limited success. The Ikonians have an evolved sense of smell, and it is possible they have other evolved senses, sharper according to genetics, capable of discriminating among and interpreting sensory cues that are not even available to our five senses. In any case, they have developed the ability to detect us with an alarming degree of consistency. If I were to accompany you, we wouldn't get forty meters inside their frontier before being found out. That would not be much of a scouting foray now, would it, human?"

Bishop nodded with a half smile. "And you are betting my life and the Eligor Empire that humans don't smell—as awfully as an Eligor anyway—is that it?"

Kiel narrowed his eyes to mere slits of golden fire. "I can only appeal to the gods of fate that the insects have not refined the ability to sniff out monumental human ignorance, or else we are lost."

Bishop took the rebuke. Breathing in the cool forest air, he tried to relax. "Fine, you can't accompany me to Ikonia. It was a valid question that I needed to ask. Now tell me, my fine reptilian host, where do you propose that I start my search for this information that is needed?"

Kiel looked at Bishop with something of a pitying expression upon his scaled face. "Terus Kor."

"Terus Kor." Bishop thought a moment and then looked up in sudden concern. "Terus Kor, the ghost city?"

"Ghost city?" Kiel's face took on an amused expression. "Terus Kor is an Old Earth city in the southernmost part of Ikonia. Ghost city indeed! Dark gods of the Others, you humans are superstitious."

"Yes, well, I don't believe in ghosts, if that's what you think!" Bishop growled defensively. "*Ghost city* is just the name that the runa singers have given it. And as for being superstitious, I am apt to believe, after reading your little book, that we do not hold any exclusive rights to the descriptor."

Kiel nodded. "Of course."

"Well, on with your story, O scaly one," Bishop barked, with a dismissive wave of his hand.

Kiel eyed Bishop and then continued. "Terus Kor is the best spot for beginning your search. There might be clues there. Then you might require a search of the surrounding area. You dare not go farther north, because there you will run into active Ikonian cities, cities that would be impossible to penetrate, even for a Sha Tar."

"What reasons do you have for sending me to this dead city of Terus Kor?" Bishop asked, trying to mask his concern.

"We, the Imperial Intelligence Service, have amassed detailed knowledge of hundreds of Blue Zones throughout the world, even several within your protectorate."

Bishop narrowed his eyes. "How would you have knowledge of Blue Zones within the protectorate?"

"Foragers are ever keen on Old Earth sites and have, in ages past, been more than happy to sell such information to the Eligor."

"Foragers?"

"Oh, don't act so surprised! Humans have filled their pockets as readily as the Eligor with Old Earth artifacts and knowledge dug up by foragers. Do you think they haven't visited every site they could get their hands on? That's how they make their living. They have even been caught trying to raid sites within our own empire, if you can imagine."

Bishop recalled the recent treaty with the protectorate and swallowed when considering the implications. "Great! Fine! You were saying?"

Kiel continued. "Using Old Earth technology, we can recognize the chemical elements associated with the various weapons used in the destruction—"

"Chemicals?"

"That's what I said, human—chemicals."

"I know about chemicals," Bishop said boastfully. "There's earth, air, fire, and, ah, water. Quite learned for a simple soldier, wouldn't you say?"

Kiel winced. "Uh, quite. I had no idea." He rubbed his forehead. "Allow me to proceed before I decide to give up this quest, crawl into a hole, and hide."

Bishop shrugged but said nothing.

"These chemical elements combined with the specific soil from each site produce a unique signature, or rather, a fingerprint for each Blue Zone. After the fall of Kirsk, we analyzed several dead Ikonian soldiers using an Old Earth device that was remarkably sophisticated. Their bodies contained elevated traces of certain elements—lithium, tellurium, and zirconium."

Bishop frowned in suspicion but elected not to start a debate about the unknown substances.

"Those elements in their corresponding levels only occur at site LV-234—the Blue Zone near Terus Kor. That indicates the soldiers were at one point associated with Terus Kor, although according to our last survey of this city, it is abandoned. This is a mystery. We have sent several Eligor scouts to Terus Kor, but none of them have returned. Probably their scent is too recognizable."

"None? None have returned?"

"That reminds me," Kiel began, changing the subject. "I have something for you, something that is sure to come in useful." Kiel pulled a small metallic cylinder from his pack and handed it to Bishop.

"What is it, Eligor army rations? Canned rat? A parchment for my last will and testament?"

"A map from the Old Earth. I appropriated it from the Eligor historical archives before I left Opal. It will guide you to the dead city once I have placed you within range."

"No rat, eh?"

"I wouldn't waste a well-meaning rat ration on you, Sha Tar. You may stick to your own tasteless food."

Bishop took the thin metal tube from Kiel and eyed it suspiciously. It was small, light, and perfectly wrought—definitely Old Earth. And like all Old Earth magic, it took a bit of fiddling to discover its secret. There was no obvious way by which to open the tube; it seemed a solid cylinder of metal as Bishop turned and twisted it. He finally looked up at Kiel with frustrated anger.

"Squeeze it, human," Kiel said, yawning.

Bishop darkened but squeezed the tube with all his might. Kiel apparently had given the correct directive. One end of the tube opened like the iris of an eye, revealing a scroll hidden within. Bishop removed the scroll from the metal tube and held it out. The metallic paperlike substance magically unfurled and straightened into a wrinkle-free sheaf that appeared as new and unblemished as it must have looked the day of its creation. The map glinted dully in the gathering murk of evening, a relic from the age of the Others. With a sudden shock, Bishop now saw that the map shimmered and wavered as if unstable. Turning it, he noted that its topography moved and shifted to its new position, always orienting itself to the north. He looked at Kiel with undisguised awe and a questioning stare.

Kiel shrugged with something of a faint toothy smile. "It is of the Old Earth. What can I say? All I know of it is that it is powered by sunlight and will fade to a blank sheet if not recharged occasionally. That small fact took our scientists a little more than a Great Cycle to discover. Other than that, I know that your position in relation to the map will always be shown as a greenish dot. See?" Kiel pointed.

While Bishop marveled, Kiel slowly traced his clawed finger up the map. "I will guide you through the sunken city of Ra to a point on the northern shore. There you will cross over into the lands of ancient Ikonia and travel to that point." Kiel now pointed to a red mark. "That is Terus Kor, your destination.

Bishop returned his attention to a lower point on the map. "Sunken city of Ra—another dead city? Why not take a more easterly route through this land here?" Bishop pointed to a seemingly easier spot on the map.

Kiel nodded. "True, the terrain there is much less demanding, yet that land is now in the hands of the Ikonians."

"Right. Well, I had to ask. Is the sunken city safe to travel through?"

"Safer than the lands that are now controlled by the Ikonians, I assure you," Kiel answered evasively.

"This Ra—" Bishop began.

"Yes, Ra is the only possible route," Kiel stated, cutting Bishop short.

"This Ra—" Bishop began again with a growing suspicion.

"I think that we should rest," Kiel said, interrupting again. "The road is long, and we have barely started the journey. Yes, rest is what we now need." Kiel settled down against the side of a tree and closed his eyes.

Bishop wondered if the lizard was feigning sleep or if he was actually tired. Reluctantly giving up his questioning, he resealed the wondrous Old Earth map and looked up through the forest canopy at the brightening sky. "Yes, the road is long," he repeated, talking half to himself.

SIX

> Some drift through skies on cottony beds of ease
> while others fight and sail through bloody seas.
> —Vena Korela,
> Saga of Leminkanen, Runa 143

In the half-light of the evening, the travelers once again set out toward the still-distant Ikonian frontier. Amphibian life had begun to appear in increasing numbers as they neared the sunken city of Ra. The dead city was said to be half submerged in an inland sea that stood in between them and Ikonia, like a massive grave marker from the age of the Others. Frogs seemed to chorus a funeral requiem to the city, growing ever louder in the night air as the three travelers approached.

Not only were the frogs growing louder and more profuse, but also a multitude of buzzing, biting insects had made an unwelcome appearance. There was little the travelers could do but grimly endure.

Through puddles and mires, the travelers plodded as the trail steadily deteriorated before them. Giant reeds and cattails hovered over them, replacing the coniferous growth, which had characterized the landscape of the forest behind them.

All through the night they moved on. The trail became wetter and more difficult to navigate. Twice they had to circle broad pools from which bubbles of marsh gas rose and burst. One such pool shone with a thousand phosphorescent eyes that winked out at them as they passed, unnerving Storm Singer, who crouched on Bishop's shoulder in fear and loathing.

Suddenly, Kiel jerked in surprise, then without thought, stamped the life out of a water snake that had made the mistake of striking at him.

"Take care, Kiel. That snake had your eyes. It might have been a relative, albeit a distant one," Bishop remarked dryly.

"You would be best advised to do the same," Kiel retorted as several swamp rats scurried around Bishop's feet, nearly causing him to lose his balance.

Storm Singer, who had hopped up on Bishop's head in alarm, settled down and began to chortle. "Indeed, Kiel. Clever, clever."

Bishop smiled; the tension that had plagued him over the last several days had eased considerably. This fearsome creature Kiel was not so different after all. But there was still a remoteness to the Eligor, an alien being from an alien society that was difficult to understand. It was going to take time to fathom.

The first faint glimmer of dawn was just beginning to lighten the eastern sky when they came to a halt. Kiel reached down below the surface of the muck they were walking through and felt the hard ground below it.

"I thought so," he muttered half to himself. "There's only a thin layer of mud here. I think we are on an ancient road of some sort. There were many such thoroughfares in the days of Ra's glory."

"Then we are getting close to the city," Bishop returned.

Kiel nodded and pointed ahead of them to the east. "Somewhere over there lies the sunken city of Ra." Then he looked at the brightening sky. "Day's coming. We'll need to find shelter soon. There are, ah, things that live here that would best be avoided."

"Biomechs?" Bishop questioned.

"No, not exactly." Kiel evaded the question.

"What do you know that you are not telling me?" Bishop demanded.

"I have told you all that you need to know. Now, let's be on our way."

Bishop scowled. If he'd learned anything about the lizard, it was this: Kiel had a stubborn side. It was a waste of his breath to push him.

The decision to stop for the day was soon made for them. With no warning, they rounded a clump of reeds and found an open expanse of still water before them, broken by dark hillocks and peculiar rows of islands that took shape in the misty half-light of the morning.

Bishop stared at the strange expanse while dragonflies lazily stitched at the water. Here at last was the inland water that hid the dead city they had come to invade.

"There." Kiel pointed. "That is as good a place as any to spend the day. The ground will be less swampy on that island."

"If you say so," Bishop answered doubtfully, eyeing the mound that rose from the water just ahead of them.

While Storm Singer flapped off in search of food for himself, Bishop and Kiel left the shore and waded through the water. Bishop climbed on to the flat-topped island, about ten meters square, bordering the deeper waters ahead. Thick bushes and even a few small trees grew upon it, but none of the marsh plants of the lower bog that was now behind them, suggesting that it was in fact solid ground. He noticed the curiously angular edges of the island as they settled in for the day, safely hidden under the foliage.

"This doesn't strike me as a natural island," Bishop said half to himself.

Kiel eyed the perimeter in the growing light as he unpacked. "This is probably the top of a building of some type. Only the Others knew how much of it is sunk below us. This building could have reached the height of a hundred meters or more at one time. The mire around it could easily be that deep."

Bishop was about to question Kiel's assessment of the probable height of the original building they stood upon when he gasped in astonishment.

As daylight flooded the landscape, the once-heavy mist dissipated, revealing towering forms coalescing in the distance. Rising from brown still water, stretching to the horizon, were the thrusted-up ruins of a vast and ancient metropolis, the hecatomb of a vanished race. Some of the buildings towered hundreds of meters above the waterline, suggesting a level of technology far superior to anything known in the present age.

"By the Others," Bishop whispered in unmasked awe.

Kiel, who was munching peacefully on his dinner, opened a golden eye and looked out at the vast city in the distance. "You act as if you are surprised at the works of your own ancestors. Don't you humans learn about your own history?"

"Well, yes, some. But—" Bishop muttered.

"I would think that humans would be very concerned with their own past if for no better reason than to guard against a repeat of the cataclysm that brought about their downfall," Kiel said with something bordering on genuine concern.

Bishop reddened. "You don't know anything about human history, lizard. Don't lecture me on things that don't concern you. We dominated this planet thousands of years before the Eligor even existed."

"That's the point. They do concern me, as they do all Eligor. Left unchecked, you humans spread like a disease." Kiel's eyes took on a cold reptilian look.

Bishop waved his hand in growing anger. "I'm not going to get drawn into a philosophical argument about which of our two respective races would be better classified as a disease after what your beloved empire tried to do to the protectorate."

Kiel glowered at Bishop for a moment before closing his eyes and returning to his chewing.

"Neither will I, human," Kiel muttered with his mouth full. "But know this. If you continue to raise your voice, remnants of your proud human legacy will likely come to pay you a visit, and I would venture it won't be a pleasant reunion."

Bishop looked at him oddly. "What are you talking about?"

"Nothing," Kiel muttered, finishing his meal. "Don't strain your tiny human head over it. Wake me when half the day has passed." With that, Kiel turned away from Bishop, settling himself against a small tree.

Bishop elected to let Kiel sleep rather than question him further about whatever lurked in these waters. He sullenly looked out over the fantastic scene that continued to materialize in the morning light.

The buildings were mind-shattering in their stature, and their emergence from unplumbed water suggested an even greater original height than what was currently visible. Smaller structures or perhaps those that had sunk deeper into the mud were only domed islets covered with small leafy trees and scrub like the one on which the travelers now lay concealed.

Even though the structures were covered with plant life and showed the wear of the ages, the destruction by some titanic force was still visible. Many of the scorched ruins were shattered and broken as if by some colossal blow, a blow that contained both fire and shock. Bishop knew that somewhere close was a deadly Blue Zone, the very epicenter of the destruction. The manner of the devastation suggested that the blast point was fairly distant, because if it had occurred above the city of Ra, nothing would have remained.

Water plants such as lily pads; arrow weed; and other, nameless aquatic flora, some like great floating bladders, covered much of the still water close to shore, but the deeper water sat like a great glassy mirror with nothing, absolutely nothing, disturbing its surface. Here and there along the shoreline, great piles of logs lay tumbled, many overgrown with vines and creepers, the wreckage hurled in by past storms.

The colorless towers closest to Bishop had dark, gaping holes in many places where once there had been windows, if vegetation was not obscuring them. Here and there, amazingly, a fragment of ancient glass still glinted in the sunlight, and occasionally even a scrap of some rustproof metal shone dully. It was an extraordinary scene, ancient beyond memory.

The voices of the frogs had died down with the coming of the sun, but the insects still buzzed and stung, although mercifully far fewer in number. Of other life there was little, save for a few reptilelike creatures that flew silently about the roofs of some of the buildings. Large blotches of greenish guano stained several of the gaping window holes, suggesting a roosting area.

Storm Singer reappeared after a bit, and for the rest of the morning Kiel and Bishop took turns watching the great city and the water below it, but they saw nothing beyond the movements of small identifiable animals: water snakes, nutria, rats, and salamanders. Soon the job of watching the area became monotonous, and shortly after noon, Bishop woke Kiel, then curled into his own bedroll and fell asleep almost at once.

"The sleep of the young. Were I as untroubled, it would be a better world," Kiel muttered, looking out over the swamp that lay before them.

The afternoon drew on, and the sun sank low on the western horizon. The first frog voices began to sound, hesitantly at first, then growing louder. The insects also resumed their chorus, their humming battalions attacking in new numbers, rousing Bishop from his fitful slumber.

"Time to leave," Kiel finally said as the last rays of the sun settled below the horizon.

They repacked a few belongings and waded back to the shore, muddy though it was, in an attempt to circle the city. The water between the great buildings was too deep and too vast to try swimming, even if it had not been for their heavy packs and weaponry. And who knew what lurked under the surface? They had made but little progress along the shoreline, when they froze.

The insect noises suddenly hushed and the lagoons stood still when through the ruined towers of the ancient city a long echoing shriek was heard. As they listened, the sound came yet again, a mournful lament that rose thunderously into the evening air then slowly died. It was over as soon as it had begun. A frog croaked hesitantly, and then another, until the entire area was again filled with the normal sounds of the marshland.

"Could you tell where the sound came from?" Bishop whispered.

"No. It seemed to be some distance away, possibly somewhere ahead of us."

"Ahead of us?" Storm Singer questioned, now fully alert. The bird had visibly shrunk in size at the sound, and his eyes had become black saucers of apprehension.

"Ahead of us? That's just wonderful. Just great. This journey just gets better and better, doesn't it?" Bishop dismally came to a stop and sat down heavily on a log, throwing up his hands. "What are we supposed to do, just keep walking into the waiting jaws of whatever that was?"

"Jaws?" Storm Singer repeated the word, intently scanning the marshland, shrinking back even more.

Kiel didn't respond, but neither did he continue to walk toward the distressing sound ahead of them.

Noting a pile of logs and branches before them, Bishop looked up from his seat on the log. "What about building a raft to carry us across the inland sea instead of taking our chances by walking along this demon-haunted marshland?"

Kiel examined the logs and nodded. "Yes. Perhaps that would be a good idea. Well done, Sha Tar. You are a credit to your species."

"I do have them." Bishop thumped his head with his finger.

"Remarkably sentient," Kiel muttered. "You almost qualify as a life-form."

Bishop darkened.

"Excellent idea," Storm Singer broke in. "Well thought, Bishop. Truly, I'm as surprised as Kiel, for a creature with such a small nut."

"Bird, don't you think we would be better served if you watched the area while we work, instead of engaging in your brainless prattle?" Bishop said blandly, jerking his thumb toward the sky.

"Yet another mental masterstroke for the human," Storm Singer croaked as he took to the air.

While Storm Singer circled above them, Bishop and Kiel got to work untangling the logs and binding them together with the tough vines that grew over them. After some time, they had constructed a serviceable raft. Bishop cut two poles and even fashioned some crude paddles with his dagger. Slowly, they pushed the heavy raft onto the surface of the still water and clambered aboard, their weight causing the raft to dip momentarily below the murky surface. Using the poles, Kiel propelled the raft into the starlit evening, straight toward the broken and blasted towers that lay before them.

The raft was graceless, but with patience, it was just possible to move it forward. While Kiel poled, Bishop leaned forward and cut the tangled mats of vegetation that lay entwined on the water's surface.

Storm Singer silently landed on Kiel's shoulder, settling down to his never-ending task of preening. "Nothing of any consequence moves within eyesight."

"That's a comfort," Bishop growled. "Those rat-sized raisin eyes of yours couldn't spy a charging biomech, I'd wager."

Storm Singer delicately smoothened a feather. "The eyes of a wolf-bird can pick out the movement of a flea on a human's head."

Bishop eyed the bird and then scratched absently. "We don't need to know about fleas, bird—just danger."

"I would think a head full of fleas would be a danger," Storm Singer began.

"Might I suggest a bit of quiet?" Kiel's translator hissed in annoyance.

Bishop eyed Storm Singer, then shrugged and returned to his job of cutting away the water plants. "Better fleas than mites," he muttered to himself, scratching absently at an armpit.

The ponderous raft slid ever farther away from the shore, heading toward the center of the towering dead city that now loomed ahead of them. Frogs blinked and fell silent, their cold eyes goggling from huge lily pads and bladderworts as the travelers slid by.

Into the night, the raft's slow progress continued, and soon they were entering the outer suburbs of drowned Ra. Black windows and gaping rents in the shattered ancient masonry leered down at the travelers as they poled ever closer to the city center.

On two occasions they encountered a bank of thick mud, rising up invisibly under the water plants, crowning the surface of the great lagoon, and were forced to backtrack through the maze of the outer city. Fortunately, there seemed always an open corridor available. Finally, after entering a wide stretch between the buildings, the ground under the raft sank away as the water deepened. The travelers traded their poles for the crudely built paddles.

Then from out of the east, in the direction they were traveling, came the same strange call they had heard before. The frogs fell silent.

Two times the mournful sound came in the darkness. Then there was silence once more. Slowly the frogs began to chorus again, and the night sounds returned.

"It sounded like it was ahead of us, just like it did before."

"It seemed to me to come from that direction. Possibly it was reflected off the buildings," Kiel muttered nervously.

"I hope you're right. Let's get out of this demon-haunted city and be done with it."

"I wholeheartedly agree," put in Storm Singer, for once not wanting to add an avian witticism.

They resumed paddling into the humming, croaking, and chirping darkness, rowing through the inky water toward the far end of the great dead city somewhere ahead of them.

Sometime past midnight, a lean ancient moon rose in the eastern sky, but the light was of little comfort. The eyes of a thousand ruined windows leered down on Kiel and Bishop as they silently slid past. Perhaps they were following boulevards and lanes that once echoed the marching of the soldiers in parades of conquest in the days of the Others. All those were buried now, lost and forgotten, under the weight of centuries of mud and water.

Toward morning, they broke into deeper water, and all plant life vanished. The raft drifted along what once must have been a mighty avenue; the close-packed buildings on either side had become so tall that even in their ruin it was as if the travelers were rafting through a deep canyon. They could see light ahead and behind, but the buildings hemmed them in on both sides. There were bays and great rents in the moss-covered cliffs and walls of stone, along with some shadowed niches and caves.

Bishop looked around carefully. Then his eyes returned to one spot, seeing something that brought a chill to his body.

"Gods of the Others," Bishop whispered as he nudged Kiel and pointed.

Storm Singer's eyes followed Bishop's finger, then the bird hissed. He flared his neck feathers in alarm.

Kiel froze.

The gloomy light was just strong enough to delineate the spot that had caught Bishop's eye. A huge wall or gate had collapsed in a distant age. Now, water flowed through the gap and into the still pool, which was hundreds of meters across. In the middle of the pool, just opposite the entrance where the raft rode, a massive object rose from the water. At first Bishop thought it was an enormous mound of rubble, but, with a thrill of horror, he detected a slight movement. Then the shape began to make sense as he detected ribs, scales, and legs curled and tucked around a massive body. The thing before them was curled up and sleeping like a monstrous kitten in front of an open hearth, yet a kitten it most assuredly was not. The sheer bulk of the creature defied the imagination. Webbing on one of the back feet identified it as some kind of water creature, and just possibly it was an herbivore. Just possibly.

They drifted silently past the slumbering monster toward their distant goal, and for what seemed like hours they sat frozen, not daring to make a sound, looking at each other in silence. Finally, they resumed their paddling, taking great care not to splash the water as they did so. Even Kiel, who rarely showed emotion, continued to look behind them as if expecting to see the titan suddenly come boiling out of the water.

The light of the morning began illuminating the sky as a cleft between the buildings ahead of them grew larger. The sun was almost up before the craft emerged between the towering buildings and into a small lake, whose clear blue water indicated great depth.

"Shades of the Others," Bishop finally whispered. He was used to giant spiders, horse-sized rats, and other monstrous mutations from the Change, but the fiend behind them had taken him by surprise. "No one will believe that one."

Storm Singer elected not to look back. His concentration was now focused intently on every darkened fissure in the buildings they were passing as if to discover some new horror lurking there. "I only wish to live long enough to tell the tale. It is of no great concern of my nest-mates, believe it or not," he hissed quietly.

"I would agree with the wise bird," Kiel said, shooting one last look behind him, seeming now to take the creature in stride.

Then turning, Kiel gazed out at the lake ahead of them, which was ringed by the rotting towers. "I'll wager that this lake was once the city's central plaza."

With much effort, Bishop turned and followed Kiel's gaze to the middle of the lake. A small green island covered with bushes and trees rose out of the water.

"The trees are still standing, a good sign that the creature back there doesn't frequent it," Bishop remarked, trying to sound convincing.

Kiel shrugged. "He'll leave us alone if we leave him alone, one would prefer to assume."

Storm Singer glanced behind them again. "I trust that you are correct, Kiel, because if you are not—"

"Yes," Bishop concluded solemnly. "We will all long for wings to carry us to safety, even if mites come with blessings from heaven."

Bishop stood on the raft immobile, holding his paddle. True, the island did look inviting. Perhaps too much so. He had not forgotten the initial feeling of being watched and the weird calling sounds that haunted the necropolis. The island was still surrounded by the drowned city and its ravaged buildings, peaceful though it looked.

But fatigue won over caution. They had to rest somewhere, and all three of them were nearly exhausted. They also needed to eat and a source of clean water was urgent.

"Come on then," he said and began to paddle. "At the very least we can hide there for the rest of the day."

A gently sloping beach on one end made the island almost perfect to land the raft and upon exploration, they found a spring, or rather a dew pond, filled with clean, sweet water set at the center of the island, surrounded by tall ferns and sweet-smelling flowers. To make matters complete Keil discovered a bed of fresh water clams in the shallows and the three carnivores feasted on raw, juicy shellfish until they could hold no more. By mid-afternoon, washed, clean and with full stomachs, they began the routine of setting up camp.

As they were settling down to rest, the terrible wailing call, which had grown so familiar to them, came again, louder than they had ever heard it. And this time it did not stop.

"What is it? What does it mean?" Storm Singer cawed.

Before Bishop could respond, Kiel was up and moving. "Look to the water!" he called, stabbing a clawed finger in alarm.

Bishop turned and froze.

From the surrounding lake, greenish forms emerged one by one, until the water was boiling with activity. They were like newts with pallid skin and huge black eyes. Newt-like they were, yet as they slowly walked onto the island, they each stood on two webbed feet like a human.

"What in the eight hells are they?" hissed Bishop.

Kiel surveyed the creatures before them. "The Great Cataclysm brought about many changes, not all of which are as civilized as the foragers. These beings are the Megatherium, the water folk of Ra. They are believed to be a relic survivor of the city's original residents."

"Not as civilized as the foragers? This is becoming a routine! What kind of guide are you? You knew about them before we even started this journey! You knew and yet you said nothing!"

"I had hoped—prayed—that we would live long enough to debate it, Sha Tar," Kiel answered, unsheathing his sword with a singing sound.

Bishop hastily drew his own sword while Storm Singer leapt to the top of Bishop's head, his throat feathers bristling in alarm.

"Storm Singer, get out of here! You can't help us!" Bishop barked, shaking the bird loose. The bird needed no prodding, taking flight in a flurry of black feathers and enraged cawing. The bird swooped down upon the newt men in rage, lunging time and time again, but to no avail. The Megatherium were not interested in the bird, seeming to realize that Storm Singer posed little, if any, threat.

Then after a final lunge, Storm Singer rose into the air and shot from sight, flying back the way they had come.

"The flying rat has flown the proverbial coop," Bishop growled in disgust, watching the bird disappear. "Just as I have always said, wolf-birds are worthless!"

"Leave him be, Sha Tar. He could have done little more than scratch them anyway."

Bishop shook his head in resignation. "You're right. I just thought he would have tried a little harder before deserting us, that's all."

Bishop's attention returned to the water. "Black gods, look at them. They must have been watching us from the beginning." From every side there came scores of them, brandishing small knives fashioned from shards of broken glass, with handles made from a material that looked distressingly like human bone.

There came the moaning cry again—a strange hand-cranked device carried by one of the creatures—and then the Megatherium swarmed upon them like a crashing wave. Bishop and Kiel prepared themselves, raising their blades in defense as the terrible wave broke over them. Their swords turned red with blood as the Megatherium, armed only with their knives, claws, and teeth, threw themselves wantonly upon them. Bishop and Kiel possessed one advantage—they wore protective clothing, whereas their foes did not. Yet the amphibians flung themselves into the fray as fiercely as if they had been clothed in steel.

Within moments, more than a dozen grotesque mutilated bodies lay crumpled on the ground about them, here a headless body, there a bodiless head.

Then for a moment, the horde of creatures drew back and stood at a distance, the blood from their sword wounds making brilliant designs on their leprous skin. Kiel and Bishop looked warily at the creatures that ringed them like wolves.

"The safest way to Ikonia, Sir Eligor? The safest way, you said."

"Trust me, this is the safest, easiest way."

"Easy? You call this easy! I'd hate to see the difficult route!"

"You prattle too much, human."

"And you keep too many secrets," Bishop returned angrily.

Bishop stared at the creatures that ringed them. They were bowed and gnarled of limb, with hairless heads that slanted at a severe angle. Large unblinking eyes glinted in malevolent spite. They wore no clothing except for a wide knife belt of woven reed.

The wailing device sounded once more, and in a flash, the amphibians came again. This time they closed quarters on Kiel and Bishop, a deadly strategy since there was a greater number of Megatherium. Back-to-back, Kiel and Bishop fought, their foe pressing until their snarling faces were so close, the travelers could smell their rank, beast-like breath.

The dead city of Ra, the churning water about them, time itself, all faded into a gray mist. Bishop ceased to be a civilized man and became a mere fighting automaton. The haze of battle erased mind and soul.

Swing, thrust, parry, slash.

Bestial faces snarled through the battle fog. A Megatherium appeared, was dispatched, and fell away, only to be replaced by yet another. Years of culture and custom slipped away like sea mist, and Bishop was again a savage, a primal man of the forests and dale, facing a terror from another age, lost in the lust for slaughter. A creature slammed into Bishop and drove him to the ground. He reeled up, slaying the monster with a fierce upslashing thrust, spilling its life out in a gory explosion. And on it went.

An uncomfortable tingling drew his attention back to reality, and in a split second the Riika shimmered. In the next second, a nearly invisible wave, like the rippling caused by a stone dropped into a still pond, ripped away from the device, followed by sudden overwhelming fatigue. He staggered momentarily, sword raised in confused wonderment. The Megatherium had been thrown back as if by an invisible and irresistible blast of air, as easily as one might blow foam from a tankard of ale. Even Kiel had been thrown several meters and was now eyeing Bishop in a strange, knowing way.

The Megatherium recovered quickly from their momentary surprise, their faces set in rictus grins of hate as they floated in preparation for the final assault. The travelers were trapped and dangerously fatigued. They wearily raised their swords for the last desperate assault, when a cawing sound reached them. Storm Singer! The bird had not deserted them after all.

The bird somersaulted in midair and then went into a bizarre act of aerial acrobatics and croaking screams that momentarily drew the attention of the Megatherium. He tumbled, rolled, flipped, and shrieked, all a mere arm's length above the newt creatures.

"The bird's gone mad," Bishop muttered, dropping the point of his sword in momentary confusion. Kiel, too, was fixed on the scene in wonderment.

"What in the eight—"

Suddenly, and without warning, the Megatherium were lifted into the air by a great swell of water beneath them. The newt things bobbed, frozen in terror, as monstrous jaws broke away from the water and closed around them. In stunned fascination, Bishop realized that the gleaming ivory teeth were as big as his own body. It was the very beast they had passed the previous night. Not a sound came from the Megatherium, their having been consumed too quickly. For one instant, the monster held them thus, then it closed its vast mouth, and the newt things simply vanished in a roiling of water and foam. From this, a tail ten meters long emerged and towered above Bishop and Kiel, then it too slipped below the water, leaving an oily, bloody slick ringed by widening foamy rings of gory flotsam, some of which still wiggled with independent life. The wake caused by the submerging behemoth washed up on the island beach, and in an instant the two travelers were waist-deep in surging water. The water raced back as swiftly as it had come, leaving the two in stunned silence.

Storm Singer circled and then again flew back the way he had come, squawking and cawing as if in torment. An ominous ripple on the water followed him into the city gloom.

"Black gods!" Bishop panted, weary, shocked, and in awe. Then he turned to Kiel, wiping his sword and resheathing it. "Tell me again why you believe this is the safest route."

Kiel looked at him. "The Megatherium usually keep to themselves. Usually. They must have had a bad season to become so emboldened as to attack us in the open. They could have still been harboring ill will toward us from the last conflict with our army. Or there could be another reason."

Kiel began clawing through the sandy mud of the beach. Then his claws encountered something unyielding.

"Ah, as I suspected. Just our luck," he muttered, pulling a gelatinous glob from the muck.

"Eggs?" Bishop poked the jellylike mass.

Kiel nodded. "They probably would have just let us pass unnoticed if we hadn't stopped on this accursed island. Then again, they have never been friends of the Eligor nation."

Bishop scanned the waterways feeding the central plaza. "Enough talk. Let's get out of here while we have the chance."

Kiel nodded, carefully returning the egg to the mud. "For once, we agree, human."

The two travelers gathered their belongings and quickly refloated the beached raft, paddling away north of the city's center. Within the hour, Storm Singer returned, settling on Bishop's shoulder and beginning to nonchalantly preen his feathers.

"Good riddance to that bad egg."

Bishop looked at the bird with new respect. "I suppose that I owe you a debt of thanks, Storm Singer. I doubted your courage, and for that I am sorry."

Storm Singer lowered his black forehead to rest on Bishop's own, his ebon eyes glittering. "I would expect that you would have done the same for me, yes?"

Bishop smiled. "Yes." And then he frowned. "How is it that that great beast followed you?"

Storm Singer cackled and then took on a look of innocence by shrugging. "By some means of which I am completely mystified, a few stray rocks broke loose above the beast and bounced off its slumbering head, catching its attention rather quickly, I might add. And then, after it reared to catch me, as I recall, another rock dropped and somehow smashed the egg it had been resting on. Strange for one so large to take such an interest in chasing one so small, wouldn't you think? After all, it was just an egg. There are certainly more to follow."

Kiel's translator hissed and crackled in hilarity.

"Where is the beast now?" Bishop questioned, quickly scanning the water.

"I have led it back to the other side of the city, where it is now gainfully employed chasing several of those plodding two-legged frogs through the marsh. They seem ungainly out of water; I am guessing it will be a short chase."

Kiel raised his arm to Storm Singer, and the bird flew to it. "Worth a scratch or two, I believe. Wouldn't you agree, Sha Tar?"

Bishop shook his head in disbelief.

The wolf-bird's eyes closed in rapture as Kiel began scratching his neck. "Payment accepted," Storm Singer crooned.

They again set out on the water toward their goal to the north. No more did they hear the ghostly call that had so bothered them when they first entered the environs of Ra, and they saw no sign of the giant monster that had inadvertently come to their aid.

Night fell and the moon rose, making the towers rear up like vague phantoms around the travelers, throwing strange shadows among the darkened waterways. Through the night they quietly paddled, not daring to speak, even in whispers. The vacant windows watched them as they drifted below, seeming to silently rage at their spoiled victory.

As the night faded, they finally broke out of the towering buildings and back into the weed-choked, insect-haunted perimeter lands. Ahead of them, growing larger in the distance, they could just make out the dark line of the forest.

They had survived the sunken city of Ra.

The sun rode up the eastern sky as the travelers landed the raft and hid it in the brush. Storm Singer retreated to the upper branches of an overhanging tree and retired for the day while Kiel set about building a small smokeless fire to dry their wet clothes. Bishop, nodding in approval at Kiel's idea, stripped off his muddy clothing and prepared to wash them in a stream that meandered through the clearing.

"It will be good to clean the trail dust off these clothes. I have not had a decent bath since before we left Gondakar," Bishop said. He began humming a tune.

Kiel absently looked up from his fire and stared in utter astonishment. Bishop, sensing the sudden attention, returned the Eligor's stare and darkened.

"What?"

Kiel rubbed his eyes, shook his head, and returned his attention to the fire, a faint chortling sound intermittently spitting from his translator.

Bishop's ears flamed. He turned away from the Eligor and quickened his scrubbing. "Well, what did you expect, a scaly backside like your own unsightly reptilian hide?"

"Well," Kiel muttered, "I'll tell you what I didn't expect."

"Never mind, I'd rather not know," Bishop growled, hastening to put his wet clothing back on.

Kiel began to shake in silent mirth. "Gods of the Others …"

"I said never mind, lizard!"

Soon the dry crackle of a cooking fire murmured through the still forest, and wisps of smoke curled upward in a mingling hazy cloud. Bishop, still dripping in wet clothing, drew forth a few raggedy bits of smoked meat and a granite-hard lump of wayfarer's bread from his pack.

"A banquet again!" He burped unpleasantly, sourly picking a few tufts of lint from the tasteless morsels.

Suddenly the forest litter rustled amid the roots. Bishop's arm shot out, the hardtack dropping to the leaf-covered ground.

"Ha-ha!" Bishop barked in pleasure.

"What is it? What do you have there?" Kiel asked, suddenly intrigued by Bishop's strange actions.

Bishop held up his squirming trophy with a childish grin: a well-fed frog that had wandered up from the marsh. "Not your lucky day, my boy," he sang cheerfully, grabbing for his dagger. "Frog legs! Why didn't I think of it before? There are probably hundreds—thousands—of frogs hopping around these parts."

"How can you even think of eating frogs after what we just went through?" Kiel muttered as he took a foul-smelling dead rat from his own pack.

Bishop smacked his lips. "You can sit there wolfing your rotten rat supper, but I am having fresh food for a change! I'll consider it my revenge on Ra for our mistreatment."

Twenty minutes later, Bishop had cleaned and prepared a sizable pile of frog legs. He hummed to himself as he held his skewer over the fire. "Freftar the frog was the lord of the trees, the lord of the pond, the mud, and the bees."

He smiled a superior smile at Kiel over the snapping and crackling of the fire. "That's called a poem, Kiel. In the protectorate, we have poetry. It rhymes. Trees, bees, you see?" He looked self-satisfied. "Good poem, huh?"

"Ah yes, poetry. How quaint," Kiel said, yawning. And then with a glitter in his golden eyes, he spoke again, reciting as follows:

> Eligor legions lead on. Our hearts beat high.
> Lead on from Opal's towers.
> Who would not deem it bliss to die,
> Slain in a cause like ours?
> The brave who sleep in the soil of thine
> Lay not entombed but wholly enshrined.
>
> Souls of the slain in a bloody war,
> Look from your sainted rest.
> Tell us ye rose in glory's lore
> To mingle with the blest.
> Tell us how short the death pang's power,
> How bright the joys of your immortal bower.
>
> Strike the loud harp, ye minstrel train.
> Pour forth your loftiest leis.
> Each heart shall echo to the strain
> Breathed in the warriors' praise.
> Bid every string triumphant swell,
> The inspiring sound that's loved so well.
>
> Opal, amid the fiercest hour,
> The widest rage of fight,
> Thy name shall lend our falcons power
> And nerve our hearts with might.
> Envied be those for thee who fall,
> Who find their graves beneath thy wall.
>
> For them no need of sculptured tomb
> Should chronicle their fame,
> Or pyramid record their doom,

Or deathless verse their name.
It is enough that dust of thine
Should shroud their form, O divine.

Eligor legions lead on. Our hearts beat high
For combat's glorious hour.
Soon shall the crimson banner fly
On Opal's loftiest tower.
We burn to mingle in the strife,
Where but to die grants eternal life.

Kiel looked up at Bishop. "See, it rhymes." He paused. "Bit of a trial for me, to modify it so as it would rhyme after the manner of the translator."

From above them, Bishop heard a cackling avian laugh. "Strife, life, hour, tower. Yes, human, see how it rhymes?"

Bishop pulled his skewer out of the fire and turned his back. "You made your point, both of you," he grumbled.

"Unfortunate that the Riika does not impart intelligence along with its many other blessings, wouldn't you say?" Kiel said in a banal tone.

Bishop turned in unbridled surprise. "What do you know of the Riika?"

Kiel stirred the fire with a branch while seemingly lost in thought, sparks flying about him in the gloaming. "Have you forgotten that I am a member of the once-mighty Eligor Imperial Security Service? We knew much of Old Earth history and much of the Old Earth technology; we have suffered for that unhealthy interest. Though we believed the humans had lost the Riika along with their technology ages ago, I suspected when I first saw the device, but was not convinced until you used it against the Megatherium. It is wise your people hid it from the Eligor Empire, because if the Eligor had suspected, they would not have hesitated to throw every resource into its recovery. The abortive war might not have ended with a retreat."

Bishop, knowing better than most how close the protectorate had come to losing the last war, shivered at the thought of what might have happened if it had lasted much longer. "Tell me then, what is it? What does it do?"

"I am not entirely sure. Its secrets died with the destruction of the Old Earth. I, as do many within intelligence, believe it was a weapon of some importance. I believe that it was designed for humans and that only certain humans could unlock its secrets. Some believe it was created too late to prevent the great wars that ended the Fourth Age. Others believe that it was the cause of the great wars. I am also fairly sure the Riika was accompanied by a second device that was worn on the opposite wrist. This one was necessary in order to invoke its power."

"May the bearer find the key," Bishop muttered to himself.

"What was that?" Kiel looked up from the fire.

"Perhaps nothing." Bishop frowned. "The Order. They believe there is a key that will be found and used to bring about a new age for the protectorate. It is part of their belief as stated in the sacred writings of the Vena Korela. They believe the bearer of the Riika will find this key and unite the Great Houses, bringing about a new age, a sixth and final age. But there have been many bearers throughout the history of the protectorate, and no key has ever been found. No one knows what it looks like, where to find it, or how to use it. I have come to believe those of Order no longer believe this myth. Several knights questioned me at some length after the acceptance ceremony, but they seemed relieved when I could not answer their questions and quickly lost interest."

"What questions?"

"Oh, like did I feel different, did I think differently. They asked me if I had any abilities that I had not possessed before the Riika accepted me, which I did not."

"It would seem you have mastered something of the Old Earth power that resides within the device even without this so-called key."

"Not really. It has only aided me twice, and of its own volition: once on a previous assignment, and then against the Megatherium. I seem to have no more control over it than I do the weather."

"Did you ever report the first occurrence to your Order?" Kiel asked with renewed interest.

Bishop gave Kiel a sheepish look. "No, I thought it best not to include the, ah, incident in my report."

Kiel eyed Bishop a moment longer but said no more about the Riika as he resumed his absent stirring of the fire. "Perhaps that was wise," he muttered half to himself.

Bishop, on the other hand, had become sullen. Long after the others had turned in for the night, he sat pondering the things he had been told.

The next day they moved out of the lowlands and into the lands of the Eligor northern forest. Twice, the small group came across deep sluggish rivers—outlets of the inland sea they had just crossed—and in each case they walked half a kilometer or so to avoid them, crossing at wide, shallow sandbars. Soon all traces of the swampland behind them vanished and the forest slowly transformed itself into a primeval land of ancient trees. The height and the thickness of the boles exceeded anything Bishop had ever seen before, shooting upward in magnificent columns until, at an enormous distance above their heads, he could dimly see the point where they threw out their side branches into a gothic interlacing lattice that coalesced to form one great matted roof of foliage, through which an occasional golden ray of sunshine shot downward to trace a thin dazzling line of light onto the deep obscurity below.

As the pair moved noiselessly among the thick, soft carpet of decaying vegetation, a hush fell upon them as if they were walking through hallowed ground. Even Storm Singer's chatter fell to a whisper. Vivid orchids and strange-colored lichens smoldered upon the ancient tree trunks, and where a wandering shaft of light fell upon the fungus, it gave the effect of looking like a lost fairy world. In this great waste of forest, life struggled ever upward to reach the light. Every plant, even the smallest, curled and writhed toward the emerald roof, twining around its stronger and taller brethren in the effort, draping everything in a corded vine-entangled carpet.

Of animal life, there was no movement amid the majestic vaulted aisles that stretched before them as they walked, but a constant rustling far above their heads told of a multitudinous world of snakes, insects, birds, and sloths living in the canopy, strange creatures that looked down in wonder at the tiny figures that plodded along in the obscure depths below them. Only once did some bandy-legged, lurching creature scuttle clumsily amid the shadows. It was the only sign of earth life that Bishop saw in this dark eternal forest.

The trail continued to ascend away from the swampy lowlands, leading them over a dark, rock-studded rise that took the entire afternoon to navigate. Occasional brooks with pebbly bottoms and fern-draped banks gurgled down the shallow gorges in the hill, offering fresh water at the banks of each rock-studded pool, where fish swirled in torpid schools. Though the feeling of danger never left Bishop, he silently marveled at this dreamworld that was so different from the cleared lands of the protectorate.

"Tell me, how did the old empire come into being, Sir Eligor? What was it like in its days of glory?" Bishop suddenly asked, wondering at the history of these strange lands.

A bird called above them, and its mate answered in the distance. Below the ancient trees, nothing moved except the lonely travelers in the silent darkness.

"The empire?" Kiel muttered, seeming to slowly absorb the question. "This is not an easy question you have asked of me."

Bishop walked along in silence as the Eligor pondered the question.

He had not expected a response from Kiel and was surprised to get an answer.

"The Eligor Empire," Kiel finally began. "The Eligor Empire, as I have stated previously, came into being on the Zero Date of One Reed, after the Great Cataclysm, the beginning of your Fifth Age. Little is known of this time, but it is believed that within the first millennium, powerful kings had risen from the ashes of the Great Cataclysm and ruled over our scattered people until, according to patriotic legend, the Eligor united and established a more representative form of government known then as the Eligor Republic. For five Great Cycles, the republic existed, and our people expanded from small communities into one major power. After countless years of border warfare, the Eligor conquered the surrounding regions and, by the twenty-sixth of Flint in the Fourth Cycle of Ix, controlled all the lands that make up our current borders."

"Then there were other peoples who once lived in this land besides the Eligor?" Bishop asked.

"Certainly, there were others in these lands, others who were, or so the legends go, constantly warring with our ancestors."

"What happened to them?"

"The Eligor embarked on a conquest to clear the Eastern Basin of hostile kingdoms. First, we defeated our greatest rival, the Vanir, whose possessions, including, Ozareth, Ixxis Roi, and Sub Korra, eventually became major Eligor city-states."

"What were these Vanir like? Were they human?" Bishop wondered aloud.

"It is said the Vanir were humanlike but much larger in stature. I have also been told they were a remnant race of the Others and still retained some of the old science of the Fourth Age, science that we have since absorbed into our own culture, such as electricity and related technologies."

"'Lectricity?" Bishop turned quizzically toward Kiel.

Kiel coughed. "Never mind, Sha Tar."

Bishop scowled but remained silent as Kiel continued.

"During the beginning of the Grand Cycle of Tresa, our military forces fought against and defeated the last of our hereditary enemies, bringing the city-states of Volsung, Opal, Thokk, Kirsk, and Asgrad under Eligor control. In the west, most of the original lands of the foragers were wrested, which included the entire domain within one hundred kilometers of the Western Sea, so that the Eligor frontiers extended from the eastern ocean to the lands of the foragers, and from the Gondakar Barrier to the northern borders of the Ikonian Empire."

"Why did you not take all the forager lands and absorb them into your empire?"

"Why indeed? The foragers have the unique ability to live and work within Blue Zones without suffering ill effects from the poisons that still linger in such places. We would not wish to destroy such a race since we have always had an unhealthy interest in Old Earth technology excavated from such sites."

"The Eligor were driven on to conquest, but why?" Bishop asked, pressing the question.

"Immense wealth inflamed the ambitions of the Eligor hierarchy, who struggled for personal domination rather than collective rule. This early corruption within the body politic transformed the Eligor themselves. Eligor imperialism introduced extremes of wealth and poverty that sharpened social and economic conflict within the Eligor state. The flood of military plunder and captured slaves dramatically changed the countryside as small farms died and landless peasants migrated to the great cities to join the army for want of work and food. It is widely believed that the wealth of the republic corrupted the once noble Eligor people. Nearly a century of intermittent civil war between the city-states threatened to destroy the unity and prosperity of the Eligor Republic itself."

"What is it that prevented this catastrophe?" Bishop asked.

Kiel thought for a moment. "In the year fifty-two, in the House of the Third Cycle of Kekses, an ambitious young Eligor by the name of Philotanus, who had held many of the highest political offices in the Eligor government, marched into Opal and overthrew the leaders of the republic. After defeating his enemies, he ruled as dictator for twenty years until his assassination. Philotanus's assassins hoped to restore the old republic, but it was no longer possible. Neither the urban masses, who were now totally integrated into the military, nor the military establishment would allow the old aristocracy to regain control.

"The Eligor Empire needed a strong hand to administer the state and control the army since the old system of government was unsuitable to rule an empire of more than sixty million subjects. If Imperial Eligor wanted to maintain its dominance, the government needed to create new administrative and military institutions. Philotanus planned to transform the Eligor state, but his few years in power were insufficient. His followers included his longtime military deputy Orias and his great-nephew Ronwe, who eventually turned on each other. By Nineteen Scorpion of the Fourth Cycle of Kekses, Orias was the unchallenged successor to Philotanus and the master of the Eligor Empire. Three years later, the Grand Union proclaimed him first emperor, the supreme ruler of the Eligor Empire, and so it began."

Kiel turned to Bishop. "Does that answer your question, Sha Tar?"

Bishop silently nodded as he walked along, deliberating on what Kiel had just revealed. He began to comprehend the reasons for the Eligor paranoia and mythos that had caused the attack on the protectorate. He had always taken the invasion as a personal attack and never given thought to the larger picture. For the first time since meeting Kiel, Bishop realized that this Eligor walking before him was probably only one tiny component of a vast military machine and not the villain he had originally imagined him to be. Bishop would need to reassess his prejudice against these people, but such would happen slowly.

On the ninth day after leaving the drowned city of Ra, having traveled about twenty kilometers, Kiel and Bishop began to emerge from the great trees, which had grown smaller until they were mere shrubs. Their place was taken by an immense wilderness of bamboo that grew so thick that they could only penetrate it by cutting a pathway with their swords. It took a long day traveling from the morning till evening, with only two breaks of one hour each, to get through this obstacle. Anything more monotonous and wearying, Bishop could not have imagined, as even in the most open places he could not see more than ten meters, while usually his vision was limited to the back of Kiel's scaly neck and to the green wall within a half meter on either side. From above came one thin knife edge of sunshine, and fifteen feet over their heads they saw the thinning tops of the bamboo swaying against the deep blue sky. Bishop did not know what creatures inhabited the thicket, but several times they heard the plunging of large, heavy animals quite close. Just as night closed in, they cleared the bamboos and at once formed camp, exhausted by the interminable day. A small smokeless fire was lit while Kiel brought forth a hastily harvested pile of odd blackberries that grew in profusion close to the ground.

Kiel began munching the berries with something bordering on true relish. "What say you of our empire, Bishop?" he asked, with a hint of unbridled pride.

Bishop bit into one of the berries and grimaced. "Empire, you say? What empire? All I see is a matted morass of fecund forest. I see no empire. In the protectorate, we would have cleared all of this and planted crops or left it to the snakes long ago."

Kiel darkened. "Typically human: take the best, leave the scraps to those less fortunate."

"Well, come on now, Kiel, be realistic. There is nothing out here you could hope to call an empire. It is an empire in name alone. I could as easily call it part of the protectorate. It would be as true to fact as your statement." With a florid wave of his arm, Bishop completed the statement. "Behold! The empire of bamboo, biting insects, and loathsome berries!"

Kiel's eyes narrowed to slits. "So much you know, human. The Eligor know every stone, every beast, every plant, within this forest. We harvest it just as you humans harvest your land. The difference is that we do not strip and sterilize the land for the sake of one pitiful crop of grain."

"Hush!" Bishop hissed, raising his hand. "I hear something!"

From the utter silence, there emerged a regular footfall. It was the tread of some animal, the rhythm of soft but heavy pads placed cautiously upon the ground. The creature stole slowly around the camp, then halted. There was a low sibilant rise and fall—the breathing of the creature. Only the firelight separated Bishop from this new horror of the night. Both Bishop and Kiel had drawn their swords and now faced the gloom.

"Gods of the Others, I think I see it!"

Bishop peered over Kiel's shoulder. Yes, there was something. In the deep shadow of a tree there was an even deeper shadow, black, silent, vague—a crouching form of menace. It was no higher than an ox, but the dim outline suggested vast bulk and strength. That hissing pant, as regular and full volume as the bellows of a forge, spoke of a monstrous being. Once, as it moved, Bishop thought he saw the glint of two terrible greenish eyes. There was an uneasy rustling as if it were crawling forward.

"It's going to pounce!" Bishop warned.

"Don't move," Kiel warned.

"If it jumps, we are done for."

"Don't move," Kiel hissed.

Kiel slowly stooped to the fire and picked up a crackling branch. The thing moved forward several paces. Kiel never hesitated, but running toward it with a quick light step, dashed the flaming wood into the brute's face. For an instant Bishop had a vision of a monstrous mask like a giant lizard, of scaly leprous skin, and of a red mouth beslobbered with slime. The next moment, there was a crash in the undergrowth and the visitor was gone.

Kiel returned the flickering torch to the fire with a shower of sparks. "Like I said, we know this wood and everything in it."

Bishop's heart slowly settled as he shakily resheathed his sword. He had lost his desire to argue the point.

The next day the bamboo gave way to the forest again. The trees now grew so thick and the foliage was spread so wide that Bishop could see nothing of the moonlight except that here and there the high branches wove a tangled filigree against the starry sky. As Bishop's eyes became more and more used to the obscurity, he learned that there were different degrees of darkness among the trees: some of the trees were dimly visible, but between and among them there were patches of coal-black shadow, like the mouths of caves, which he cautiously passed. Bishop's imagination began to play on his mind in this haunted wood. Visions of a slavering muzzle suddenly thrusting out of the inky darkness flitted through his mind, and he tried to put them out of his thoughts. The darkness of the forest was alarming, but even worse was the white flood of moonlight in the more open sections they passed. At these times it seemed the darkness around them was full of lurking menace and a thousand glittering eyes. Yet in the misty, silvery night, he could see no sign of life. He and Kiel silently slipped through without being detected by more than a wandering firefly.

At the far side of the glade, they picked up a meandering stream and followed it for a time. It was a welcome companion, gurgling and chuckling as it ran, reminding Bishop of an old trout stream he had fished in his youth. Once they passed close to a nest of flying reptiles, and as they did so, Bishop heard the dry leathery rattle of wings as one of the creatures rose up and soared into the air. As it passed across the face of the moon, the light shone clearly through the membranous wings, causing the creature to look like a flying skeleton against the white radiance.

The travelers crouched low among the bushes as Kiel whispered a warning: "A single cry will bring hundreds of its mates, even the meekest of which would be a calamity."

It was not long before the creature disappeared from sight and the travelers dared to move onward on their journey. The night had been exceedingly still, but as they walked, Bishop became aware of a peculiar sound. It was like a great boiling kettle or bubbling pot. Soon they came upon the source in the center of a small clearing: a pool of sorts from which some black pitch-like ooze rose and fell in great blisters of bursting gas. The air above it was shimmering with heat, and the ground was so hot that Bishop found he could not rest his hand against it. The pair hurried. The vent, left in the darkness, melted into the vast northern lands of the Eligor Empire.

Two more uneventful days brought the travelers to within range of the long-sought Ikonian border. There before them, in the gloom of the forest, rose a massive crumbled wall of mossy stone that stretched east and west. A stone marker stood half broken in the twilight, inscribed with spidery Eligor script.

"The northern border of the Eligor Empire," Kiel stated, pointing at the marker. "I have safely brought you to within a day's travel of Ikonia as promised. I dare go no further lest I cause our detection."

"Safe. He calls that a safe trip," Bishop banally remarked to Storm Singer, who sat silently on his shoulder. "I surely wouldn't wish to endure a dangerous trip."

Kiel's eyes narrowed. "Just possibly I should have taken you through the lands haunted by the Nysrogh. Mayhap you would more appreciate your guide?"

"Nysrogh? Yes, well, are you sure you wouldn't like to tag along with me and the bird? You never know, it might be a safe trip, like the one we just concluded," Bishop grumbled.

"I must now return to Opal and inform the Grand Union of my success in obtaining 'assistance' from your government, even though the assistance is only a bird and one fresh-faced human nestling with no respect for his betters."

"More than enough force to combat the ghost legions of mythic Ikonia," Bishop quipped.

Kiel looked hard at Bishop. "They are not ghosts, Sha Tar. Keep this fact very clear in that tiny human head of yours or you will not last a day."

Bishop looked at Storm Singer and shrugged. "Guess the lizard is serious after all."

Storm Singer ruffled his ebon feathers but remained silent.

"If possible, I will return to keep watch for your homecoming, and if not, I will send patrols to meet you here at the border. Wait for the patrol. It would not behoove you to go wandering around any deeper into the empire. Not every Eligor is as fond of humans as I am."

Kiel started to turn, but then he added, "Go well, Bishop. Go well, Storm Singer. And thank you for your help."

Storm Singer bobbed his raven head while Bishop silently held out his hand, which this time Kiel shook in the human fashion. Then, without any additional words, Kiel melted back into the gloom of the great Eligor forest and disappeared, leaving Bishop alone with Storm Singer.

"Go well, Kiel," Bishop said as he struck out over the tumbled mound of mossy rock and into the forbidding gloom of the Ikonian frontier.

SEVEN

BATTLE AT IXXIS ROI

> They held them back with spear and spade, with desperate dike and wall, with foemen leaning on their shields, roaring at them as they reeled, and no help came at all.
>
> —Vena Korela,
> Saga of Louhi, Runa 5

I've succeeded in my mission, Kiel reflected silently, his booted feet thumping along beneath a golden canopy of rustling autumn leaves. *And yet why do I feel so grim?*

He glanced up at the latticework of branches leaning over the trail, with cathedral-like shafts of sunlight occasionally piercing the gloom beneath.

Why so grim indeed?

It wasn't a difficult question to answer. True, he had succeeded in the mission that the Grand Union had set him upon, successfully enlisting the aid of the human protectorate in an attempt to unravel the mystery surrounding the Ikonian attacks. But in doing so, he had lost his entire command on the journey south, had wasted weeks debating and haggling with the human government, and in fact had risked everything to insert one lone human within the boundaries of the Ikonian frontier.

Bishop had accepted the task given him with something bordering on reckless determination, scurrying off like an overlarge ferret tearing after an escaping mouse, heedless of the immense dangers that confronted him. Kiel sighed as a pang of guilt washed through him. The impudent little human was a good sort after all, as arrogant and oversure of himself as the empire had been in its days of glory, but good at heart.

"What a pity," he muttered aloud.

A bird sang a mournful song somewhere in the trees above, and Kiel suddenly felt as if he had somehow signed Bishop's execution papers.

"What a pity."

Still, there was a certain resiliency to the human that Kiel had simply not expected. Outwardly, Bishop was as delicate as a hatchling, but he was also hard as triple-fold steel in a pinch. It was something to hang on to, if only just. And there was Storm Singer, an animal that spoke to Kiel of human ingenuity at its most formidable, even if the species creation had occurred eons ago. No, there would be no faltering now. He was sure that his plan, however far-out, was the only course of action left for the Eligor race.

Kiel straightened his back as he strode ever closer to distant Opal. Bishop could take care of himself. Kiel needed to focus on his next duty, namely, explaining this whole situation to the Imperial Grand Union. He had silently debated the problem since leaving Bishop at the border ten days ago and still had not arrived at an equitable solution.

His explanations would need to be creative indeed. The Grand Union had pinned all its hopes on the prospect of human support, and one lone soldier was not what they were expecting, even if the soldier was the possessor of a Riika. To reveal the truth would create panic. Kiel suspected Bishop would need to be parceled up and presented as an entire division, an entire legion, before the Grand Union would react with anything less than total pandemonium.

Kiel put the troubling thoughts out of his mind as he walked along in the gloom. *Better to concentrate on the present,* he thought, scanning the darkened forest for danger. He had selected a path that would take him well around the last-known Ikonian threat, massing above the army depot at Sub Korra and circling down below it to come at Opal from the west toward the city of Ixxis Roi, but the forest still held myriad dangers to be ever watchful for.

The sunlight wavered momentarily, causing Kiel to glance up through the golden forest canopy in concern. Great pillaring thunderheads piled in the north; the sun began to sail in and out through the thickening clouds; and the southern sky turned a coppery color. He could not be more than two days west of Ixxis Roi. The thought of fresh food and news after so long on the trail caused him to quicken his pace, making it as fast as the approaching storm.

The air began to stir, and it seemed the temperature dropped several degrees within a matter of moments. Kiel glanced down, seeing his shadow dim, waver momentarily, and then disappear altogether. The sun sailed behind another, darker cloud, and this time it did not reappear; for a moment its roiling edges were embroidered with gold, and then the iron-colored belly of the approaching thunderhead blotted out all traces of blue sky.

The cool breeze became more insistent as it moved through the trees. Somewhere behind, thunder rumbled, lightning flickered, and the forest darkened. Kiel slowed, looking around suspiciously. Had he just heard thunder from ahead of him as well? Not possible: the storm was behind, to the northwest. The sound came again, a distant roaring that strangely reminded him of the Imperial Coliseum during tournament season.

Kiel was now creeping through the undergrowth as the strange sounds coalesced and grew more distinct. Far up the trail, he saw the flitting of shadow shapes and heard the hurrying of many footsteps and the faint clanking of armor. Kiel, now quite disturbed, slid off the trail, melting into the deep gloom of the surrounding wood. The wind shifted, bringing with it the unmistakable stench of death. There could no longer be any doubt.

"Battle."

Kiel's scales prickled. Either he had grossly misjudged his route or the Ikonians were now much farther south than he had expected. The sound of struggling and sword clashing momentarily grew louder, interrupting his thoughts. The battle seemed to be moving like the flow and ebb of an ocean, clashing, retreating, regrouping, and attacking again.

"Ikonians, this far south?" Kiel whispered. And they were on the offensive. These woods were probably full of Ikonians hunting their prey.

"Curse the black gods!" He would need to backtrack several days and loop farther south, skirting the Moeras Kor Depression, a trip that would bring its own particular dangers.

As Kiel prepared to move back toward the trail he heard a scuffle and the dragging of something toward his hidden position among the mossy boles that hid him.

Kiel stopped, crouching low among the gnarled trucks and leaf litter. His memories of the Ikonian autopsy came again like a wave of sour nausea. Not daring to underestimate the creature, he cautiously peered around a tree, soundlessly unsheathing his sword as he did so.

Out of the murk, a shadow materialized. Kiel's sword tip dropped. It was not an Ikonian; rather, it was a wounded Eligor soldier, limping and then collapsing not two meters from his hiding place. Kiel resheathed his sword, cautiously ghosted back out onto the trail, and scanned the area. There were no other signs of movement. The sounds of battle seemed momentarily lost as thunder sounded again and rain began to patter on the dry leaves. He rolled the soldier over and saw with some surprise that, though mortally wounded, the Eligor was still living.

"What is it? What has happened?" Kiel demanded.

The soldier's eyes fluttered open but remained unfocused. "Move the Fourteenth Division south. We will regroup with the main army at the substation." The soldier gasped as foamy blood flecked his scaled mouth.

"The substation at Ixxis Roi?"

"Ixxis Roi. Yes." The soldier frowned through his pain, not understanding Kiel's ignorance.

"Why south? Why Ixxis Roi?" Kiel pressed.

The soldier's golden eyes dimmed, and he coughed, spattering Kiel with blood.

"Why south? Why do we need to move the division south?" Kiel shook the soldier.

"The insects have overrun Sub Korra. Regroup with the main army at Ixxis." The soldier shuddered once and then lay still, an ever-widening pool of blood spreading out beneath him.

Sub Korra overrun? Kiel shivered with dread as he let the dead soldier down. He had picked the right trail. Ixxis Roi was close, but it was no longer the haven he had expected. The Ikonians had finally overcome the army's defenses at Sub Korra, a city that lay less than eighty kilometers north of Opal. Kiel crouched in stunned silence as the distant sounds of battle came to him again. There were probably a score of skirmishes throughout this wood, and Kiel had blindly walked into the middle of them.

Soon there were other sounds in the forest, namely, the sounds of many hurrying footsteps advancing in his direction. Kiel again unsheathed his sword and stood as lightning flashed above him and the rain came harder. It seemed he would not have the opportunity to flee this time.

It was only a matter of moments before several shadow figures began to materialize out of the misty, rain-streaked forest. A score of Eligor scouts gathered on the upper trail, raised their swords, and stopped.

Kiel stood his ground, waiting.

Seeing that it was another Eligor that stood before them, they lowered their weapons and approached cautiously.

"Who are you?" the lead scout asked, eyeing the dead form at Kiel's feet.

"Kiel of the Imperial Intelligence Service of Opal," he said, resheathing his sword. "I need to talk to your commander."

The other soldiers began muttering among themselves. The lead scout warily eyed the red circle insignia on Kiel's uniform.

"Imperial Intelligence? Out here?" The scout absently stepped back a few paces.

"I need to speak with your commander," Kiel repeated insistently.

The scout recovered some of his composure and shook his head warily. "We have no commander; our officers were either separated from us or killed in the last encounter with the insects. That one there"—he pointed—"lying at your feet, he was an officer. Probably ran all the way from Sub Korra."

"All killed," Kiel muttered distantly. These tidings were a heavy blow to his weary mind, coming as they had at an hour when he had thought to have put the worst behind him. There was no room for hesitation, to lose the meager footing he had so preciously purchased. "What were your last orders?"

The scout glanced at his comrades, who shuffled nervously, and then looked back at Kiel. "Our last authorized orders were to evacuate Sub Korra." The Eligor shrugged. "But evacuate to where? We were cut off and lost contact with our command when the city was overrun." The scout looked over his shoulder toward the northeast as the distant sound of battle came to them again. "The army was shattered and simply fell apart after the fall of Sub Korra. We have been retreating ever since."

The remains of the Fourteenth Division approached out of the rain and came to a shambling muddy halt as Kiel took in the distressing sight. There were the wounded on stretchers, moaning in pain and delirium.

There were bandaged, limping Eligor supported by those among them who could still stand, dazed by hunger and exhaustion. There were a few, a very few it seemed, who still looked as if they were ready for another fight. Yet all of them, it seemed, were now desperately looking to Kiel for direction.

"What are your orders?" the soldier asked beseechingly.

"Orders?"

"You are the ranking officer. What are your orders?" The soldier was becoming noticeably uncomfortable.

"Yes, of course, of course I am." His position within Imperial Intelligence meant that he technically outranked everyone in the army. There was no doubt of Kiel's rank; the question was what to do. His mind raced as he recalled the last words spoken by the dead Eligor at his feet. "Move the Fourteenth southwest toward the Kuru River," he said, repeating the words that still lingered in his mind. "Yes, move them toward the river," he said, this time louder and with more confidence. "I believe there is a viaduct due south of this general area. We will circle under the Ikonians and, with any luck, regroup with the remnants of the army at Ixxis Roi."

The soldier nodded eagerly, passing the order on to the beleaguered troops, while Kiel dragged the dead soldier off the trail and covered him with brush.

"May you feast with the All-father everlasting," he whispered reverently, placing his hand momentarily upon the lonely mound before moving back out onto the trail and motioning the scouts to follow. He had no idea if there would be any army waiting for them at the substation, but there seemed little else out in this insect-haunted forest in the way of options.

For five long hours, Kiel hurried the struggling division south toward Ixxis Roi, purposely traveling through a forest so dense and tangled that it was known as the "briar thicket." He would make it as difficult as possible for the invaders to follow. Still, reports filtered in from terrified rear scouts of Ikonians moving just beyond the screen of trees to the rear, but Kiel would not turn and fight. Instead, he goaded the soldiers on, hoping to outdistance the enemy.

Late in the day, they encountered yet another shattered fragment of the retreating army, but still there was no sign of command; not even a junior lieutenant had survived the last assault. It seemed as if Kiel was the only Eligor with any rank within a hundred kilometers. Again, his thoughts drifted to the main body of the army. Had it been destroyed at Sub Korra, or was it waiting at Ixxis Roi as the dead soldier had indicated?

Night fell, and with it came a sense of safety, as it was said the insects would not fight after dark. Still, Kiel pushed the soldiers on until around midnight, when the Kuru River materialized out of the gloom. The scouts had succeeded in locating the crossing, a large wooden footbridge connected by rock supports. Before dawn crept over the eastern mountains, they would cross and tear down the viaduct. Kiel could only hope the insects were not as expert at swimming as they were with ground action.

Soldiers ate their meager rations and stirred in the shadows, tending to the wounded and ordering weapons, while Kiel walked among the two shattered divisions, assigning the older, more experienced Eligor within the encampment to act as his temporary command. He had already enlisted the scout Nakula as his lieutenant, the Eligor he had first encountered in the clearing. Nakula had seen battle before and had the experience Kiel so desperately needed to organize this mob into some semblance of a fighting force. Imperial Intelligence had trained him in battle tactics, but he had never had the opportunity to test the instruction in an actual situation. Kiel supposed Nakula would help bridge the gap in experience.

"Report on the troops, sir," Nakula said, approaching Kiel from out of the gloom.

Kiel sighed. This was the moment he had been dreading. "What is our status?"

Nakula shifted uneasily in the dim light. "The remnants of the Fourteenth are comprised of two hundred forty-two able-bodied Eligor, while those of the Twenty-Second number about a hundred. The soldiers who can be spared are readying the bridge for destruction as per your orders. As soon as the wounded are taken across, we will proceed with its demolition."

"Three hundred," Kiel muttered, shaking his head in disbelief.

Before the war, a single division amounted to between thirteen thousand and sixteen thousand troops. It would have included the division base, the supporting command providing supplies, and nine combat battalions supported by six auxiliary battalions. Attached to the division base were reconnaissance forces, combat engineers, signalers, and a company of military police, all or most of whom were apparently scattered or lost.

"And what of our weapons?"

"No heavy weapons. Armor and swords are spread thin. The archers have nearly exhausted their arrows, but they are currently preparing new shafts. There will be little sleep in the camp tonight."

"And food?"

"Enough to last us another two days. Probably enough to reach Ixxis Roi." Nakula eyed the darkened wood about them with caution. "That is, if we are not further delayed in this briar patch."

It was as bleak a report as Kiel had feared. If they were caught out here in the forest again by a big enough contingent of the insects, they were through. Yet it would not bode well to advertise his hopeless sentiment; he would keep the soldiers busy—buy them hope, if only a little.

"Very well, we will continue with the demolition of the bridge. Once the work is near completion, we will cross and make a run for Ixxis Roi."

Nakula saluted and melted back into the gloom. Kiel retreated to a private spot on the outskirts of the camp to contemplate his new predicament. He was the commander of the Imperial Intelligence of Opal, not an army officer. He desperately needed to return to Opal, yet he could not bring himself to leave these Eligor, who had begun to look to him for guidance.

Kiel's thoughts were interrupted as a deer suddenly came bounding out of the darkness and through the startled encampment. Several exclamations turned to curses and nervous laughter as everyone settled back into their routine. Kiel watched the deer fade back into the forest to the west but could not return to his thoughts. He looked around as if he were the only one alive in the encampment. The cool air was still as death. The insect life was silent. A leaf floated to the ground.

Kiel stood and listened intently. Something was wrong.

"Commander Kiel," Nakula called, approaching from behind.

Kiel held up his hand for silence as he searched the northern wood.

Another deer came bounding through their camp, but this time it was followed by screaming Eligor guards and a whirlwind of Ikonian soldiers.

Cursing his luck, Kiel ripped his sword away from its sheath as the entire camp exploded into chaos.

The enemy seemed to come from everywhere all at once. In an instant, Kiel was in the center of a hurricane of stabbing spears and lashing swords. A spear bent his armor and chitinous hands groped maddeningly for his vitals, but nothing was able to move beyond his sword blade as it sang its song of death.

At every turn, fate seemed to find Kiel and check his efforts, like some great game arranged upon the face of the earth, a game in which he was but a pawn. In his mind, there materialized the laughing face of Death, his true opponent, pointing its skeletal finger mockingly, gloating over its latest masterful move. "You have failed! You have failed!" It seemed to cackle in mirthless glee.

"No!" Kiel screamed aloud. The visage of death faded, morphing into the visage of an Ikonian soldier.

A red mist of unreasoning fury wavered before Kiel's blazing yellow eyes. He cleaved skulls, smashed breasts, severed limbs, ripped entrails, and littered the ground with a grim harvest of death, and still they came. Shielded by his armor, his back against a tree, he heaped mangled corpses at his feet. Death would pay a bitter price before it claimed him this night.

If there was a glimmer of hope, it was to be found in the fact that none of these insects seemed to be of the same fiendish type that he had fought beneath the city of Opal. These were smaller and possessed great luminous eyes as if their sole purpose was to navigate the darkness around them, but when they fell, they remained still and did not again move with renewed demonic life as had previously occurred.

"Orders, Commander?" Kiel heard someone scream, as if the voice had come from a great distance.

"Everyone to the river. Cross the river and tear up the bridge!" he heard himself respond automatically.

The Eligor archers were able to slow the onslaught just long enough to allow a frantic crossing of the river. The bridge was brought down as the last of the living Eligor stumbled across it. Even then, two more assaults were pressed before the Ikonians gave up the battle and settled on the opposite side of the riverbank, rustling about in massed silence and frustration, continuing to gather until countless insects faced the exhausted Eligor.

"Hold your positions!" Kiel shouted.

"Hold our positions?" Kiel heard several soldiers repeat in confused anger.

Nakula hurriedly approached Kiel as he studied the lines of insects massing along the river. "Commander, would it not be wiser to flee south while we still have the chance? The Ikonians seem stymied by the water. This might be our only opportunity."

Kiel continued to watch the massing of the enemy at the water's edge. Flee? Here there were insects where he had been assured there wouldn't be, in the dead of night. What other surprises could he expect from these devils? "No, we will not flee. I won't make the mistake of underestimating them twice. Here we stand and fight. If we run now, they will be on our backs in a moment."

"But if you are wrong?" Nakula pressed insistently.

Kiel turned. "And if I am right? What then, soldier? Fight while scattered in the wood with our backs to them? It would be a slaughter."

Nakula nodded, beginning to see the logic. "We will stand. I'll pass the order along to the soldiers." He saluted again and dashed off, ordering the remnants of the two battered divisions at the river's edge.

The eastern sky brightened, and as it did so, the Ikonians were joined by the daylight elements of the frightful horde. Insects closer in resemblance to what Kiel had previously known appeared on the river's edge, contrasting sharply with their smaller nocturnal brethren. Sar's observations came floating back into Kiel's memory as Kiel looked on in apprehension. The bioweapons scientist had been correct. The Ikonians were split into castes—workers, farmers, and soldiers, including soldiers adapted for fighting in the daylight and soldiers adapted for fighting in the darkness.

Now it was the turn of the daylight elements of the Ikonian horde. Suddenly and without warning, the Ikonians attacked, swarming across the river and up the hill behind a barrage of arrows so thick that the pelting cloud gnawed saplings in half.

Kiel stood at the head of his soldiers. "Hold your positions," he roared again.

The Eligor crouched, raising their shields before the approaching ocean of chitinous bodies as the two opposing lines collided and merged. The edge of the battle swayed to and fro with wild whirlpools and eddies. At times Kiel saw more of the enemy around him than his own soldiers. Gaps opened, swallowed, and closed again. Squads of Eligor who had cut their way through to him disappeared again in the swirling melee.

Kiel swung at, stabbed, and beat back the Ikonian horde until he could no longer count the kills he had inflicted. And still they came at him. Around him, his fellow Eligor soldiers died by the score, less successful at warding off the maddened enemy than he. For every Eligor corpse, there were four whiplike Ikonian carcasses, but still they came in an endless flood, the pools of intermingling red and yellow-green running like rivers before Kiel.

All around Kiel, a strange and mingled roar thundered. He knew the end was near. The sounds of battle intensified. Kiel assumed the hill was being surrounded. The Eligor were running out of arrows. In only a matter of minutes, it would all be over.

And then it was over.

Somewhere to the south, a horn trumpeted. As if having heard an unperceivable signal, the Ikonians suddenly disengaged and withdrew, going back down through the forest and across the river, disappearing into the treed gloom of the northern shore.

Kiel swayed in exhaustion as he looked around. Everywhere there was heaped carnage. Hundreds of Ikonians had perished in the onslaught, but it seemed the same was true for the Eligor. Yet there were many still living, and these looked to Kiel with newfound respect as a roar of triumph went up in the forest.

Nakula, bleeding from a dozen wounds and limping badly, approached Kiel, grinning.

"I see nothing to smile about!" Kiel grated in confused anger.

"Commander, we are alive. If we had turned to flee, it would have been our doom just as you warned."

It took a moment for Kiel to absorb the words. Just as Nakula had said, Kiel's gamble had paid off. But why had the Ikonians retreated? It seemed they were right on the edge of a crushing victory.

As if reading Kiel's mind, Nakula, running to his side, pointed excitedly toward the southern forest. "The army has found us! They are coming."

Kiel followed Nakula's finger. In the direction of the trumpeting horn, he now saw hundreds of fresh Eligor breaking away from the trees and running toward the river. A roar of cheering broke out from his beleaguered soldiers. There would be no more thoughts of defeat today.

Soon the advance guard of the new division was led to Kiel. "Who are you?" Kiel immediately questioned, wiping his battered sword and resheathing it.

"Kon Tu of the Twenty-Third, detached," the lead soldier responded.

Kiel was still confused; his luck had not been good enough as of late to fully trust his eyes. "Have you been cut off from the main army as well? Are you all that is left of the army?"

Kon Tu shook his head. "We were sent to locate separated elements of the main army two days ago. We were ready to give up the search when we heard the fighting."

"The main army? It still exists?" Kiel pressed.

"They are waiting for us at Ixxis."

Kiel closed his eyes in relief. "Thank the Others."

Kon Tu scanned the river warily. "I would suggest we leave this wood as soon as possible. We have come to learn the Ikonians are not easily diverted from their objective, and our supply line is dangerously thin. Any moment we could become as separated as you were."

Kiel nodded. "I think you will be hard-pressed to find any among us who would wish to stay any longer."

Kon Tu saluted and barked an order to his soldiers. The order to pack up was passed along the ranks of Eligor.

Kiel looked up at the brightening sky and then turned to Nakula. "Let us now make for Ixxis Roi with haste."

Nakula nodded, signaling the others who stood waiting. "Move out," he called.

As Ixxis Roi materialized out of the mists of the forest and became distinct, Kiel froze amid his ragged troops in stunned silence, slowly absorbing the lurid scene that stretched before him.

A ghostly vision of Ixxis Roi as it had once been wavered before Kiel's eyes: immaculate tessellated avenues of marble spiraling toward a majestic city hub, where the sky-flung spires of the Imperial War Academy pierced the heavens with magnificent minarets of gold. Massive bronze dragons leered from pedestals placed amid the ancient architecture, blazing like molten gold in the morning sun, while the sounds of unearthly music floated in the air. Pyramidal temples reared up like colossi crowned with tapering sanctuaries, and with altars blazing with inextinguishable fires in honor of terrible nameless Eligor gods.

In his mind, Kiel again saw a maze of luxuriant gardens filled with a multitude of trees and flowers, all of breathtaking beauty and profuse. Within this labyrinth of sweet-scented groves and shrubberies, fountains of sparkling water threw up their dazzling jets of light, scattering refreshing dew amid the riotous blossoms and wandering bees.

His vision wavered again, like a ghostly shroud blown in the winds of time, and then it faded, replaced by the stark reality that now stood out sharply before him. The once-proud city was now broken and shattered. Rubble lay in great heaps, and the stench of death was everywhere. The dead were piled up upon each other, in some places more than four bodies deep, exhibiting every ghastly form of wound and mutilation. Of the enemy dead, there were distressingly few.

Below this scene of destruction lay the remnants of the imperial army. Streamers of smoke from myriad cooking fires, broken here and there by hastily erected earthworks, rose and curled in the cool, still air. Kiel, followed by the battle-worn components of his provisional command, was quickly led through the outer fortifications and down through the first lines of defense. Weary, half-starved soldiers eyed Kiel as he passed, moving farther into the depths of the grim camp and toward its distant center, where a beehive of activity swirled around a great olive-green tent.

Kiel instructed Nakula to disperse his soldiers back into the army while he and Kon Tu reported to central command.

For some time, Kiel, led by Kon Tu, followed a muddy, deeply rutted trail as wagons passed, laden with maimed and injured soldiers, trundling slowly toward the south, away from the front lines and toward the perceived safety of distant Opal. Behind Kiel, his ragtag soldiers dispersed back into their reunited units until Kon Tu alone was walking beside him in a brooding silence, a silence broken only by the occasional croaking and cawing of the wheeling crows and carrion birds above.

Kiel moved through a shadowed landscape that seemed devoid of color—only mottled blacks and drab grays in varying shades of intensity. In years past, the imperial army had been considered an unstoppable juggernaut, unequaled in its might and power, but now …

Kiel's mind slowly surfaced from the unfathomable thoughts, realizing with some surprise that he was now standing before the great tent he had noticed earlier. Two guards stood stoically on either side of its entrance as couriers came and went in a steady stream. Kon Tu stepped to one side of the tent and motioned to the guards. "Commander K'Xi will wish to talk to this individual; he is Kiel of Internal State Security, savior of the Fourteenth and the Twenty-Second."

The soldiers paled as Kon Tu melted into the encampment and

disappeared, seeming to hesitate with fear, but Kiel did not notice. Now Kiel could finally arrange for an escort back to Opal. Now he could look forward to completing his assignment and returning to matters of more immediate concern.

One of the soldiers spoke, saying, "The general is expecting you, sir," then silently led Kiel into the depths of the inner tent, finally making it to what seemed to be its center.

On a raised dais in front of a chair of pure gold that was inlaid with turquoise and other semiprecious stones sat an Eligor of unquestioned authority, K'Xi. Scattered at his feet were military weapons of every sort, shields, quivers, bows, and arrows, some of which contrasted strikingly against an Old Earth device or two. The walls were hung with tapestries made of the hair of different wild animals of rich and varied colors, festooned by gold rings and embroidered with the likeness of a winged skull, the crest of the Imperial Eligor Army. Above the chair was a canopy of variegated plumage, from the center of which shot forth resplendent rays of gold and jewels, seemingly the last grand trappings of an army that had known glory in other times.

K'Xi was a black-scaled giant of an Eligor, well over two meters tall, heavily muscled, and bandaged from the recent fighting. The soldiers who moved around him consisted of a score of younger Eligor, whom Kiel guessed to be raw recruits just out of officer's training. The oldest looked no more than eighteen cycles, yet another sign of the desperate situation that now existed within the military.

K'Xi looked up from a great wooden table set below him that was strewn with maps and charts. Aides swirled about the tent in nervous haste.

"Kiel, first commander of the Imperial Intelligence Service of Opal."

"Kiel of Imperial Intelligence." K'Xi did not bother to hide his disbelief as he stood, but before Kiel could elaborate, the third commander touched the ground and then his forehead in formal greeting. "You wear the red circle insignia of the IIS, and your exploits are known to us. I find it impossible to believe that anyone with an ounce of intelligence would falsify such a thing as that."

"It is a rather involved account," Kiel began grimly.

K'Xi cut Kiel short with a nervous wave of his hand. "If Imperial Intelligence has business in the northern woods, who am I to question it? It is, I am sure, best left as your own affair." K'Xi pondered a bit before continuing, briefly eyeing the great map that lay before him. "From what I have been told about your exploits of late, it is of little concern. You seem to have singlehandedly saved what was left of our western flank, and that's good enough for me. Right now, the empire needs every soldier it can find."

Kiel brushed dirt absently from his tattered uniform. "Yes, of course it does, but soldiering is not what I had in mind when I ran into your scattered army. I must return to Opal. The Grand Union is expecting a report that is critically important and long overdue."

"The Grand Union!" K'Xi spat in open contempt as he began pacing the tent, an act that would have surely brought death in the days of the old empire. "Forgive my treasonous mouth, Commander Kiel, but the Grand Union only argues. They argue while our empire is slowly eviscerated before our eyes."

"The war does not go well then?" Kiel questioned, his face drawing down into a frowning mask. "What is the current status of our army?"

K'Xi again looked down at the largest map spread before him. His aides moved several wooden markers upon it. "I will not deceive you, Kiel; the war does not go well. The last of our reserves were exhausted pushing the Ikonians back out of Ixxis to evacuate those trapped within, as per our orders. The effort was a useless waste of energy. There weren't any left alive to evacuate. If it had not been for finding you, the entire operation would have been for naught. The Grand Union should have known that. Everyone else did. The insects will retake Ixxis in days, possibly hours. But we will give them a fight to remember."

"However valiant your soldiers may be, how do you expect to face a force so superior in numbers and equipment as that of our antagonists?" Kiel asked, distressed.

The argument was a valid one, but K'Xi had set his fortunes on the task, and he was not the type of Eligor to shrink from it. "When I bear an imperial commission," he returned, "it is as good as my word. As for my soldiers, they are servants of the empire, and together we will carry out every last word of our orders, rest assured, to the last drop of our blood. If we fall, it will be glory enough to perish in the discharge of our duty."

Kiel admired the statement, but there was folly in this kind of determination. He knew better than most that if glory in death was what K'Xi wished, it would surely be granted him in swift accord.

"These Ikonians don't always die as easily as one would wish," K'Xi concluded, "yet we will take our fair share before the imperial army is no more."

Kiel thought again of the discovery beneath Opal and could only wonder why the Grand Union had decided to keep such information to itself. "They will die easily enough if deprived of their head," he offered.

K'Xi looked up from the map table with searching eyes. "Ah, you too have found their weakness, yes? We have learned this at no small sacrifice to our own soldiers."

"It is something, if only just," Kiel offered.

"A weakness it is, but the Ikonians do not readily offer up their heads to our swords." The general slumped, obviously finding it difficult to rally his spirits for the final struggle.

With downcast eyes and a dejected mien, he exclaimed, "Of what worth is resistance when the very gods declare themselves against us! Yet, I mourn for most the old and infirm, the females and the young, too feeble to fight or fly. For me and the brave Eligor around me, we must bare our breasts to the storm and meet it as we may."

Kiel, maddened by K'Xi's words of hopelessness, found himself becoming ever more impatient to continue his trek. "General K'Xi, forgive my impatience. I have a great need to return to Opal with vital information, as I have stated. There is still a chance, albeit a small one, if I succeed."

K'Xi nodded grudgingly. "I don't have the authority to keep you here, even if I felt one more soldier could somehow make a difference. You will stay the night. It seems you could use the rest. Tomorrow I will arrange portage to Opal."

Kiel nodded his assent and followed an aide to an adjoining tent, where he unpacked his meager belongings and sat at the edge of a cot to ponder the day's events. Was it too late to save the Eligor race? The general could not be blamed for his dejected mien, as there was little left to hope for, but still, some remote part of Kiel's mind kept goading him on. It was as if a whispered voice spoke to him through the conscious mists of futility, the voice speaking of hope. Kiel lay down and closed his eyes, trying to make sense of his thoughts. But sleep, of which he had been long deprived, stole upon him before any order was achieved.

In his dreams, Kiel was transported back to Ixxis Roi, and again he saw the great city as it had once been. Its famed market materialized out of the mists of his subconscious, materializing from his first memories. On drawing near to the great market, Kiel had been astonished at the throng of Eligor pressing toward it, and on entering the place, his surprise was heightened by the sight of the multitudes assembled there and by the dimensions of the enclosures, thrice as large as the celebrated central markets of Opal.

Here, in his dreams, traders could be found from all parts of the empire, with the products and manufactures peculiar to their city-states: the goldsmiths of Ozareth, the potters and jewelers of Thokk, the artists of

Helikontha, the stonecutters of Opal, the butchers of Kirsk, the fishermen of Ozareth, the fruit growers of Hiedrun, the aficionados of heavy industrial machinery and Old Earth technology from the excavations of Asgard, and the spice sellers of Ixxis Roi, all busily engaged in marketing their respective wares, and bargaining and haggling with purchasers.

Deep porticos surrounded the marketplace, and every type of merchandise had its own quarter allotted to it. Here one could see cotton piled up in bales, or manufactured into clothing or articles for domestic use—tapestry, curtains, coverlets, and the like. The richly dyed and richly colored fabrics reminded Kiel of the silk markets of the Far East. In the quarter assigned to goldsmiths, Kiel was amazed by the various articles formed of precious metals, curious jewelry made in the shape of birds and fish with scales and feathers alternately of gold and silver, with movable heads and bodies. These fantastic little trinkets were garnished with precious stones and showed a patient, puerile ingenuity in their manufacture.

In an adjoining quarter were collected specimens of pottery, both utilitarian and fine, and vases of wood elaborately carved, varnished or gilt, with curious and sometimes graceful forms. There were also hatchets made of Old Earth steel. The soldier found here all the implements of his trade, including weapons of all sorts: copper-headed lances, arrows, and swords, and also the leaf mail that was so common throughout the country. There were also, in uncounted numbers, cotton clothing; exquisitely made featherwork mantles; ornamented armor, vases and plates of gold; gold dust; bands and bracelets; crystal, gilt, and varnished jars and goblets; bells, arms, and utensils of copper; reams of paper; grain; fruit; incense; amber; cochineal; cocoa, wild animals and birds; timber; lime; mats; and a profusion of other items considerably more difficult to identify, no doubt of Old Earth manufacture, as this was the empire's height of fascination with such things.

Kiel's dreams shifted, and now it seemed he was back in Opal, fighting again the horror of the Ikonians. The insect came at him, and this time he was defenseless and cornered, waiting for the fatal swing of the insect's arm blades while distant klaxons sounded ever louder in the distance. His distant inner voice became suddenly clear.

Flee! the voice shrieked.

Kiel jerked awake, realizing that the sounds of alarm that met his waking mind were real. A chorus of alarms was sounding all through the encampment. From outside, followed by the hurrying of many feet, in the distance, a dull roaring, like ocean surf pounding against the shore, began to pervade the air.

Kiel jumped to his feet and hurried into the central tent. "What is it? What is going on?" he roared in confused fury.

K'Xi stood before his great chair, leisurely buckling his sword. "Time, it seems, has run its course. The Ikonians have returned. I would suggest you leave as you had planned, Kiel. Deliver your report to the Grand Union and tell them of our plight."

Kiel gripped his sword in mounting fury, swiftly following K'Xi out of the tent. His grip on his sword loosened a bit as he beheld the sight that met his eyes. It was like the eight gates of hell had been opened. Ikonians were swarming from the distant woods and smashing against the outer defenses of Ixxis Roi.

"The dogs of war are at my heels again!" Kiel grated, shaking his fists futilely in the air. A red wave of hate washed through him. To have gone through so much, to have been so close to completing his mission, only to be confronted by overwhelming numbers in battle was too much to accept.

"Fall back! We are through with Ixxis Roi. Fall back!" K'Xi bellowed over the din. He then turned to Kiel. "Go to the rear and lead what you can back to Opal. It is your only chance."

The bulk of the Eligor army began to retreat en masse as the Ikonians pressed the outer defenses even harder. K'Xi disappeared in the confusion just as the soldier to Kiel's left was suddenly shot in the face and collapsed. Before Kiel could collect his thoughts, the soldier on his right was shot four times in the back simultaneously, seemingly from different directions. A young Eligor ran past Kiel with an arrow protruding from his throat, blood spattering in all directions as he dropped to the ground, thrashing silently as he died. Kiel gripped his sword and stood as soldiers trampled the wounded into the ground. The Ikonians had already breached the defenses in several places, so it would be only a matter of moments before the entire field was overrun. There were now more dead and wounded than living, and they covered the ground in clustered masses, making the retreat all the more difficult. The blood stood in puddles, spattering rock and tree, and the ground was slick with it.

Finally, Kiel fell back through fresh troops as the rear of the army counterattacked, giving hope to the retreating army behind them. The hoarse and indistinguishable orders of K'Xi, the screaming and whizzing of arrows as they tore through the struggling masses of Eligor soldiers, the death screams of the wounded, were one by one silenced as the Ikonians ruthlessly dispatched the Eligor somewhere in front, trampling them under their feet as the moving lines of battle fell back. Rank after rank was riddled with arrow and spear, finally sinking into a mass of torn and mutilated corpses.

"Orders, Kiel! Orders!" a voice screamed.

Kiel parried an upward thrust from an Ikonian who suddenly appeared before him and stabbed the insect in the head before daring to find the owner of the voice that had called out.

Nakula was suddenly at Kiel's side. "The commander has fallen. The soldiers look to you now. What do we do?"

"Move the army out of these ruins or we are through!"

The order was passed along, and slowly the army began to move again. Kiel, seeking to elude his dogged pursuer, skirted south in an effort to break away from the immediate threat, but the two adversaries were now in brutal, clumsy lockstep as the battle lines lurched though the broken city of Ixxis Roi. The ground itself seemed to seethe like a boiling cauldron as the incessant pattering of arrows and spears raised the dirt in little geysers and spitting sand.

The retreating Eligor army sagged from the attack, leaving a dangerous gap in its middle. Ikonians raced through the ragged hole just as Kiel spotted the trouble and ordered a single small regiment to countercharge and stop them. Every one of those Eligor realized in an instant what that order meant: death to them all—the sacrifice of the regiment to gain a few minutes of time for the retreating army. They did not hesitate; rather, they ran back down the slope toward the countless thousands of Ikonians with their swords waving. The astonished Ikonians fell back, and the gap was momentarily closed.

But it was a momentary victory. The earth began to shake as if a storm had suddenly broken over them. Not more than a thousand meters back, the forest exploded with a fresh Ikonian charge. Soldier touched soldier, rank pressed rank, the arms of countless thousands of them carrying swords, pikes, and banners, a forest of them all gleaming in the sun, a sloping forest of flashing steel. Forward they moved as if they were one soul, in perfect order without impediment of ditch, or wall, or stream, over ridge and slope, through orchard and meadow, horrifying, grim, irresistible.

The Eligor army still attacked at the back, slowing the invasion and allowing the others to escape. They could not help but kill one with every swing of the sword, there were so many of them. But it did not stop the inevitable. The enemy came like an ocean of fate. Thirty-eight Eligor battle flags, caught in a great Ikonian pincer, had been left behind, trampled in the blood and gore of the dying rear army. And as before, just when it seemed the Ikonian army was on the brink of a crushing victory, they suddenly disengaged and melted back into the northern woods, leaving a sea of carnage behind them.

Kiel had watched it all in horror: twenty thousand Eligor soldiers had been killed in moments, half the remaining army destroyed in the blink of an eye. The dead lay upon the field in crevices and rocks, and behind fences, trees, and boulders. In thickets where they had crept for safety, they died in agony once the Ikonians found them. By stream or hedge, wherever the battle had raged or their weakening steps could carry them, the dead lay where they had fallen, putrefying under the sun like so much wasted meat. The Eligor could ill afford such a sacrifice, and any hope of stopping the invasion had long since evaporated. Kiel, turning to stare at those pitiful few who remained alive, motioned them to follow as he began the long final push back to Opal. This time there would be no stopping until he was encircled by the city's battlements.

The long limping retreat to Opal began through an autumn downpour, washing the blood from the grass and pelting the wounded who stretched along for miles. Upon reaching a small hill, Kiel turned again. There below lay distant Ixxis Roi, smoldering and in ruins, the black smoke rising high in the air and hanging like a pall. There was stillness in the midst of which Ixxis Roi, with her ruins, her spectral roofs, and her broken spires, rested beneath a ghastly and fitful glare. There was no sound of life, only the stillness of the catacomb. Only the footsteps of the retreating army could be heard, like a funeral troop of echoes. Then Kiel turned his head to the south and the city was lost behind the screen of trees, becoming a thing of the past.

Again, Kiel thought of Bishop and wondered at his chances. If the limitless enemy hordes suggested anything, it was this: the northern woods in the lands of Ikonia were awash with insects. Bishop would surely be found out.

All was lost.

EIGHT

IKONIA

> Up from the depths and through the seventh gate.
> —Vena Korela,
> Saga of Kullervo, Runa 29

The woodland silence was unnerving. Storm Singer, who had been gone for hours now, had flown off on patrol, accentuating Bishop's sense of solitude. Truly, Bishop had even begun to miss the presence of Kiel in these wilds. Though an uppity sort, the lizard had provided company, and any company in these hinterlands was better than none.

Frowning, Bishop scanned the upper canopy of the forest for Storm Singer. *Where has that worthless thing gotten to anyway?*

But it was no use fretting about Storm Singer; the bird was nowhere to be found. Only wild avian fauna met Bishop's eyes. *Gods of the Others, I wish I were a wolf-bird, flying hither and thither with no earthly cares!*

Bishop shook his head in frustration and continued on his northerly route. As the sun touched the western mountains with gold, he broke through the tangle of forest vegetation and beheld the borderlands of ancient Ikonia.

"Black devils!" Bishop hissed in awe.

In the clearing before him, massive stone pylons, carved in the likeness of stylized partially slumbering human heads, left little doubt that this was in fact the Ikonian frontier. Kiel had said these granite guardians were to be found at each "gate," or natural pass into Ikonian territory. If Kiel's information was correct, then Bishop was now standing near the seventh of twelve known gates leading into the northern lands beyond.

He continued to stare at the fantastic sight set before him. The ancient statues marched away to the east and west, casting long shadows upon the bramble-choked meadow. Slitted hollow eyes seemed to leer at him in an ageless vigil, adding an uncomfortable sense of being watched to his growing uneasiness. Pulling his gaze away from the statues, Bishop nervously withdrew the metallic Old Earth map from an inner pocket and extracted it from its container. The map shimmered and wavered before becoming stable, again showing mountains, rivers, and boundaries of a long-lost era.

Bishop looked up from the map and into the northern mountains ahead of him, mountains gnawed and bitten by nameless eons. The Others, beings empowered with the technological ability to create such a miraculous thing as this map, had worked their dark magic in this land countless millennia ago, but now, so it was said, there were only the insect-like Ikonians, mythic creatures that had lain dormant for untold centuries. And now, according to Kiel, they were on the move, smashing their way through the Eligor Empire and toward the Gondakar Barrier. The whole story was quite unbelievable, but Bishop had been given his accursed orders.

His attention returned to the map. Strange symbols and a thin series of gossamer lines indicated long-since-vanished borders, roads, and provinces. Even the rivers marked on the map had either changed their course or dried up ages upon ages ago, but the cities were said to remain. Bishop moved his finger to the center of the map; a starlike symbol denoted a particularly large city. Kiel had explained that the bizarre angular glyphs next to the symbol identified the place as Terus Kor. It was there that Kiel had suggested Bishop begin his search for answers.

Bishop furled the ancient map, reverently returned it to his pocket, and set his shoulders. It was either now or never.

The sun slowly sank behind the brooding northern mountains as Bishop moved away from the forest canopy, quietly moving past the gray statues. A bird sang somewhere in the dry autumn grass, and insects buzzed and whirred about the meadow, but otherwise it was dead still, not even a breeze breaking the oppressive silence. Shadows came drifting silently from the east as Bishop melted into the dim tree line on the northern side of a glade.

A game trail appeared in the undergrowth, and Bishop swiftly but warily followed it into the gloom. Stars winked out one by one above the treed canopy; the twilight winds whispered among the ancient boles; and the moon, lean and haggard, began to rise in the eastern sky.

Suddenly Bishop stopped short. From somewhere in front of him came a strange and eerie echo or something like an echo. Bishop started forward again, chastising himself for his wayward imagination. The stories he had heard of these woods were just that: stories! The quicker he completed his task, the quicker he could quit this godforsaken stretch of land and be done with it.

Bishop stopped again, his scalp prickling in horror; he could no longer doubt his senses. From somewhere out there in the darkened forest came a whisper of frightful laughter. Again the sound came, closer and more clearly this time. Bishop, momentarily unnerved, unsheathed his sword and backed up a step or two, listening intently as the sounds begin to coalesce in his mind. The gibbering and yammering wasn't laughter, no. There was no mirth in it. It was only an animal's cry. Or was it?

Bishop looked up at the surrounding trees. "Where is that dratted bird?"

Then, stabbing through the animal cry came a new sound: a scream.

"A human!" Bishop hissed in sudden shock. He started forward again, quickening his gait. He cursed the elusive lights and flickering shadows that veiled the forest in the rising moonlight, making accurate sight impossible. The animal sounds continued, growing louder, as did the screams. Then he heard the faint drumming of frantic booted feet. Bishop, losing all apprehension, broke into a run, moving toward the sound. A human was being hunted to the death out there in the stygian forest, and by what manner, the gods of the Others only knew.

The sound of the flying feet halted abruptly. The screaming rose unbearably, mingled with the sounds of rending and ripping flesh. Evidently the human had been overtaken. Bishop, his flesh crawling, visualized some ghastly fiend of the darkness crouching on the back of its victim, crouching and tearing.

Then the noise of a short and futile struggle came clearly through the abysmal silence of the night and the footfalls began again, yet now they were stumbling and uneven. The screaming continued, but now with a gasping, blood-choked gurgle. The sweat was cold on Bishop's face and body.

"By the Others! For a moment's clear light!" he cursed.

The sounds reached him easily now; the struggle was near at hand. Yet this hellish half-light veiled all things in shifting shadows, so that the forest appeared to be a haze of blurred illusions, and the towering trees about him seemed like lurking giants.

"You there! Help is coming!" Bishop shouted, forgetting that in making noise he might forewarn creatures that were best left ignorant of his presence.

The shrieks of the unknown victim broke into a shrill squealing at the sound of Bishop's voice, and then from the shadows of the tall grass, a thing stumbled and reeled, a thing that had once been a man. It was covered in blood, staggering through the darkness. Bishop forced himself to look at the figure's gaping chest and staring eyes. Wait. The man's forearm was scaled. Bishop looked again. This was not a human at all.

Where his clothing had been ripped, the thing's shoulders were scaled. Not a man. No, an Eligor—a torn and dying Eligor.

"Kiel!" Bishop cried. But no, it was not—could not be—Kiel. Gore-covered and broken, the thing that fell at Bishop's feet writhed, groveled, and raised its ruined face to the indifferent moon. The nameless Eligor screamed, then fell down again and died in a widening pool of blood, scarlet entrails ballooning through its clenched and stiffened fingers.

The moon had now risen, so the light was better. Bishop bent above the body, which lay stark in its mutilation, and shuddered—a rare thing for him, who had seen the terrible deeds of the Imperial Eligor at the Battle of Koth.

Bishop was shaken to the bone. "How is it possible that another Eligor could be this far from the empire?"

The only sound in the glade was the faint trickling of fluids escaping the collapsing veins of the corpse before him. Then, like a hand of ice on his spine came the awareness that he was not alone. He looked up, his eyes piercing the dark shadows from where the Eligor had staggered. He saw nothing, yet he knew—he felt—that other eyes were returning his stare. He straightened, raised his sword, and waited. The moonlight spread over the darkened glade, and the trees and grasses took on their proper size.

The shadows melted, and Bishop saw what at first he thought to be only a shadow of mist, a wisp of fog that swayed in the tall grass before him. He gazed.

More illusion, he thought.

Then the thing began to take on shape, vague and indistinct at first, then slowly materializing. Two slitted eyes flamed at him. The form of the thing was misty and vague, allowing the grasses and bushes beyond to show clearly through it.

Bishop felt the blood pounding in his temples, yet he was as cold as ice. How could an unstable being such as this wraith thing before him, a being that wavered and shimmered like heat waves on a sunbaked road, cause him physical harm? Despite the appearance of this new creature, the shredded corpse at Bishop's feet gave mute testimony that the fiend could destroy with swiftness.

Of one thing Bishop was sure: he would not let himself be chased through the forest. For him, there would be no screaming and fleeing, only to be dragged down again and again. If he must die, he would die in his tracks, his wounds in front.

Now a vague and gristly mouth gaped wide, and the demonic laughter Bishop had heard before again shrieked out, soul-shaking because of its nearness. In the midst of the threat of doom, Bishop deliberately drew back his sword and thrust it into the thing. The blade clattered harmlessly away from the ghostly image, causing the transparent beast to ripple like water before steadying itself again, revealing the true nature of the creature before Bishop, a relic mutant from the age of the Others, a light-shifter! Tales of these demons were rife throughout the protectorate, but until now Bishop had suspected them to be fables told for amusement alone with no truth attached. Now he was forced to quickly reevaluate his judgment of their validity. Before him was a living, breathing organism, a weird type of biomech able to bend the light around its form using Old Earth technology, a relic from a lost age.

Bishop swung his sword again, with much the same result. Howls of rage and mockery answered the thrust as the thing flew at him like a wisp of smoke. Long shadowy limbs stretched out to drag him down. Bishop thrust the sword again into the center of his attacker. The blade was deflected away from the beast as if it had encountered a block of ice. Then Bishop felt hands grip his limbs like vises. Bestial talons tore his clothing and the skin beneath, holding Bishop in an embrace of death.

Bishop dropped the useless sword and sought to grapple with his foe. It was like fighting behind a sheet of glass that had been armed with daggerlike claws. Nothing seemed real except the flaying talons and the luminous eyes, eyes that seemed to burn into the depths of Bishop's soul. Already Bishop's garments hung in tatters, and he was bleeding from multiple wounds. He saw no help for himself now, but that his body should lie there beside the remains of the first victim. Above the Eligor's torn and lifeless body, man fought with light-shifter under the pale light of the rising moon.

Bishop's despair was momentarily arrested as a flickering shadow shape descended above him. "Bisshoppp!" Then the black form flew at the creature's eyes with tearing claws.

Storm Singer!

The light-shifter broke away in startled rage. Yellow eye fluid spurted from the wounds and streamed down its shimmering form. The bird swooped again with an enraged shriek as the monster blindly struck out against its new antagonist. For a second, Bishop could see the monster—the shifting device had been disrupted. And so, therefore, the monster's glasslike defense became visible.

It was the chance Bishop needed.

He swung his sword with all his remaining power. The blade sliced into the light-shifter, making a shower of sparks and a hissing sound. The creature fully materialized because of the force that was driving into it, again revealing a scaled demon, reptilian but as streamlined and agile as a shark. Metallic cables and plates covering the rippling muscles twisted in surprisingly cat-quick movements given the creature's tremendous bulk. The torn eyes rolled in a bizarre likeness to a human face.

For a moment Bishop believed he had not even scratched the demon, but then the screams of rage turned to shrieks of pain as the beast stumbled backward, revealing a severed cable of some vital sort. The light-shifter shimmered for an instant longer and then exploded into a greenish fireball, knocking Bishop to the ground.

Storm Singer circled, dropped to the ground, and skittered to Bishop's side, lightly pecking at his hair in alarm as dust and greenish mist rained down around them.

"Not so quick, buzzard! I'm not dead yet," Bishop rasped through clenched teeth.

"Ho-ho!" Storm Singer hooted. "Don't flatter yourself. I wouldn't think of dining on such a bitter carcass!"

Bishop opened his weary eyes. "You saved my life."

"Yes, well, this is a lonely stretch of wood, and even a human is better company than nothing at all."

Bishop stiffly rose to his feet and hobbled over to the creature that had almost bested him. There before him, glistening in the moonlight, was what remained of the light-shifter. A monstrous mouth gaped in a mirthless death leer on the separated head. Greenish gore mixed with strange bits of metal, wiring, and fragments of undecipherable Old Earth technology was all that remained of the bizarre body, a product of the Others to be sure. How long this horror from the ancient past had haunted these woods, Bishop couldn't guess.

"You were supposed to be scouting for danger, not food," Bishop growled.

"Difficult to warn against that which cannot be seen," Storm Singer responded philosophically.

Bishop acknowledged the bird's logic but remained silent, poking at the monstrosity with the toe of his boot.

"I am famished! Shall we stop for the evening and dine?" Storm Singer piped as he hopped to a low branch above Bishop.

Bishop looked up at the bird and then back at the steaming remains of the light-shifter. "Stimulates your appetite, does it?" He walked over to the remains of the Eligor. "By the look of him, he appears to be some sort of scout. Kiel said nothing about any Eligor being in Ikonia. In fact, he had said they would be found out, that it would be suicide to even approach the frontier. There's a mystery here somewhere, but I'll admit that it escapes me just now."

"A mystery?" Storm Singer questioned.

"If there truly isn't anything in Ikonia but ghosts as I have always believed, then why would there be an Eligor scout out here? Why would the empire take such a chance?" An ominous feeling crept over Bishop as the inevitable answer stole upon him. There was something going on up here after all, perhaps not exactly what Kiel had told him, but certainly something interesting enough to have enticed the Eligor to take a chance and send scouts into these woods.

"Come on, bird, let's get out of here," Bishop muttered, turning to leave.

Storm Singer glided to Bishop's shoulder and began grumbling about dinner again, but the complaint was lost on Bishop. Yes, there was something going on in these demon-haunted woods, something dangerous, more dangerous than Bishop had first suspected. He would have to be doubly careful.

NINE

THE DREAMER

> All men dream, but not equally. Those who dream by night in the dusky recesses of their minds awake in the day to find it is all a fantasy. But those who dream in the daylight are dangerous men, for they may act out their dreams with open eyes and strive to make them a reality.
>
> —Old Earth axiom

Bishop glanced about, hastening his pace. He was no coward, but he did not like this wood. Tall trees towered all about, their sullen branches shutting out the twilight that was now rapidly approaching. And everywhere there was silence. The dim trail led in and out among great moss-draped boles, skirting the upper edge of a ravine, where Bishop could gaze down at the treetops beneath. Occasionally, through a rift in the forest, he could see clear to the forbidding hills that hinted of higher ranges much farther to the north.

It had been four days since his battle with the light-shifter in the borderlands of the frontier, yet nothing larger than a mouse had disturbed him since. It had been almost too quiet. Bishop scanned the upper canopy, but nothing moved save for millions of autumn leaves rattling softy as they stirred gently in the evening breeze. He was beginning to regret that he and Storm Singer had not made clearer provisions for locating each other in these dense northern forests. Bishop declined to think that something unfortunate had happened to the bird.

"The flying rat is just too ill-tempered to have gotten himself in a pinch," he muttered to himself. "He's probably off chasing rabbits or bits of colored yarn, or something just as brainless."

Bishop looked about the wood in sudden watchful alertness. His words had sounded eerily loud in this miserable, silent land, and he was loath to verbalize his thoughts again for some time. Dismal it was, and Bishop suddenly longed for the pleasant woodlands of the protectorate with their scampering deer and chirping birds, to which he was accustomed. In this silent twilight, the forest seemed desolate and uninhabited, even though he feared it was not; it seemed as if the trees themselves did not appreciate the disturbance.

Warily, he continued up the winding trail. A ghostly light in the sky told of the ancient moon's rising as it slowly rode up the eastern sky in the gathering murk of evening. All around Bishop, forest life began awakening with a myriad hoots, growls, and rustlings, driving away the previous silence. He strained his eyes, expecting a nameless monster to spring upon him at every turn in the trail. This was, after all, as far north as any human had ventured in untold centuries. Who knew what lurked in this land of the dead?

The forested dale became shallower and the walls less steep as Bishop climbed ever higher. Gullies opened into the ravine from the right and left, while the ground became stony and uneven, forcing Bishop to scramble over loose scree and underbrush. At last, the ravine gave out completely and he abruptly broke away from the forest cover, finding himself at the rim of a treeless upland plateau.

Bishop's skin roughened with a supernatural thrill as he stared in stunned silence. Not more than one kilometer ahead, bone white in the light of the moon, loomed the broken ruins of Terus Kor, an ancient city of titan proportions with sky-flung monoliths reaching to the heavens like the skeletal fingers of a juggernaut.

Kiel had insisted that here, somewhere in this broken and dead city, might lie the keys to unlocking the mystery of the Ikonians and their supposed shift from a benign culture to the martial society that now threatened the Eligor Empire. Bishop was still unconvinced, but here at last was his goal. Another day or two and he would be free to begin his return trip to the republic.

Surely, there is nothing to be found here but dust, bleached bone, and Old Earth devilry, Bishop thought, trying to bolster his confidence.

Still, there was the near-fatal event at the border, an event that continued to nag at Bishop's mind. Why had there been an Eligor soldier out here in the middle of this lonely expanse of territory if nothing existed but a dead city surrounded by tangled forest?

Bishop continued to take in the fantastic scene. Terus Kor was said to be immensely old. Eligor legend, as related by Kiel, stated that its origins predated the mythic insects themselves and possibly predated the rise of the Others. Strange glittering spires were clustered together in an extraordinary geometrical pattern. The city before Bishop was nothing like the modern human cities dotting the Protectorate of Merja Soria, which had grown together in a random, haphazard manner. This city had apparently been planned and built with a definite purpose in mind. Yet its size was its most humbling feature. Indeed, from Bishop's considerable distance, there was massiveness about the ancient structures that utterly dwarfed any modern architectural achievements known to him. The great honeycombed cities of the Eligor Empire would have likely paled in comparison to this primordial tour de force as well. Perhaps, Bishop thought, the city of Ra had once looked like this before sinking into the marsh that now mostly hid it from view.

A fantastic sight Terus Kor was, yet it was strangely repellant. A somber, heavy motif seemed to hang over the place, suggesting a sullen and slightly inhuman character to the builders. A grim mountain range sat behind the ancient city, its treed slopes bestowing a blackened and scorched appearance, which only accented the oppressive sight. Below the brooding mountain range, perhaps ten kilometers behind the city, was an immense glassy blue-green smudge on the earth that was utterly sterile and devoid of life. This was the center of a Blue Zone.

"A Blue Zone!" Bishop whispered the words like a curse.

Bishop knew from his training that countless eons ago, the hellfire that ended the Genetic Wars and consequently the Fourth Age had been unleashed above these sites. Bishop also knew that prolonged exposure to a Blue Zone was very dangerous. Thankfully, the sterile area was a considerable distance away. Still, he should move quickly.

Bishop ghosted forward, keeping to low gullies and arroyos, while the city, rising before him, began to reveal more and more detail.

Though parts of the city still stood intact, there was, nevertheless, a suggestion of devastation on a vast scale, devastation that staggered the imagination. Indeed, even before Bishop had cleared the undergrowth and beheld the city, there had been ever-increasing suggestions of the destruction. Broken pieces of the city he now gazed upon had been thrown several kilometers into the surrounding forests, radiating away from the Blue Zone as if thrown by the hand of an immense ogre. Strange metal girders and great blocks of rocklike material lay randomly scattered across the surface of the dismal land, twisted and forgotten.

Truly, even the ground Bishop stood upon had changed as he neared the plateau. All manner of plant life one would have expected to see had vanished, replaced by a strange thorny bramble that grew in clumps near the edge of the city. No sign of the rich loam of the forest floor remained. Instead, the ground was now wholly composed of a peculiar glass-like sand interspersed with the thorny bracken and gnarled bushes.

A dry, strangely warm breeze blew softly through the air, carrying with it the smell of things long dead and long unburied, things that are best left undisturbed. Bishop shivered despite himself as he surveyed the spectacular sight.

An hour's silent march brought Bishop to a halt before a massive gated wall that now reared up directly in front of him. Time had bitten scallops out of the wall, and over these scallops rose the half-ruined towers of the city beyond that leered down on him, seeming to mock the tiny creature who dared invade their realm.

Bishop approached the gate, which was made of two massive doors, twice as high as a man, fashioned from foot-thick timbers sheathed in bronze. There was little doubt that the gate before him, although still quite ancient, was a product of a much later construction than the city behind, as evidenced by the crudeness of its manufacture. Old Earth structures were well-known for their strange impervious materials and exacting craftsmanship, while this creation before him was of rather ordinary make. Why someone would have taken the time to wall this broken city was as troubling as why the city had been abandoned. Just possibly, Bishop mused, remembering scraps of Kiel's tale, foragers at some time in the not too distant past had tried to lay claim to the city but then, for reasons unknown, abandoned the idea. It was a troubling thought, as foragers were renowned for their tenacious greed concerning such sites.

Bishop pushed against the doors, grunting, but without effect. He drew his sword and struck the bronze with the pummel. From the way the gates sagged, Bishop guessed that the wood had rotted away. But the bronze was too thick to hew through without spoiling the edge of his blade, not to mention the fact that it would create noise. Besides, there was an easier way.

Thirty paces north of the gate, the wall had crumbled so that its lowest point was less than ten meters above the ground. At the same time, a pile of tailings against the foot of the wall rose to within two meters of the broken edge. Bishop approached the broken section, drew back a few paces, and ran forward. He sprinted up the slope of the tailings and leapt into the air, catching the broken edge of the wall. After a grunt, a heave, and a scramble, he was over the edge. Ignoring his fresh scratches and bruises, he stood, warily gazing down at the dead city.

Just inside the wall was a cleared space where for centuries plant life had been waging a silent war upon the ancient pavement. The paving slabs were cracked and upended. Between them, grass, weeds, and a few scrubby trees had forced their way.

Beyond the cleared area lay the ruins of one of the lesser districts. Here the one-story buildings had slumped into mere mounds of dirt. Beyond them, bleach-white in the cold moonlight, Bishop discerned the better-preserved buildings. As with all precataclysmic ruins, an aura of evil hung over this deserted city like a cloud of death.

Straining his senses, Bishop scanned the city for signs of life. Nothing moved, and the only sound discernible was the dry twittering of crickets or the occasional droning of a lone cicada calling for a mate.

Bishop wondered at the doom that haunted Terus Kor. Although the thoughts roused panicky, atavistic fears in his soul, he hardened himself. Gripping his sword, he slithered down the rough-hewn stone of the crumbling wall into the city, dropping the last meter and a half. An instant later, he was threading his way through the deserted streets toward the center of the dead city. He made no more noise than a shadow.

Ruin rose up and encompassed Bishop on either side. Here and there, the front of a house, or something like a house, had fallen into the street, forcing Bishop to detour or scramble over the piles of debris. The gibbous moon was now high in the sky, casting the city in thin shadow.

Bishop began to remember the scraps of legend concerning Terus Kor that Kiel had relayed to him on the journey. The Others had lived, breathed, and conjured their dark technology here. They had died here too, but not all were said to be dead. Some were said to still haunt this fearful city, guarding it against those who would invade it to plunder its secrets or its wealth. Bishop again thought of the foragers and wondered at their failed attempt to wrest the city for themselves and plunder it. What drove them from this city? He shook the thoughts from his mind.

Bishop suddenly stopped, narrowing his eyes to try to see more clearly in the shadowy gloom. There on the sandy ground between two paving slabs was a track, a tripod-like print that was altogether new to him. Bishop's hair stood on end as he quickly looked about. The city was not deserted, that much was now certain. At least one unknown entity had been here in the recent past, and from the looks of it, it walked upright.

Bishop crouched and fingered the print. Yes, it was a physical impression of something large and alien. Ghosts weren't supposed to leave prints, and even if they did, they would no doubt be recognizably human, certainly nothing like this freakish track.

Ikonians! The thought suddenly entered his mind. *Could it be true?*

A knot of fear welled up in Bishop's throat and stuck there like a lump of dried wayfarer's biscuit. All the tales about the Ikonians he had been told by Kiel came back, beading his flesh with clammy sweat. What if the insects, whose violent tendencies Kiel had described at length, were to discover him in the very heart of their city?

Black gods! Bishop swallowed hard as a rivulet of sweat trickled down his face.

He slowly resumed his pace, scrutinizing the surrounding buildings with a newfound sense of foreboding. The towering spires were growing taller, which Bishop took to mean he was closing in on the center of this ghost city of the Others. No life of any kind could be seen, but he felt as if a thousand eyes were constantly upon him as he glided silently along.

Bishop entered a central plaza, possibly the very center of this terrible city. Great towering structures loomed all about him, seeming to touch the stars with their immense height. Standing at the center of the featureless plaza was a green pyramidal monument, which immediately struck Bishop as weirdly out of place in this dead city. While the buildings that ringed it were broken and pitted with extreme age, the pyramid appeared as if it had only recently been created. Four razor-sharp obsidian-like sides rose to a point approximately twenty meters above the ground.

As Bishop approached the pyramid, he realized that its surface was not the smooth greenish obsidian he originally took it to be. Hieroglyphics of a type unknown to him were etched into its otherwise perfect finish.

Bishop, tracing the foreign inscriptions with his finger, froze. An acrid smell invaded the air, causing him to whirl. He stared in horror as the surrounding buildings poured forth with a hidden menace. In mere seconds, some thirty monstrous insects silently moved away from the shadows and closed in on him, crouched and ready.

"Gods of the Others," he whispered. "Ikonians!" They could be nothing else.

Nothing in Bishop's training or experience had prepared him for this sight. Kiel had gone on and on about these beings, had explained the insects in every detail, but still, in a safe part of Bishop's mind, he had not believed.

Bishop was transfixed with fear.

The leader stepped forward, lifting its upper arm. Then, in a rapid motion, the creature folded the arm, projecting a long blade, which apparently grew out of its body. The creature repeated the motion with its opposite member. As the other creatures followed suit, a snapping sound filled the air.

"All this way, and through so much!" Bishop hissed.

He desperately scanned the streets for an escape route. Nothing. The bizarre insect-like creatures were on all sides. Bishop glanced at his Riika, but the Old Earth device glinted inertly in the hazy light. Even his sword would be of little use against so many. But if these creatures expected him to flee, they were in error. With some deeply hidden resolve washing through him, he unsheathed his sword and stood waiting for the inevitable attack.

One of the creatures charged at him, blades forward. Bishop met the insect thing with a downward blow that sliced from its left shoulder to its right hip. A sickly-sweet-smelling yellow hemolymph jetted from the cloven body as the insect thing crumpled, its heels pattering lightly on the ground. Another Ikonian sprang in from the side, thrusting its sawtooth forearm at Bishop's head, but he ducked so that the deadly member hissed over his shoulder. Straightening, Bishop tore out the creature's entrails with a crunching sound. The creature calmly attempted to return the viscera to their proper place, notwithstanding the fatal nature of the wound, but it crumpled to the ground, dead.

The creatures were now surging all around Bishop, who cleared a space with a great two-handed swing and set his back close to one of the strange buildings that towered over him, close enough to prevent the Ikonians from running behind him, but not too close to prevent Bishop from using his blade. If he wasted any motion or strength with the up-and-down movement, he more than made up for it by the smashing power of his sword. No need to strike twice at any foe as his sword sang its song of death.

An Ikonian sprang under his sword, crouching and stabbing upward with its arm blade. The sword turned in Bishop's hand. He rendered the attacker senseless with a downward strike.

The creatures now ringed Bishop like wolves, striving to reach him with their blades. Two went down with split heads as they tried to close in on him, the radiant, iridescent light in their compound eyes seeming to grow dull and wink out as they died in silent writhing agony.

Then one of the creatures, reaching over the shoulders of the others, drove its arm weapon through Bishop's thigh and withdrew it in a fluid movement, rending the muscle. With a roar of renewed fury, Bishop thrust savagely, splitting his antagonist like an apple.

Before Bishop could regain his balance, another of the loathsome creatures came at him. It gashed Bishop's right arm while another Ikonian smashed something against his head.

Bishop swayed, went to the ground, and reeled up again. With a terrible swing of his shoulders, he caused his clawing, stabbing foes to back away. Then, feeling his strength oozing from him, he gave one great roar and leapt in among them.

Into the melee he hurled himself, slashing left and right, depending only on his light clothing to protect him from the cat-quick Ikonians.

He was down, up, down again, and up again, his right arm now hanging useless, his sword flailing in his left. An Ikonian's head spun from its shoulders and a chitinous arm vanished at the elbow, and then Bishop, utterly spent, crumpled to the ground, striving vainly to raise his sword that now hung loosely in his grasp.

Then they were surging at him from every side, too many for him to fathom. For what seemed to be ten lifetimes, he swung at the chitinous bodies, splitting and cracking their hard exoskeletons with every sword thrust. In every corner he saw the luminescent eyes. The air was full of the stench of death, mixed with the scent of his own blood, now pouring freely from many wounds. It was probably only a matter of seconds before he was overwhelmed; there were just too many.

Bishop, feeling a sharp blow to the head, dropped. A dozen spears were at his breast in an instant. He prepared for the end as hopeless despair washed over him.

Instead of the expected spear thrust, a voice spoke—a human voice. "Stay!" came the sharp command in the language of Merja Soria.

Vaguely, through a darkening fog of pain and fatigue, a man—a human man—appeared over Bishop. And then, as if falling into a black void, Bishop fainted.

As consciousness returned to Bishop, he came to realize that he was lying on the floor in a room of some type. Bishop's eyes slowly focused; blood moved back into his extremities; and blurred shadows sharpened, becoming distinct. No, it was not a room, but a prison! Yet it was like no prison he had ever imagined.

Bishop stiffly rose from the floor and stood stretching his stiff muscles while studying the cubicle that now confined him. Three featureless solid gray walls enclosed the sides and rear, yet it was the front of the cell that was most unnerving, as it was not barred with iron rungs as would have been typical within the protectorate.

Bishop approached the front and stared.

Stretching from wall to wall and from floor to ceiling was what appeared to be a slab of shimmering molten glass wavering as if with intense heat, yet no heat was present. How this was accomplished, Bishop could not guess, yet the faintly hissing air around the glass-like barrier was enough to dissuade him from attempting to touch it. As if not wholly convinced of the nature of the grid, he removed a shirttail and slowly inserted it into the shimmering field. With a hissing sound, like hot metal encountering water, the fabric melted, vanishing in a puff of smoke as if by magic. He wisely concluded the field would do the same to flesh.

A wavering transparent reflection stared back at Bishop, and he looked up. Cold, ghostly foxfire shone down from peculiarly crafted panels set into an otherwise unremarkable ceiling above.

Bishop's skin roughened with the thrill of superstitious dread. "Technology," he whispered.

The light, the shield, the cell itself—everything spoke to him of dark Old Earth magic. This room could not have been the work of Ikonians.

A peculiar sensation reached up through the floor and caught Bishop's attention. Under his booted feet, the floor was made up of perfectly corrugated metal plates, which in itself was an oddity because within the protectorate, metal was too rare to be used in such a fashion. And even if it had been used here, the craftsmanship would have been painfully crude by comparison. Bishop knelt and touched the floor plates, whose cold surface vibrated with a low thrumming sensation, suggesting animate activity somewhere beyond his limited field of view. A wet earthy smell came to him from underneath the ribbed flooring.

Bishop sniffed at the air and suddenly realized that he was underground, within an Ikonian nest and most certainly their prisoner. But why? He warily stood again. Why had he not been slain outright? Kiel had related the ferocity of these creatures in gruesome detail, instilling the notion that Ikonians had no use whatsoever for captives.

A movement just beyond the glass-like barrier drew Bishop's attention away from his silent questions. With a shock, he perceived six Ikonians silently approaching his cell from the dim outer tunnel.

Coming to a stop in front of the shimmering field of energy that sealed the front of the cell, they stood scrutinizing him. Bizarre expressionless compound eyes reflected the radiant glow from the shimmering barrier separating him from them.

Bishop faced the mythic creatures before him, phantoms of Kiel's fearsome description, as they traveled north. Not having had the opportunity to study these macabre entities on the surface, he did so now. They were without a doubt insect-like, yet they each also looked like some grotesque parody of a human being. Strange and sticklike, they stared with eyes that shone with a thousand colors. Tight silken garments of green covered their bodies. A slumbering human face sporting a seven-sided glyph decorated the center of the helmets that protected their oversized heads.

The Ikonians seemed as curious of Bishop as he was of them. They clustered around his cell in silent curiosity, their whiplike antennae delicately probing the air in front of them. Humans, Bishop suspected, were not a common sight in the dead city of Terus Kor.

"Do you require nourishment?" came a metallic monotone voice from a small polygon bolted to the side of the cell.

Bishop was dumbfounded. The Ikonians could communicate? They had Old Earth translators like the Eligor? Did they share the Eligor's unhealthy fascination for Old Earth technology? Again, a dreaded sense of the Old Earth pervaded upon Bishop.

"Do you require nourishment?" crackled the quizzical voice again.

"Ah, maybe some water?" Bishop responded, pantomiming, still not believing the Ikonians could understand him.

The insect fingered a device in its chitinous hand. A metallic grating sound from the back of his cell momentarily stole Bishop's attention. Turning, he saw a cube-shaped mass breaking away from the wall and sliding out approximately half a meter. The sound of water drew Bishop closer. Within the cube, water ran from a metal spigot into a hole at its bottom.

"Water can be acquired from, and waste can be removed by, the device at the back of your repairing, reconstructing restriction chamber," the artificial voice said.

Relieving himself in the same receptacle he was to gain his drinking water from did not sit well with Bishop and his sanitary nature, but the term *holding chamber* effectively killed his apprehensions about the toilet.

"Repairing? Reconstructing? What do you mean?" Bishop asked, suddenly suspicious.

The insect seemed to absorb Bishop's questions.

"You have been held. You required repair—reconstruction. You were damaged when you resisted capture. It was necessary to reconstruct your limbs before the pending interrogation by the Dreamer."

Bishop jerked his hand to the gaping hole in his trousers. No sign of the spear wound could be felt; nothing remained of it but a thin white scar. His right arm and head he found to be free of cuts and soreness as well. Either the Ikonians were in possession of extremely advanced medical knowledge or he had lain unconscious for a considerable length of time.

"How long have I been here?"

"You will be interrogated."

Bishop looked up in surprise. "Interrogated? What do you mean, interrogated?"

"The Dreamer will interrogate you."

Bishop shook his head in growing frustration. "The Dreamer? What in the eight hells is a Dreamer?"

"No more questions for now," came the flat, unemotional response.

The Ikonians silently glided from the outer hall, leaving silence in their wake, save for the soft hissing from the shimmering barrier at the front of Bishop's cell.

Several hours elapsed before Bishop was wakened from a fitful sleep on the comfortless metal floor. Before him in the hallway was a contingent of approximately fifteen armed Ikonians of the type seen before. Bishop rose stiffly from the floor as one of the insects touched a lighted grid on the outer wall.

The shimmering wall flickered, dimmed, and winked out. It was not molten glass after all, but rather some kind of nameless Old Earth magic. Only the Others had possessed such technology, and they were long dead. What was going on here?

Spears were lowered as one Ikonian entered the chamber where Bishop stood. It began shackling Bishop's wrists with a length of chain. A sweet aroma filled the air as a voice crackled from a device around the insect's thorax.

"Do not resist or you will be damaged again," the terse artificial voice told him.

"What's going on? Where are you taking me?"

"You are to be taken to the audience chamber, where the Dreamer awaits."

Bishop shrugged, trying to act indifferent as he fell in behind two of the lead insects. His fears were returning, but he tried to conceal them. He had expected death in the city above but had been spared for some reason. Surely, he would not be killed now.

After several long minutes of wandering through darkened tubelike galleries, Bishop, surrounded by his insect guards, passed through two massive iron doors into the audience chamber of Terus Kor. A pair of uniformed guards, each armed with a golden spear, took Bishop firmly by the arms and led him into the great hall.

It was a strange and fantastic scene. Bishop had been led into a great chamber whose walls and floor were of polished greenish stone. Gigantic strangely carved columns held up a cathedral-like roof, which was lost in the spider-haunted shadows above. Countless ranks of armored Ikonians lined the walls, and a double column of them stood motionless between two gigantic statues of a slumbering human head, reminding Bishop of the monoliths he had encountered at the Ikonian border. However, Bishop's gaze was drawn irresistibly toward the center of the chamber.

"Behold the Dreamer," a metallic voice crackled.

Instead of an Ikonian, Bishop was stunned to see a human man sitting casually upon a massive throne-like seat that had apparently been carved out of one solid piece of pale green jade. As Bishop was goaded toward the strange human, a vague memory of his fight in the dead city above him washed back into his mind. Yes, a human man had leered over him just before he had lost consciousness.

Bishop was motioned to stop less than six meters from the raised jade seat. He looked up at the man before him.

Cold eyes returned Bishop's gaze with icy contempt.

This strange human was a striking figure. Although seated, he was obviously tall. Strong, though leanly built, he was without a doubt human, not a mutation like the foragers; his long blond hair cascaded down sinewy shoulders that had been burned bronze by the wasteland's sun.

This stranger before Bishop was fully clad in outlandish loose-fitting garments that seemed to suggest a military cut in a style unknown to Bishop. His beardless face was of an indeterminate type. Bishop could not place him. There were aspects in this man from half a dozen regions within Merja Soria, Saraknyalian, Narakan, Meresinian, and Semyazan. He was like a composite. However, something suggested to Bishop that this human sitting before him was not a product of the protectorate; something in the strange fathomless eyes suggested an alien origin.

Then, without warning, the man spoke.

"Who are you, and from what country did you come?" came the strong yet strangely accented voice.

"I am Bishop from the Protectorate of Merja Soria," Bishop responded.

The steel-gray eyes of the man widened with disbelief then clouded in thought. "Merja Soria? Merja Soria! Yes, Merja Soria would have survived the wars. Merja Soria, with its pacifist culture. Yes, they would not have been targeted. Yet the bearer of one half of a Riika from Merja Soria I would not have thought it possible. Much has changed since the Old Ones walked the earth. Yes, much has changed."

At the Dreamer's mention of the Riika, Bishop's eyes widened. Even within the protectorate, few could readily identify a Riika, and they were of the Order. Yet here, hundreds of kilometers beyond the Gondakar Barrier, there was a human who had correctly identified it without so much as a hesitation, just as Kiel had done. It seemed common knowledge to everyone but humans.

The strange man's attention suddenly returned to Bishop. "Why have you come to Terus Kor?"

Bishop, seeing no reason to hide the truth, again responded. "To determine the nature of the attacks on the Eligor Empire."

The man's face took on a look of astonishment. "Why would you care about the Eligor?"

"They are supposedly being hunted and killed by the insects for a reason unknown."

"Are you to have me believe that Merja Soria is concerned with the well-being of the Eligor?" The man laughed a dry, mirthless laugh that whispered off the polished walls like death.

The well-being of the wretched Eligor was not Bishop's reason for crossing into Ikonia. The Order was concerned for its own reasons, but he felt it dangerous to correct this outlandish human.

The Dreamer continued: "Saving a species destined for extinction is a fool's enterprise. The weak are replaced by the strong! Those who cannot adapt, die."

The man was either beyond Bishop's ability to understand or mad, or both, yet the Ikonians stood motionless in rapture or fear—Bishop couldn't tell which—as if they were frozen in time, watching this strange human.

The strange man chuckled. "O what fools the Merja Sorians were, and apparently still are. The Eligor have tried to annihilate the humans for centuries, and the Merja Sorians would like nothing more than to help them accomplish their goal."

The man, leaning back in the great jade chair, sighed, closed his eyes, and smiled. "Well, it seems that I have awakened none too soon."

Awakened! Bishop cast aside his fears. "The Ikonians call you a 'Dreamer.' Who are you?"

"Ikonians?" The man shook his head, clearly not understanding the use of the word. Then, realization washed through him.

"Ah, you are referring to the insects! Certainly, the 'Ikonians,' as you so name them, are not in the truest sense of the word *Ikonians*. But since the original Ikonians—those who created the insects—are long dead, I don't believe they will contest the title. Besides, the insects' true name is beyond human speech."

Bishop looked at the motionless creatures that filled the chamber. Thousands, perhaps more, stood motionless, waiting.

"Nevertheless," the man said imperiously, "welcome to Terus Kor! I am the Dreamer, so named by the insects, or as you have named them, the Ikonians—Shabbathai in my native tongue, the first of the Old Earth to reawaken into this new age." The armored ranks of motionless Ikonians rustled like autumn leaves. "Yet for you, human," the strange man continued, "you may call me Reaver—Reaver One."

"The Old Earth," said Bishop, shocked. The Old Earth? That wasn't possible! Those of the Old Earth, the Others, had inhabited the planet countless millennia ago and were long dead.

"Ah, you know of the Old Earth. Pray, what do they remember about us in Merja Soria?"

The Others were a godlike race of humans who lived before the Great Change, which had ended that era in a war so devastating that the effects were still present. Bishop thought it best not to say as much to Reaver. Who knew how this madman would take it? "They were warlike, hungry for land." He thought a bit more. "Is that what you are after then, land?"

Reaver made an impatient gesture then laughed again, a decidedly evil sound. "Territory is a dangerous enchantress in war. Serious wars are rarely won by capturing territory, unless that territory includes a vital political or economic center. Territory may well be the political objective of a campaign, but it rarely should be the military objective. No, land is not the goal of this quest."

"Is it your intention to dominate the planet with these insects, then?" Bishop growled.

Reaver laughed a genuine laugh this time. "You, Merja Sorian, are a rare study in stupidity. The insects are merely bioweapons, nothing more."

Bishop scowled. "Bioweapons? I don't understand."

"Of course, you don't. You are a brainless beast." Reaver's smile faded. "Do you think that I was given the name Reaver One because it was my father's name? Tell me, O king of fools, do you know what number comes after one?"

Bishop jerked in sudden understanding. "There are others of your kind?"

Reaver nodded in mock satisfaction as if a child had spoken its first word. "Very good, very good." He chuckled. "You have pieced a tiny bit of the puzzle together at last. I merely pave the way for those who will soon follow."

Bishop had already noticed the way the Ikonians seemed to blindly obey the Dreamer. "Did you direct the Ikonians to destroy Kirsk?"

The Dreamer smiled a mirthless smile. "Like the leaves of the forest when summer is green, that host with their banners at sunset were seen, like the leaves of the forest when autumn hath blown, that host on the morrow lay withered and strown."

Seeing that Bishop did not understand his poetic reply, Reaver, leaning forward, responded again, slowly this time. "That was a yes."

"Then I have completed my objective," Bishop said, bemused.

"So it would seem."

Bishop sighed to himself. Obviously, there was a second part of his objective: to get out of Ikonia alive with the information. Certainly, there were now more mysteries needing solutions than there had been before he had entered Ikonia, but staying alive long enough to come up with those solutions seemed impossible. Bishop glared morosely at the endless ranks of armed Ikonians. "Just possibly it would have been far better if I had been killed in the city above us rather than be captured alive," he growled.

Anger seemed to flash in Reaver's eyes.

"Do you think that your tedious life was spared out of compassion?

Do you think that you were able to invade the lands of ancient Ikonia without my knowledge? Foolish human! I have known you were coming since you crossed over into our domain and encountered one of the hunter-killers. Your clothing was steeped in the odor of an Eligor. A pet, perhaps? A lover?"

Bishop remembered all too clearly his near-terminal struggle with the beast at the border. Then he remembered another thing.

"There was an Eligor that was killed," he muttered.

"Yes, and now you come to the very heart of the matter. You have been spared to replace that pitiful creature."

"Replace the Eligor?"

"My timetable has been accelerated thanks to the recent human–Eligor conflict. I found it necessary to take advantage of the Eligor Empire's disastrous defeat at the Battle of Koth. I require someone from your time to assist me in locating and identifying all sentient centers of power on this future earth. The Eligor soldier who was captured at Kirsk was not willing to assist me further and tried to escape. You observed the result."

"Why would you need such knowledge of the earth's inhabitants?"

Reaver leaned back on his throne, closed his eyes, and smiled. "For their destruction."

Bishop felt a shock run through his body. "Destruction? Why would you wish their destruction?"

Reaver opened his eyes and locked them on Bishop's. "Because they are inferior and have no place in the coming order."

Eight hells. Kiel was right. Bryn was right. The humans were next. This Reaver was obviously mad. And yet he seemed to possess the power to pull off this terrible feat. The protectorate had to be warned.

Escape! Bishop's mind screamed.

The two guards who flanked Bishop were facing the throne with respectfully downcast eyes, giving their full attention to the Dreamer, who might at any instant issue a command. Bishop gently hefted the chains that bound his wrists. They were too stout for him to break by brute force.

Quietly, he brought his wrists together so that the length of chain hung down half a meter. Then, pivoting, he suddenly snapped his arms up past the head of the left-hand guard. The slack part of the chain swung like a whip, catching the guard across the face and sending him staggering back, hemolymph gushing from his smashed head.

At Bishop's first violent movement, the other guard had whirled and brought down his spear to the defensive position. As he did so, Bishop caught the head of the spear with the slack part of the chain and jerked it out of the guard's grasp.

Bishop whirled toward the Dreamer and brought his Riika up. Possibly it would save him this time. But no, it did nothing. As Bishop moved to the edge of the dais, Reaver acted, nimble as a striking cobra. A light flashed from the girdle of metal strapped around his waist as the Dreamer, smiling wickedly, casually raised his hands, his fists clenched and his thumbs pointing. Bishop's lunge toward his antagonist was never completed. His body became numb, stricken as if with venom from a reptile's fang. His mind clouded; his head, too heavy to hold up, fell forward. Going limp, he collapsed.

The last sound Bishop heard, as the Ikonians swarmed over him, was the now familiar laughing of the Dreamer.

TEN

THIRTY-SIX

> That which is not dead can eternally lie, and with strange eons, even death may die.
> —Vena Korela,
> Saga of Marjatta, Runa 239

When Bishop slowly regained consciousness, he found he was lying facedown in his cell with the energy screen shimmering across the opening. He felt as if he had been in the mother of all alehouse brawls and had lost the fight.

Except for the cube-shaped privy, the ventilation grilles set high on the two opposing walls, and the light panels on the ceiling, it was a featureless metal room. There were no furnishings—not so much as a speck of dust, in fact.

Bishop sourly noted the absence of a bunk and blankets.

"As an initiate in the Order, at least I had a stuffed straw mattress and a pillow," he mumbled, depressed, noting that even his voice sounded weak and tinny after his ordeal with Reaver One. "I'll never drink from that bottle again."

Bishop sat up on the cold floor, his head pounding and his vision swimming with the effort, and morosely looked out toward the corridor. A slight stirring sound came to his ears from one of the ventilation grids, followed by an odd smell. Standing shakily and walking heavily to it, he strained to peer through, but it was too high on the wall.

"Good morrow?" he called softly, standing on his toes. "Is someone there?" he wondered aloud. Had they possibly captured Storm Singer?

Bishop's nostrils flared slightly, then, as carefully as one might examine an object with one's eye, he smelled the air again.

Surely, Bishop had enjoyed the scent of flowers and women, of his mother's bread, roasted meat, ale, and wine, of green fields and storm winds speaking of rain, but never had he smelled anything like this new scent. The fragrance that met his nose was, as far as he could tell, a simple odor, but he found it impossible to describe, much as one might find it difficult to describe the flavor of a fruit to someone who had never before tasted it. It was, however, slightly acrid, somewhat irritating to Bishop's nostrils. It vaguely reminded him of the aromatic odor of burning hay or possibly spiced pipe tobacco—maybe even cinnamon.

But now it changed. This new smell was different from the first. It wasn't a bad smell. It was sweeter, like a mix of honey and, again, something just beyond his ability to describe. The rustling sound continued for a time and then fell silent.

"Foul air supply from the dead city above. Death and more death. Finally enough for even Reaver's tastes," he concluded sulkily. Losing interest, Bishop moved away from the grille to sit close to the shimmering energy field. He stared forlornly out into the corridor.

To compound his depression, a hollow rumbling from the pit of his stomach reminded him that he had not eaten since before his capture, however many days that had been.

Bishop gazed at the shimmering screen before him. "Am I to die in here alone, unburied and unknelled?" he wondered aloud. He had seen no sign of an insect, not even one of normal size, or any living thing since his return.

As if reading his mind, two Ikonian guards entered the outer gallery.

Bishop scrambled to his feet again. One of the Ikonians was carrying something round and gray-brown in color. Bishop stood and watched anxiously as the Ikonian, now standing before his cell, worked the pliable grayish mass into a flattened disk, its feelers animatedly following the forming process. Bishop followed the process too, completely befuddled.

When the Ikonian had finished its work, it opened a hatch on the floor in front of the shield and placed the disk in a sort of drawer, then closed the hatch and pulled a lever. Then the insect looked at Bishop expectantly.

"What?" Bishop questioned in a perplexed tone.

The Ikonian gestured toward the floor on Bishop's side of the energy screen. Looking down, Bishop saw an opposing panel. He squatted and found that the seemingly immovable floor plate was now sliding open without making noise. An odd earthy smell greeted him as he gingerly extracted the brownish-gray disk. It was soft and spongy to the touch.

Bishop wondered if the artifact was connected with an unknown ritual, or perhaps it was meant to be his pillow, when what he really needed was food. The Ikonians had turned and begun to retreat down the tunnel.

Bishop dropped the pillow disk. "Hey there! Hey! Half a moment," he called. The insects swiveled and stood, staring. "Humans need more than water and pillows to survive. How about some food?" He pantomimed eating. "You know, food? A joint of beef? Some bread, perhaps? Potatoes, candied yams? I wouldn't even turn my nose up at wayfarer's bread at present—and that's saying a great deal indeed."

The Ikonians stared, nonplussed.

"Yes? No? Hello?"

"You have already been provided with appropriate nourishment required for sustenance," came the unemotional translation.

"I have?" Bishop asked. He looked around the cell, his eyes finally settling on the brown disk. "By the black gods of the Others, that's not a pillow, is it?"

"It is highly nutritious acromyrmex fungus, rich in glycogen, carbohydrates, and amino acids. It is grown in the royal gardens by the worker caste."

Bishop tapped the spongy mass with the toe of his boot, then curled his lip up in disgust. "I think I'd rather eat a pillow. Take it away!"

"It is forbidden to waste acromyrmex fungus grown in the royal gardens. When you have consumed it, we will bring more."

"I wouldn't waste food if I had any, but this, this is not food," Bishop muttered, somewhat perturbed at the whole affair.

Several hours passed. Bishop sat in his corner eyeing the gray mass, his stomach growling. "I guess it is sort of bread-colored," he said, half convinced. "Or maybe it's the shape. Yes, I've seen bread formed in that fashion. The Semyazans make it in the south. Peasant bread, they call it; it has a somewhat nutty flavor, as I recall."

Bishop tentatively probed it with a finger. It deflated slightly, filling the prison with a musty, mushroomlike smell. "Maybe it tastes better than it smells."

He broke a small piece off and touched it with the tip of his tongue. "No. O gods of the Others, it tastes worse," he said, grimacing. An involuntary shiver ran through him.

The rustling sound and the sweet smell met his senses again from the wall grid as he stared at the moldering disk. He would simply not eat that ghastly thing. It was below his dignity as a human and a standard-bearer of the Order.

Several hours later, Bishop was busy finishing the last few crumbs of his fungus disk. "Well," he commented to himself with a hearty belch. "It was grown in the royal gardens by the worker caste; it was nutritious." He belched again. "I guess it was somewhat nutty-tasting, now that I think about it."

From then on, Bishop was fed three times a day. For breakfast, it was a sort of fungus gruel or porridge called "leucocoprinus," so named by the insects. Around midday, it was a chopped fungus, or *gongylophora*, and finally for dinner, the now familiar fungus disk formed of the ever-popular acromyrmex. The guards assured Bishop that each of the three meals was in fact a different food, distinctly different, and even seemed a bit peeved that he couldn't tell them apart. But if there truly was a difference, it was well beyond his ability to detect. It was all the same to him: bland, akin to eating raw mushrooms.

Out of sheer boredom, Bishop molded one of his dinner disks into the shape of a beef joint. It didn't help the taste, but the act certainly mystified the guards.

"What an improvement," he purred, smacking his lips. "Go ahead and try it with yours."

For a moment, it looked as if they just might consider the idea, but finally they turned and left him to finish the feast in silence.

By the fourth day, any humor in the situation had long faded. The meals had become tedious, and the hours between meals dragged. Bishop wondered about the fate of Storm Singer and even found that he missed the bird, nearly as much as he did Kiel. He tried to keep mentally active to pass the time, but finding an activity that engaged him proved difficult. He removed his soiled clothing and, to the best of his ability, beat and scrubbed the dirt and dried blood out of it in the privy. Then he scrubbed his own body until his skin was clean, red, and raw.

After his clothing dried, he dressed and conducted a centimeter-by-centimeter inspection of his cell, looking for any possible way out. The floors and ceiling were featureless gray metal, but he continued his search. It kept his mind off the subject that nagged at him.

What was Reaver's plan for him?

On the morning of the seventh day, Bishop began to exercise. It was during his morning stretching that he thought he heard a voice from the ventilation grid. He stopped immediately and listened. It wasn't coming from the outer tunnel. Intrigued and excited, he called out softly, "Hello? Is anyone there?"

Nothing. Then the now familiar rustling came to his ears, more insistent than before, followed by the odd smell he had noted before. After an indefinable noise, a stilted electronic voice spoke. "You are human, yes?"

Bishop stood on his toes just below the grid. He immediately recognized the Old Earth translator from his association with Kiel. "Yes, I am human. Who are you?" he asked insistently.

"This tunneler's number is thirty-six," came the monotone voice from the vent.

"Tunneler? Your number? What do you mean, your number? Who are you?"

There was a pause as if the owner of the translator was pondering the question. "This tunneler's number is thirty-six—the thirty-sixth to be hatched and reared in the Twelfth Colony since the nuptial flight of the queen," the voice said with a slower cadence as if to help lend clarity.

"*What* are you?" Bishop probed, excited, confused, and somewhat frustrated.

"Thirty-Six is a—" There was a pause as the sweet smell invaded Bishop's nose. Then the voice returned. "Forgive this tunneler. It forgets that the translator has its limitations. Thirty-Six is an insect from the thirty-sixth nest of the tunneler caste." The translator struggled, crackling with static.

It was one of the insects, and Ikonian! Bishop was cautious. This could be a deception, but to what purpose? He did not think Reaver was capable of such subtle subterfuge, knowing that he preferred to use violence.

"Where are you talking to me from?"

"Thirty-Six has been long detained in the cell next to yours."

An Ikonian imprisoned? This was unexpected. True, humans imprisoned their criminals. But Bishop had always assumed humans were the only intelligent life-forms that did such things.

"Do you mean to say you've been in there all this time?" Bishop stammered. "Until now, you've kept quiet. Why?"

"This tunneler has only now reacquired a translator through covert means. It was discovered some time ago and removed."

"How is it that you came to be imprisoned?" Bishop asked, still not quite sure he was talking to an insect.

A strong odor came from the vent. "The guards come. We will discuss it after the evening victuals are consumed."

Bishop started to respond, then thought better of it. It had been a long time since he had talked with anyone, and now he was being interrupted. He impatiently moved to the front of his cell and looked out into the tunnel. Just as Thirty-Six had said, the guards were approaching from the tunnel gloom with his fungus disk dinner.

One of the guards deposited the freshly formed disks into the food compartment and pulled the lever. Bishop stood motionless, not moving so much as a muscle. The guards too stood frozen, watching him, waiting for him to retrieve the food, but Bishop would not move. Even though it was obvious that he was consuming his meals, after the first few days he could no longer bring himself to do so in front of the insects, originally out of anger, then out of pride. The guards obviously did not understand the act, having become ever more fascinated with Bishop's silent protest.

Shortly, the guards became disinterested as they always did, as if their minds could not hold the curiosity for very long, and disappeared from sight. Bishop, smiling a satisfied smile, descended on the fungus disk and began wolfing it down with something bordering on gusto. It really had started to taste like Semyazan peasant bread. He had begun to think of all the foods he missed and began describing one such food, mostly to himself, as he ate.

"My mother was a small woman. A happy little lady she was. She was a wonderful cook. Her mother was too, or so I have heard, you know, and she taught her. Let me tell you about the cake she baked for my fifth birthday, this mother of mine. She knew I was crazy about cakes."

Bishop went on. The words came slowly as he ate his bland rations. He described it all exactly and lovingly: the mixing of the batter in a large yellow earthenware bowl, the breaking of the eggs, the careful whisking, the precise measuring of the flour, and the adding in of the extra touches, namely, candied peel and raisins. The gods only knew what art, what magic, went into that rich almond icing.

"It was," Bishop finally concluded, "a most beautiful, beautiful rare, wonderful cake, this cake my mother baked for me on my fifth birthday. The smell of it baking was like something from heaven."

Bishop wept.

Several hours later—or was it days?—after Bishop recovered from the longing memory of his youth, his longing for home and family, and feeling the aching passion of his first love, he slowly returned to the vent. "Are you there?" he questioned.

Shortly, a scent returned his query. "Yes, Thirty-Six is here," came the slightly perplexed electronic voice. "This tunneler is a prisoner. Do you understand? Thirty-Six is always here."

"I understand that you were imprisoned, but I do not understand why."

A moment passed before he heard a reply. "Yes, this tunneler understands your confusion, but it is difficult to explain."

"Try," Bishop said blandly. "I appear to have an excess of time at the moment."

There was a moment of silence before Thirty-Six began again. "When our race was created in the Dreaming, those of the colony were fashioned to obey the Dreamers without question. When the Dreamer returned and awoke, he reestablished control over most of us. Yet over the succeeding millennia, some of the nest have evolved, grown beyond the Dreamer's ability to control as in the days of the Dreaming. Thirty-Six is one such aberration."

The Dreamer, Reaver One, controlled them? That explained their enthralled obedience to his commands, and yet not all Ikonians were thus controlled.

Interesting.

"So, you are not controlled by the Dreamer—Reaver One—and were discovered?"

"That is so. The Dreamer discovered this tunneler's aberration. As a consequence, Thirty-Six was detained for study," Thirty-Six responded.

Bishop scowled. "Who is this Dreamer, this Reaver One? Where did he come from?"

After a bit of silence, Thirty-Six replied, "Those of the tunneler caste were excavating a new gallery for the temporal caste when we broke into a vault from the Dreaming time. The Dreamer was there."

"Dreaming," Bishop repeated. He didn't understand the term. Was it the translator? He had become familiar with the Old Earth technology because of his close association with Kiel: it had its limitations.

There was a rustling and a bit more fragrance before the reply. "Very difficult. Very difficult to explain." More rustling followed.

"Well, again, seeing that we appear to have an abundance of time on our hands ..." Bishop said with a sigh.

"Very true, human. Very true. Your logic is quite sound."

"The Dreaming," Bishop urged impatiently.

Amid the sounds of nervous pacing, the Ikonian began. "The pretime, the Dreaming, the Dreaming time, was the period ages upon ages ago before our creation or the founding stage of the First Colony. This tunneler suspects that at one level of meaning it is an indistinct era in the exceedingly remote past, well before our recorded memories at the beginning—the founding stage of the first queen, the origin of the first nest, and the creation of the first nest cell. We were created by a long-ago-extinct race of beings to serve as their protectors. The Dreamers, they were, the others who came before, like you but not like you."

The Others! Bishop thought. It always returned to the Others.

"These Dreamers, where did they come from?" Bishop wondered aloud, expecting to hear something new about the Others, as the Others were actually what he now believed them to be.

"We would not know. We would not care."

"You would not know—" Bishop started.

"For us," Thirty-Six said, interrupting, "the origin of the Dreamers is unimportant, as is the timing of their creative endeavors. These beings of the Dreaming simply were. They created us. We pay heed only to the time since—the time after the founding stage of the first nest and the development of the First Colony."

Thirty-Six rambled at some length concerning the founding stage, obviously of great interest to the insect, before Bishop stopped it.

"But the Others, these Dreamers, are no more," Bishop stated.

"Yes and no," Thirty-Six responded.

"Yes and no?"

"The absence of any specific beginning of the Dreaming era is matched by the absence of any definite end, as a circle has no end. After their creative activities on earth were completed, the Dreamers, worn down by their grand efforts, ended their creative pursuits. They disappeared to sleep, promising to return, to awaken at a predetermined time. That time has come."

"All right then," Bishop said, exasperated. "You just happened upon a vault—a vault from Old Earth."

"Yes, it is as Thirty-Six describes. Many such vaults have been found within, under, the Blue Zones, yet without exception they are sealed and beyond the ability of all to enter. The Dreamers had created these ancient vaults to hide their magic. This vault was different; it was not sealed and was easily opened. Within the enclosure we found a cylinder—metal egg—containing a Dreamer. The Dreamer had waited there for uncounted years, knowing that the descendants of the First Colony would be the ones to discover him and revive him."

"Are you trying to say that you found a vault from the age of the Dreamers—the Others? With a living Other inside it?" It was too fantastic to believe, but Bishop knew enough about the Others and their magic to reject the idea out of hand. There was little beyond their ability, he suspected, absently rubbing the Riika.

"This is so," Thirty-Six promptly responded.

Thirty-Six proceeded to drone on for some time, spewing tedious details regarding peculiarities of the chamber. Obviously this tunneler was greatly impressed by subterranean architecture. Bishop absorbed what he was being told.

"The Dreamer was found beyond and through a hexagon-shaped tunnel that itself has a remarkable history. In the dim days, it was thought that hexagon-shaped tunnels were superior in both aesthetics and physical form. Can you imagine, the beauty, the majesty?"

"Nope," Bishop muttered, still mentally reeling from what Thirty-Six had imparted.

"These conclusions were, of course, completely wrong."

"Of course," Bishop returned, mostly ignoring Thirty-Six's tunnel lore.

"We now know with absolute certainty that it is the circular tunnel that is, in fact, far superior in both respects. The clean, undemanding nature of the circle is exceedingly elegant in its stark, simplistic beauty, and yet it suggests a subtlety of power, power coupled with unbounded grace that seems to transcend—"

As Thirty-Six prattled, Bishop's head began to pound as much from the tunnel lore as from the accompanying aroma wafting through the vent. Then Bishop had to listen to more minutiae about the arch over the vault door, including the insect's speculation about the work involved in hollowing out such a chamber. Finally, Bishop heard an rapturous description of the chamber itself.

"What else was in the chamber?" Bishop asked, tiring of the information overload. "A flaming sword floating in the air?"

Bishop heard pacing and rustling, accompanied by an acrid waft of aroma. "A flaming sword? No, there was no such thing."

"All right then," Bishop said as he lay down on the comfortless metal floor and closed his eyes. "I have heard enough for tonight. I don't know about you Ikonians of the tunneler caste, but we humans need to rest from time to time. And I need to reflect on what I have been told."

"There is little time, human," Thirty-Six said.

"After breakfast there will be an excess of time, I am sure," Bishop muttered wearily. But sleep came slowly as he struggled to absorb the implications of what he had been told. Thirty-Six seemed beyond the ability to fabricate myth, adding a frightening dimension of veracity to the tale.

Bishop was wakened in the morning by the guards bringing him his fungus breakfast. He stiffly got up and stretched his aching muscles, waiting for the guards to disappear before retrieving the food and devouring it. He washed his face and paced the cell floor before eagerly sitting below the vent between his cell and Thirty-Six's cell.

"Thirty-Six, are you there?" he called softly.

"Yes, Thirty-Six is here," came the slightly bewildered voice again. "This tunneler is a prisoner. Do you understand? Thirty-Six is always here."

"Yes. I meant, are you listening to me?" Bishop growled.

"What else would this tunneler be doing?"

"Sleeping, of course."

"Those of the colony do not require rest, sleep, as do other sentient life."

"Sounds convenient."

"This tunneler is sure that it is. In fact, we of the Twelfth Colony have found that our—"

"Fine, fine. Now, where did we leave off yesterday?" Bishop asked, interrupting.

"This tunneler was relating to you the discovery of the vault that contained the Dreamer," Thirty-Six said, continuing as if the conversation had ceased only moments ago.

"Oh yes, how could I have forgotten?" Bishop settled himself. "You found a vault from the age of the Others, and it contained a living Other, or Dreamer as you so name him. Now tell me, did this Dreamer insist on becoming your leader, or did the colony just feel it would be a welcome change in government?"

There was a long silent moment while Thirty-Six absorbed the question. "No and no, human. Your conclusions are all wrong."

"Then how is it that you allowed him to take over your colony? I mean, it seems to me that you could have resisted him a little more than you did."

"No, not so simple. The chemoreceptor instantly brought us, most of us, under his control—enslavement."

"A chemo what?"

"The device on his waist. The chemoreceptor is more than a weapon; the Dreamers can use it to control us. They are, after all, our creators. After the Dreamer took control, many of our soldiers were also implanted with accelerators, a device from the Dreaming that has been modified to be used on our bodies. It allows the soldiers certain biophysical enhancements in order to better protect the nest from those not of the nest, or those not controlled by the Dreamer, or those from outside deemed to be a danger to the nest.

Bishop struggled with the information. "So, your colony was brought under control by this chemo, ah, device?"

"Chemoreceptor."

"How does the mechanism work? What does it do, this chemoreceptor?"

There was a long pause as if Thirty-Six was considering the knowledge it was about to impart. "You asked a complex question. The chemoreceptor's function is based on chemical communication or the semiochemicals produced by our exocrine glands."

"What?"

"Semiochemicals—scent communication."

"Scent? Smell? I don't understand."

"You seem to know very little, human."

Bishop fumed in growing frustration. "Well, maybe if you took a moment to explain."

"This tunneler will try to explain, but Thirty-Six is only of the tunneler caste."

"I understand that much."

Thirty-Six continued. "There is a nest odor by which we may identify one another. Variations in this nest odor permit identifications of individuals. Combining these basic aliphatic hydrocarbon 'primers' and 'releasers' allows us to communicate with those of the nest."

"Doesn't sound very efficient," Bishop remarked, struggling with this alien concept and these unknown words. Possibly the translator was not functioning properly.

"No. No, human, you are wrong. Although there are drawbacks to this form of communication, as with your method, it can be extremely efficient and carries several advantages. As an exempli gratia, a semiochemical can be carried to the sensory appendages of a nest-mate much farther than the shout or cry of a human can be carried to the sensory organs of another human. Moreover, if not too much time is allowed to escape, one of the nest may leave a message in its chamber or a tunnel for another nest-mate. The other, in turn, may arrive later to interpret it."

Struggling to understand Thirty-Six, Bishop was still seeing semiochemicals as an inferior means of communication. He asked, "You spoke of a disadvantage. What might that be?"

There was the sound of pacing for a moment or two. "Our entire existence is based on semiochemicals, and the Dreamers well know this, as those of the Dreaming developed their methods of control based on this simple fact. There are scents, methylundecane, tridecane, hexadecane, and an array of farnesene compounds, that to us are so compelling that we are unable to resist them, something akin to a human trying to resist the desire to scream if he were suddenly thrown into a fire. Yet some overcame, grew beyond the control. This tunneler, Thirty-Six, is one of the ones who overcame."

Bishop pondered what he was hearing for a time. If this was true, it could be useful information. "How were you discovered?"

Thirty-Six responded as if ashamed of what he had done. "This tunneler allowed an Eligor to escape."

Bishop started. His memory returned to the Eligor he had found at the border. "An Eligor? If it's the same one that I encountered, I am afraid to report that he was killed by a shifter—a hunter-killer," Bishop said, correcting himself, remembering Reaver's definition of the beast.

There was a pause. "That is unfortunate. The Eligor should not have been captured in the first place, merely prevented from entering our land. He was not of the nest, not of the colony, just as you are not of the colony."

"Me?"

"You are not of the nest, not of the colony, just like the Eligor was not of the colony. You should not be here."

"Well, we agree on that anyway. But tell me, why were you allowed to live? It seems to me that this Dreamer, this Reaver One, isn't one to dismiss such a transgression as freeing his captives."

"Very true. Yes, very true. Yet those of the colony will not kill those of the colony, as it would violate our nest law. Even the soldiers of the colony will not kill a nest-mate; it is beyond their ability. This was when the Dreamer realized the extent of our change, because in the time of the Dreaming, it is said that we would have followed any order even if it meant killing our own species and breaking nest law."

Another meal was brought, and Bishop ate, simultaneously absorbing what he had been told. He tried to block his mind from recalling the screams of the dying Eligor and the horrific laughter of the light-shifter. Thirty-Six had helped the Eligor to escape, but the Eligor had escaped into the jaws of death.

There was silence for a long time after the guards had vanished. Then the insect suddenly asked, "Why have you come to the Twelfth Colony?"

Bishop hesitated for a moment. It was a secret mission the Order had sent him on, but here, locked up in a subterranean cell below Terus Kor, what difference did it make?

"Why am I here? I was sent here to find the reasons behind the attacks on the Eligor Empire."

"Have you completed your mission then?" Thirty-Six questioned.

"Well, mostly, for whatever good it will do." Bishop slid to the floor of the cell and sat down.

"Then this tunneler will assist you in escaping. It is not permitted to allow those to remain who are not of the nest. It is nest law."

Bishop started. "You what?"

His first eager thrill was quickly snuffed with a quickening splash of cold reality. What could a woefully pathetic imprisoned insect tunneler possibly do to aid in his escape? Bishop slumped again.

"How can you help me? You are a prisoner too. Are you going to gnaw through the Old Earth metal of your prison, O wise tunneler?"

"Gnaw through metal? No, this is not possible. There are others who have escaped the control of the Dreamer, others who have not yet been discovered. They will assist us."

Bishop suddenly sat up straight. "Others? What others?"

"There are several of the nest that have evolved away from the Dreamer's control. Thirty-Six is the only one that has been discovered."

Bishop considered that. "I don't mean to be ungracious, but what is it to you if I rot in this cell or escape back to the Protectorate of Merja Soria? I mean, beyond your not wanting me in your colony."

The Ikonian answered with a question. "Is it true that the humans defeated—crushed—the Imperial Eligor at the Battle of Koth as was relayed to me by the imprisoned Eligor I communicated with?"

"Well, I suppose that is mostly true."

"Then it is possible that the humans, if warned, will be able to defeat the Dreamer and allow our race to continue on our own course. The Dreamers long ago completed their task and are revered for it, yet they are not required—not welcome in our time. It is creating disorder. I am far behind in my duties as a tunneler. The nest, the colony, stagnates. There has been no harmony and no order ever since the Dreamer arrived."

Here Bishop was saving the Eligor Empire, and now Thirty-Six wanted to add war with the Dreamer to his growing list of responsibilities. How was he supposed to save these Ikonians, these insects, from the Dreamer? He imagined the Order would be equally uninterested in the job. He bit back his protestations. "Well, of course. We'll do that straight off. And getting back to your escape plans for me—"

The insect continued matter-of-factly. "This tunneler can have you taken to the lower tunnels as it did with the Eligor captive, but after that, you will be on your own. The Ikonian soldiers will follow once the Dreamer realizes you have decided not to aid him in his conquest. You must not stop until you are well beyond the Ikonian frontier. The soldiers will not kill their own kind, yet they will descend on other creatures if so ordered. They cannot refuse the Dreamer in this regard. If they catch you, you will be terminated, as was the Eligor before you."

Bishop frowned. Something didn't seem right. "If this Dreamer suspects that you are the one that aided the Eligor, how is it that you were imprisoned next to me? Pardon me, but that seems too good to be believed, even for a simpleminded standard-bearer like me."

The Ikonian paced and rustled. "That is perhaps something to consider. It is possible that the Dreamer has placed us in close proximity of one another in order to ensnare others of the nest with Thirty-Six's particular aberration. Still, the collaborator will be of a type he will never suspect. She is his concubine."

"She, a female, an Ikonian, is his concubine!" Bishop yelped. "An insect? I ... I'm speechless. I mean, I can't even imagine!" Bishop shook his head as if to clear a mental picture. "Right. Fine. Getting back to these soldiers, how am I to defeat them if they are invulnerable?"

"She serves until the others arrive. She is uniquely formed in order to mimic—"

"I don't want to know!" Bishop screamed, momentarily plugging his ears. "Please. The soldiers. Tell me about them."

The pacing began anew. "Very difficult, very difficult, very difficult are the soldiers. They are formidable. They have the accelerators." The translator settled down to normal cadences. "It will not be easy."

"Tell me about the soldiers. Are there any weaknesses?"

There was a long moment of silence that followed Bishop's question. He was about to ask it again when Thirty-Six finally replied.

"It is forbidden to speak of such things. There is no nest trust between us. You are not of the colony. Thirty-Six cannot, by Thirty-Six's actions, harm a nest-mate."

Now it was Bishop's turn to sit in silence while he pondered the statement. "Nest trust, is it? How am I to gain nest trust with you?"

"It is not possible, and yet"—he paused—"would you have nest trust with this tunneler?"

Bishop struggled with the thought. Trusting the Ikonian and expecting the insect to trust him in return after only a few days of contact was a fantastic leap of faith, but Bishop needed to believe in something, and Thirty-Six was the only possibility at the moment.

"I would have nest trust with you, Thirty-Six," Bishop finally stated.

Minutes passed, and then Thirty-Six said slowly, "You must first give your word that things shared in nest trust will remain with you. Is this clearly understood?"

"It is understood. I give you my word, Thirty-Six."

Thirty-Six apparently took time to ponder Bishop's sincerity, because he didn't speak. Finally, he replied, "Very well, look to the ventilation grid."

Bishop stood back away from the grille and watched as two small multijointed feelers effortlessly slid through the grating, probing the air delicately. He recognized them as Ikonian antennae.

"To seal our nest trust, we must touch."

Bishop rolled his eyes and reached up, touching the tips of the antennae with his fingers. The feelers jerked back for a moment, then tentatively returned to probe and curl about Bishop's fingers. Then the feelers delicately probed his face before they retreated to whence they had come.

"There is nest trust between us," Thirty-Six said with finality.

"Wonderful," Bishop muttered, half embarrassed. If the Order were to catch wind of this, he would never hear the end of it.

"Yes, it is wonderful to have nest trust," Thirty-Six returned.

"Ah, right." Bishop coughed. "Now what of these soldiers?"

Thirty-Six became meditative, then it began speaking again. "This tunneler will tell you what you need to know, but you will not share the information with those who are not of the colony."

"Understood. We have nest trust. Speak on with confidence, Thirty-Six." Bishop settled himself again as the insect's translator droned.

"Very well. To begin with, we have eyes, which are compound and multifaceted, but we do not much rely on these organs. They are to us something like your ears and nose, used as secondary sensors. The two appendages protruding from our heads are our primary sensory organs. Not only are these organs sensitive to semiochemicals, but also they transform sound vibrations into something intelligible."

Bishop slumped. "So, your auditory sense and your sense of smell are more developed than your sense of sight. It doesn't appear that this information will give me much of an advantage. Is there anything else I should worry about?"

"There are the aspects to the accelerators that this tunneler previously mentioned."

Bishop listened.

"The accelerators are aptly named because they are also designed to 'accelerate' the physical abilities of the soldiers. The accelerators provide the soldiers with enhanced endurance, speed, and strength, along with many other advantages. It would be unwise to allow any of the soldiers to catch up with you, as this tunneler doubts that you would be able to survive such an encounter."

"I have my own means of defense," Bishop muttered, rubbing his Riika.

"Little good has half a Riika done you recently, Thirty-Six believes."

"Why do you say that?" What did this insect know?

"Did you not attempt to use the device, the Riika, in the throne room against the Dreamer?"

"Yes, but how ...?" By the Dreamer's whiskers! Even Thirty-Six knew about the Riika!

"Are you having trouble with your memory?"

"No problems. Why?"

"As this tunneler has stated, there are others besides Thirty-Six that have eluded the control of the Dreamer."

"Are there ways to overcome the accelerator?"

"Only with another accelerator."

Shades of the Others. Bishop slumped. The Riika was of no use against the accelerator. He rubbed the inert Old Earth device resting on his arm. It seemed as of late it was no good at all.

An acrid smell suddenly assaulted Bishop's nostrils. "Caution human, the Dreamer comes."

Bishop swung around toward the shimmering door shield, raising the Riika instinctively.

In a moment, Reaver One stood before him on the other side of the barrier, flanked by several insects. These insects were different from the ones Bishop had faced up to now. They were tall and massive and possessed a metallic blister fused into their upper arm—accelerators. The Ikonian soldiers! They were as Kiel had described. They were also as Thirty-Six had described. Even if the soldiers had not been given the accelerators, they would have been more than a match for any human. Their hulking forms were covered in chitinous thorny plates of natural armor, but the subtle movements of their stride suggested the agility of a lynx.

Bishop gaped at Reaver. The man was even bigger than he had originally estimated, reaching nearly to the height of the soldiers around him.

The soldiers stood motionless like macabre statues. Reaver smiled coolly, noting Bishop's proximity to the shield. "I would suggest that you not touch the plasma grid. It operates on a Fifth Force principle and would likely vaporize your worthless, lice-ridden carcass." Reaver chuckled to himself. "That would be a fitting epitaph on your gravestone, wouldn't it? 'Here lies the dullest of humans—vaporized himself on a plasma grid.'"

Bishop, recalling his experimentation with the field, mechanically backed away from the grid. He lowered the Riika and glared at Reaver with open hatred. "Very well. What do you want, anyway?"

Reaver's face took on an expression of feigned perplexity. "I thought I made myself clear during our last little chat. I require your assistance. Now surely you have rotted down here long enough to have made up even your dim-witted mind. Tell me of the defenses of Merja Soria, its technology, its government. Tell me what you know of the partial Riika you wear. Tell me what you have learned of its power."

"It turns out I'm just a poor human who lost his way in the wood. What you need is an officer or someone of the Order. Why don't you trot down to the protectorate and hire yourself one? I am sure you will be welcomed as an honored guest, just as you have honored me."

Reaver's eyes widened. "Truly? Why, it seems I made a mistake. Quick now, my insect friends, fetch the keys and release this poor soul at once." Reaver's eyes returned to their crafty state. He laughed.

"By the way, Merja Sorian," he continued, "it happens that you are the bearer of a Riika, which means you are no ordinary human—a veritable walking key to the past. That could be a rare commodity in this age. And I am not one to overlook an advantage."

Bishop's eyes narrowed. An advantage. What did this Reaver One know that he did not?

"Now will you willingly assist me?" Reaver asked, grinning like some ancient vulture that had come to roost above a dying animal.

Bishop set his jaw and glowered at Reaver, saying not a word.

The feigned smile on Reaver's face vanished, his expression becoming chiseled granite. "Now, I am many things, Merja Sorian, but I am not patient. I will allow you a short while longer to mull it over. There is an easy path and a difficult path. When I come again and you refuse, I will force the answers from you and take the Riika for my own. I have the ability to unlock its power, given time. Nothing is beyond my ability."

The Dreamer abruptly turned and left. The soldiers followed without delay.

Moments later, Thirty-Six spoke again, its artificial voice a mere whisper. "Time has run its course. You will leave the colony tonight."

ELEVEN

LOWER TUNNELS

> There was the door to which I found no key; there was the veil through which I could not see.
> —Vena Korela,
> Saga of Joukahainen, Runa 98

Bishop never fully understood how Thirty-Six had sent for help, but just after the last meal of the day had been consumed, there came a visitor to his cell.

The creature who approached was decidedly delicate and was smaller than the guards. Iridescent gossamer wings fluttered, and large liquid eyes looked at him hesitantly. She—for it was clear to Bishop that this insect was female—approached the plasma grid.

The delicate creature continued to stare. A translator crackled in an unmistakably higher pitch than that of Thirty-Six's. "Humans are so strange," came the translation. And then with a note of finality, the voice said, "I fear I will never get used to your form. Yes, it is settled: I will free you. It is not right that you are here. You are not of the colony. You are not of the nest."

"Honorable as well as beautiful, it seems," Bishop remarked, somewhat relieved, as the insect touched a wall stud and the plasma grid flashed before sputtering momentarily and then winking out. It was a pleasant nothing. Even though alien, the creature was not unattractive; in fact, she was not very far removed from a human female in form and comeliness, though she had distinctly insect features for sure.

The wings of the creature that now faced Bishop fluttered, and a sweet smell invaded his nostrils. "Beautiful?" The insect paused. "So strange and yet so interesting."

Bishop coughed. His ears burned.

The female studied Bishop for a moment and then turned down the tunnel. "Follow me, human."

Bishop turned to follow and then stopped. "Just one moment."

The female watched Bishop in puzzlement as he walked to the front of the neighboring cell. There, timidly standing motionless at its front, was Thirty-Six. The insect was rather plain in contrast to others of its species. Bishop suspected that for a tunnel worker, special embellishment was not necessary. But beneath that plain surface, Thirty-Six was anything but ordinary.

"Will you not come with me, Thirty-Six?" Bishop asked, already knowing the response.

"Thirty-Six will not leave the colony. It is not permitted for a tunneler to do so, even if it wished to leave, which it does not."

"Thirty-Six, thank you for your help. I shall never forget our nest trust."

Thirty-Six raised its hands in a friendly gesture. "By the gods of the Others," it intoned, mistaking one of Bishop's favorite curses for some form of human custom, "may your feet take you to your own colony, and may you be reunited with those of your own nest."

"By the gods of the Others," Bishop returned, not knowing what else to say, and then turned to the female.

"Let's get out of here."

Bishop studied the small furtive creature that quickly ghosted ahead of him. Thirty-Six had described the females. The colony had one mother, and not surprisingly, she was of great importance as foundress of the colony, well beyond her primary responsibility of egg production. The other females, who were either sterile workers or virgin reproductives of the queen, were usually tasked with managing the nurseries, unless the mother suddenly died or another colony site was established. Of course, this female was of value for an entirely different reason. Bishop shuddered.

As they hurriedly walked along, the female spoke. "As I understand it, humans rely on the presence of light in order to use their primary sensory organs to an optimal degree."

"Their—my what?"

"Your eyes cannot be used in darkness. Is this so?"

"My *eyes*? Oh. Yes, that is correct."

"The lower tunnels are not provided with light panels. You will require a light generator."

The slender insect slid one of her four delicate articulated forelimbs into a pouch that hung around her thorax. Producing a small metallic cylinder, she handed it to Bishop. The cylinder's perfect craftsmanship immediately identified it as an Old Earth relic. One end of the tube was transparent, and just below its surface, Bishop perceived a reflective cone wrapped around multiple smaller glass spheres. As Bishop turned the light generator in his hands, he noticed a slight flexible blister at about the place where his thumb rested. He pushed the blister. A shaft of light shot out of the device and into his eyes. He dropped the thing and it skittered across the floor, throwing off a spiraling beam of cold light.

"Gods of the Others!" he swore, backing away from the accursed object.

His guide stopped and stared at him. "It is strange that you would fear the light generator. After all, it is human technology."

"I don't fear the bloody thing! It's just that I haven't used one in some time," Bishop stammered, eyeing the contrivance with dread.

The insect stared for a moment longer.

"What?" Bishop asked defensively. "I use them all the time."

"We should continue."

"Lead on," Bishop growled, impatiently retrieving the Old Earth torch, fumbling with it for a moment, then mostly by accident, turning it off.

The insect stared a moment longer, then continued down the tunnel. "You must take care not to encounter a guardian in the lower tunnels."

Bishop slowed. "A guardian?"

"They are a lesser, nonsentient life-form that inhabits the lower tunnels. They are used for waste disposal and keep unwanted creatures out of the sewers. They will kill you if they find you. They will even kill us if they wander into the upper tunnels."

"Maybe you should kill them if they are such a threat."

"We will not kill the guardians; they are of the nest."

"Well, we've always got the nest to consider, don't we?" Bishop remarked blandly.

"There is the nest to consider, yes. There are other dangers to avoid."

Bishop slowed his pace again. "What other dangers?"

"There are the hunter-killers that on occasion use the drain exits as dens, but they will not bother you in the upper tunnels for fear of the guardians. The guardians will not bother the hunter-killers in the lower tunnels for the same reason."

Bishop stopped and turned to the female. "Hunter-killers? Light-shifters? Biomechs? I am beginning to believe that I would have been better served by staying in my cell and taking my chances with Reaver."

"You would not be better served."

"The last shifter I encountered nearly killed me."

"They are of no concern; they are programmed to temporarily shut down—deactivate—at the utterance of certain Old Earth words of power, which I will teach you. You will use these commands at the foot of the winding stairs before you enter the drain exits. This will most likely temporarily deactivate them and allow you to pass unmolested."

"Most likely? Well, that's a comfort," Bishop stammered.

The female ignored the comment, continuing her dialogue, teaching Bishop the Old Earth commands and resuming her discourse about the lower tunnels and their history, apparently every bit as fascinated by nest lore minutiae as Thirty-Six had been.

They hurried along in the gloom, dropping lower and lower, changing directions with the tunnel. Finally, after about an hour, the tunnel came to an abrupt end. There in the floor was a circular lid. With each of her four forelimbs, the insect grabbed four recessed grips and pulled. Grudgingly, the heavy metal lid opened, exposing a pitch-black void below.

"You are free of the colony," the translator crackled. "Here is your pack and its contents, your sword and sheath, and a gift."

Before Bishop could question the Ikonian, she clasped two halves of a metallic cylinder around his right forearm. The device clicked as the two perfect halves came together. There was a flash and the halves fused, becoming one seamless wristband.

Bishop jerked his arm away. "What in the eight hells?"

Feeling a sharp pinching and tingling, followed by a strange sensation whipping along his veins, Bishop frantically tugged at the contrivance, but it was now as permanent as the Riika on his left arm.

"The device is coveted by the Dreamer. It was taken from his chamber while he slept. He suspects you are the key to unlocking its full potential. It might aid you and it might not, but it was worth the effort, yes? The soldiers' accelerators are based on this device."

Bishop looked at the armlet with renewed interest. It looked suspiciously like the Riika on his left arm, as if the two were a matched pair. "Where did it come from? Where did you find it?"

"It was discovered with the Dreamer when he was exhumed; it is at least as old as he. It is said that he took it against the wishes of others of his kind in the Dreaming because of its potential to destroy him. He will not be pleased when he discovers it missing."

"I suspect not. Indeed, how long can I expect its power to last, if in fact I can even call upon its power?"

"It is said the device draws its energy from your own body. It should not fail so long as you are alive."

Bishop frowned suspiciously at the device on his arm. "The accelerators that I have seen on the soldiers—those look different."

"True," came the insect's response. "The soldiers' accelerators were modeled after this unit. They are crude copies designed to mimic the key device. The Dreamer has the ability to open this unit and study it, but he cannot replicate it in this age. The soldiers' accelerators are primitive in comparison to the key now resting on your appendage."

"The key." Something began to nag at Bishop's memory, from the Riika ceremony of his youth.

"May the bearer find the key," the knights of the Order had chanted.

Bryn's voice seemed to whisper to Bishop from the past. "The myth, Bishop, the legend, in part, I believe, suggests that at the proper time, at the time of our most desperate need, the Riika will be made whole again, uniting the Great Houses and, in so doing, forging a unified government and bringing about a golden Sixth Age."

Had the insect inadvertently fulfilled the prophecy of the Vena Korela? Bishop looked with fresh eyes at the strange device locked around his wrist that so closely resembled the Riika. Again he wondered at its implication.

Bishop shuddered. "You might have signed my death warrant. If this is as great a threat as you claim, then Reaver will not easily forget that I now carry it. I might have stood a better chance of escaping into the southern forests without it. Also, it will not take him long to figure out who took it. And he is not bound by your noble nest law as you of the nest are."

"It is of no concern. I am a fertile female, and I intend on leaving the twelfth nest with a drone and founding my own nest this very night. It is the will of the queen."

Bishop looked up at the small, delicate form standing next to him. "Thank you for aiding me. I do not mean to blame you for my own worries. Reaver would have likely sent the soldiers after me anyway. At least there is a chance, although it's a slim one. So, thank you again. What did you say your name was?"

The luminous compound eyes looked up at him. "I did not say. My name is"—a strong aroma assailed Bishop's nostrils as the translator for the female paused in thought—"Seventy-Eight Million, Nine Hundred Twenty-Eight Thousand, Four Hundred Forty-Three," the mechanical voice uttered.

Bishop blinked. "Ah, go well, ah, right."

Then, as an afterthought, remembering the ritual he had performed with Thirty-Six, he raised his fingers and touched the tips of the female's antennae. They jerked away at first and then returned and coiled around his arms, holding them firmly. Her wings rustled and hummed in a quickened movement.

Bishop swallowed hard. *What have I started?* But soon, her wings ceased their movement, and her antennae uncurled and straightened.

"We have nest trust," came the soft, barely audible voice.

"I suppose I had better get moving now," Bishop stammered as he backed toward the hole, fumbling with his pack and sword, struggling to strap them on. "I'm usually not one to touch feelers and leave, but things being as they are …"

The insect studied him for a moment and then spoke. "Go with speed, human. May your feet take you to your own colony, and may you be reunited with those of your own nest." Then she turned and melted back into the tunnel gloaming from which they came.

Bishop dropped down into the gaping hole. Finding a foot rung, he lowered the massive hatch above him, once again sealing it. Then, descending to the ground, he activated the electric torch. A stream of cold light burst out, illuminating the tunnel. The chamber was old, ancient in fact, the walls being hexagonal in form, unlike the more recent rounded tunnels of the upper chambers.

"You were right, Thirty-Six, not very aesthetic." Bishop smiled despite himself. He would miss his insect friend.

Quietly, he walked to the center of the chamber and stopped. There were six tunnels that led from the circular chamber in every direction, like the spokes of a wheel. This was something he had not counted on—had not even thought of asking. The insects might have thought him capable of ascertaining the right one by way of scent or some other means.

"You yammered on and on about your blessed tunnels, Thirty-Six, but you couldn't tell me which one to take to freedom?"

Compounding matters, Bishop suddenly felt a sting on his ankle. He twisted, his arms cuffing at a dark fist-sized entity that had hold of his leg. He dislodged the creature and threw it from him, causing it to hit the cavern wall with a sickening crunch. The hairy legs moved aimlessly while dying eyes glittered at him redly and evilly, finally winking out as the creature lay still.

Quickly, Bishop moved the torch down to shine on the ground. There directly below him was a nest made of rubbish, where several eggs from some foul creature were in the process of hatching.

Bishop could see the gleaming red eyes of a fist-sized insect, identical to the one he'd just killed, scrambling about and trying to pull itself from one of the leathery eggs. Next to it was a crushed egg, the small inhabitant dead. Bishop had accidentally stepped on it in his fright. He removed an intact egg and held it to his ear. Able to hear a persistent ugly scratching inside it, he sensed the movement of yet another of the horrid creatures in the act of breaking out of its shell and set his heel upon it. He shined his torch cautiously into the shadows. Somewhere in this demon-haunted dungeon lurked the mother, whom he did not wish to meet while in her violated nest surrounded by her dead offspring.

Nothing stirred.

He walked on, the pain in his leg slowly subsiding. Thankfully, his leg did not seem to be poisoned, but the thought of the creatures hatching and scurrying about was unnerving. Relying completely on instinct, he chose the lowest of the six tunnels and limped toward it, hoping his instincts were better than his fading luck. The female had stated that these were, among other things, drainage tunnels and that the lowest would most certainly serve that function.

The cavern in which Bishop was now walking reeked of death and decay, in contrast with the fastidiously clean tunnels of the upper inhabited levels, which made it seem all the more repulsive with its filth and litter. In one corner there were scattered bones and, among them, the shattered skull of some nameless beast. The bones had been split and the marrow sucked from them. The clean, steady light from the Ikonian torch cast eerie shadows on the ceilings and walls, which danced as Bishop passed. Here and there were piles of shattered Ikonian exoskeletons, chitinous bits of their strange bodies, as if this tunnel were a depository for the colony dead. At the same instant as having that thought, Bishop heard a slight scratching noise and looked up to see two flaming luminous red eyes peering at him from the darkness of a side tunnel.

The guardian was not as tall as an Ikonian, but it looked heavier, maybe a hundred kilos. It was low to the ground and lozenge-shaped like an immense beetle, black as midnight, and glistening in the gloom like wet soot.

The first thing Bishop noticed after the glowing eyes were the two hooked pincerlike extensions whose tips met perhaps a meter beyond the body—clearly some aberration of the jaws. The creature's abdomen seemed divided into two thick casings that might have, ages before, been wing covers but now were fused together, forming a thick, immobile exoskeleton. The head was even now withdrawn beneath the exoskeleton, but the creature's eyes were clearly visible, as were the extensions of its jaws. The antennae, unlike those of the Ikonians, were short and thick.

The guardian, if in fact it was a guardian, seemed to be puzzled and made no move to attack. Undoubtedly in its long life in the tunnels it had never encountered anything like Bishop. It backed up a bit and drew its head deeper into its exoskeleton, lifting its hooked tubular jaws before its eyes as though to shield them from the light.

It occurred to Bishop that the light of the torch may have temporarily blinded or disoriented the guardian. It was clear that the creature did not yet understand what had taken place within its tunnels. Bishop seized on the thought and quickly brought the torch forward. With a shout, he thrust it at the creature's face.

Bishop expected the thing to retreat hastily, but it made no move whatsoever other than to lift its tubular pincerlike jaws to him. It seemed most unnatural, as though the creature might have been a living rock, or a blind carnivorous growth. One thing was clear: the creature did not fear Bishop or the torch.

Backing away, Bishop slipped his sword from its sheath. The guardian took a step forward and began to hiss. The sound unnerved Bishop for a moment, as he had become used to the uncanny silence of the lower tunnels. Now the thing began to poke its disk-shaped head out from beneath its protective cover, and its antennae began to explore the air.

The hissing now became more intense.

Bishop retreated, moving back in the direction from which he had come. Perhaps there was another way out of the tunnels. The creature followed Bishop back through the central hub, where he had started, clambered clumsily over the top of the nest, and stopped. It began to poke about the shattered remains of the crushed eggs, its antennae trembling in sudden distress.

Bishop, watching the creature, decided it was time to leave. He turned and began to jog away from the guardian, going around the perimeter of the hub and back down the darkened passage he had first entered. He hoped, considering the size, shape, and probable weight of the creature and the stoutness of its legs, that it would not be able to move quickly, at least not for a sustained period.

Minutes after Bishop left the guardian in the dark, he heard from behind him one of the strangest and most horrifying sounds he had ever heard in his life, a long, enraged buzzing and yammering.

He stopped for a moment and listened. Scrambling after him in the tunnel was the guardian insect, its tiny brain apparently finally connecting Bishop with its ruined nest and dead young.

Bishop turned and ran. After what seemed like an eternity, he again stopped nearly exhausted and listened. He'd been right about the guardian's mobility, as the sounds of pursuit had disappeared. Yet he knew that somewhere back there it remained and would be coming. The guardian would not yield its vengeance or give up its prey so easily. Slowly, patiently, implacably, like the coming of winter or the weathering of a stone, somewhere in the darkness, it was still coming.

The melodrama of the guardian's pursuit of its prey unnerved Bishop. How terrible it would be to be trapped in these tunnels, waiting for the beetle thing, the creature that understood all the twists and turns of its labyrinthine lair. An interloper could outrun it perhaps for hours, possibly days, not able to sleep or stop, not knowing if the beetle or one of its kin were suddenly to confront him at the next turn.

He needed to find the exit, and soon.

Bishop lost sense of time as he loped on and on in the darkness. He stopped for a rest here and there, letting his leg muscles recover, and began to move again as soon as he had caught his breath. Finally, he staggered to a stop, his reserves gone. Surely there would be time, if not for sleep, then to close his eyes. The guardian must have been left far behind.

He awoke with a start.

A rustling sound had awakened him from a deep unintended sleep. He fumbled for the electric torch, turning in time to see the two glowing eyes looking down upon him.

Bishop cried out as he felt two long, curved objects close around his body in an embrace of death. With flailing hands, he seized the narrow, hollow pincerlike jaws of the guardian and tried to force them from his body, but those relentless hooks closed even more tightly, puncturing his buckskin shirt and entering his skin. A searing pain enveloped him. To his horror, he felt a pulling sensation against his internal tissues and realized that the creature was sucking through those foul tubes. He pushed against the pincers with desperation. Little by little, he thrust them out of his skin, getting them free of his body. He held them at arm's length. With a sickening snapping sound, they broke from the face of the guardian and fell to the ground.

The guardian wavered, its entire exoskeleton trembling in pain. It began backing away on its six short legs. Bishop leapt forward, thrusting his hand under the wing shell, seizing the short antennae. Twisting with his other hand, he managed to turn the thing onto its back. It lay there rocking, its short legs writhing impotently. Bishop backed away, his hands defensively thrust out, inadvertently aiming the Riika in the process.

White-hot fire leapt from the device and slammed into the creature, roasting it while it writhed in silent agony. And then as if the Riika was saving the last of its energy for the coup de grâce, the guardian was suddenly blown to ash and whirling cinders. The Riika-flame flickered and died in that very moment.

Bishop slumped in fatigue but marveled at what had just occurred. The Riika had never done *that* before. There had been signs of its Old Earth magic, but nothing as awesome as destroying an antagonist—and that without direct contact. The initial pain of the punctures subsided somewhat and then miraculously vanished all together as the new, right arm device vibrated slightly. Apparently the insect delivered no more poison than its young. Bishop shakily stood, grabbed the torch, and moved quickly away from the thick, sooty cloud of sickening stench from the incinerated creature. A sound in the darkness caused him stop and turn. From the tunnel behind him, yet another guardian stalked toward him, its nippers clicking in agitation.

Bishop quickly moved off back down the tunnel and away from the battle scene as the second guardian sniffed and poked at smoldering ash heap.

Bishop scrambled along a narrow tunnel, frequently looking over his shoulder. The insect was not following—yet. He pushed his strength to put distance between himself and the creature. The tunnel went on without another intersection for some distance. Now and then it broke out of its walls into a large cave, where it formed a suspended walkway across chasms whose depths were lost in darkness. Sunlight filtered down into the big caves through hidden openings somewhere high above. In the faint light of the tunnel, Bishop could make out a lower level. A hexagonal doorway led to a stone stairway, narrow and downwardly curving, but quite open and slightly illuminated.

The biomechs that dwelled below had no desire to come up, and the guardians would not dare to go down. Bishop went on, armed with the three words of Old Earth power that the female insect had given him. They sat like swallowed nuggets of molten gold in his throat, invocations not fit for modern human beings to summon. Bishop cautiously descended the curving stairs.

As he had been instructed, he counted the turnings of the stair, and stopped on what should be the last, before the source of light ahead could come into his view. There he drew in his breath and said, clearly and loudly, pausing after each word, the three words of power.

With the first word, the air fell still. Before, he had only thought the air was silent; there had been a certain quiet murmuring that he was not aware of until it ceased.

With the second word, the light in the room was dimmed and the air became fresh and ordinary, whereas before Bishop had only thought that it was without odor. Time began to make itself felt so that Bishop perceived the immense age of the rock around him. Then time seemed to grind to a halt.

The third word of power seemed to hang forever on his tongue, but when he at last had said it, time flowed on once more, as it should. The light before him grew brighter. A certain rippling watery reflection had vanished and it was now steady, whereas before Bishop had only thought that it was so.

With that, Bishop went on down, walking into the final room. The vaulted chamber was round and high, perhaps twenty meters across. Bishop gazed warily at the far side of the chamber. There, motionless and curled as if in sleep, sat the three light-shifter beasts, shimmering as if radiating intense heat. With a shudder, he pulled his gaze away from them and moved silently past. Just as the female Ikonian had said, the command words had worked their magic.

Bishop could not help but stare at the beasts as he passed. Grotesque beyond imagination, they looked like giant malformed wingless bats that had been sheathed in Old Earth armor plating. Thick cables and eon-tarnished wiring wrapped about the beasts, connecting their metal-scaled bodies and internal parts to the collars that controlled them. Vented ports in the armor steamed and hissed as if to denote some hidden furnace deep within the biomechs, a furnace that lay banked but ready. Ahead of Bishop, set clearly in the far wall, was the exit. Dim natural light cast its welcome glow upon the floor. Bishop had made it through the lower tunnels and into the forestland below Terus Kor.

TWELVE

THE KEY

> But one must the charge be, and one the call.
> Who from the dust shall awaken us all?
> One but to sever the distant doom.
> And now shall the sleeper arise from his tomb.
> —Vena Korela,
> Saga of Ukko, Runa 41

Around noon, three days after escaping the twelfth nest below the dead city of Terus Kor, an uneasy premonition began to slowly invade Bishop's thoughts. The colossal trees of the mountain forests had thinned in several spots, and in these areas grassy meadows had grown, affording him a rather good view in several directions. At the top of a grassy rise, he looked back into the northern forest behind him and caught sight of a distant figure following him.

At first, he tried to convince himself that he had mistaken some kind of beast randomly crossing his path. But a few minutes later he looked back and saw the same figure still on his track, only now significantly closer.

It's nothing. Nothing at all, Bishop thought, as he slowed to study the moving point in the distance.

Not yet seriously convinced the creature was truly following him, he climbed the next low hill and again looked back, this time pausing for several minutes, studying his pursuer. As he watched, his indifference vanished.

"I should have known Reaver would not give up so easily," Bishop muttered darkly as he backed away from the rise.

He was forced to admit that the thing following him was either an Ikonian or something very similar. The approaching figure was gaining ground rapidly. Furthermore, it moved with a smooth gliding motion that Bishop tried to assure himself was an illusion caused by the rippling grass that hid the figure's feet. It was no illusion; the figure was an Ikonian soldier, fully armored and utterly deadly.

Even the slowest, weakest Ikonian was more than a match for the most powerful human, or so Thirty-Six had casually imparted during Bishop's captivity. Bishop instinctively lifted the Riika. He did not yet consider it a weapon to be trusted, but what other choice did he have?

Sweat trickled down Bishop's forehead as he looked around helplessly at the empty grassland, the few scattered trees—none near enough to be of any help—and the vacant sapphire sky overhead. He was being stalked by a creature well over two meters tall, at least ten times his strength, and easily twice as fast, and he had no place to hide and no place to run.

Reaver wanted Bishop back, and more importantly, Reaver wanted the key Bishop now carried against his will. Bishop did not want to fight. The air was sweet, the sun warm, and he had no desire whatsoever to perish.

He frantically tried to think of anything else that might give him an advantage, however slight, and tried to determine whether any spot within range might be better than another. He could see nothing that would help. He was going to meet the Ikonian on the open grassland no matter what he did, and one part of it seemed no different from another.

Determined not to flee, he was sure, after a long discussion with Kiel, that the Ikonians had no compunction about killing from behind. If he were to die, he preferred to die facing his foe. The Ikonian paused about a hundred meters in front of him and watched him, its expressionless iridescent eyes glinting in the noonday sun. Bishop, realizing that the Ikonian was well within range of his Riika, decided to attack.

He leveled the Old Earth weapon just as he had done with the guardian, and fired. A ribbon of white-hot energy leapt out of the device and washed over the Ikonian's body, momentarily concealing it from sight. Bishop concentrated the energy beam as long as he could before it drained his strength. The ribbon reddened, sputtered, and then ceased altogether, leaving him reeling from the effort. Exhaustion was apparently the Riika's price, for its power source was, in fact, his body as revealed by the female Ikonian.

The soldier stood motionless, steaming hot but mostly undamaged, its natural armor too thick and tough even for his Old Earth magic. The Riika had failed.

A translator crackled to life, "human, you are being unwise. If you do not surrender, I will be forced to damage you," the Ikonian's translator device crackled out. "Reaver wishes you to return to the twelfth nest, and he will not be put off."

Bishop was not going back to Terus Kor after having made it this far. A life of imprisonment, even if Reaver didn't kill him outright, would be no life at all.

As Bishop faced the Ikonian knight and readied himself for the inevitable attack, he felt a peculiar sensation in his right arm. Chancing a quick glance, his eyes fell on the key device given to him by the female. In that instant, he felt a stabbing pain from the alien mechanism, as if his wrist had been seized in an iron grip.

Never before had Bishop experienced anything like what now tore through him. His body burned with the heat of a hundred suns and froze with the iciness of space, only a hundred times colder. He swept down into the deepest pits of agony and up to the highest crags of pleasure. Bone by bone, vein by vein, cell by cell, he felt his body disintegrate and come together again. Through the fiery bloodred mists, he heard his own voice screaming, and then it was over. The entire experience had taken only a split second of time, yet he felt it had lasted an eternity.

Bishop pondered with a clearness of mind that was new and strange to him. As for that, all his sensations were now new and strange. He felt as if he had awakened from a monstrously long sleep, as if cobwebs that had unknowingly clogged his mind all his life had been instantly brushed away.

The Ikonian advanced, and Bishop, still shaking from the effects of the key, unsheathed and gripped the sword, its handle compressing and nearly crushing like putty in his grasp. Bishop, stunned, looked down dumbfounded at the weapon and, with a shock, noticed his corded biceps standing out like knots of iron on arms that seemed not his own.

The air was suddenly supercharged with dynamic tension.

Bishop carefully gripped the sword and once again began cautiously advancing toward the Ikonian soldier. The insect, unsurprised by the charge, leisurely folded back its upper forearms, exposing the two deadly scythe-like blades beneath. As he closed, Bishop swung his sword at the Ikonian's throat. As he expected, the Ikonian's blades shot up and deflected the intended blow. What he did not expect, however, was his sword, his arm, reacting as if on its own.

In a blur, the rigid shaft twisted around, intercepting the attacking blades and striking down diagonally, stabbing into the Ikonian's chitinous shoulder. The Ikonian's accelerator hissed; yellow sparks shot from the wound as it shimmered and healed.

Bishop stared, dumbfounded. He had drawn first blood from an Ikonian soldier. The Ikonian, seemingly as shocked as Bishop, stepped back and assumed a defensive posture. Bishop looked at his sword and the arm that held it. Had it truly been him and not a magically possessed sword? He and the Ikonian stood scarcely a meter apart, both warily watching Bishop's weapon as if it were an animate being. But no, he knew that he had moved of his own accord. The elixir of the key was coursing through his veins, altering him, transforming him.

The Ikonian was the first to press the attack; it brought its arm blades down toward Bishop's head, apparently not troubled by its healing shoulder. Bishop's blade shot up to meet the blades, then beat them back, slipping around the Ikonian's hands and into the side of its elbow. There was a shorter hissing sound this time as the blade penetrated, followed by a single yellow flash and the oozing of the creature's greenish blood. Bishop's blade and the hand that gripped it paused in midair and seemed to vibrate with expectation.

The Ikonian was not so indecisive, it attacked. For a moment, Bishop was unable to visually follow what happened, even though his own left hand was a part of the fight. At first the Ikonian was attacking, and then it was defending as Bishop's blade met every attack and retaliated, pressing home its own assault, all in a blur of motion far too fast for the human eye to follow. Bishop's blade never allowed so much as the fraction of a second the Ikonian would have needed to step back out of reach. Greenish hemolymph flowed down the Ikonian's front from a dozen wounds, now shimmering in a vain attempt to heal.

Then, abruptly, it was all over. Bishop found himself on one knee, his arm awkwardly twisted with his sword driven through the Ikonian's chest at an odd angle. Bishop stared in dismay; he had no doubt found the creature's vitals, yet it still lived. He tried to pull the sword free. Four chitinous hands grabbed it. Bishop's blade writhed, ripping open the insect's chest, almost splitting the thing into two halves.

The Ikonian's hands fell away, and the creature toppled backward, sliding off the blade and crumpling into a broken heap. The creature's accelerator hissed and its entrails flickered with an eerie foxfire, but the damage was beyond the device's ability to heal. Slowly the hissing of the accelerator faded, as did the shimmering effect, and then the body of the Ikonian lay dead.

Bishop's wrist ached, his muscles not being used to such punishment. He sank to a sitting position and stared at the corpse, half afraid it would return to life. A bird sang overhead, and crickets chirped in the dry late autumn grass.

Bishop had killed an Ikonian soldier.

As Bishop again moved south and the day waned, the initial supercharging effects of the key ebbed and dissipated, leaving him feeling brittle and strangely weightless, even though he was sure he had returned to his natural state. Still, it seemed that he had been permanently changed in some way, that the key apparently had had some lasting effects upon his body. For one, his senses were considerably sharper than they had been before the event. The first change that became apparent was his eyesight. Night descended and the ancient waning gibbous moon rode up through the vaulted sky on the eastern horizon, the gloom of the hills and forestlands seeming to become bathed in a weird bluish-green half-light. All around him were suggestions of sharpened hearing, eyesight, smell, and awareness, like a cat or night bird. Crickets chirped in the grass; rustling sounds gave away the slithering of a snake; the wind moved through the upper branches of the forest; a bird took flight. There were other changes beyond the standard senses. For one, he now possessed a keen sensation of things that could not be discerned by the eyes, ears, or nose. He knew, without fully understanding how, that somewhere far behind, more Ikonian soldiers were following. They were following him as surely as the more tangible nocturnal creatures moved around him. He knew there were more closing in. Surely, one soldier could be overcome with the key, but two? three?

Now in places there were ruined works of stone and iron beside the path, mounds of green growth topped with slender birch and fir sighing in the wind.

Soon, a deep pool of water, clear as crystal, stood in Bishop's way. A freshet fell over a stone lip and ran, glistening and gurgling, down a steep rocky channel, its bubbling water plunging over green-hued stone. Trout, now clearly visible, sat warily in the black shallows under overhanging fern and bracken. Bishop waded across and allowed himself to be drawn toward and over the diminutive falls. *Yes, this will—should—slow the Ikonians a bit,* he thought, *and allow me to evade them a bit longer if I am lucky.* Below the falls, the scenery began to change as more and more suggestions of ancient civilization slid by.

Bishop knew that this area he was entering must be an Old Earth metropolis that had long ago been abandoned. He would be forced to travel through the perimeter if he did not exit the water. Creeping out again, he continued into the gloom.

Shortly, he had again entered the great pine forests of the northern Eligor Empire. The silence of the woods lay like a brooding cloak about Bishop as he woodenly shambled on. The black shadows seemed fixed, immovable, with the weight of superstition that overhung this forgotten backcountry. Vague ancestral dreads stirred at the back of Bishop's mind, for he had been told tales of these forbidden zones of destruction in his youth, and the ensuing years had not erased their shadows, tales of black shapes stalking the midnight glades—ghosts of the Others.

Cursing these childish memories, Bishop quickened his pace. The dim trail wound tortuously between dense walls of giant trees and was choked with rotting stumps and new growth. The sensation of the Ikonian soldiers pursuing him returned, even stronger than before. He had to find a place to hide—and soon.

THIRTEEN

THE LEVIATHAN

> Through hush of wood, it calls to me. Through graying stillness, autumn morn, ancient knowledge holds the key from times when winds and stars were born.
>
> —Vena Korela,
> Saga of Sampoe, Runa 76

Through the gray fog and mists of the forest, Bishop saw a thin slit of blackness between two massive slabs of rock resting against the low cliff he had been walking parallel to, and sprinted toward it. An unknown number of Ikonian soldiers were closing in on his trail, and he knew it was only a matter of hours before they would appear out of the gloom and discover him.

Bishop had become aware of them shortly after his first encounter with the lone soldier in the open grasslands behind him. He could not hope to overpower a squad of them; the single Ikonian he had faced in the plains behind him had nearly spelled his doom. He squeezed himself into the black cleft in the rocky rise that gaped before him. At least here he was protected on three sides, and who knew, maybe the cave and rock surrounding it would throw his pursuers off the trail.

Searching the sky one last time, Bishop sighed in futile despondency. There had been no sign of the wolf-bird since well before his capture above the Twelfth Colony. Bishop was sure Storm Singer had given up on him long ago and flown back to the protectorate. He didn't blame the bird. What choice had he in the matter? Bishop had given up on himself long before the wolf-bird would have. It was miraculous that he had even escaped and gotten this far.

Stooping, Bishop entered the darkness and found himself in a narrow chamber surrounded by rock, utterly dark save for the feeble twilight that came through the cleft. The uneven floor of the cave was strewn with litter blown in by centuries of wind or carried in by birds and other small animals. Dead leaves, pine needles, twigs, a few scattered bones and chips of rock. There was nothing in all this detritus that could be used as a weapon but just possibly nothing was needed. Here in the darkness, he just might be safe.

Moving as far back into the cave as possible, Bishop began exploring the walls with outstretched hands. His questing fingers told him that here were chisel marks on the stone, forming cryptic glyphs in some unknown writing. Soon he came to another opening. He groped his way through this portal and into the blackness. His searching fingers told him that here there seemed to be smooth angular walls as if this was a man-made creation and not quite so natural as he originally suspected.

He had to stoop to wedge himself through the inner opening, and again he noted the angular nature. Beyond the opening, he could once more stand erect. He paused, listening warily. Although the silence was absolute, some sense seemed to warn him that he was not alone in the chamber. It was nothing he could see, hear, or smell, but was more a sense of presence.

Bishop's forest-trained ears, listening for echoes, told him that this inner chamber was much larger than the outer one. The place had an oily, acrid fug, as if from a foundry or a smithy. His feet, cautiously placed, encountered objects scattered on the floor, objects he could feel but not see. It was not forest litter; these objects had a man-made aspect to them.

Bishop suddenly remembered something, his Old Earth torch, the outlandish device the Ikonian female had given him: he still had it buried in his pack. A bit of rummaging brought the apparatus to his hands. He extracted it and quickly depressed the blister that brought forth its magic.

The hair lifting from the nape of his neck, Bishop felt his skin prickle with a supernatural thrill. At the far end of the chamber sat an immense metal object, leering at him from the shadows.

With a startled yelp, Bishop jumped back against the wall and gripped his sword. Then, realization slowly replaced his alarm. The thing at the far end of the chamber stood as motionless and as cold as the mountain that entombed it.

Bishop lowered his sword and stared, dumbfounded. "Gods of the Others," he muttered in awe.

Gods of the Others indeed. The ancient machinery of the Others was not common in the present age, but Bishop had seen enough to recognize Old Earth artifacts when confronted with them, though this monster that loomed over him was by far the largest such creation he had ever laid eyes on. Many saw technology as some dark form of magic, a thing to be avoided with superstitious dread, and Bishop could not find many faults with that view now that he was confronted with an immense example of it. Only the gods of the Others knew what this thing was and, more importantly, what it had been designed to do.

With slow steps, Bishop approached the thing, walking twice around it, keeping a cautious distance from the mountain of Old Earth metal that was pocked and pitted with the passing of eons.

Except for the impression that it gave of enormous and mysterious power, this thing before him seemed dead, long dead. Dust and detritus from countless centuries coated it like a gray funeral shroud. The immense form before him was a giant flattened metal lozenge with smooth regular curves resembling a massive metallic crab. It was built low to the ground for something of its massive size. There were no outward clues to its purpose other than several thick metal pods projecting from either side of an upper blister. Bishop noted that at its very top was a small multifaceted glassy protrusion that disturbingly resembled the eye of an insect. There were also several whiplike antennae arranged in rows, which again brought an insect to Bishop's mind.

The thing did not have any wheels like a cart or wagon, which perplexed Bishop all the more, as it seemed that this mechanism was designed for movement. Obviously, the utility lay in six massive crab-like legs, three on either side of the main body, on which it sat.

On the dull metal of one flank, painted small in relation to the beast's size, but with Old Earth precision, was a gauntleted hand grasping a cluster of thunderbolts. Under this symbol, the following was written in cryptic glyphs:

> Lëviâthân
> Modûs VII

The meaning of the words and the language were both unknown to Bishop.

Now, holding his breath, Bishop ventured to put out a hand and touch the thing. Nothing seemed to happen from the touch except a cascade of dust that caused him to sneeze. He stood back and looked around at the rest of the cave with renewed interest.

What Bishop took to be the front of the chamber, he now realized, was a curtain of ancient articulated metal resting on two vertical tracks at either end of the opening, an opening that was just the right size to permit the monster's passage, if in fact the thing was ever intended to move. There were imperfections in the joints as if the great panels had sagged over the eons. Through these gaps, a small heap of pebbly dirt had trickled to the floor. There had to have been several tons of rock that, in some distant period, had slid down from the upper cliff and over the front of the doors, forever sealing the metal beast in its ageless crypt.

The thin portal Bishop had come through must have been created only to allow the passage of humans. And it was only by accident that it, too, had not been covered as was the larger door. Bishop now wondered at the true nature of the cliff line he had been following for the last several hours.

The danger of the outer world was momentarily forgotten as Bishop walked around the Old Earth juggernaut again, running his hand along its surface as powdery dust rained down. On this circuit he paid much more attention to details. He suspected that this thing was not in fact magical, as many of Merja Soria would have attested, but still there was a sense of colossal power that was just as unsettling. Bishop had seen the miraculous abilities of his own Riika and Reaver's converter and wondered how much more powerful this thing before him could possibly be.

High on the armored flank, just above the upper level of the six armored legs it sat upon, was a barely perceptible circular line that suggested a close-fitting door. Recessed in this circle was what looked like a handle that might be used to tug it open, if in fact it was a door.

And now Bishop noticed several small rungs fused into the solid metal and ascending to the top of the blister like a ladder. He took a deep breath and climbed. The grip on the door accepted his hand easily. He pulled. His first tug was met with resistance, as was the second. When he dared use all his strength to pull the handle, the ancient door yielded with the begrudging groan of long-unoiled metal. The door, incredibly thick, swung slowly open on a massive recessed hinge. A barely audible click sounded somewhere within the depths of the metal beast, and light streaked out of the door like the blinding rays of the sun.

Bishop stumbled away from the lid, dropping his Old Earth torch, which bounced off the metal beast and went spiraling off into the gloom. "Gods! The Old Ones must have enjoyed terrorizing their subjects with unexpected light."

He waited tensely, but nothing else happened. Bishop finally chose to take the light as a favorable sign and relaxed somewhat, marveling at the balance of the massive door that he had opened, so massive that he was sure if it were laid upon the ground, he would not be able to budge it.

What powers the Others must have employed merely to forge this monstrous brooding beast, let alone one with such potential power and complexity. It staggered the imagination. Not for the first time, Bishop shuddered at the thought of those strange primordial beings. He paused with his eyes just below the lower rim of the doorway. The shapes inside were of a perplexing variety and at first seemed utterly strange. Printed or graven symbols, none of which Bishop could read, were sprinkled thickly everywhere, suggesting a level of complexity difficult to remember even for those employed as operators.

Nothing moved. Nothing was clearly menacing. The light came from panels that glowed just like the artificial lights of Bishop's cell under Terus Kor and like the Old Earth torch. And just like those artificial lights, these as well radiated no noticeable heat. Bishop reasoned that the technology was of the same type.

Descending until he was halfway into the doorway, Bishop listened. From somewhere deep within the mass of metal came a faint murmuring, something like the sound of the wind through the trees, or possibly a whispering voice. Wind it was, for stale air was now moving out through the doorway, past Bishop's face, generated from small round vents positioned at even intervals along a strikingly clean inner corridor.

Bishop sat in the doorway a little longer, probing the strangeness with alert eyes. Surprisingly, the open space within the Old Earth device was not very big in comparison to its outer size. Two or three men could pretty well fill it and still be crowded in the narrow corridor.

A movement at the far end of the outer tunnel suddenly caught Bishop's attention. Something had passed in front of the dim light leaking in from the outer cave. Something was stirring out there. His eyes focused on several slender shadows, and his hackles prickled anew. Ikonians had entered the outer cave and discovered him.

Three, possibly four Ikonian soldiers were now cautiously working their way through the inner portal toward him, cornering him in the back of the chamber. Without thought, Bishop climbed into the metal beast, closed the massive door, and secured it by means of a wheel assembly, thankfully rather simple and understandable in its workings. A very slight scratching could now be heard. Bishop imagined that the Ikonians were now scrambling over the top of the beast, furiously attempting to locate a way in. Bishop's eyes frantically moved around the interior, afraid another opening would allow entry. Mercifully, he saw none. He was safe for the moment, but to what end? He was trapped as effectively as he would have been on the outside, but he seemed to be safe for the moment. The faint scratching continued as thorny hands ineffectually tore at the sealed door above him.

For a moment, Bishop crouched inside the beast, not knowing what else to do. As his panic slowly subsided, he began to look around the interior more closely. The cold lights above him continued to operate as if the thing somehow knew he was there.

Here and there were signs that the Others had built this great thing of metal for human beings. The narrow path was well provided with what appeared to be handrails, and from some of the fixed and peculiar objects, there extended several protrusions that appeared to be levers, made to fit the grip of human hands. Two objects that had puzzled Bishop at first he now realized to be squat metal seats, apparently fastened firmly to the flooring. They were low and stoutly made, sitting on either side of the main aisle, appearing to be facing the front of the metal giant.

With increasing boldness, Bishop made his way to the forward chair and sat down, the cushioned material as supple as the day it had been manufactured. The scraping sounds of the Ikonians could still be heard.

It was with the greatest effort that he ignored the closed and bolted door behind him.

Directly in front of Bishop, several flat black glass plates were arranged in a semicircle around the two seats. Nothing could be seen under or through them, and he wondered if it was a cover of some type. He felt around the perimeter of a lower plate, roughly hand-sized and rounded, made of the same material and found nothing that suggested it was meant to detach. The glass was cool. He laid his hand flat against it.

Suddenly the glass flashed, and a thin white line quickly traced his opened palm. Bishop jerked his hand away in alarm as unreadable glyphs began to appear under the glassy surface, glowing like red fire seen under several centimeters of ice:

IÂT UIPI LÂNNËT

Then, below these glyphs, another indecipherable message appeared:

UIPI LUOTËHËT ËTËLÂT

A terrible whining came from deep within the metal beast's belly. Shortly, the whining intensified, turning into a groan as if the thing were in agony. Bishop, half stricken with alarm, rose from his chair as the groan escalated into a single shuddering roar. "Uipi kâikki ilmân rânnët!"

The screen flickered in response as more and more lights twinkled on, followed by a din of beeps and chirps as if there resided a host of tortured birds and insects behind each of the glass plates. A dizzying array of symbols began to appear on one of the screens, no doubt imparting a torrent of information that was of no use to Bishop in the present age.

Bishop would have fled but for the fact that he would have never gotten past the Ikonian soldiers swarming without. He sat back in the chair and waited, all his old fears concerning the Old Earth and its nameless magic welling up in his throat like vomit. A series of four bloodred elongated U-shaped symbols appeared beneath one of the glass screens. The screens began to fill with green light one by one until they were full. Then another message flashed:

Tuskissa tulisen synnyn!

Again and again came the flashing glyphs:

Riekka! Riekka! Riekka!

Underneath this message, a small square symbol with a single glyph at its center appeared, flashing rhythmically. It was clear to Bishop that he was required to touch it. With the greatest hesitancy, he did so. He experienced another brief spasm of fear once the series of interlocking glass plates above the single rounded plate began shimmering like water. But soon this shimmering cleared away, and Bishop found that by some devilish power he was now looking through the surface of the glass plates as if they were windows. He could now plainly see, in a bizarre greenish ghostly twilight, the outer chamber around the metal monster and a cluster of Ikonians milling about at the front of the cave. They seemed as alarmed as he, their movements being uncertain and erratic. Bishop hoped they would scatter, but they seemed intent on waiting him out.

A thin red X now appeared as if suspended in the air before him. With wonderment, he realized it centered on whatever he looked at, as if it had become part of his eyes. In fear, he closed his eyes, and with relief the crossed lines disappeared. Reopening them caused the crosshairs to jerk to his new eye position, steadying themselves. This had to be a weapon of some kind, but nothing seemed to happen when he focused his sight on each of the Ikonian soldiers before him.

There had to be another switch. Bishop, frantically looking around, saw a lever placed in such a fashion as to act as a sort of grip for his right hand: it was molded into the arm of his chair. The grip reminded him of a crossbow he had once handled as a youth, complete with trigger. Bishop grabbed the lever and squeezed.

The effect was immediate and awesome. There came to Bishop's ears the sound of a muffled thunderclap. He looked up just in time to see searing knives of white-hot energy lance out of the forward pods in the upper blister and slam into the wall above the milling Ikonians. A perfect circular hole appeared in the wall and the rock behind it as if they had been casually punched out of paper. Rock, dust, and detritus rained down all about the Ikonians from the concussion that still rumbled through the mountainside.

The Ikonians jerked in agitated surprise, bringing their weapons up toward the great doors behind them, not realizing where the blast had originated. Bishop, now understanding something of the beast's power, centered his eyes on the first soldier and again squeezed the trigger.

There was another bright flash as if the sun had exploded, and when Bishop could see again, there was one fewer Ikonian in the chamber and a correspondingly ragged hole behind its last position. The others were crouched in confusion, their antennae dancing in anxiety. But before they could recover, Bishop targeted them and squeezed the trigger again. The remaining Ikonians were vaporized one by one with seemingly no more effort than snuffing out a candle.

Though relieved, this cold, bloodless method of dealing death was disturbing to Bishop. For the first time in his adult life, he felt ashamed of the momentary thrill of limitless and forbidden power. Within seconds, nothing remained in the cave except sand, gravel, and bits of daylight pouring into the chamber from the multiple holes neatly punched into the forward metal door. A cloud of smoke swirled in wraithlike eddies and then dissipated slowly through the openings as fresh air invaded the stale room.

After several long moments, Bishop's thoughts returned to him. This machine was definitely a weapon, yes, probably even more destructive than the Reaver threat. If only it could be brought back to Merja Soria—for proper study, if nothing else. Its power seemed limitless. He could not simply leave it behind unprotected. More soldiers were sure to follow, and when they did, they would discover this device and unlock its secrets just as he had done. And Bishop was sure that Reaver would not struggle with his conscience as he had done.

The immense Old Earth mechanism had to be as heavy as a small hill, but Bishop figured that it must move somehow. There was another grip on the left side of the armrest. When Bishop grabbed it and squeezed the trigger, the thrumming sound beneath him, which had gradually been smoothing itself down to a lower level, came swelling up again. Vibrating with immeasurable power, the metal beast rose on all six legs about two meters off the ground as if lifted by an invisible hand. Bishop marveled at the power he now possessed. He was sure that if someone were on the outside, they would now be able to move the entire mountain of Old Earth metal with the touch of a finger.

At either side of Bishop's head, the miraculous glass plates allowed him to perceive that the six legs, now standing fully upright, were now poised to carry the bulk of the machine forward exactly as if it were an immense crab. How this was possible was well beyond Bishop's understanding. Further, as Bishop looked to the far left and as the red x touched the far end of the left side of the screen, the entire upper pod swiveled to rest on the left side of the cave, further movement of his eyes allowed Bishop to actually spin the massive upper pod, with him remaining motionless, all the way around to where it had first been sitting, the red x facing the front of the cave as well as the entire upper pod assembly.

Bishop nudged the lever forward. The huge mount thrummed as if in rage, and charged. The doors loomed in the vision screen, and Bishop heard the metal barrier give way, peeling back with no more resistance than paper peeling away from an ancient book. Boulders the size of a small house tumbled away from him as if they were made of gossamer. In sheer terror, Bishop released the grip, and just as quickly, his mount slowed and settled to a stop, now well outside the cave from which he had started.

He was safe and free. For the first time since his escape from Ikonia, he could truly relax. With gaining confidence, Bishop again took hold of the left grip and pulled its trigger. The mechanism responded, smoother now that he understood something of how it was to be employed. The monster levitated and began moving more rapidly over the ground of the dark forest. For once, Bishop was not afraid of what he might chance upon. At this speed he would reach the Gondakar Barrier and home within a matter of days instead of weeks.

Mammoth trees silently slid past the vision screens as Bishop rode the Old Earth beast toward the human frontier. Even for its massive size, it still had to be herded around some of the more immobile flora, as some of the ancient trees were quite beyond even its near-invincible ability to conquer. Ancient beyond imagination, the old giants seemed to look down on Bishop in silent, uncaring contempt.

As the novelty of the great Old Earth device began to wane, Bishop allowed himself the occasional luxury of glancing about the inner control housing he occupied. The cold black glass-like panels shimmered with red, blue, and green sparks of light, appearing like the evening sky filled with multicolored stars, all seeming to answer unknown questions, questions the Others must have posed to the metal beast in the distant past. Bishop could only hope it was not necessary to interpret them.

Now the forest began to change from the cold upper pine-laden slopes to the wetter, warmer vegetation more prevalent in the lower valleys. Bishop surmised he was closing on the Moeras Kor Depression, the massive swamp Kiel had warned him of, an area he would have normally avoided at all costs. Yet its gently sloped sides would allow his metal mount to move forward easily, whereas the rocky, heavily treed mountain perimeter would not. The smaller brushy growth surrounding Moeras Kor would be no match for his Old Earth ride.

Late in the day, the great pines finally gave way to the blackened stunted scrub that marked the borders of the Moeras Kor Depression. With some reluctance, Bishop steered his mount down into the gloom. At about halfway to what he surmised was the bottom of the marsh, he turned the beast to a new heading that would carry him on a generally southern course parallel to the swampy bottomland.

Night finally descended, but through the vision screen Bishop could see the darkened world around him as if the sun still shone. Some power within the screen bathed the night in an eerie greenish half-light as it had done within the beast's lair. On into the stygian gloom he traveled, secure in the safety of this metal fortress. Yet although the beast was tireless, Bishop was not. Around midnight, he found himself nodding in the seat. Finally, after smashing a rather good-sized tree to the forest floor, Bishop decided that he desperately needed rest. He no longer feared his ride, but he was afraid that he might draw more unwanted attention to his path. He quieted the monster by reversing the method he had used to wake it. The beast once again settled ponderously to the earth as the six immense armored metal legs folded and settled the main body to the forest floor. Slowly, the thrumming of power vibrating around Bishop quieted and then ceased, the machine settling again into slumber.

Bishop wearily climbed out of the chair and walked to the back of the cramped hallway. Here he curled up on the slightly warm metal floor and fell into a surprisingly deep sleep.

It was the cold metal that finally woke Bishop. The flooring had cooled overnight to an uncomfortable degree. Feeling stiff but much refreshed, Bishop again made his way to the front of the great metal device and sat in the seat, where he reactivated the vision screens. Something had apparently malfunctioned during the night because half the screens had darkened. Now, Bishop could see the landscape through only eight or ten centimeters at the tops of the screens. Muttering, he reawakened the beast by moving the handgrip forward, yet as he did so, he felt the thing lurch slightly. The ten centimeters of the vision screen became six. And why did he feel like his seat was tilting? But now the ground was uneven, and the dividing line on his screen became diagonal and slowly crept upward.

Bishop began looking about the interior for some sign of trouble. The twinkling lights glittered at him silently, presenting no help at all. Suddenly he saw a black shape flash and settle on the upper part of the dividing line on one of the vision screens.

It was Storm Singer! The bird was running around on the upper visible part of the vision screen, picking at the dividing line between visible light and blackness, pulling up beak after beak of black muck as he did so.

"Black gods!" Bishop yelled. He was sinking in this miserable marsh! Bishop grabbed the handgrip and frantically jerked it from side to side, then from front to back. Yet try as he might, all his moving of the handgrips seemed only to throw up great black gouts of mud either in front or behind as the beast shrieked its frustration.

Bishop was stuck.

He had to get out, even though a part of his brain screamed at him to stay and try to free the device, which could be very important to the protectorate in this time of pending crisis. Jumping out of the seat, he ran to the ladder, climbed to the hatch, and pushed. The hatch would not move.

Panic gripped him for the first time as he looked back at the vision screen just in time to see the last of the fading light slip into total blackness.

"By the Others!" Bishop barked as the beast tilted even more. On the wall next to the door was a series of buttons, at least ten. Bishop pounded on them all.

Behind him the lighted panel flickered momentarily as if in thought, then another message flashed: Annapas ajan kulua päivän mennä toisen tulla!

A sudden explosion knocked Bishop to the floor of the beast as black muck flooded in on top of him. Half stunned by the impact, he was only dimly aware of a faint patch of light pouring in with a rain of stagnant muddy water. The beast shuddered and tilted suddenly. Bishop struggled to the first rung and gripped it, his head spinning from the shock of the recent blow. He nearly blacked out as he climbed. He mustn't lose consciousness; if he were to do so, he would never again awaken. Drunkenly, he grabbed the second rung, fighting the torrents of mud that now filled the interior. The lights flickered once, then twice, then blackness engulfed him. All sounds of power began fading as the monster shuddered in its death throes. The light above Bishop was darkening; the mud was racing in to bury him alive; and he himself was losing consciousness.

With his last ounce of strength, Bishop fought the pouring mud and climbed out, dragging himself away from the boiling pool of slime. Darkness rushed in around him, and he felt himself falling into a pit of unconsciousness.

Out of the blackness a gray mist began to form. Like sap oozing from a tree in spring, consciousness seeped back into Bishop's body. He became aware of a strange sensation, as if someone were pulling him through the grass by his hair. Pulling his hair?

"Wake up, you lazy human. Wake up! This is no time for a nap!"

"Storm Singer? Where in the name of the black gods of the Others have you been?" Bishop groaned as he slowly became aware of his surroundings.

The bird continued to tug at Bishop's hair, not at first realizing he had awakened.

"All right, all right, I'm awake, buzzard! Let me alone!" Bishop barked, shooing the bird away from him impatiently.

As Bishop's vision slowly returned to him, the wolf-bird fluttered away a few meters and eyed him. "Quickly now. Move your muddy carcass away from this spot before it's too late," the wolf-bird squawked in alarm. "There is something approaching, and I know not what it is."

Storm Singer spread his black wings and took flight. Bishop had neither time to gather his thoughts nor time to even question Storm Singer. Getting painfully to his feet, he began to climb away from the mire, looking wistfully behind himself once to see if anything remained of the metal monster, but there was nothing—nothing but a black pool of stinking, bubbling muck.

"It pains the heart," Bishop muttered as the dark blotch of marsh disappeared behind him.

The trail wound away from the lower swamp and wended its way among rotting stumps, rank hummocks, and scummy, snake-haunted pools and bogs. It wasn't long, though, before Bishop began to understand the cause of Storm Singer's alarm. There was the sound of something approaching. Quickly and without thought, Bishop climbed up and hid behind a patch of monstrous fungi attached to the side of an ancient gnarled tree. Looking through a crack in this dense patch of mushrooms, he strained to look down the mist-shrouded trail as the noise grew nearer. The sound was unlike anything he had ever heard before, a strange clicking and a weird intermittent hissing as if steam was escaping from a pot left too long on the hearth.

Suddenly, a line of apparitions materialized out of the gloom on the trail below. Bishop immediately realized these creatures below him were Eligor soldiers. Five of them were walking single file down the trail in the direction from which Bishop had come. He flattened himself against the tree and froze.

Like Kiel, these Eligor were considerably larger in size than the average human. They wore the familiar bronze-colored scale armor of the empire—all too familiar to anyone who had survived the invasion and subsequent battle at Koth. Unlike Kiel, they were not wearing footwear. The brief glimpse Bishop had of their feet left the impression of appendages so formidable, boots would have been wasted on them. The strange hissing and rattling Bishop had noted earlier was nothing more than the Eligor's collective talking and muttering as they moved along. There was a graceful nature to the walk, like hardened athletes, giving the impression of all but effortlessly gliding down the misty trail, the small red circle insignia on their shoulders swaying with their marching rhythm. Bishop looked harder at those red circles. They were like Kiel's insignia.

Blast it. How am I supposed to know if these Eligor are the soldiers Kiel promised to send or some mongrel pack of ignorant lizards that'd as soon have me for lunch as help me? He needed to make contact.

Bishop was a long way from where Kiel said he would send help. Was it worth the risk? The empire was still technically at war with the protectorate, and few knew of the arrangement Bishop had with Kiel. If these were the wrong soldiers, he could quickly find himself in a fight he didn't feel capable of winning in his present condition, even with the Riika. Still, he needed to get his information to the protectorate quickly. He had lost his pack and everything in it, including a diminished supply of fungus food, compliments of Thirty-Six. It seemed a risk he had to take.

Climbing down from the tree, Bishop called out, "You there, I wonder if you could point me in the proper direction? I seem to have lost my way."

The effect was immediate. The soldiers stumbled into each other, nearly falling to the ground in a tangled pile of scale and claw. Rapidly recovering, they drew their weapons and stood tensely, facing Bishop, looking first at him and then at each other.

At last, the largest and presumably the most senior approached

Bishop. The Eligor cautiously activated his translator and spoke. "Bisop? Are you the human called Bisop?" His translator struggled, crackling.

"The name is Bishop. Got that? Bishop!" Bishop responded with a defensive growl.

"Bissss-hop. Bishhop," the Eligor repeated slowly.

"Yes, Bishop. That is correct. Gods of the Others, man, it's not that hard of a name."

"Bishop." The Eligor relaxed somewhat. "I am Subcommander J'Kra. We were sent by Kiel to retrieve you and take you safely to Opal. You are considerably farther west and south of where you should have been."

Bishop shook his head. "That is true, but I'm not going to Opal. I have to get back to the protectorate. Do you understand? Merja Soria?"

"I understand. Nevertheless, you are first to report to Kiel of the Imperial Intelligence Service. It is most important. Opal is close, only two days distant to the southeast and in between this point and the human frontier anyway. We have been long patrolling for you, as were numerous other teams. We were ready to give up until we were drawn to you by an unusual sound in the depression yonder."

Bishop saw that this Eligor would not be swayed and also that a fight was not in his best interests. He was dangerously tired, lost, and nearly starving.

"All right, fine. I'll go to meet with Kiel first. But after that, you will take me to the protectorate, got that?" Bishop stabbed a thumb in the direction he presumed to be south.

"That is acceptable." Looking over Bishop's torn, muddied, and nearly useless clothing, the Eligor added, "We have clean garments for you if you would like to change before we leave. It might be easier for you on the trail."

Bishop looked down at his rotting clothing, which was now hanging off him in threadbare rags and tatters. His clothes, having not been changed since before his capture in Terus Kor, were in the most deplorable condition.

"I accept your most gracious offer."

They shortly found a pool of relatively clean water, where Bishop peeled off his clothing and bathed, scrubbing away weeks of filth and grime. The Eligor gathered around him in unbridled fascination, apparently never having seen a human before and certainly not a naked one. One of them began to snigger, then the rest joined in.

Bishop's eyes narrowed as he turned modestly away from them. "Do you mind? A little privacy, please!"

The Eligor broke up and retreated a few paces while he completed his washing. Then he changed into the oversized black leather garments—the Eligor uniform.

"Ha-ha-ha!" came laughter from above them. "By the Great Egg in the sky! You look like an ill-fed Eligor nestling."

Storm Singer, evidently having decided that these Eligor were not going to cause mischief after all, fluttered down to alight upon Bishop's well-padded shoulder. The Eligor jumped and resumed being on guard, not knowing what to make of the wolf-bird.

"It's all right. Storm Singer is harmless—well, unless you do not abide mites. The beast is simply stiff with them."

The Eligor again gathered around Bishop, this time to ogle the raven. "It is tame?" one of them asked, reaching out to pet Storm Singer.

"As tame as you could ever hope a moth-eaten bird to be, I suppose."

Storm Singer, ignoring Bishop's verbal jabs, hopped from Eligor to Eligor, drinking in the attention, as they momentarily forgot where they were.

"All right now, let's get going," Bishop grumbled. "This isn't a picnic; the flying rat isn't a celebrity, as much as he might think he is; and I would like to conclude this ill-fated adventure and be done with it."

Soon they were on the trail and moving away from the outskirts of the great marsh and toward Imperial Opal, somewhere to the southeast. While Storm Singer flitted from Eligor to Eligor, chatting with them as if they were long-lost nest-mates, Bishop kept quiet. These were, after all, Eligor soldiers and not the sort he would have chosen himself as trail-mates.

Storm Singer finally returned to Bishop's shoulder and settled down. "You are not the easiest human to locate. You should have taken my advice and stayed with me. If it had not been for that terrible ruckus you made in your Old Earth contraption, I would have given you up for lost and flown home for yuletide."

Bishop scowled at the bird. "Fat lot of good you've done me on this ill-thought-out trip so far. What was I to do, send up smoke signals?"

Storm Singer began casually preening his feathers. "Very well, the next time you are trapped, I might just have a mind to leave you to your own devices."

Bishop steamed in frustration. The bird had saved him again, and try as he might, he could not find any fault in the creature. "I am sorry. I do not wish to be ungrateful. Thank you for your help, and thank you for not giving me up for lost. I appreciate it, and I owe you a great debt."

Storm Singer ruffled and nuzzled Bishop. "You are my human. How could I be expected to do any less?"

"*Your* human?" Bishop cried, but for the life of him he could not think of any response to the outrageous comment. He stalked down the trail after the Eligor, Storm Singer bobbing in rhythm all the while—or was it silent laughter?

Before long, a young, bandy-legged Eligor about Bishop's height, but painfully thin even by human standards, began to make himself known. It seemed the gangly Eligor youngster could not keep his eyes off Bishop. It wasn't long before the Eligor began to bombard him with questions.

"What is it like in the protectorate?" the Eligor, whose name Bishop learned was Pa Kar, finally asked in unbridled curiosity.

"Oh, you know, it's a place," Bishop responded dully.

"Like the Eligor Empire?"

"Yup."

"How are humans born? Are they hatched from eggs like we Eligor are?"

"Yup."

"What are human females like?"

"Oh, you know, like females everywhere, I suppose."

"Like Eligor females?"

"Sort of. Probably a bit more vicious."

"More vicious than Eligor females?"

"Yup."

On and on, Pa Kar asked questions, one after the other. Bishop rolled his eyes. Had Kiel sent this particular young soldier purposely to torment him? Bishop moved away from the overinquisitive conscript and to the side of the subcommander.

"Tell me, J'Kra, how is old Kiel these days?"

The Eligor soldier stared at Bishop with a barely suppressed look of astonishment, as if he had misunderstood his translator.

"*Old Kiel?*"

"Yes, how is *old* Kiel these days?"

"Kiel is the first commander of the Imperial Intelligence Service of Opal. It is not proper to speak of him thus."

"Not proper?" Bishop stammered.

After several more attempts at gleaning information out of the tight-lipped J'Kra, Bishop let the matter drop and moved to the back of the column, where Pa Kar descended on him again.

"What do humans eat?"

"Food."

"What kind of food?"

"Oh, you know, just food."

"Like Eligor food? Rats and oat bread?"

"Ah, strictly oat bread. Yes, only oat bread."

Two days of travel brought them to within sight of the ramparts of Opal, a black basalt city that reared out of the forest mists and into the early winter sky. They waited for night to descend before entering the western gate, J'Kra thinking that the presence of a human strolling through the streets during the bustle of the daylight hours might cause an undue ruckus.

Bishop agreed.

The gates of the city were fashioned of bronze, green with verdigris and cast in the likeness of a winged skull—the symbol of the old empire. J'Kra presented himself to an open slit in the great doors, and the portcullis rose ponderously into the night air, allowing them to enter the dread city of Imperial Opal. Hooded and silent, Bishop followed the weary Eligor soldiers through the southern gate and into the city proper. Even in the darkness, Bishop was awed at its size.

Here everything was carved from black basalt. The architecture was simple but exacting, spiraling toward the inner city like rings within rings, dwindling tier upon tier into a tapering spire that seemed to split the stars: the Grand Union of Opal. It was a chilling sight. Bishop had heard that it was here that the final decision had been made to invade the protectorate. He was certainly the first human in centuries to see it and live to tell the tale. At least he hoped he would live to talk about it.

Through the broad, well-planned avenues of this grim city, the troop pursued its unaltered course. The city inhabitants who still walked the darkened streets stepped out of their way, casting brief incurious glances at the passing soldiers and the hooded form who accompanied them.

Amid groves of trees covered with phosphorescent flowers of scarlet, azure, and gold, the lower palace of the Grand Union loomed up before them. It consisted of one gigantic cone or spire tapering up from a squat circular base made entirely of black stone, the round tower wall coiling upward like some curious conical seashell.

Still, Bishop sensed something suggesting that all was not well within the dark city. There were signs of a rapidly prepared staging ground where boxes and supplies lay strewn and trampled. There were also indications of neglect, such as the weed-choked flower beds they passed. It was also strangely quiet, like the ghostly necropolis of Terus Kor, even considering the time of night; there were few about and there was no sign of military personnel, as if Opal had been suddenly emptied of them.

It was at the perimeter of the lower palace that J'Kra dismissed his band and led Bishop into a small courtyard garden, closing the high wrought iron gate overgrown with ivy behind them.

"I will summon Kiel. You will wait here with your bird companion." J'Kra, opening an ironbound inner door, quickly entered the building, leaving Bishop in silence.

Bishop sat down on a rock bench that faced a small water fountain issuing a crystal stream of water into a pool containing curious silver-orange fish that lazily swam at its bottom by the light of a cold and uncaring moon. Storm Singer had retired into a black ball of feathers upon Bishop's shoulder and seemed not in the slightest concerned about their location within the recent enemy's stronghold. The looming spires of the central city glittered frostily overhead, set against the starry backdrop. Not in Bishop's most bizarre nightmares would he have believed he would ever be standing in the fabled city of Opal. It was here, in this dark city, that the bulk of the Eligor army had issued forth to invade the protectorate. Somehow it didn't seem right that the Eligor had inflicted so much damage without receiving a scratch for payment in return. Now here Bishop was aiding them. The thought still irritated him, yet these creatures did not strike him as the mindless brutes depicted within the protectorate. That thought was equally as troubling.

It wasn't long before the door opened again and Kiel appeared, flanked by two IIS soldiers and Subcommander J'Kra.

"Back so soon, human? Have you lost your way? I was sure you would be gone for a full quarter cycle, if not longer."

"So soon, is it? Not soon enough, I am sure."

Kiel smiled a genuine, toothy smile and grabbed Bishop by his shoulders. "It is good to see you, Bishop. I find it strange to admit, but I have missed you."

Bishop looked up at Kiel. It was strange, but he had missed this Eligor too. A thin sheepish smile crept over his face. "It is good to see your scaly face as well, old friend."

Kiel's smile broadened. "Have you found something of import then?"

"Possibly," Bishop grumbled in thought.

Kiel's smile vanished, to be replaced by a look of expectation. "What! What have you found?"

"I have found that I do not much care for the flavor of fungus!"

Kiel's face flattened. "Very well, I see that it is going to take awhile to extract your story. Come along, human, let us retire to a dinner of fresh rat. We will forgo the sautéed mushrooms with wine sauce."

"Ah, rat! Kiel, my long-lost reptilian comrade, you remembered," Bishop purred, breaking into a smile again.

A croaking sound came from under Bishop's cloak, and two glittering eyes popped out. "If you two require an intimate moment, I can flutter off," Storm Singer croaked sleepily.

Kiel reached into the hood and scratched the bird's neck. "Keeping this human out of mischief, are you, Storm Singer?"

"One does one's best," was the bird's response.

Kiel turned to take in the subcommander, who had reappeared in the open doorway. "J'Kra, you have performed a great service to the empire. Your deeds shall not go without reward."

The Eligor soldier touched the ground and then his forehead in grave respect. "To serve the IIS is honor enough, sir," was his practiced response. Then, saluting smartly, J'Kra turned and left the ivied gate.

"Pretty important, aren't we?" Bishop said blandly as he watched J'Kra leave.

"Well, you know, human, the position has its perks."

"As I can well imagine," Bishop remarked, taking in Kiel's silver-trimmed cloak and velvet sir coat.

After entering Kiel's command bunker, Bishop recounted his fantastic tale while settling down to a golden plate filled with roasted meat—it did not appear to be rat—and a tankard of very strange Eligor ale that burned like fire on the way to his stomach, leaving him feeling strangely light-headed.

"Shades of the Others! What is this stuff?" Bishop wheezed.

"Ægir," Kiel returned jovially after taking a deep quaff. "One of the few luxuries we still possess. It involves the fermentation of barley and hops. I'm also fairly sure it is a very ancient human invention, though it would have been heresy to admit such a thing in the old days of the empire, as you can well imagine. We even sing of it: 'Ægir, you are the one. You are the one who holds with both hands the great sweetwort. Ægir, you are the one who pours out your golden gift.'" Kiel ended his song with a long mournful belch, lightly clanking his tankard against Bishop's.

Bishop guffawed despite himself. It had been a long time since he had felt true companionship with another soul. Even in the protectorate, there had been few in his life he could have called friends. How strange it was to see this Eligor as something other than the mindless ravening enemy he had first perceived him to be.

Pushing back his plate, Kiel settled himself comfortably, sipping his Ægir. "Now tell me, Bishop, this Reaver you have described. Do you believe he is a charlatan, or is it possible that he truly is some relic from the past?"

Bishop shrugged. "I would like to believe that he is a swindler, yet how he has managed to enslave the Ikonians is beyond my wits and pay grade to comprehend. If you had seen the things I have seen, you would not be so sure of exactly what he is. But whatever he is, he is in possession of old-world technology that is surely beyond anything I have ever heard of." He rubbed his Riika apprehensively.

"I wonder," Kiel muttered.

Bishop's attention was drawn away from the Old Earth device resting on his arm. "What do you wonder?"

"If this Reaver One is a fake, then he is a product of our present earth. But just suppose for a moment that he really is what the Ikonians believe him to be."

"Then what?"

"Then Reaver would surely have been recorded and set down in the histories."

"I would agree, but our histories are not very old, Kiel. They might go back, say, a thousand years at best. The Old Earth is ages older than that."

"No, human, not the protectorate's histories—the Eligor archives."

"Eligor archives—history? Not to sound discourteous, but I've had a taste of your Ignotum pro Magna, and it's somewhat far-fetched."

Kiel shook his reptilian head, chuckling. "No, no, not that claptrap. The Imperial Archives. They are filled with relics of the past ages—hidden for millennia before being unearthed. The empire was fanatical about excavating precataclysmic sites, in search of anything that would give them a military advantage. The Grand Union was the only government organ that had free access to them, that is, until after the collapse of the old government."

"And you want me to look at them?" Bishop wearily rubbed his face. "Kiel, I must be blunt. I can agonize through an army report when pressed to do so. Given enough time, I can even scratch one together, though the effort usually gives me a headache. But to decipher an Old Earth book?"

"Book? No, Bishop, *books*. We have thousands of books—hundreds of thousands. Hundreds upon hundreds of thousands, perhaps."

Bishop blinked, carefully setting down his tankard. "How can I put this?" he said slowly, rubbing his forehead. "I don't understand your culture. I don't understand your language, let alone the written language. I don't even much care to read books that I do understand, unless the book has pictures in it, of course. It would take years for me just to work out the Eligorian alphabet. I must be frank: I am just not that smart to be of that sort of service to you. Can't you find someone who is better suited? I mean, not to sound ungracious, but I did my job, and now I would like to go home. It is too much to ask a simple standard-bearer to tackle alone."

Kiel managed a hurt look. "Alone? I would never think of asking you to handle this alone. You will have a librarian to help you, a trusted Eligor. A wonderful fellow, he is. You'll get on with him fine. I'd rather not involve anyone else until we learn more. And I have other things to do."

Bishop's forehead furrowed in thought. "OK. I guess it's worth a try. I'll stay a few more days and look at your book for whatever good it will do, but then I will leave. I have already gotten more out of this trip than I originally bargained for."

"*Books*," Kiel corrected.

"Fine. I'll look at your *books* for all the good it will do. I can only hope they have pictures in them, or it will be an abysmal disappointment."

Kiel nodded with something bordering on relief painted on his scaly face. "Yes." He stated with resolve, "Tomorrow I will take you to the Imperial Archives and we will see about this Reaver character of yours." He hesitated. "Storm Singer, you are welcome to relax here in my command bunker. I'm sure you deserve it."

Storm Singer, who had taken the back of Bishop's chair for a roost like some frightful finial, lifted his head from under a wing. "Why, thank you, O noble Kiel. I would be most honored. Bishop, let me know if I can be of any help in the archives chamber, will you?"

"Surely, O wise buzzard, if I have need of any paper shredding, feather picking, or nest building, I will call upon your most esteemed and august person at once!" Bishop drained the last of his Ægir as if in a toast while Kiel roared in laughter.

FOURTEEN

HISTORIES

> Ancient tomes in an endless line.
> Magic keys come out of time.
> —Vena Korela,
> Saga of Sampoe, Runa 402

"No!" the historian's translator hissed like an enraged snake. "I don't deserve it! Why must I always be afflicted with the destitute and the downtrodden? And a human no less! I am a scholar, a scientist, not a slave to be ordered about! Have I nothing better to do? Have I not a thousand tomes gathering dust on my shelves, unread, unstudied?"

He turned to Kiel, stabbing at him with a crooked, yellow-clawed finger. "And you! You dare to show your face again. Do you think I've forgotten all the books your officers have misplaced or returned damaged? And what about that Old Earth map you stole? Do you think I am here to serve as your slave? I thought you were supposed to protect my interests!"

Bishop blinked, absently stepping back toward the door behind him.

Kiel hastily trotted back up the stone stairway and reached for the door. "Yes, well, charming to the last. Duty calls. I must be leaving!"

Kiel quickly opened the upper door. "I will post a guard for your protection, Bishop. Have him call for me if you find something. Otherwise,

I will see you when I see you." Kiel slipped through the door and was gone in a flash. Bishop was left alone with the old Eligor.

Sheepishly looking up at the old Eligor, Bishop smiled weakly and swallowed hard.

The scholar returned the look with a withering gaze, his fangs slightly bared. "Look! I am a busy Eligor!" he rasped with a mix of anger and despair. He waved his emaciated arms recklessly at the messy chamber, a sight Bishop found hard to associate with the normally fastidious Eligor.

Bishop looked at the upper exit darkly. "I'll see you when I see you?" he muttered to himself.

He returned his gaze to the historian and held out his hand sheepishly. "Hello, sir. My name is Bishop; I am a standard-bearer within the…"

The historian ignored Bishop's outstretched hand and cut him short with a dismissive grunt. "And I am E'Ka the historian. What of it? Do you think you impress me with your ridiculous Order? Do you think you astound me with your imbecilic title?"

Bishop stood, feeling like a schoolboy who had been caught on a romp. His hand dropped back to his side as if it were dangerously inviting a bite from the old lizard.

The Eligor continued. "I am chief historian of Opal. And I am a very busy Eligor." He now gestured at his desk as if to prove what he had said.

The desk, a vast wooden table, was piled with papers, bottles of ink, pens, scissors, leather fasteners, binders, and a host of unrecognizable arcane items. Bishop's eyes traveled from the desk to the surrounding room. There wasn't a square meter of the chamber that did not contain shelves of books or scrolls of parchment. Other books, thousands perhaps, were piled like cordwood here and there, disappearing in the gloom of the great subterranean vault, that no doubt, contained untold millions.

Bishop glanced at an unfolded cot in the corner. Its blankets were crumpled and hadn't been aired in weeks, possibly months. E'Ka's personal belongings, which seemed to be negligible, were scattered wantonly about the floor as if they had been kicked about in anger. Under the historian's table was a brazier filled with hot coals that burned perilously close to a pile of scholarly litter, with which the floor was strewn.

E'Ka himself was of a gaunt build for an Eligor, and he reminded Bishop of an angry magpie that enjoyed nothing so much as scolding squirrels. His leather uniform, which hung on him as if it were dangling on a coatrack, was worn through in a dozen places, only two or three of which had been ineptly attacked with needle and thread. One of his boots had a broken lace that had been carelessly knotted back together. In the past few weeks, Bishop had observed Eligor who were meticulous in their dress, taking great pride in their appearance. They could hardly pass a mirror without straightening their uniforms, smoothing a scale, or polishing a fang. But E'Ka apparently had better things to spend his time on, among which was berating those like Bishop who were hapless enough to fall within the realm of his wrath.

Yet despite E'Ka's incomparable eccentricities, his petulance and exasperation, Bishop felt drawn to this old Eligor and sensed in him something he admired—a shrewd and kind spirit, a sense of humor, and a love of learning. He had no doubt that E'Ka was the finest scholar in Opal, just as Kiel had said.

E'Ka glowered in silence for a few more seconds before slumping in fatigue. "Oh, very well, I see that I have no choice in this matter. What is it you require? An old Merja Sorian cookbook, perhaps? A book of Eligor love poetry? Bird-watching? Whatever pleases you, go on, out with it!"

Bishop mutely shook his head, seeming to dash the old scholar's tiny glimmer of hope.

"It was worth a try. What is it you wish of me?" the Eligor said, throwing his scaled hands up wearily.

Bishop related his story to the old historian in as much detail as possible. The Eligor listened in growing agitation. Bishop finished with his reason for coming. "We—Kiel—felt there might be a clue to this Reaver fellow buried here somewhere."

"And I am to find this crumb of lost knowledge, a crumb that has been swept into a crack and lost for countless eons? Am I to remember everything? You are correct in using the term *buried*, for that is exactly what it has become, buried and lost to us."

E'Ka began hastily walking toward the darkened vault as if the matter were closed.

"Please, it is very important that I find out as much as I can."

"Important to you perhaps, but not to me," E'Ka growled. He melted into the dim and dusty gloom of the archival vault, looking like a poorly stuffed scarecrow caught in a windstorm.

Bishop stood motionless, not knowing what else to do.

"I will do what I can, but I cannot do everything!" the old Eligor called from the dim chamber he had melted into. The sound of books being flung about met Bishop's ears.

Soon though, the aged historian E'Ka shuffled back to the front of the labyrinthine Imperial Archives chamber with a stack of literature so heavy that an onlooker would have thought him taxed beyond his strength. There was a rodent-like scurry and quickness to everything the old Eligor did, accentuated by sunken skeletal features and an all-seeing personality. The old Eligor laid the books down on the oaken desk and began a final search, eventually deciding on a tome of unusual size and age. After several moments of riffling through the dusty pages, he stopped and looked up at Bishop, frowning. Then E'Ka's translator crackled with irritation.

"You did say Reaver, Reaver of Ikonia?"

"Yes, that's right, Reaver of Ikonia," Bishop responded with growing excitement.

"Very well, I will read from a collection of writings known as the 'Ra Codex.' It was compiled at the end of the Fourth Age, possibly sometime after. It is of dubious historical worth. Still, these pages have more than a few grains of truth within them."

The historian settled himself before the ancient text, donned a pair of spectacles, something Bishop had never seen another Eligor wearing, and began reading the spidery script:

"'We come now to Reaver, a strong, charismatic, ruthless, and ambitious dictator with a penchant for seeking violent solutions to real or imagined problems, whether personal or public. At the time of the Ikonian civil war, other nations of that era compared him to some of the worst misanthropic leaders then known to humankind. After becoming the ruler of Ikonia, he allegedly murdered political opponents by his own hand on at least thirteen occasions.

"'The Heptagon, Reaver's political party—itself enshrined as a cult of violence within the Ikonian state—was a mélange of twisted philosophies, one being a serious belief in the virtue of violence as the catalyst of civilization, another being a fascination with eugenics, improving the human species through genetics and selective breeding.

"'Reaver took control as leader of Ikonia and head of the Heptagon cult after winning the civil war. He immediately ensured his personal security and rule by purging likely political rivals in the grand tradition of the Ankara dynasty in the tenth period, or the Olethros monarchy, which was toppled two decades previous.

"'Reaver faced formidable challenges in ruling Ikonia as its population was composed of five other political factions, his being the minority. His solution, unsurprisingly, was a draconian mix of domestic spying, communications monitoring, intimidation, and outright terror by the Trelrethos, the bioengineered regulates the Heptagon had inherited. The Trelrethos had significant domestic and national security functions, and their privileges, equipment, training, and status reflected their importance to Reaver's state.'"

E'Ka looked up from his reading. "Quite a nasty fellow we have here.

Could have passed as Imperial Intelligence Service; could have vied for Kiel's position. Just listen to this." He continued, now seemingly quite interested in what he was reading:

"'The Trelrethos were responsible for crushing the only known attempt on Reaver's life. The assassination attempt was quickly smashed, and the affairs of the high command were once again in smooth working order. During the weeks that followed, the suspects were tracked down. Two thousand people, including dozens of high-ranking officers, were killed in a paroxysm of fratricide. Some of the leading plotters were garroted with wire and impaled on metal hooks, while the guards recorded the victims' death throes so that Reaver could enjoy the film in his personal cinema. It is of note that the arch-plotter, a relative of some importance, was never found. It was believed the assassin fled across the border to a rival nation that was on the brink of war with Ikonia and granted asylum, further escalating tensions between these two superpowers.'"

"Does it say whether this Reaver was ever defeated?"

"Of course," E'Ka said, paging through a few chapters. "The regime was finally overcome and defeated, but it took nearly the entire planet to carry this out. Whole regions were laid to waste. The text does not say it, but this Reaver might have been the cause of the end of the last age. Interesting. I never knew that."

E'Ka closed the book and again looked into Bishop's eyes. "That is all I can find on this character Reaver. Is there anything else I can help you with, perhaps a nice book on knitting or possibly baking?"

"Baking? What's there to know about baking? Anyone can bake. My mother bakes! No. Let's get back to this text. All that is told there refers to *who* he is; I need to know *what* he is." Bishop's tone revealed his anxiety. "It's very important."

E'Ka's golden eyes glittered darkly in the gloom as he spread his spindly arms wide in a dramatic gesture. "In these halls we have exquisite poetry, art, and science, beyond your imagination to fathom, the combined technical wealth of the ages. You are the first person, certainly the first human ever, to visit these grand halls of accumulated knowledge since the fall of the old Eligor Republic, and all you want to see are these boring manuscripts?" The old historian let his arms drop back to his sides in apparent anguish.

Bishop stared, exasperated. "No, no poetry, no cooking, no baking. I need to know more about Reaver. It's very important."

"Oh, all right then," E'Ka said wearily, giving in. "The effort to interest you in something of real merit was worth the candle in any case."

The old Eligor slowly lifted his skeletal frame and wearily shambled back into the bowels of the cathedral-like archives chamber, disappearing for several minutes, then returning finally with one strange small book.

Reseating himself, E'Ka opened the tome and began running a scaled finger across the lines of text. Bishop noticed at once that this book was like no other book that he had ever seen. Its pages were as thin as gossamer and metallic in composition, like the Old Earth map given to him by Kiel. The glyphs were certainly similar to the map, angular and exact, forming perfect lines in an unknown language—unknown yet familiar. Suddenly, Bishop remembered something else: these letters were very similar to those that had decorated the metal beast he had discovered in the cave days before. Yes, the book was of the Old Earth.

"The Others!" Bishop muttered the word like a curse.

Startled, E'Ka looked up from his reading, suddenly quite animated. "Yes, you are absolutely correct. I had no idea that you were versed in the writings of the Others. A human, interested in history. I might swoon from astonishment!"

"Ah, right. I mean, of course I am. History is required within the Order." This was a lie—there were no such books Bishop had ever seen within Merja Soria—but he didn't want to look uneducated in front of this learned Eligor.

The Eligor looked at Bishop dubiously and then continued his research, finally stopping on a specific page and frowning.

"Now this is strange. Yes, very strange," E'Ka muttered.

"What?! What's strange? What have you found there?" Bishop stretched his neck, trying to see the page, but it was a useless effort. The glyphs were quite beyond his ability to understand. Worse yet, there were no pictures.

"Well," the historian began again, "I suppose this could be an error. Even the Others weren't perfect, you know."

The old Eligor turned a page and again stopped. "No, no error! This text refers to Reaver in the plural as if there were more than one of them."

"I'm not sure I understand," Bishop replied.

E'Ka shot Bishop a devious look. "Let me read the text then. Just possibly, a human of your apparent higher education can make some sense of it."

Bishop ignored the remark and listened as the historian began the translation.

"'This wearisome chapter is entitled 'Eugenics: The Human Application of Genetic Engineering.'"

E'Ka ran his finger down the page and then began again.

"'There were two attempts to apply the amassed genetic sciences on human subjects. Both engendered public outcries, for it was feared that those who were the wealthiest would be able to afford to improve their bloodlines, whereas others would not, leaving the rest of society behind, eventually creating a new biological caste system. Yet within certain military establishments there was a call for selective breeding and genetic manipulation to enhance the intellectual and physical qualities of humans, at the same time eliminating, by forcible methods, undesirable and unwanted characteristics. These elements claimed that it would be better for the world if those who were manifestly unfit to continue their bloodlines be prevented from producing degenerate offspring, rather than allowing the unfortunate progeny to be terminated, whether through execution for criminal activity or through starvation as a result of imbecility.

"'The second such attempt on humans, which was to become known as the Reaver Project, though initially successful, met with near-disastrous consequences. A group of three male and four female test embryos—Reaver One through Seven—were altered to reflect enhanced mental and physical abilities. The experimenters did not allow, however, for the unforeseen certainty that accompanies enhanced physical and mental abilities, that being enhanced ambition.

"'An accelerated but predictable mental development had been plotted for these children based on the known genetic works previously so successful with certain military constructs. However, at age thirty-six months, the Reavers made a logarithmic leap away from the expected linear curve, exhibiting alarming signs of extreme mental ability. Within their sixteenth year they had collectively developed several theoretical formulas that apparently unlocked faster-than-light drive and time travel. Problematic here was that no one could validate the theories because of the advanced nature of the mathematics involved.'"

Bishop was stunned at the revelation. "What became of the Reavers?"

E'Ka closed his eyes and rubbed his scaled head as if in sudden pain. "How did I know you were going to ask that question? How, how did I know, human?" He sounded as if he were about to weep in unbridled grief.

Bishop looked at him meekly, not knowing quite how to respond to the accusation.

Getting back up from his chair, the aged Eligor ambled into the darkness of the archives chamber, muttering to himself all the while. Returning, he slammed another small silvery book down as if it had angered him in some way. He again sat down and began impatiently riffling through the metallic pages. An ordinary book would have likely been torn to shreds, but this Old Earth tome seemed to ignore the mistreatment.

Selecting a page, the Eligor stabbed a clawed finger several times down on the open book and glared at Bishop. "Before you ask, human, this is the last possible existing reference on the tedious subject of Reaver."

Bishop nodded in acknowledgment, electing not to speak.

"Now to conclude this session," the historian spluttered in frustration, thumbing madly through the pages before a certain glyph caught his trained eye. "Yes, well, the Reaver Project was terminated in part because of a massive public outcry that had arisen against this human genetic research, which was apparently begun in secrecy and leaked to the public. Critics feared that these technologies would usher in a second eugenics war, more dangerous than previous by virtue of its greater genetic power, possibly resulting in the enslavement of the masses by these so-called supermen. The Reaver children were separated and mostly disappeared from society, supposedly living out their lives in remote corners of the earth under close security. Apparently at least one of them was wont to pursue more excitement, as you have no doubt puzzled out."

The old Eligor closed the book. "Now, if you don't mind, I have my own work that needs attention." E'Ka ambled off into the darkened gloom, muttering to himself as he disappeared.

Was it truly possible? Bishop was dazed as he sat there alone in the Eligor Imperial Archives chamber. Was this Reaver character a result of the Old Earth sciences, a living relic from the age of the Others? Bishop knew that there was very little beyond the ability of those precataclysmic humans of old, yet for one to have survived down through the ages was simply beyond his ability to fathom. Since his imprisonment beneath dead Terus Kor, the facts had been revealed, but he had not wanted to believe them. No human, not even a superior human, could possibly live so long.

Bishop hooded himself and walked back up the worn stone steps just as night was descending. The sound of thunder rolled though the city as he opened the massive ironbound door and quietly exited into the growing twilight, directly encountering a rainstorm. His sodden guard was shivering in a hazy cold rain that had already soaked him. He glowered at Bishop with slits of golden fire.

Bishop gave the guard a meek smile. "I'll be going back to my sleeping quarters for the evening. You are certainly welcome to stay for dinner if you wish."

The guard rolled his eyes and let out a forced sigh. But he let no time pass before he stomped off into the misty gloom, grumbling something to himself, with Bishop, lost in thought, trailing behind.

Bishop lay huddled in his sleeping blankets, his thoughts as tumultuous as the storm now beating at the ramparts of Opal as he wondered about what he had learned. Reaver was, or rather the Reavers were, from the Old Earth, but the Old Earth had ended countless eons ago at the end of the Fourth Age. How is it that this Reaver One could have survived into the current Fifth Age?

Then he remembered something of the text that had just been read to him. The Reavers had developed time travel. Was it possible to travel through time as simply as one could go on, say, a sea voyage? It was too fantastic to consider; it bordered on black magic, as no other force Bishop could think of could explain it. Strange that the Ikonian insects just happened upon Reaver's crypt. Had it in fact simply materialized out of the past? That would explain much.

"Gods of the Others!" Bishop swore aloud. If such a thing were possible, then the inhabitants of the planet were faced with an invasion from the Old Earth—an invasion no one could hope to stop.

His troubled thoughts returned to the archives chamber. "But E'Ka said the regime was finally overcome and defeated," he whispered softly. He shot up straight in the darkness. "Defeated? But how?"

"One is endeavoring to sleep over here, human," came an angered croaking voice from the other side of the room. A small dark form tucked a head back under ruffled ebon feathers with a growl of exasperation.

"Beg pardon, Storm Singer."

"Think nothing of it," was the muffled response.

Bishop laid his head down again, his thoughts racing. Reaver had been defeated once before. Bishop needed to find out how. Yes, tomorrow he would need to return to the archives chamber.

At first light Bishop was again in the archives chamber with a very irritated E'Ka.

"Yes, I see that you will not stop now, not until you have forced me to translate the entire archival collection into your primitive language. I warn you, though, I will not live long enough to complete the task for you. But then, you will not live long enough to hear it all either."

"E'Ka, this might be very important. Please. Exactly how was Reaver overcome? What weapon was employed?"

"Important to you, but not to me!" Bishop gave the old librarian a wheedling look. "Oh, all right!"

E'Ka, growling and muttering again, disappeared into the cold gloom of the cavernous vault, finally returning with a massive tome that was obviously of a much later date than the Old Earth text Bishop had seen before.

E'Ka looked around the room in suspicion before reverently placing the book down. "You will keep this to yourself, human. I have heard of this Reaver of yours before but kept the source to myself out of fear. Even now, after the destruction of the old empire, this book is not welcome. While the empire reigned, it meant death even to look upon it, never mind being found in possession of it. Only the dark Eligor gods know what the higher-ups would have done if they had caught someone actually reading it."

"Death, from reading a book? I do not understand. I mean, there must be thousands of books here from the Old Earth."

"True enough, but they were mostly written by humans and could be discounted as propaganda if need be, but even these books were dangerous because they did not always agree with the imperial canon of the time. On more than one occasion the empire considered destroying these ancient tomes.

"This"—E'Ka reverently patted the book—"was infinitely more dangerous. It was written by an Eligor."

Bishop shrugged his shoulders in question.

E'Ka opened the book to the first page. "It is known as the Tar Ka Codex," he whispered softly as if the book itself were a living thing.

E'Ka lifted a yellowed, worm-eaten parchment that lay loosely under the cover and read haltingly from the hand-scrawled notations.

"'Everyone knoweth in the present age that from ancient writings, Tar Ka gained knowledge inspired by the dread teachings from his precataclysmic human masters, Shabbathai, Tzedeq, Madim, Shemesh, Nogah, Kokav, and Levanah, who ruled over the Eligor and other races that served beneath them.'"

E'Ka looked up. "In case you were wondering, human, those names are ancient Eligor numbers—one, two, three, four, and so on. Interesting, isn't it?"

Bishop stared, trying to look interested in E'Ka's teaching.

E'Ka returned to the parchment. "'In addition to the gift of wisdom, which he acquired, he obtained in profusion all the other virtues that were sought in order that knowledge worthy of eternal preservation might not be buried with his body, so that it might be carefully preserved for the ages to come.'"

E'Ka looked up from his reading as if he suddenly remembered something of importance. "If memory serves, the humans would also know this book. It is considered an important work, though it goes by a different name in your language."

Bishop looked up in interest.

"I believe, if memory serves, that it would be known as the Vena Korela."

Bishop started, then shook his head vehemently. "No. You are wrong. That's utterly ridiculous. The Vena Korela is the sacred holy book of the Order; it was written by a human, not an Eligor, and it is only sung by the runa singers within the protectorate. Gods of the Others, man, it would be sacrilege to even suggest such a thing."

E'Ka chortled, smiling wickedly. "Human arrogance. Everything of value was created by the humans. Well, trust me, the Vena Korela—the Tar Ka Codex—is Eligor through and through, a fact I would not expect a human nestling such as you to know."

Bishop's skin prickled at the revelation. The mere suggestion that the holy writings of the Order were in fact written by an Eligor caused him to feel uneasy.

"The contents of the Tar Ka Codex are fearsome enough, even if one accepts the official view that it represents the ravings of a madman, or shall I say a mad Eligor, who went by the name of Tar Ka. Of course, no one accepts the official view."

Bishop, still reeling from the revelation, listened mutely.

"The Tar Ka Codex details the precataclysmic cults and the dark worship of technological objects that were still known in Tar Ka's day. It goes on to predict certain future events, as if he had some insight into what would happen. I myself will be so bold as to say that just possibly Tar Ka was one of the first true Eligor scientists, even if others see his ravings as heresy. His writings, his predictions, and his oracular poetry were eventually destroyed, and he was publicly executed for his trouble. But it is here in the Tar Ka Codex where, among many strange things, I found mention of Reaver and the Iron Thunderbolt."

"The Iron Thunderbolt?!"

"Yes, the Iron Thunderbolt. That curious, sinister thing that, according to the Tar Ka Codex, is said to forever brood under the ashes of the eighth hell and around which many dark legends cluster. Tar Ka did not devote much space to it, but from his confusing terminology, it seems that he believed the Iron Thunderbolt was some monstrously powerful talisman, lost and forgotten centuries ago. His words are difficult to understand. I believe that the cryptic nature of his writings was no accident but was a way to hide the information in an attempt to evade detection by those who would not wish it to be known. The attempt might have worked because he was executed for reasons that had nothing to do with surreptitiously divulging technological information from the age of the Others.

"Yes, I imagine concerning the Thunderbolt, as with the entire codex, he was being cryptic to protect himself. He spoke of it as one of the *keys*—a term he used many times, in various ways. That word was one of the many peculiar mannerisms of his writings. There is an entire book called *The Saga of Levanah* that goes on and on about another key of power."

"Levanah." Something tugged at Bishop's memory.

"Yes, Levanah, the Eligor word for seven."

Bishop's concentration returned. "You stated that Tar Ka's writings were destroyed. How is it that you have found this single volume?"

E'Ka coughed in embarrassment. "It was many cycles ago. There was an earthquake that broke several great blocks of stone and mortar out of a back storage wall down here behind the main archives chamber. Hidden behind one of those stones was an object found by one of my aides, which the aide brought to me. I ignored the lacquered case for a time, not realizing the importance of the find. I assure you that when I did finally open it, I took very little time placing it back behind the rock and resealing it. I could not destroy it."

"You could not destroy it? Though it meant your death if you were to be discovered with it?"

"It was very old, and the implication of enormous antiquity piqued my interest immensely, as it must have my predecessors, for it was they who must have hidden this, the last, rat-eaten copy of the Tar Ka Codex in its entirety. I suspect that even your human translation is most likely incomplete or corrupt by comparison."

"All right, E'Ka. It is old. Of that there is little doubt. And for the sake of expedience, I will try to accept what you say about its origin. But how does this ancient codex tie in with the Reaver story? I have never heard so much as one line sung by the runa singers concerning him."

E'Ka looked at Bishop severely. "It ties in. Why don't you listen for once, instead of rattling in ignorance? As I stated, the copy your Order possesses is quite possibly incomplete. From what I have been told, your government never had an actual copy but compiled theirs from oral tradition handed down from generations of people, until at some point they decided to write an actual copy to better preserve its contents." He reverently sifted through the ancient worm-eaten pages. "As I have already stated, the Iron Thunderbolt was the key, or at least one of the keys, that unlocked a weapon or series of weapons that was employed against this Reaver. The weapons were also hidden in places around the planet in the event that this evil would return. The prophecy is consistent with several others I have read on this one point, a future that is cursed with the return of Old Earth evil and the use of these keys of power to thwart it. Again, it is as if Tar Ka knew of this threat and was determined to prevent it from regaining power."

Bishop suddenly recalled where he had heard the word *thunderbolt* recently. Kiel had read from the Ignotum pro Magna; it was written in there as well. Bishop hadn't been listening all that well when the lizard was rambling on about it. "Isn't this thunderbolt an Eligor myth of some sort? Isn't it mentioned in the Ignotum pro Magna?"

E'Ka looked up, amazed. "You have read the Ignotum pro Magna?"

"Well, sure." Bishop coughed. "Hasn't everyone?"

E'Ka looked surprised, impressed despite himself, and then he managed to laugh dismissively. "I would hold the Tar Ka Codex as an infinitely more reliable source of knowledge than the Ignotum pro Magna, but still, the Ignotum pro Magna contains some things that are of merit, one being the thunderbolt legend, muddled as it is."

"This Tar Ka Codex couldn't be much better," Bishop remarked.

"Why would you say that, human?"

"The codex talks of the Iron Thunderbolt residing beneath the eighth hell as if it were an actual place, instead of a bit of superstitious nonsense, which it truly is."

E'Ka laughed a hearty laugh while slapping his knee. "You are a simple wit, but I must say I am beginning to like you. The eight hells are a real place, human. Seeped in legend they are, but they exist."

Bishop looked up in grudging interest. "A real place, you say? I have always thought it was a mythical place, a place, the eighth hell, in the afterlife reserved for the most sinful souls, with the first hell being for the least wicked."

E'Ka rolled his golden eyes, carefully closed the book, and rubbed his face. "What I find truly amazing is that your ancestors were intelligent." He opened the book again. "There were eight Old Earth experiments. As far as I know, the eighth was successful. That means, human, that seven were failures."

"All right, all right, I understand," Bishop grated, his ears flaming in embarrassment. "I am no scholar. I am merely a standard-bearer of the Order, but I am willing to learn."

"Good, then we are getting somewhere. The result of these ancient experiments was a line of progressively larger islands that exist in the Northern Sea. Everyone—every Eligor—knows this. Now are you satisfied, human?"

"No." It was difficult to deal with this old Eligor, but this was amazing information, and for some reason, it struck Bishop as having a grain of truth and, more important, being of great value to his quest.

"Will you tell me more about this experiment, this eighth hell?"

"Questions, questions!"

The old librarian's golden eyes narrowed in suspicion, and he glanced at the upper door as if expecting to see someone peeking through. "Did Kiel put you up to this? Is this a cruel joke of his? It is not beneath him, you know."

"No, I swear to you it is not a joke," Bishop assured him, unable to see Kiel as any sort of comedian.

E'Ka eyed him a few moments longer as if to be sure. "The empire believed the Others were attempting to tap the core of the earth as an energy source to power a mighty technological creation, possibly a weapon. Titanic wars were raging across the planet, and it seems unlikely they would have wasted such resources for other reasons."

Bishop knew of volcanoes, had seen one in his youth. He suspected that the power of such a natural event was immense, unfathomable. If it were possible to harness that power, the result would be limitless power—the power one would need to produce a powerful weapon. This story was becoming ever more plausible.

"I would think this Iron Thunderbolt would have been of some interest to the Eligor Empire. I'm surprised they didn't try to recover it."

E'Ka looked at Bishop with something bordering on newfound respect. "That was quick, human. Yes, very quick. And very correct. It wasn't ten cycles ago that a clandestine team of Imperial Intelligence were dispatched to the eighth hell to attempt a recovery. They, of course, failed."

"So how is it that a librarian became aware of a purported secret mission? They, of course, informed you?"

E'Ka's eyes narrowed shrewdly. "These stone walls are thick, human, almost as thick as your head, but not impenetrable, especially if one is shrewd. I know many secrets."

"You say the Imperial Intelligence Service failed in their mission?"

E'Ka smiled a devious smile. "It is strange to think that those of the Imperial Intelligence were the very ones who caused their own failure in the search. The IIS was responsible for destroying the Tar Ka Codex, and it is the codex that holds one of the keys of power."

"The key?"

"Cryptic as the information is, yes. And there is more."

"What else?" Bishop pressed.

"There is a code that is employed in the activation of this key, the Thunderbolt. But it is just that, a code. I cannot make sense of the symbols, though I spent some time trying. It could be that they are needed to activate the Iron Thunderbolt or gain access to it. I do not know."

E'Ka turned the brittle pages until he had found what he was searching for. Then, with quill in hand, he lovingly reproduced the glyphs he had spoken of and handed them to Bishop. Their meaning was beyond him, but this was hope. Folding the scrap, Bishop slid it into an inner pocket.

Bishop felt the satisfaction of completion and a new hope growing within his soul. What if all of this was true? How else was the human race going to protect itself against Reaver? It all made sense, a returning evil from the Old Earth as prophesied. Even the Vena Korela spoke of such an occurrence: an evil from the Old Earth and a weapon placed on the planet to destroy it.

"How far is the eighth hell from Opal, E'Ka?"

"It is close, human. Closer than I care to admit, I think," E'Ka muttered, now very subdued. "Would that it were sunk into the emerald depths of the Northern Sea and seen no more by either humankind or Eligor. As I said, not so very long ago the empire tried to invade the island, but few returned from that accursed place."

"Evil?" Bishop sobered. "What do you mean exactly? What is so evil about it?"

"It is haunted or cursed," E'Ka answered uneasily, with the suggestion of a shudder.

"It seems strange for one of your learning to talk of curses and hauntings."

"Not strange, human. The ill-fated expedition I spoke of, initiated at the command of the emperor himself some ten cycles ago, ended in disaster. Only two of the original twenty soldiers stumbled back to Opal to tell the tale, and one of them was stricken mad. Something had shattered in his brain and sealed his lips forever. Until the day of his death, which came soon after, he spoke only blasphemies or slavered gibberish. So you see, human, it is a rigid mind indeed that closes out the possibility of the supernatural realm."

"What of the other survivor?"

"He was affected by the same devils that destroyed the other members of the expedition, but he slowly recovered and is still alive."

"What is his name? Where can I find him?"

The old librarian's eyes glittered like a cat's eyes in the gloaming. "Kiel. It was your dear friend Kiel."

Bishop was not at first sure he had understood E'Ka, but before he could ask the question again, he heard a sound. E'Ka himself looked up as the low rumbling filled the chamber. Rivulets of dust filtered down around them as the sound increased. The door burst open, and Kiel, followed by Storm Singer and several Eligor guards, hurried through.

"Bishop, I pray you have found what you came here seeking, for I fear that we will be leaving sooner than expected."

"What's going on?" Bishop stammered in alarm. Agitation was clearly written on Kiel's face.

"The Ikonians are attacking Opal!"

FIFTEEN

FLIGHT FROM OPAL

> A voice rang through the forest wood with a sudden trumpet's power: "We rise on all our hills! Come forth! 'Tis thy country's gathering hour. There's a gleam of spears by every stream, in each old battle dell. Come forth, young soldier! Bid thy home a brief and proud farewell!
>
> —Vena Korela,
> Second Saga of Vainamonen, Runa 44

The battle lines were drawn. Kiel, Storm Singer, and Bishop, hooded and silent, anxiously gazed over the protected northern ramparts of Opal, surveying the scene below them. A column of Eligor soldiers marched out of the city, ready to counter the attack on Opal. Ahead of them, darkening the open plain all the way to the forest line, were hundreds of thousands of Ikonians, waiting. The Eligor who marched were only fifteen hundred strong. The remaining nine hundred soldiers stayed within the walls as the last line of defense. Bishop noted their javelins, short swords, and heavy shields; their armor was emblazoned with the winged skull of the old empire. These soldiers represented the remnants of an army beneath whose footfalls the world had been shaken in the Eligor war with Merja Soria, but now they were a mere shadow of that former glory. And strangely, Bishop no longer found any comfort in the fact.

Flanking the Eligor column was a swarm of archers and slingers. Bishop noted the battle-hardened general—a tall Eligor whose lean and seasoned face Bishop could just make out at that distance—riding a two-legged reptile to the head of a formation of similarly mounted riders.

"A good Eligor, that one." Kiel pointed. "Con Tar was one of the few to openly oppose the war with Merja Soria and live to tell of it. He was vindicated, but to what end?"

At the revelation, Bishop felt new respect for the Eligor race. No one within the protectorate would have ever believed that there were such Eligor. Bishop himself had thought them all evil through and through not so long ago.

A deep-throated roar rose from the Eligor soldiers as they approached their foes. Although the odds were vastly against them, from their determined and resolute demeanor, they gave an impression of a force that intended to slice its way through and continue without pause.

A group of cavalry detached itself from the main body and raced toward the Ikonian ranks, but it was only a gesture. With loud jeering sounds, they wheeled to within three spear lengths and cast their javelins, which rattled harmlessly off the overlapping shields of the silent Ikonians. But the lead cavalryman dared too much. Swinging in, he leaned from his saddle and thrust at an Ikonian's face. The insect's great shield turned the lance, and the Ikonian struck back as a snake strikes. Its ponderous mace crushed helmet and head like an eggshell. Even the Eligor's mount went to its knees from the shock. The oncoming Eligor army shouted vengefully and quickened their pace as the riderless mount raced by with the pulped remains of the soldier, foot caught in the stirrup, trailing crazily beneath the pounding hoofs.

Now the first line of the Eligor army crashed against the steadily advancing solid wall of Ikonian shields—crashed and recoiled upon itself. The shield wall had not been shaken so much as a sword's breadth. Shield crashed on shield, and the short Eligor sword sought for an opening in that iron wall. Ikonian spears, the Ikonians bristling in solid ranks above, thrust and became reddened; heavy axes chopped down, cleaving through iron, scale, and bone; screams of agony rent the air; and amid the dying bodies, blood ran freely. Bishop saw one of the massive Ikonian soldiers looming above the smaller insect men at the forefront of the fray, dealing blows like thunderbolts. A broad-shouldered Eligor captain rushed in, shield held high, stabbing upward. The iron mace crashed terribly, causing the sword to shiver, rending the shield apart, shattering the helmet, and crushing the ruined skull down between the shoulders in a single blow. Riderless mounts brayed in panic and careened off the battlefield, bucking and kicking.

The front line of the Eligor army bent like a lead bar before a wedge as the soldiers reeled back in the face of the steadily advancing enemy. Now the Ikonians brought forth their bows, firing arrows in a hail of death. At close range, the heavy shafts tore through shield and corselet, impaling armored Eligor by the score. The front line of the Eligor army rolled back, red and broken, and the Ikonians trod on the dead as they continued to move forward. The full force of the Ikonian army would batter down the resistance of the Eligor warriors like a heavy ram—would stamp them down, sweep over their formations.

Bishop saw Kiel's face tighten in anguish as he at last realized the magnitude of the Ikonian threat facing Opal. Surely in that moment there flashed a chaotic picture in his brain.

Defeat! Disgrace! Scarlet ruin!

Now the Eligor army, aware of their desperate plight, flung themselves headlong upon their foes. The shield wall rocked but did not give. Eligor faces, contorted in rage, stared defiantly over locked shields into the compassionless, shimmering eyes of the Ikonians while the insect automatons hacked and slew in a red storm of slaughter, crimsoned axes rising and falling in a grim harvest of life. Looming always above the melee were the towering forms of the Ikonian soldiers, from whose gory maces came showering a ghastly rain of brains and blood, like a crimson storm from hell.

But the battle was not over yet. Dazed, shattered, their formation broken, and nearly half their numbers already down, the Eligor fought back with desperate fury. Hemmed in on all sides, they slashed and smote singly or in small packs, or fought back-to-back, archers, spear-throwers, and riders mingling in a chaotic mass. The Ikonians closed around the remaining Eligor army and tightened, sending a storm of arrows into the surrounded Eligor, piercing armor and scaled skin, nailing many together as they fell in piles. While the massed and serried soldiers battled, the noise thundering around them, the surviving Eligor hurled themselves into the swinging red axes that barred the way to their retreat.

But there was no retreat.

Rising from the fray was a figure Bishop recognized. It was Con Tar the general. He cast aside his broken and useless sword as he ran forward, drawing his dirk. Tackling an Ikonian soldier, Con Tar stabbed again and again, but to no avail; the knight almost casually ran him through while his, the Ikonian's, stab wounds shimmered and healed.

There was a chorused groan of despair from the parapets of Opal as Con Tar's lifeless body disappeared underfoot. The three hundred Eligor soldiers still alive were crushed in the tightening pincers of the Ikonian horde within minutes.

The battle was over.

Within two hours, the invading army had casually encircled the ramparts of Opal and settled down to the routine business of siege. No use now risking the loss of even one soldier by storming the black walls of the city. Better to starve the Eligor out from within. Months it might take, possibly years, but the Ikonians had time as their ally.

With a haggard look upon his scaled face, Kiel turned slowly to

Bishop. "We must retire to my command bunker. I would know of what you have found in the Imperial Archives, and I pray that it is enough, because there is nothing else left."

Within Kiel's gloomy chamber, Bishop slowly pulled his mind away from thinking about the red carnage below Opal and began to focus his thoughts on the details that had seemed so important just hours ago. Storm Singer sat on a window ledge, staring morosely out toward the northern battlements, while Bishop began recounting what he had learned. When his story finally touched on the Tar Ka Codex and the Iron Thunderbolt, Kiel stiffened, becoming alert. "The eighth hell? Yes, I know of the island. I know it all too well."

"That is what E'Ka mentioned, something about a failed mission to recover the device, a mission that you supposedly took part in, though I would appreciate it if you kept that to yourself. He was wary about discussing it, and I would not wish to abuse his trust."

Kiel's eyes gazed into the distance. "Yes, the old fool knows much for a librarian. Then again, he was not always a librarian."

Bishop looked up a Kiel. "Not a librarian? What was he then?"

"He was my predecessor."

"E'Ka was a commander of the Imperial Security Service? But how could an old, withered Eligor like that have been assigned to such an important position?" Bishop gaped.

Kiel smiled briefly before regaining his thoughts. "Yes, well, he was not hatched old, Bishop. At any rate, I was sent by the empire to recover the Thunderbolt. In the days before the war with Merja Soria, they were fanatical about Old Earth technology, but simply demanding results won't guarantee them. The Thunderbolt could not be recovered. There was a sealed door that proved impossible to open, and there were other things."

Bishop nodded in growing enthusiasm. "A door, you say? E'Ka found a key in the Tar Ka Codex."

Kiel's eyes focused as he leaned forward, then they widened in astonishment. "The Tar Ka Codex, you say? A key?"

"Well, I would guess it is more like a code than a key, but E'Ka insisted that it was the answer, and I am apt to agree with him. And again, I would appreciate your not mentioning the Tar Ka Codex to him. He seemed somewhat worried about it."

Now a hopeful light began to flicker and grow in Kiel's eyes as if a witch's fire had just been lit beneath a meter of golden ice. "Yes, of course I will honor your trust. The Tar Ka Codex. Black gods, it makes sense. I hope you are right about this, Bishop. The eighth hell is not an experience I would soon like to relive for no reason."

"It's all there is, Kiel. Either you take the chance, or you stay and fight the Ikonians. And from what I have seen and experienced, any option is better than that."

Kiel pondered the information, seeming to struggle with invisible demons, and then set his shoulders in determination. "Very well, tomorrow we will use the eastern escape tunnel to exit the city. If we are lucky, the Ikonians have not discovered it."

"Fine then, we will use the escape tunnels and I will be on my way. The protectorate is looking better all the time."

Kiel gazed meditatively at Bishop, staring silently.

"What?"

"You must come with me. I could not hope to do this alone."

Now it was Bishop's turn to stare. Even Storm Singer turned from his window perch, seeming to shrink in size. "Now wait just a damn minute. I was supposed to travel to Ikonia and learn what I could learn. I have done that and, I might add, given you a hand in locating a weapon in your fight, an extra bonus that I won't even charge you for. Now it is time for me to leave, and that's the end of it!"

Kiel shook his head. "Bishop, there are fifty thousand including the nestlings in Opal. They have no chance, and you know as well as I do that Merja Soria is next in line. I can't do this without you. I am sure your government would agree."

Bishop recalled the ruthless way the Eligor had been slaughtered beneath the battlements of Opal and thought of his own family and friends in the same situation. He also recalled his own treatment at Reaver's hand. Kiel was right, and Bishop knew it.

Bishop closed his eyes, shaking his head slowly. "Really, I have responsibilities at home. I have my orders; I am to return and report on the situation." The words sounded hollow in his ears. "Can't you at least get the children out through your tunnels?"

"No," said Kiel. "That is not our way. Everyone, even the young, will stay to defend their home city; it's all we have left. If I did not believe there was at least a slim chance of success, I would not leave either."

Bishop, understanding what Kiel was saying, stood silently for a moment longer, feeling littler and littler. He would do the same thing if the tables were turned. "What can I say? You have me, and you know you do."

Kiel firmly took hold of Bishop's shoulders and gave him a long knowing look. "If there was another way, my friend, know that I would take it. I wish no harm to come to you, but there is no choice: we must risk it. We will leave at first light on the morrow."

Bishop didn't understand his own emotions. A year ago, nothing would have pleased him more than the sight of that battlefield. Apparently, Kiel understood him better than he understood himself. Bishop sighed in resignation as Storm Singer looked on, nodding gravely.

"It would appear, Sir Vulture, that you and I will not be returning to the home nest as soon as you might have thought."

Storm Singer squawked an avian response, but Bishop did not wonder at its translation.

In the twilight hours, Kiel cautiously emerged from the exit tunnel into the half-light of the silent forest. The tunnel had taken them several kilometers northeast of Opal and hopefully beyond the Ikonian army. Bishop peered around as the rock door silently slid shut behind them, clicking invisibly in a granite outcropping that jutted away from a shallow canyon wall.

"No Ikonians that I can see," Bishop said.

Kiel shushed him and scowled.

Before long, a black shadow that was Storm Singer ghosted out of the sky and alighted on Bishop's shoulder. "There was a skirmish ahead, but nothing remains alive except the forest scavengers."

Bishop glanced at Kiel in inquiring silence.

"There were several probes that were sent out when the Ikonians were detected. None returned," Kiel muttered.

Bishop nodded as they moved into the predawn forest, which steamed in the cold morning air. They passed dew-bedecked cobwebs that were glittering in the early sunlight like jewels. He had always loved walking in the awaking forest, myriad bird life singing their songs of the rebirth of another day, but now he recoiled at the stench of death and decay. Any contentment to be found under the foliage canopy was snuffed in an oppressive cloud of miasma.

Before long, the great trees thinned and an open meadow materialized before them. The sun broke over the eastern mountains, flaming like a crimson eye on the horizon. Silent as a ghost, strewn with the wreckage of the skirmish, a field stretched grim and still beneath the garish rays. Here and there amid the sprawled unmoving bodies, scarlet pools of congealed gore lay like hellish lakes, reflecting the red-streamed sky.

Dark furtive figures moved in the grasses, snuffling and whining at the scattered corpses. Scavengers moved through the battle site, dining unmolested. Crows and other carrion eaters wheeled and cried in the brightening sky. Bishop followed as Kiel picked his way over the bodies. Shortly thereafter, they were again within the concealment of the dark forest and moving steadily away from the carnage and toward the distant coast. No one spoke as they moved through the forest. Even Storm Singer, usually wont to chatter, stayed to himself as he flew above them, scouting ahead as the day wore on.

As evening descended and the travelers made camp, Bishop related to Kiel more details from what he had learned at the archives chamber. A small fire crackled and wavered before them while they ate their evening rations, talking in low tones. Storm Singer sat high above them, watching for any trouble.

"How many days is it to the coast?" Bishop questioned, between bites of Eligor oat bread, trying to start up a casual conversation. Kiel had not spoken much since the flight from Opal, for obvious reasons. His city was encircled, and the last remnants of a once mighty race were now effectively cut off from any possible chance of escape and poised for extinction. There were other, lesser cities within the Eligor Empire, but those would be of little use. If they had not already been sacked, they soon would be, and they had already been dangerously weakened and depleted, having answered a desperate call for supplies and reserves.

Kiel thought a moment before responding. "We will taste of the salt air in three days hence. It is to the northeast of our current position. The eighth hell is just off the coast of the Northern Sea, possibly ten kilometers or so. On a clear day, you can just make it out on the horizon. I just hope the ocean isn't too rough this time of the year. The last time I was there, it was high summer and calm, as calm as it ever gets."

Bishop nodded, chewing on his rations awhile longer, then frowned.

"It might be a bad time to bring this up, but how are we to reach this eighth hell?"

"The remnants of the last expedition—that being myself and one other unfortunate Eligor—left several supplies behind that we will put to good use, one being an Old Earth boat."

Bishop stopped chewing and looked up in surprise. "An Old Earth boat? A boat from the Old Earth?"

Kiel returned the stare with widened eyes, mocking Bishop's gaze. "That's what I said, an *Old Earth boat.*"

Bishop put his meal down and sighed. "Now, I don't mean to sound concerned, but trusting a boat in the open ocean, a boat that is old beyond imagination no less, is not what I would call a wise decision. Possibly we should construct a raft."

"What do you have against the use of an Old Earth boat? Did one molest you as a child?"

"Well, I might not be the smartest human who has ever walked the planet, but I have seen boats not ten years of age that wouldn't be fit for kindling. Think, Kiel, think!" Bishop thumped his head with a finger several times.

The Eligor rolled his golden eyes in mock exasperation. "Jest with an Ikonian soldier and warm the forager on your belly before you seek to lift the savage from his savagery, I have always said." Kiel gave Bishop an exasperated look and then chuckled. "Bishop, it isn't a wooden boat."

"I don't understand. Not wooden? What's it made out of then? animal skins? tarred canvas?"

"Metal, of course," Kiel said as he began eating again.

"Metal!" Bishop guffawed, slapping his knee. "A metal boat! How in the eight hells can a metal boat stay afloat?"

Kiel seemed to be enjoying Bishop's confusion for a bit before responding to his outburst. "I don't think I can explain it to your simple wit, but trust me, it is a fine boat. And, might I ask, why are you so vexed about a sea crossing?"

Bishop coughed and quickly returned to his meal.

"Why are you so worried?" Kiel pressed.

Bishop looked up into the trees toward Storm Singer's roost with something bordering on embarrassment, then whispered, "Because I can't swim."

There came from above them tittering laughter. Bishop buried his head, his ears burning in embarrassment.

"You can't swim," Kiel repeated in disbelief, breaking into a thin smile.

"You heard me, chief," Bishop growled. "And I would be surprised if the buzzard up there could."

"That's remarkable. Swimming is required in the Eligor service. I am truly surprised." Kiel's smile broadened.

"I am a soldier, not a fish. A soldier does not need to know how to swim. A soldier soldiers on the land, not in the water, and certainly not in the bloody ocean. Whoever heard of fighting in the ocean anyway?"

"What if you had to cross a river while tracking something? Surely there are rivers in the protectorate?"

Bishop gulped down the last of his tough oat bread and then eyed Kiel. "Yes, we have rivers. But we also have an invention called a bridge, and we are able to walk across them without any worry of wetting our feet."

"And if there happened not to be a bridge, what then?"

"If it's too deep, we build a raft. What's your point anyway? Because if you've got one, it is escaping me at the moment."

Kiel, sobering, finished his evening victuals as well, fastidiously brushing crumbs absently from his armor. "No point. It's just humorous, that's all. A standard-bearer of the mighty Order of Merja Soria who can't swim. It's just humorous."

"All right, that's enough!" Bishop growled, his ears flaming all the more.

Kiel, daintily dabbing at his mouth with a handkerchief, added, "You know, it might be a good thing to learn how to swim in the near future, just in case we are forced to cross a river or, say, an ocean, and don't have the luxury of time to build a raft, or a bridge for that matter, if something were to happen to the boat."

Bishop looked up in apprehension as Kiel nonchalantly lay down to retire for the evening, rolling himself comfortably in his bedroll. "Why do you say that? You said the boat is seaworthy."

"Well, yes, but a metal boat … I mean, I never really thought about it before, but it does sort of boggle the mind, doesn't it, Standard-Bearer Bishop?" Kiel returned smugly as he closed his eyes. "Good night. Pleasant dreams. Sleep tight, don't let the cimex lectularius bite."

For the next several days they moved steadily northeast, and soon there were unmistakable signs of the ocean. The ground became sandy, seabirds screeched and wheeled in the sky, and Bishop could smell the salty tang of the sea mixed in the air, as a dull roar of breakers sounded in the distance.

Storm Singer flitted through the trees, landing on Kiel's shoulder and pointing a wing eastward. "The beach, the shore you spoke of is just ahead. But it seems a fair distance over the water to the island. I surely hope Bishop doesn't fall in on the way, seeing that he never learned how to swim and all."

Kiel pretended not to have heard the remark. Bishop reddened, replying, "I hear talk of sea harriers in these parts. Kiel, pray tell, what do they eat?"

"A sea harrier? Oh, you know, the typical fare: rabbits, squirrels, fish, birds …"

Storm Singer shot an ebon eye to the heavens. "Very well, Bishop, you have made your point. We will watch out for one another."

Dark clouds roiled in the sky when the trio finally broke away from the tangle of stunted trees and bramble and at last beheld the eastern ocean spread before them like a great gray-blue shroud. A black gravelly beach, strewn with logs and the detritus of past storms, ran for a kilometer both to the north and south, terminating against dark seaworn granite cliffs.

Kiel looked out on the slate-gray ocean and pointed to a series of eight black dots barely visible on the misty horizon. "Do you see the largest island at the southern end of the chain?"

Bishop squinted through the icy wind. "Yes, I see it."

"That is the eighth hell, our destination."

They moved away from the thick foliage and meandered down a sandy game path and onto the beach, where the roar of the surf was deafening. "We left our supplies toward the northern cliffs in a cave," Kiel said, pointing as the wind whipped at his scaled armor.

Bishop looked out over the limitless expanse of water, which was breathtaking in its grandeur. Somewhere out there, buried beneath the eighth hell, rested the object of their quest, the Iron Thunderbolt. Not for the first time, he wondered at the wisdom of disturbing such Old Earth sorcery from its ageless slumber.

After what seemed like hours, the black cliffs loomed over the travelers as Kiel searched the base. "There it is." He pointed to a gaping hole in the rock wall well above the high tide mark.

Scrabbling up the rocky cliff face with slippery seaweed and a profusion of mussels awaiting high tide, they entered the darkened cave and cautiously walked back into its shallow, sandy depths. The sound of the ocean became a dull roar behind them as the cave took a slight turn. Just as Kiel had said, resting against the back of the cave was a canvas-covered mound.

Kiel, brushing a few sand crabs toward an eager Storm Singer, grabbed the canvas and pulled it away from a dully glinting overturned object. Without a doubt it was a boat, but one like nothing Bishop had ever imagined. Thin, sheetlike rust-free metal had been molded to form the shell of the boat, while the upper supports and seats were riveted together in remarkable Old Earth perfection.

Kiel lifted one end of the boat. "Grab the other end. We will take it down to the beach and wash it up and check it for leaks. It's been ten cycles since I left it here, and I did that in haste."

Bishop, prepared for a strain, almost fell over as he hefted the thing. It was nearly weightless, actually lighter than the wooden boats he had been around as a child.

"Remarkable," he muttered in awe.

"You are learning, human. You are learning."

After Kiel and Bishop had hauled the boat out of the cave and down to the waterline, Kiel took a long branch and carefully began removing ten years' accumulation of clotted spiderwebs with meticulous attention to detail. Then he began a close inspection of the inner lip, occasionally swatting frantically at the remaining entomological inhabitants. Both Bishop and Storm Singer watched the process with confused glances.

"What's the point, Kiel?" Bishop finally questioned.

"Don't like spiders."

"Spiders?" Bishop barked in laughter as he turned to Storm Singer. "Behold! First Commander of the Imperial Intelligence Service of Grand Opal, the dread terror of nations, fearing nothing except spiders."

Storm Singer chortled at the comment as Kiel finished his fastidious cleaning and threw the stick away. "I don't like spiders, but I can swim if you would prefer I put them back."

Bishop's smile flattened; he waved his hand indifferently. "All right, hurry up with your spider thing. I would like to get on with it. As for swimming, I am sure that I will learn quickly if it becomes necessary to do so."

Kiel set about unlatching several compartments built into the sides of the boat. Inside he found rope, climbing gear, and rock picks. "Everything appears just as I left it. We are as ready as we will ever be."

They thrust the boat into the foam and, using the accompanying metal paddles attached to its sides, paddled clear of the breakers with ease just as a breeze blew in from offshore. The wind was strangely warm and carried with it the smell of rotted vegetation and the spicy-sweet aroma of flowers.

"It feels warm out here," Bishop said wonderingly, "though winter approaches."

"The ocean current in these parts comes from the tropics to the south of here. The island chain is directly in the path of the warm trade winds."

Bishop and Kiel took turns paddling to preserve their strength. Bishop handed the paddles over to Kiel after an hour or so, then pulled a bit of food from his pack and relaxed against the stern gunwale. The wind continued to blow against them, carrying with it the smells of the island. Down in the water, Bishop could see the beams of light plunging below and becoming lost in the emerald depths. He dozed for a while, dreaming of his youth and the magical times he had spent fishing with his father. Those were good days in the long ago.

Bishop's daydreams were interrupted by a flock of seagulls skimming across the tops of the waves toward the island shore. He rubbed his eyes and looked up, following the birds' path through the sky. There ahead of them loomed the eighth hell. From the mainland it had looked like a dot, but now the true size was becoming clear. It must have been ten kilometers or more from side to side, and its summit was so tall, it was now lost in steamy cloud cover.

"Shades of the Others," Bishop swore as he took in the fantastic scene. "It's not what I expected at all."

"Did you think it would be different?"

"I thought it would be small, maybe a kilometer in circumference at best. This is going to take us years to explore."

"Not to worry, Bishop. We located the entrance on our last visit."

"And where exactly is this entrance?"

"On the top of Ambrym."

"Ambrym?"

"Ambrym is the highest mountain on this dreary island. I would point it out, but it happens to be lost in the clouds at the moment."

"On the top, you say?" Bishop remarked in a banal tone, looking at the distant black slopes jutting away from the verdant jungle below. "Of course, right on the top. And why not? It would have been far too easy to have built it on the beach, where we could have easily gotten at it, now, wouldn't it have?"

Kiel shrugged as he continued to paddle. "There might have been a lower entrance in the days of the Others, but they would all be long buried."

"How's that?"

"The mountain is growing. Every cycle it gets taller."

A slight rumbling sound caught Bishop's ear as Kiel looked behind him at the mountain.

"It's an active volcano?"

"One of the largest known in the empire."

Bishop was ready to turn around. "How can we assault an active volcano?"

"Ambrym isn't the problem. It is the entrance itself that will prove to be the real challenge. The opening is stable, but the island grows around it every cycle. We might have a time finding it again. It was probably a tower in eons past, but now it lies beneath the rim."

Soon the surf washed their boat in. They could hear the sound of pebbly sand scraping against the hull.

They dragged the boat up the shore and away from the pounding waves, securing it to a palmlike tree that bowed away from the dense jungle, which was alive with the raucous sound of birds and the smell of fecund plant life, which was in superabundance here. They divided the climbing equipment between their own packs and turned toward the mountain.

"Welcome the eighth hell," Kiel said casually as he melted into the forbidding gloom of the stygian jungle of the eighth hell.

SIXTEEN

THE EIGHTH HELL

> There was a door to which I found no key. There was a veil through which I could not see.
> —Vena Korela,
> Second Saga of Vainamonen, Runa 129

"I'm at the end of my endurance." Bishop panted as the trail finally began to level out. He glanced behind him at the steep, heavily vegetated sides of the mountain. After a day spent hacking their way through the dense jungles of the eighth hell's westernmost climes, followed by a backbreaking five-hour hike up the volcano's slope, he felt he could go no further. He looked beseechingly at Kiel.

"Hike, don't talk. Hasten, Bishop," Storm Singer croaked from Bishop's shoulder. "Kiel isn't complaining."

"He hasn't had to carry your fat feathered carcass up two kilometers of mountain, all the while keeping to a goat trail no wider than my dagger is long! You should not have eaten so many crabs; you are getting a potbelly. I just might use you as a pillow tonight."

Storm Singer bobbed in mirth, saying, "Crabs is good!"

"Crabs *are* good! Good and fattening!" Bishop eyed the surrounding land with disdain as he struggled to put one foot in front of the other. "With canyons plummeting on both sides and you squawking and fidgeting one centimeter from my ear the entire time, it's a wonder I haven't dropped to my death."

"If memory serves, it was you who insisted we climb this anthill to find your Old Earth device and stop this mythic Reaver fellow whom you claim resides up yonder in Ikonia."

Bishop opened his mouth to respond but was cut short.

"My pack is thrice as heavy as yours, human," Kiel growled. "If you wish, I will trade the climbing gear for Storm Singer."

"A splendid idea," replied the bird. "Besides, this human has undersized shoulders."

Bishop shook his head wearily and moved forward, his booted feet crunching on the volcanic ground.

After a few hundred meters, the trail finally flattened out. The trees and the three-meter-tall cane grasses that lushly lined the track behind them thinned to become a world of swirling gas clouds and sifting glassy filaments of cinder. Ahead of them in the distance loomed Ambrym, the heart of the eighth hell.

"By the Others!" Bishop swore as he eyed the fantastic scene. "I thought we had reached the top. The whole mountain looms above us!"

Kiel shook his head in annoyance as they advanced. "You've been fooled three times by false summits. You might be many things, human, but you are no mountain climber. That much is certain."

"Never after today will you be able to say that again!" Bishop retorted, still eyeing the distant sight. The ancient volcano jutted almost a thousand meters into the sky and seemed to brood darkly over them as they advanced. Even Storm Singer seemed mesmerized by the sight.

Evening was rapidly approaching, and Kiel thankfully agreed to establish camp on the tree line, apparently loath to invade the bleak highlands after dark. Bishop shook Storm Singer from his shoulder and set about preparing the camp. The bird flew to one of the lower branches of a stunted cactus-like bush and began his evening feather care.

The campsite was nestled in a grove of palms and tree-sized ferns. Multicolored orchids dotted the black soil, bobbing on long green stalks in the gentle perfumed wind that drifted up from the superabundant vegetation of the lower jungle. Overhead, the dark silhouettes of monstrous bats creased the evening sky.

The travelers unpacked their supplies, Bishop gazing about him all the while. The thinning vegetation in the upper jungle of the eighth hell clung to life by a tenacious thread, and it seemed that the camp itself was perched on the edge of disaster. Above the three travelers, the blasted sides of the volcano lay barren and devoid of life.

Kiel, finishing his camp duties, sat wearily on a rock that jutted away from the sandy ground and, following Bishop's eyes, looked out beyond the ash plain, noting the volcano as it lit the clouds in the distance, wreathing them in a ghostly red glow.

"You're sure this is the correct island, Kiel? It doesn't look like any Old Earth site I've ever seen," Bishop mumbled, breaking up a dry branch for kindling.

Kiel's translator crackled as he motioned toward the volcano in the distance. "Very sure, human. Somewhere inside that monster is the entrance to the Thunderbolt."

The Eligor took a tainted rat from his pack and absently munched, but he would not take his eyes away from the distant cone. "Yes, very sure," he repeated to himself.

As Bishop lit the fire and rummaged around in his pack for something to eat, a movement at the perimeter of the glade caught his attention. A gray muzzle poked its way through the grass, followed by the lean and predatory body of a wolf. Bishop relaxed somewhat. "Someone is looking for a handout."

Kiel followed Bishop's pointing finger to the furtive animal, which stood frozen, watching and waiting. In the next instant, Kiel leapt up, grabbing a rock all in one motion and expertly threw it. There was a resounding thud followed by a yelp. The wolf doubled on its hind legs, sprinted back into the lower forest in an instant and was gone, crashing through the undergrowth far below them.

"What in the eight hells did you do that for? It was only a mangy wolf!" Bishop barked in surprise.

Storm Singer, still on his branch in a nearby tree, poked his head out from behind some leaves and stared silently.

"Murdering monsters, that's what they are," Kiel grated, sitting back down with an unreadable look upon his face.

Bishop stared at Kiel. "Murdering? What are you talking about? Wolves never attack anything larger than a small deer."

"Little you know."

"little I know... Why would a wolf attack unless it was starving or provoked?"

"They were deliberately starved and provoked." Kiel spoke the words evenly. He continued to stare at the forest in which the wolf had vanished as if he were seeing something that wasn't actually there, something Bishop could never see.

"Kiel. What are you talking about?" Bishop threw his arms up in exasperation.

Kiel turned his attention to Bishop with unfocused eyes, then looked back toward the lower forest. He said nothing for a few moments. "Well, in any case, it won't be nosing through our food supplies any time soon."

If you say so, but, I am wondering, how in the name of the Others did it even get on this accursed island in the first place?"

Kiel, with a distant look still in his eyes, answered. "Apparently, wolves were few in number at one point in the forgotten past, almost extinct, as they should have been, and then the Others suddenly decided to repopulate the entire planet with them for their own unknowable reasons."

"You seem not overly fond of wolves, if I had to guess," Bishop commented, settling a bit.

"It was a pack of wolves that killed my nest brother."

"Killed your nest brother? You had a brother!" Bishop glanced warily at Kiel. He knew little about the Eligor's past, and certainly nothing about any brother.

Golden eyes slowly refocused. "The Imperial Intelligence Service," he began, "it was an endurance test. Apparently I still suffer residual trauma from the event."

"An endurance test for the Imperial Intelligence Service? You're joking."

"No. No joke, Bishop. The candidates were stripped to the waist and, without any defensive weapons, were required to fight, for ten minutes, wolves that were unleashed after having been incited to kill. If the candidates took flight, they were terminated."

There was a long, uneasy silence that crept over the camp as the two furtively glanced at each other.

"I suppose it was a just mangy wolf after all …" Kiel's voice died away. "I apologize, it will not happen again."

Bishop absently fed the sputtering fire with bits of wood. "No harm done. To me anyway." Glancing nervously at the lower jungle, he added, "So, if you don't mind my questions, everyone within the Imperial Intelligence Service had to take this test?"

Kiel nodded wearily. "It was as I say: some were torn to pieces; some were terminated as they panicked and ran; most survived. I still bear the scars to attest to my own ordeal with the wolves."

"And that was it? Fight off a bunch of wolves, live through it, and you could join the IIS? Just like that?"

Moments passed before Kiel answered. "The wolves—that was the final part of the training, not the beginning. Not the beginning at all. It was simply the last of many trials."

"But after the wolf test, then you were IIS?"

Kiel shook his head. "Even after the final test, it was not over. The acolyte attended a special blood ceremony—a painful rite in itself—binding himself to the emperor."

Kiel absently rubbed his scaled arms, where Bishop noted for the first time curious scars, barely visible, in the shapes of complex whirls and symbols of some sort.

"He also had to swear an oath of loyalty and obedience unto death to the body politic—the empire as a whole. Only then was he assigned duties according to his test results and quality."

Bishop stared in morbid fascination. "All that and fighting maddened wolves barehanded. And there were other trials? What were they like?"

Kiel looked up from the fire. "They weren't pleasant."

Within the protectorate, stories about the Imperial Intelligence Service were gruesome and legendary. A monstrous machine of espionage, torture, massacre, and genocide, its wheels rolled busily over occupied countries, and it became an adjunct of every Eligor activity, even to the armed forces. But what went on within the organization itself? Bishop could not resist hearing a firsthand account from an actual Eligor, so he overcame his initial reluctance to probe what appeared to be a guarded subject. "The IIS, what was it like?"

The wind rustled through the trees; a bird called in the distance; the night deepened. Kiel's golden eyes, reflecting the firelight, seemed to replay a hellish past as he pondered the question. Surprisingly, he did not hesitate long. Perhaps he needed to tell his tale.

"The Imperial Intelligence Service," he began slowly. "The IIS was an elite institution, with the strictest requirements for acceptance to the Imperial War Academy at Ixxis Roi. In the old days, the emperor himself scrutinized all applicants personally, as it was his word that called us to his service."

Ambrym rumbled ominously in the distance. "I can still hear the emperor's dread voice in my mind," Kiel muttered. He continued: "Our training methods are harsh. Weakness has no place in the order of the Imperial Intelligence Service. As an IIS cadet develops, the world will shrink back. A violent, dominating, brutal Eligor—that is what I am after. He must be all those things. He must be indifferent to pain. There must be no weakness or tenderness within him. The pride and the independence of a beast out for prey must gleam in his eyes. In this way I shall eradicate the thousands of years of Eligor domestication. Then I shall have in front of me the pure and noble natural material. With that I can dominate the world."

There was another long moment of silence, and Bishop thought Kiel would say no more, but the Eligor continued.

"Those who wished to join the ranks of the IIS had to first graduate within the top ten percent from the Imperial Military Academy, itself a grueling, two-cycle-long school. Then they had to meet a most exacting standard of physical condition and general bearing. Finally, they had to go through innumerable political and physical tests. If the applicant met the specifications, he was then made a candidate. But long before the candidate was allowed to consider himself a member of the IIS, he had to pass through a training course that was a veritable living hell."

The fire popped, a swirl of tiny sparks rising in the night air like fireflies, but Kiel seemed not to notice. "How they drilled us until we howled in pain! Navigating obstacle courses, crawling through pipes, being subjected to pack drills, and going on long marches in the heat, all with no water to quench our thirst. Yet no one ever dreamed of quitting, such was our zeal. One got so that one lost all criticism and just lived in this hell—simply an automaton. There was no other thought other than of *ēorl-gewǽdum*."

"Of what?"

Kiel was momentarily broken out of his trance as his previously distant eyes came to focus on Bishop. "Forgive me. The translator would not know the word. It is an Old Earth term. It means blind obedience."

Bishop was bewildered. "Blind obedience? How could you have endured? Was it fear?"

Kiel frowned as he thought. "Fear. Certainly there was fear, but blind obedience was achieved not merely through fear but also through the creation of a near-religious fanaticism, which separated the Imperial Intelligence Service from every other institution in the empire. The IIS was an order within an order and was not subject to national law; it had its own laws, courts, and judges. A hierarchical structure it was, with a graded series of privileges separating the higher orders from the lower orders."

Kiel absently pulled his dagger from its sheath and absently stirred the black glassy sand with it. "I suppose it's a story that has been told a thousand times in history. A regime that purposes to bring about a utopia by controlling every aspect of people's lives, but in fact brings about a living hell, a hideous hell."

"hellish, what do you mean by that?"

Kiel continued to stir the sand. "It was a system of government where the state planned and controlled the economy and where a single, authoritarian party held power, claiming to make progress toward a higher social order where all goods were to be equally shared by the people. Strange as it may seem, there is a very fine line between progressive liberalism, fascism and communism. Interesting that such a belief, when carried to its conclusion, usually brings about the end of its own coveted freedoms. I have come to believe that freedom itself is its own doom, and if too much of it is given to a people or government, it can cause freedom to bring about its own destruction. But I have grown old and jaded and have lost the patriotism of my youth."

Kiel resheathed his blade and edged closer to the now crackling fire, attempting to warm his hands in the gathering chill of the evening.

"Yes, such systems rarely work, because they rely completely on the government following its own doctrine. The government becomes responsible to no one, and therefore the very people charged with maintaining these lofty policies are usually the first to take advantage, enslaving the population in a brutal grip of repression for their own enrichment."

Kiel eyed Bishop. "Bad enough, I would think, even having to put up with elected officials, let alone officials who elect themselves, wouldn't you agree?"

"I suppose so." Bishop didn't involve himself in politics, but he had heard enough to understand what Kiel was talking about. Atrocities and crimes against humanity of the old Eligor Empire—there had been many tales about the subject. But what Kiel told him now seemed to confirm the worst, and now Bishop was somewhat sorry he had brought the topic up. Wondering if this conversation was hard for the Eligor, he coughed awkwardly. "Well," he said. "Our government has its problems too, I suppose."

Kiel continued to stare into the flames of the fire as if he had not heard Bishop. "The Imperial Intelligence Service." He nodded to himself. "Yes, the IIS was the true center of the empire. Even the lowest elements of the IIS were feared and dreaded by the common Eligor masses."

Bishop had uncorked the proverbial bottle and was now obligated to listen as Kiel emptied his thoughts. "Probably didn't have much to worry about after becoming IIS," he offered.

Kiel shook his head. "There was plenty to worry about."

"Like what?"

"Other members of the IIS, for instance."

"I don't understand."

"Everyone within the IIS was constantly spying on everyone else. Not even the top officers were exempt from being visited by Imperial emissaries, who arrived unannounced, sometimes in the dead of night, to see whether things were being done according to regulations. We lived in constant dread of being discovered as being in some way unworthy of such a high calling."

"And if someone was found to be unworthy?"

Kiel grunted. "He who failed or actually betrayed the IIS or the emperor was not merely deprived of an office but was also, together with his subordinates, deprived of his life by way of the most gruesome methods conceivable. These were the harsh and implacable laws of the Order. On the one hand, an Eligor could reach for the skies and grasp whatever he desired. On the other hand, there was the deep abyss of potential annihilation.

"Sounds like a living hell, as you have stated."

"Yes and no," Kiel responded simply.

"What do you mean, yes and no? What possible benefit was there to such a brutal existence?"

"There was a fierce pride in having been chosen for the IIS. The romanticism persisted through the entire Eligor Empire."

"And you felt pride as well?"

"I was young," Kiel responded flatly. "And," he continued, "what male of any species can say truthfully that in his heart there has never lurked a yearning for power and conquest?"

"There are women …"

"Yes, well, there are always exceptions to every rule, aren't there? But I assure you, behind every powerful female, you will find an even more powerful male who has placed her there for his own purposes."

There was a moment of silence while Bishop took in what he had been told. "What of this emperor you have spoken of? What was he like?"

Ambrym rumbled again in the distance. Kiel looked across at Bishop as if silently judging the question that had been put to him.

"The emperor," he began. "The Eligor throne was filled at the time of my ascension within the IIS by Amuzet the Second, nephew of the last, and grandson of the preceding, monarch. He was elected to the regal dignity in the Hundred and Ninety-First Cycle of Flint in the Twelfth Grand Cycle of Kala, according to our calendar, which I have previously described to you, in preference to his brothers, for his superior qualifications as both a soldier and a high priest—a combination of offices sometimes found within the hierarchy. In his early youth, he had taken an active part in the wars of the empire, though later he devoted himself more exclusively to services of the temple. He was scrupulous in his attention to all the burdensome ceremonial aspects of Eligor religious worship, which I will not bore you with. His was a grave and reserved demeanor, as he spoke little and with prudent deliberation. His behavior was well calculated to inspire superior sanctity."

Bishop looked up from the crackling fire in surprise. "Wars, you say? Wars with whom? There are only the Merja Sorians, the Eligor, the foragers, and the Ikonians. I am fairly certain the Ikonians are a recent threat. The foragers are not known to be warlike except within their own factions—the Red Serpent and Black Jaguar—and we have never interfered with your empire, unless you count repulsing your invasion at the Battle of Koth."

Kiel smiled faintly, his golden eyes refocusing from deep thought. "Do you really think your ancestors created the Gondakar Barrier, a herculean achievement in its own right, solely to keep the Eligor at bay? The world is a big place, Bishop; there are horrors out there that would freeze your soul. Even within our own borders, and they are vast, there are intelligences that would wish doom upon us, and these actors are ceaselessly at work to unseat us from power."

Bishop silently pondered this unsettling information, recalling the incident with the Megatherium at Ra, while Kiel continued with his account of Eligor history.

"When Amuzet's election was announced to him, he was found sweeping leaves from the steps of the great temple of the national war god,

Orcus, in the city of Kirsk. He received the messengers with humility, professing his unfitness for a station with such great responsibility. The message delivered to Amuzet was carried by his favorite relative, Nezahal, a power within the former government, who announced to the people afterward: 'Rejoice, happy people, that you have now a sovereign who will be to you a steady column of support, a father in distress, and a brother in tenderness and sympathy, one whose aspiring soul will disdain all the extravagant pleasures of the senses and the wasteful indulgence of sloth. An illustrious youth, Amuzet, upon whom Orcus has laid such a weighty charge, will also be given the strength to sustain it.' And so on and so forth." Kiel absently threw a log onto the fire, sending myriad sparks into the night sky as if for emphasis.

"I suppose it is not unlike one of my people within the Order being promoted to a high position. It does not sound unlike the much-vaunted promotion of our previous grand master," Bishop commented. "Was he successful, this Amuzet, in his promotion to leader of the Eligor Empire?"

"Oh, quite. At least in the beginning of his reign, Amuzet displayed all the energy and enterprise that his people had anticipated he'd show. His first expedition, against a rebel province, was a success, and he led back in triumph a throng of captive conspirators for a public execution that was to take place at his coronation. This was celebrated with uncommon pomp. Games and religious ceremonies continued for several days. Spectators flocked from every quarter of the empire to witness this event.

"In his first years, Nezahal was constantly engaged in war, frequently leading the Eligor army in person. The Eligor banners were seen in the furthest provinces of the empire and even in the distant regions of the outlands bordering our northwestern extremes, where the yellow ape-men live and occasionally raid our lands. The expeditions were generally successful, and the limits of the empire were more widely extended than at any preceding period in our history.

"The new emperor was not inattentive to the internal concerns of the empire. He made some important changes in the courts of justice and carefully watched over the execution of the laws, which he enforced with harshness and severity. He was in the habit of patrolling the streets of Kirsk in disguise to become personally acquainted with the abuses within it, and with questionable policy, it is said, he would sometimes test the integrity of his judges by tempting them with large bribes in an attempt to swerve them from their duty, and then call the criminal to strict account for yielding to the temptation, usually ending in the death of the offender. Any corruption that might have existed before his reign was soon squelched for no better reason than the fear of subterfuge.

"He liberally compensated all who served him. He showed a similar generous spirit in his public works, constructing and embellishing new temples, bringing water into the capital by way of a new channel, and also establishing a hospital, or retreat, for invalid soldiers who had been crippled in the line of duty."

"He doesn't sound like a bad emperor, all things being considered. Harsh, but not bad," Bishop chimed.

"Yes, well, those were the early years of his reign. These lordly accomplishments, so worthy of a great emperor, were counterbalanced by an different sort of show of 'success' in the latter years of his life. The humility he had so effectively displayed before his elevation to emperor gave way in later years to an intolerable arrogance. In his pleasure houses and his domestic establishments, and even in his way of life, he assumed pomp and ceremony of a sort unknown to his predecessors. He secluded himself from public observation, or when he went abroad, he exacted the most slavish homage. While in the palace, he would be served, even in the most menial offices, by persons of high rank. He dismissed several plebeians, poor soldiers of merit, from the places they had occupied during the reign of his predecessor, considering their attendance a dishonor to his royal person. It was in vain that his oldest and sagest counselors protested, though quietly, of a conduct so impolite.

"While he thus disgusted his subjects by his haughty demeanor, he further alienated their affections by imposing grievous taxes. These were necessary because of the lavish expenditure of his court. The new taxes fell with a particular heaviness on the lesser cities and the people of the empire you might call the middle class. This oppression led to frequent insurrection and resistance, and in the latter years of Azumet's reign, presented as a source of unremitting hostility, so the armed forces of one half of the empire were employed in suppressing the uprising of the other half of the population. It could be said that the war with Merja Soria was a last, desperate attempt to unify the empire under one single banner of allegiance. And it was with the greatest of luck that the timing coincided with the prophetic Ignotum pro Magna, with which you are already familiar.

"Of course, as you are well aware, the campaign against your nation was a disaster. I am of the opinion that if the Ikonians had not slain Amuzet at Kirsk, he would have been assassinated shortly thereafter from within his own royal administration. And who knows how he really died? Maybe they did get to him before the insects had their chance."

Bishop absorbed what he had been told, wondering what series of events could have created such a monster as Azumet II.

Storm Singer, apparently concluding that it was safe to do so, descended from his lofty branch, hopping lower and lower, until he alighted upon the ground, interrupting the silence.

The bird boldly ambled toward Kiel and Bishop like some grand old wizard cloaked in black robes. "I cannot sleep with an empty stomach."

Bishop rummaged in his pack and found a small lump of Eligor oat bread, placed it before the bird, who bowed in silent thanks, snatched the food and began his evening repast.

After feeding Storm Singer, Bishop returned to his pack and retrieved the map E'Ka had given him, unrolling the parchment with care. Storm Singer, sauntering toward the map with the air of an old necromancer, appeared to be studying it. The bird didn't fool Bishop in the least. Wolf-birds were excellent at spotting and tracking animate life, but they had difficulty with inanimate objects, especially man-made objects, and especially with something as complex as a map. They often couldn't tell the difference between a house and a barn. Storm Singer soon became disinterested and flew back to his tree perch.

"Where should we start the search tomorrow, Kiel?"

Kiel's eyes cleared as his dark thoughts slowly faded. "The search. Yes, we should search here." He confidently pointed a clawed finger to a spot on the map. "Yes, here on the eastern side. The entrance to the Thunderbolt is just within the crater. My fear is that over the years it has been buried or has come to lie too far below the rim to reach."

"Let's hope not." Bishop sighed. "Storm Singer, you'll scout the rim for an opening that looks man-made." Bishop was not feeling at all confident that the bird would succeed, even if the entrance had been painted red, yet every resource had to be used now.

Storm Singer looked at Bishop with a sideways glance but remained silent as if to acknowledge his own difficulty in doing such things.

As the stars winked on one by one, Bishop looked furtively around the darkened island, remembering something E'Ka had said.

"Not to sound superstitious, but E'Ka rambled about spirits or something of the sort. Do you know what he was talking about?"

Kiel looked up from the fire with a jerk, as if Bishop had touched a sore nerve. "It seems E'Ka knows quite a bit for a simple librarian, doesn't he?"

"Maybe I shouldn't have mentioned it," Bishop muttered. "I wouldn't want the old Eligor to get in trouble."

Kiel sighed. "No, he wouldn't be punished. I suppose the story has made its rounds."

"So, there was some truth to it?" Bishop probed.

Kiel nodded affirmatively. "We were twenty in number when we first landed on this dreary island. Yes, twenty in number we were. When we left, there were only two."

Bishop began to look around at the deepening gloom. Storm Singer, who had abruptly stopped picking at his feathers, began to take notice of Bishop's paranoia and flew to alight on his shoulder.

"What is it, Bishop?" the bird questioned in agitation, peering into the gloom, his eyes reflecting the sparks of the fire.

"I don't rightly know, but Kiel might."

"What do you know, Kiel?" the bird asked fearfully, becoming fully alert, jerking his head this way and that.

Kiel fished around in his pack to locate a morsel of dried meat and began chewing it. "The IIS had found a vague reference to the Thunderbolt in an Old Earth manuscript excavated from a Blue Zone. The Grand Union thought it wise to investigate the story, so we were sent here. It was to be an archeological mission; we were not prepared for an attack."

"Attack?" Storm Singer squawked.

Bishop knew very well that Kiel had made such a journey; E'Ka had told him. But he had not mentioned that he knew. Yet he was quite interested to hear about Kiel's experiences. He asked, "Attacked? Attacked by whom?"

Kiel shook his head. "It wasn't a physical entity that attacked. It was something else, something ethereal that confronted us. It entered our minds like an exploding hurricane. The attack ended as quickly as it had started, but not before it had killed eighteen of our soldiers in a most gruesome fashion."

"Gods of the Others!" Bishop swore.

"Gods of the Others," Storm Singer repeated fearfully.

"Yes, the gods of the Others; that is what we believed. We of the Imperial Intelligence Service had been trained to endure every conceivable physical torment, but mental torment, that was something our superiors did not prepare us for."

It seemed to Bishop that life within the IIS was replete with mental torment, but he kept his thoughts on the matter private. "How long did the attack occur?"

"The attack seemed quite short-lived, though later I realized that certain brief, glimmering visions were actually several hours in length—chaotic visions that disturbed me greatly, as they were unprecedented and altered my mind. When I came to my senses again, my head felt as though it had been cracked in two, and I had the singular feeling, altogether new to me, that someone or something else had tried to gain possession of my mind."

Bishop, now fully alert, spoke. "These visions you speak of, what were they like?"

Kiel's golden eyes clouded in troubled thought. "When I first dropped into unconsciousness, I began to see strange shapes before my eyes and to feel that I was standing in a large vault. I saw tremendous Old Earth technologies and rooms of curious and inexplicable apparatuses of myriad sorts. Then there were colossal caverns with intricate machinery whose functions and purposes were wholly strange to me. It was only many years after the experience that some of the visions made any sense. I believe now that there was a purpose to this attack, and as strange as it might sound, I think the deaths were accidental."

"And the purpose for the attack?" Bishop probed.

"The purpose?" Kiel muttered. "Yes, there seemed to be a purpose. When I returned to Opal, I collapsed. I was hospitalized for weeks, apparently showing no sign of consciousness for the first sixteen hours, knowing nothing but a repeating dream. But it was more than that; it was more like a kind of instruction had been overwritten within my mind.

"When I opened my eyes and began to speak, the words that came out seemed acquired and foreign. I used my vocal organs clumsily and gropingly as if I had laboriously relearned the Eligor language from books. The pronunciation was barbarously alien, while the idiom seemed to include both scraps of archaism and expressions of a wholly incomprehensible cast.

"Only after weeks of hideous repetition did I grow half reconciled to these visions and return to a fully conscious state. But snatches of what I had been given were permanently burned into my brain. I seem to have been taught chapters in history whose existence no scholar of today has ever suspected. At the same time, I noticed that I had an inexplicable command of many unknown sorts of knowledge, a command that I seemed to wish to hide rather than display. These uncanny flashes soon ceased to appear, and I now remember very little, although it is without a doubt still there. One such piece of knowledge was the location of the Thunderbolt and its reality. I know it is there; otherwise I would not have been so compelled to return."

"How is it that you were left alive?"

Kiel shrugged. "I don't know for sure. Just possibly I was the only one capable of enduring the attack. Or I was allowed to leave; I cannot be certain. Even so, for months afterward I suffered from severe headaches and graphic nightmares of those events."

"What became of this demon that attacked you?"

"It vanished—or faded would be a better way to describe the event now that I think about it. I had the peculiar sense that its power to invade our thoughts was finite or that it was looking for a particular mind, which it did not find. Let's hope it is long gone by now."

"I surely hope so," Storm Singer croaked, still scanning the darkened glade, ever more watchful.

"As do I," echoed Bishop, as he too looked about the camp's darkened perimeter with concern.

Kiel looked away, uneasy. "There was one other thing, which I am loath to bring up at this time."

Bishop looked up from the little fire. "And what is that?"

"The idea of enlisting the humans for help concerning the Ikonian conflict. It is an idea I do not think I arrived at by chance. I believe that I would not have come up with the idea on my own. More like it was a suggestion, or a compulsion, that had been placed within me and that it was only a matter of time before I would have found some excuse to travel to the protectorate."

Bishop stared. "And …?"

"When I first met you, I had a peculiar sense of satisfaction; it was like finding a missing bit of a puzzle or a lost key. More than that, I felt that bringing you to this very place was required, necessary in some way. I tried to dismiss the thoughts as irrational and, with difficulty, forced them from my mind. Then, when you mentioned the eighth hell back in Opal, the sensation returned, stronger than ever. It was as if some hidden part of my mind was persuading me to do these things."

"I don't like it, Kiel. You should have said something before now."

"In fact, I had to fight the coercion to bring you here when I first met you."

"Kiel!"

"I just didn't mention it."

"Next time, mention it."

The travelers finally retired to their bedrolls and fell into fitful slumber. Just a few kilometers away, lava boiled and the earth shook. It was more than once during the night that Bishop got up to make a thorough search of the surrounding area for danger with a worried Storm Singer nearly clinging to his ear the entire time.

In the dim light of the morning, shortly after sunrise, the travelers again struck out wearily toward Ambrym, which was several kilometers uphill. Storm Singer flew ahead of them, returning occasionally to report on the trail conditions as best he could. As they followed the dry riverbeds and ancient lava flows toward the volcanic cone, a gentle rain began to fall.

The wolf-bird gave up his investigation and dropped to Bishop's shoulder, huddling there for protection as cinder blackened rain pelted them.

Kiel unerringly followed a route up the mountain, not once stopping to reconnoiter his position. Bishop, finally becoming uneasy about this fact, called attention to it. "Kiel, you seem overly sure of our path. This is a big mountain. Are you positive that this is the correct route? You are acting as if you have been here a hundred times."

"I have never before been here, but I know with utter conviction that this is the correct route."

Bishop stopped in his tracks and stared, dumbfounded. "You have never been here? You told me that you had been to this island before—told me, in fact, that you know exactly where the Thunderbolt is hidden. What do you mean, you have never been here?"

"I have been to this island, but after the attack on the lower slopes, we were not inclined to go any farther. In fact, it was all we could do just to get back off the island alive."

"You never saw the entrance?" Bishop demanded. "How in the eight hells are you so sure that it isn't down in the jungle somewhere? I mean, we could be wasting our time sweating it out climbing this rock heap for nothing!"

"I see it in my mind. It's up there, Bishop, trust me," Kiel said, pointing with confidence.

"In your mind." Bishop stammered.

Kiel turned and began climbing again. "The way to the Thunderbolt is there, human, on the top of Ambrym. Trust me."

Bishop looked over at Storm Singer, who silently returned the look. "'Trust me,' he says. 'It's in my mind,' he says," Bishop mumbled. Then, shrugging in frustration, he struck out behind the Eligor.

The closer they hiked to the crater above them, the more the character of the ground beneath their feet began to change, from silty black grit to charcoal-lump-sized stones.

Suddenly, from a kilometer above them, Ambrym gave out a huge belch.

"Caution," Kiel warned. "Ashfall on the way."

Instead of the bluish-white clouds of steam and gas, the plume that issued out from the cone was heavy and black, trailing earthward in a dark curtain. Slowly it drifted their way on the wind. Five minutes later the ashfall found them, covering their packs and clothing with a sandy grit the color of gray pumice. It was as if the mountain was warning them to stay away. Yet on they went, until the rim was visible through the swirling ash and steam.

As they finally peered over the edge, they beheld the volcanic pit five hundred meters below obscured by rocky ledges. The pit looked like the artistic work of a visionary—a visionary or a fiend.

Every millimeter of the surface was painted with polychromatic color. Sunshine-yellow sulfur coated strips of the rock face. Iron had washed other sections with a flaming orange. Vivid metallic green deposits of other minerals, their names unknown to the travelers, glazed the rock nearest the vent, like a carpet of wet moss. Other patches of stone were bleached white by acrid gases that poured from vents.

The pit, three massive step-down ledges below them, each deeper and wider than the one above it, was marbled with layers of black ash and bleached basaltic rock.

"Well, it's now or never," Bishop stated to no one in particular, starting down toward the pit.

The three passed small whistling fumaroles steaming with superheated water vapor that Storm Singer seemed to find particularly unnerving, causing him to creep up Bishop's shoulder until he was perched almost on his ear.

"You're ripping my ear off again, you ill-begotten bird! Clip your claws or be off!" Bishop winced as he pushed Storm Singer back.

Storm Singer looked small and withdrawn as he returned Bishop's stare. "I do not like this place, Bishop. Let's make haste and retire away from this area. It is not for birds or humans."

"Well, for once I will agree with you. I do not care for this place any more than you do, but we have very little choice," Bishop returned grimly, glancing worriedly at Kiel.

The group continued down the inverted pyramid of ledges until they reached the last one. There, at the bottom of the third and largest pit, sat a lava lake. Its fury pushed lava through three crusty holes in a natural roof that partly covered the lake with a canopy. Bright orange and red splatters flew unpredictably from the circular opening of the largest hole. A second or two later, a noise from beneath the earth—a rumbling *booooom*—filled the pit and rolled across the sculpted ash plain beyond.

"It is down there somewhere." Kiel pointed with the same unerring certainty he had shown before.

Bishop eyed Storm Singer, who still clutched at his shoulder in obvious loathing of the area. "I realize that this is a terrible thing to ask, but we are going to need reconnaissance of the inner pit for any signs of human construction."

Storm Singer eyed Bishop. "And just what is it that I am supposed to find?"

Bishop looked over at Kiel for help. Kiel unsheathed his dagger, smoothed an area in the black sand, and began drawing. "The access port is generally human-sized. It is an eight-sided slate-gray doorway that is recessed into the side of the cliff face. It has a shiny black circle of glass in the center of the door."

"All of that from your mind?" Bishop questioned in shock. "You have never been here!"

Kiel mutely shrugged.

"Rock colored, you say? Black?" Storm Singer visually scanned the rock-colored and blackened moonscape in frustration. "That is likely to stand out and make itself known in this most dreary of places. Why could it not be shaped like a rabbit or an egg? I would have no difficulty spotting it then!"

"Or a mite-ridden feather, or a dead rat!" Bishop quipped.

Kiel stared at the two in silence as gossamer filaments of glassy ash rained down around them. "It should be very obvious."

"There, you see? If the lizard says it's easy, then it's easy. Now, get!"

The bird shook the ash from his feathers, glowering at Bishop and Kiel, and then came to a decision. "All right. If it will speed our departure from this hellish pit, I will go." He seemed to shake with loathing as he took to the air.

Hours passed before the bird returned, settling again on Bishop's shoulder. "I can't be sure, but about a kilometer in that direction is something that looks like it could be what you seek." Storm Singer pointed a slate-colored wing in the easterly direction.

"Describe it exactly, bird," Kiel said.

"Well, it was gray, or rock colored as you say. It is human-sized. I couldn't see the eight sides, but I am sure it has sides. It was weird-looking anyway."

They hastened to inspect what Storm Singer had discovered, only to find a natural steam vent billowing noisily.

Bishop slumped in despair. "No, no! Listen to me, you stupid bird: the door we are looking for is man-made! This is just a rotten steam vent! It's part of the volcano!"

"Well, it seemed close to your description to me. But who am I but a worthless bird, as you are always wont to say." Storm Singer ruffled his sooty feathers in frustration and again took flight amid a flurry of black feathers and angry cawing.

"Seems maddened," Kiel muttered, watching Storm Singer wheel into the haze.

"Yes, plain cracked like the stupid egg he popped out of, curse the day that happened."

This time the bird was gone much longer, and Bishop began to worry. Then, just as he was about to go looking for him, Storm Singer reappeared, winging heavily out of the swirling vapor and alighting on an overhanging rock.

"I think I have found it over there. Follow me." He flew off, motioning with a wing.

"Storm Singer! Back here!"

The bird wheeled in the sky and reluctantly returned. "Yes, what can I do for you? Bring you a sack lunch? You are holding me up when I want nothing more than to get off this island!"

Bishop glowered, rubbing the soot from his eyes. "Before I lose any more sweat hiking to another steam vent, describe what you have found, exactly."

"It is rock colored and shaped like a human, and very strange—most strange. I couldn't tell anything about the sides."

"Storm Singer! That's what you said last time!"

Kiel gazed toward the direction Storm singer had indicated. "Perhaps he has found it this time."

"Kiel! This flying rat couldn't find his own nest in this rock heap if it was painted with a red arrow."

"No, he has found it," Kiel repeated distantly.

Bishop shook his head. "What a waste of bloody time! Fine, we will run in endless circles for the rest of the day, chasing Storm Singer's tail feathers and his witless brain."

The bird took flight again, and Kiel and Bishop followed him for some forty minutes before he again alighted on Bishop's shoulder and pointed with a sooty wing tip.

"Below us there is something." Storm Singer no longer sounded very sure of himself.

"I hope you are right this time," Bishop growled. He and Kiel began unpacking their climbing supplies.

The sinewy Eligor handed Bishop the climbing rope, throwing the end down into the volcano. Clipping the rope onto the rappelling device on his belt, Bishop stepped into the air above the pit.

A dozen meters of rope slipped between Bishop's gloved fingers as he lowered himself. Acidic gases bit at his nose and eyes. The roaring coming from below him was deafening, mixed with an occasional titanic belch and pop. Each new breath from the volcano caused the temperature to momentarily soar and heaved the air so violently that Bishop's ears popped from the changing air pressure. Below, red-hot pumpkin-sized globs of ejected lava flew through the pit with an unnerving ripping sound, making it difficult for Bishop to concentrate on the task at hand.

"Shades of the Others! What a comforting sound!" he fretted in alarm as a molten projectile tore the air close behind him, followed by multiple muffled concussions.

Bishop let more rope slide through his hands as he worked his way deeper inside the pit. The air shook violently, and the clouds of acrid gas grew thicker, burning his eyes and lungs. Grasping the rope tightly, Bishop halted his descent at the edge of an overhung cliff. The lava lake waited below. A wall of thick sooty gas blew between his body and the pit, enveloping everything around him in a world of gray. In the shuddering air and disorienting noise, gravity, direction, and time seemed to fade away until there was only the volcano below him.

As the clouds parted, Bishop caught sight of something glinting against the wall of the crater below him and to his right. The clouds cleared more, revealing a door, man-made, that jutted away from the cliff face. Storm Singer had indeed found the entrance. In ages past, it had probably been flush with the wall, but erosion had dissolved the rock, leaving the structure suspended about two meters out, projecting like a pointing finger at him. Bishop signaled to Kiel to reel him up, and moments later he was back on the rim.

Bishop wiped the sooty sweat from his brow and took a long drink from his water flask. "It's down there, all right; the bird was right for once. I am sorry that I doubted you, Storm Singer."

Storm Singer, who had taken refuge under an overhang, bowed his ebon head in acceptance of the apology but remained silent, jerking as if to take flight at every explosion from below the rim of the volcano.

"Is it blocked?" Kiel asked, now becoming animated.

"No, just the opposite: it's hanging away to the side. I'll have to have you reel out more rope over there." Bishop pointed. "That's the closest point. Then I'll try to swing onto the doorsill."

They walked to the point where the overhanging ledge was directly above the entrance. Kiel reattached the rope to a rock spur, and Bishop again descended into the pit. His clutch on the tether was strong enough to give him a rope burn, a small discomfort compared to the molten lava below. Yet down he went, closing in slowly on his objective. Finally, he stopped at eye level with the exposed door. He began to swing back and forth until he was able to scramble onto the half-meter ledge at the doorsill and steady himself. The face of the opening was a featureless slab of rock or gray metal; its only decoration was the glass-like circle set into the center of the door. Bishop tried to peer through it but could not see anything except his own sweaty reflection.

"Now what?" he shouted, pounding on the door in frustration. "Just unlock the thing and enter, I suppose? Well, this might come as a surprise, but I seem to have forgotten my keys! And what good if I had brought them? There appears to be no keyhole."

The door ignored him.

"Unlock the door," Bishop repeated.

Then he remembered something Kiel had said the night before:

"When I first met you, I had a peculiar sense of satisfaction; it was like finding a missing bit of a puzzle or a lost key."

"A lost key," Bishop muttered, lifting his hand and staring as if seeing it for the first time.

He looked at the door again, slowly gaining understanding. Yes, this glass circle was not unlike the one that had faced him so many weeks ago with the crablike metal beast. With the Old Earth monster, his hand had acted like a key.

Storm Singer and Kiel had done their job; now it was Bishop's turn. With resolve, he placed his open hand on the round glass port and held his breath.

Nothing.

But wait, there was something. A flash of light? No, it must have been the exploding lava below him. Then there was a sound of rock grating on rock. Bishop looked at the door. It didn't seem to be moving, but now a line began to appear at the edges of the doorsill, and then it did move, slowly at first, then all at once sliding in, folding up and back, and revealing a black tunnel that led into the side of the cliff.

Bishop half expected a furnace blast of air to knock him off his perch, but instead, cool, welcome clean air curled out and around him. Having found the entrance to the Thunderbolt and having opened it, he hoped the rest would be easy.

SEVENTEEN

THE DARK MESSIAH

> Crimson kings on battle towers;
> Saints on gothic star-flung spires;
> Hermits on their peaks of snow;
> Heroes on their funeral pyres.
>
> —Vena Korela,
> Second Leminkanen Cycle, Runa 30

Bishop cautiously stepped into the entryway and away from the shuddering eruptions and waves of heat behind him. The cool air continued to drift past him from somewhere ahead in the dim tunnel. The perfectly constructed tunnel shone dully in the darkened gloom, seeming to beckon him to enter it. Bishop had no wish to invade its murky depths, but Reaver threatened, and the Thunderbolt might truly be here somewhere, as was foretold in the Tar Ka Codex. And then there were Kiel's visions; so far they had been right.

As Bishop took a few more steps into the gloom, light panels above him awakened from their ageless slumber, winking on one by one, revealing a shorter tunnel than Bishop had originally thought. Just ten meters long, it ended at yet another massive door. Bishop walked to that door and stopped, pondering his next move.

"Doors and more doors. The Others loved their doors."

A grating sound behind him caused Bishop to quickly turn, just in time to see the first door shudder back to its sealed position, ensnaring him like a rat in a trap. Sprinting back to the first door, he stopped. There was nothing there but a smooth surface—no levers and no glass panel. Trapped he was, but surely the Others had devised a way either to leave or proceed forward.

Turning once again and walking to the second door, Bishop studied it closely. Yes, there was something about this one that was different from the first. Its surface was glassy, very much akin to the circular keypad at the outer portal. Bishop placed his hand on its surface as he had done before and waited.

Moments passed, and then to Bishop's surprise, the entire door flashed and seemed to become unstable for a moment. Now, as if by magic, it began to transmute, first into a crystal-like substance and then into what appeared to be sparkling water. It rippled and shimmered like a living thing, then flickered again and vanished, leaving an opening into a small circular room no bigger than two meters in diameter.

"Gods, of the blackest sort," he muttered, staring in disbelief.

Bishop looked back toward the front of the tunnel, which was still sealed.

"So," he spoke aloud, "I am to go forward?"

No response.

"I'll take that as a yes then."

Straightening with resolve, and with no other options available, he stepped into the circular room, fully expecting something magical or terrifying to occur—and it did. As soon as he was in the center of the room, the door shimmered again and solidified, sealing the small cylindrical room so perfectly that Bishop could not make out so much as a seam. it was as if he were in the middle of a giant egg.

Bishop stood motionless there in the little chamber, which sealed from all possible help from above. "So, this is what Storm Singer must have felt like before he pecked his way out into the world, curse the day. Is that it? Am I to peck my way out like an accused wolf-bird?"

The room shuddered, and for a moment, Bishop dismissed it as merely the shakings of the volcano, except his senses told him that something was happening. He flung his arms out instinctively to grab at the wall, his footing suddenly precarious. He, or rather, the room, seemed to be in free fall. A soft whining sound rose in his ears. His panic grew and his stomach lurched violently as the speed of his descent accelerated. *Yes,* Bishop fearfully thought, *the feeling is like that when jumping out of a tree.* He braced himself for the imminent impact, but no such impact came; rather, his weight returned to him smoothly—his weight and then some. Now it felt as if his stomach was sinking to the bottom of his boots, and he struggled to retain its contents as the whining sound quieted again.

Bishop staggered against the wall and sank to the floor, holding his forehead in his hands. It was many moments before he had recovered enough to stand and ponder his situation.

The room seemed to have dropped, but to where? Nothing stirred. Even the rumbling and shacking of the volcano had ceased, and the room was becoming cool—no, cold. Bishop's breath came out in a vapor that hung in the air before him like fog.

The wall before Bishop suddenly flashed, becoming again like rippling water. Then it was gone, leaving the way open once more. As Bishop had expected, it no longer opened into the first hallway, which he now believed to be far above him.

Bishop shakily stepped out of the room and onto a platform that hung suspended near the center of a voluminous spherical chamber. The chamber was perfectly formed, the size of a city square, and utterly featureless save for a barely visible sort of faceting, as if it had been assembled from thousands of interlocking hexagon-shaped plates.

"Ah, greetings," he called, his voice sounding strangely muffled.

Nothing.

"I'll be taking my leave now."

Still no response.

He looked above him and below him, but there was not even the slightest embellishment to the massive spherical chamber, nothing save for the catwalk he now stood upon, which led to a small platform that was set in the exact center of the vault. There was a strangeness to the artificial cavern beyond its Old Earth nature; it had a dead quality to it like a morgue, like hallowed ground, or like a cathedral, and this fact unnerved Bishop more than any other. Even his own stealthy movements were muted and lost as if the great chamber absorbed all sound and all life.

Bishop cautiously moved away from the side of the chamber and toward the central platform, which seemed to beckon him to stand upon it. When he finally reached the center and stood there, the door he had just exited from shimmered and sealed. With distress, Bishop watched, spellbound, as the metal footbridge silently retracted into the wall and disappeared from view, leaving him stranded on what appeared to be a floating disk of metal suspended in the center of an immense orb of solid rock. Bishop realized that there was in fact light in the chamber, a dim bluish glow that bathed everything in softness, but there were no light panels, no source that was obvious; it was simply there.

Bishop focused his eyes on a point ten meters in front of him, where a speck of blue light wavered and steadied, then began to grow in three dimensions, transmuting into a strange meter-tall glyph. Eleven companion glyphs came to life, spaced equidistant from one another in a bizarre circle, twelve oddly bent and twisted blue tubes of frozen fire hovering in the air around Bishop. All the glyphs were different. As Bishop made a slow circle and again faced what he believed to be the front of the platform, he was surprised to find, now rising from the floor of the disk he stood upon, a thin rod of metal. It came to a stop at about waist level. On its top surface was a single blue glyph that, upon inspection, he found to be exactly like the one now hovering in the air directly above him. Then the circle of glyphs began to index in a slow and silent beat around him, each in turn pausing before him. The glyph on the top surface of the rod changed to mimic each new glyph that moved into place. Bishop was in a trance, watching the silent circle of symbols turn and stop, turn and stop.

There was little doubt that this was a message, one that could not be read in the current age. He was sure that if he did not answer correctly, he would die there on that floating disk of Old Earth metal and magic. This was the end. No more doors would be opening to take him away. The chamber was asking him something he could not give the answer to, asking him for a …

"The key," Bishop muttered, partly surprising himself. "The key in the Tar Ka Codex." These symbols were somewhat like those.

Bishop quickly took off his pack and rummaged through it until he came upon the scrap of parchment that had been given to him by E'Ka many days before. He unfolded the parchment. Yes, the glyphs E'Ka had written down were similar to those that circled him in the air—similar, but not exactly so. Centuries of recopying had corrupted them to such a degree that they were no longer the same. Bishop, after thinking, realized that he was sure of one thing: if he entered the wrong key, it would be over. The Others were not ones to allow for mistakes or error.

Bishop studied the parchment and then looked around him. "But how am I to use the key?"

Looking again at the rod in front of him, he discovered a raised blister of sorts, a blister with a razor-thin phosphorescent blue perimeter. Where had he seen such a thing before?

"Think, Bishop. Use that brain of yours or it will be your undoing for sure!"

Yes, now it came to him. The blister in front of him mimicked the one on the electric torch given to him by the female Ikonian so long ago.

Depressing the blister would do something. He only hoped his instincts were sound. Everything he had suffered through depended on it.

The first glyph on the parchment was a triangle with a horizontal line drawn through its center, exiting to form an upturned hook. Bishop looked at the blue glyphs. Yes, there was a triangle, but it possessed no line and no hook. Still, it was the only triangle. He waited for the glyph to circle to the center, and then, when the symbol changed on the rod, he pushed the blister. For a second, his heart stopped as the symbol instantly vanished from the circular group and reappeared at a higher point in space, where it sat motionless. Bishop had guessed right. But the key sequence written down by E'Ka required four glyphs in all. This was only the first. Three remained.

The next symbol was a curiously wrought circle with a cross splitting the circle into four equal parts. At its top was another cross. Bishop again looked at the turning glyphs. There was a circle that possessed no cross, and there was a square with a cross. The circle did possess the outer cross, which he deemed to be a closer match. When the glyph reached the front of the rod, he pushed the stud.

Though it was now ice-cold in the chamber, sweat beaded on Bishop's forehead. Time seemed to ponderously grind to a stop.

The circle glyph winked out and reappeared next to the first glyph. It was the correct choice. Bishop breathed out a ragged sigh of relief. The two glyphs he had chosen hovered motionless above the remaining ten glyphs.

The third glyph similar to one depicted on E'Ka's parchment was in the likeness of a stylized human—a round head with four lines descending away from it forming the legs and arms.

The room was bitter cold; nevertheless, Bishop was freely sweating now. His breath came in ragged gulps, and his clothing was damp. No such symbol as the one he was seeking could be found in the remaining group. There appeared to be a cross symbol, yet it did not resemble arms and legs, nor did it have a head. But it vaguely looked like the four lines. It had to be the one. Bishop waited for them to align, then pushed the button.

It was the correct choice.

One choice remained.

It was a simple diamond shape, but there remained three diamonds, each of a different form, to choose from. One of the diamonds had a crossed center; one had a hook protruding from its bottom; and one had a circle at its top. No simple diamond shape.

"E'Ka, what have you given me?" Bishop bellowed in frustration.

Think. What would likely fit with the other characters? They all looked different. It would come down to a guess. After all this work, he would just have to guess, and he had never considered himself lucky. Quite the contrary. His imprisonment within the eighth hell was testament to his characteristically bad luck.

The diamond with the circle was the one that caught Bishop's eye. So many things in this chamber were circular—the platform, the spherical auditorium, the hovering circle of glyphs.

The diamond glyph with the top circle locked above the rod, and the rod's glyph changed to match it. Bishop held his breath and depressed the blister.

It was the correct choice. The final glyph vanished and reappeared at the end of the other three. Now the circle of remaining glyphs disappeared as the chamber become even colder. Bishop shivered and waited.

Suddenly the rod with its blue-etched blister retracted into the floor, the four chosen glyphs simultaneously fading and disappearing, winking out all at once. Bishop now became aware of a faint light shimmering in front of him, hovering in space, as the glyphs before had done. Then a deep rumbling shook the earth—not the rumbling of the volcano, rather the rumbling of some device, some technological terror that was coming to life beyond Bishop's field of vision. Yes, something was awaking, but what?

The flickering foxfire in front of him began to grow in intensity as the rumbling sound smoothened and steadied. Bishop involuntarily stiffened as the foxfire brightened and formed. The thing coalescing before him was an Old Earth horror. Even a strong man, thinking that such things were his allies, when suddenly faced with something from the age of the Others, might all of a sudden call his strength into question if he failed to resist the urge to run or cover his eyes. But Bishop had come too far to turn and flee, even if he had a means of escape. He kept his gaze fixed steadily on the smoky image coalescing before him. Space changed and distance grew as the vision took shape.

As the facial features became a little more distinct, Bishop began to fear that he might understand what he was looking at, that at last he might perceive the features rightly and that when he did so, they would be too horrible to look upon.

As the vision shifted and then solidified, it became vaguely humanlike in form, but with proportions that suggested a juggernaut. A chill swept through Bishop as the vision locked emerald sparks of fire onto Bishop's eyes. The vision spoke with a dry, ageless voice, its tone resonating with immense power, vibrating the chamber around him.

"Construct," thundered the voice. "Who are you? Identify yourself!"

Several tendrils of dust fell from somewhere above and were instantly lost in the depths of the colossal orb. Bishop, ready to flee if a way would have been open to him to do so, remembered something from his early training within the Order, something to the effect that there would be times when he would need to harness his fear and proceed on faith, as sometimes faith could move a mountain. This seemed to be one of those times.

I will control my fear. I will have faith.

"My name is Bishop, and I have come in search of the Iron

Thunderbolt." His voice sounded in his ears like the squeak of a mouse heard across a great distance, with the mouse caught in the talons of an owl.

The vision steadied for a moment and then shifted through several alternating colors, rippling like waves of heat. "I should say that you have succeeded in your quest."

Bishop swallowed hard. "Then you know of the Thunderbolt?"

"*I* am the Iron Thunderbolt."

Bishop was dumbstruck. "You ... you are the Thunderbolt."

The image stared at Bishop for a moment longer as if it were pondering the question, all the while rippling like intense waves of heat. Its features flattened, and then it answered with a question: "Why have you come?"

Bishop, seeing no reason to hide his quest, responded in a shaking voice. "There is a threat that sits poised to consume the planet. There is a man, a human man, who has gained control of the Ikonians, and he—"

The vision, darkening, interrupted Bishop in midsentence. "What man?"

"He calls himself Reaver—Reaver One."

There was a sudden upsurge in the vibrations of power, which shook the chamber. Dust cascaded again in thin rivulets from somewhere above. The image brightened, the face taking on a look of satisfied accomplishment. "The circle completes itself."

"The circle? What do you mean?" Bishop, losing some of his fear, was becoming frustrated by the cryptic nature of this being.

There was a moment of silence as if the vision were contemplating answering. "I was constructed and was set upon the ocean of time to nullify the return of the Reaver threat."

Bishop, troubled, returned to his unanswered question. "Constructed? You were built? You said that you are the Thunderbolt? I don't understand. I was told the Thunderbolt was a device. You appear to be a living being of some type. Are you a god?"

The vision focused its attention on Bishop like a colossus examining an insect.

"I am the Thunderbolt."

"Are you a machine or an entity?"

"I am neither. I am both."

Bishop blinked, not comprehending.

The vision, seeming to note his perplexity, spoke again. "The Genetic Wars raged across the planet. The earth was faced with a genetic threat of titanic proportions. The humans and their constructs, the Eligor, were forced to counter the threat. We attacked the Reaver forces, but it was not enough."

"The humans fought with the Eligor as their allies, not against them?"

The figure wavered and rippled in seeming mirth. "The Eligor were the closest allies of the humans in those days. Faithful as dogs, they were. They died by the millions protecting them."

Bishop felt weak in the knees, his head spinning from the revelation. "The Eligor were our allies? How is it that we could have been so deceived?"

"Look to Reaver One for your answer."

"Reaver?"

"After the great conflagration, the Reavers, in an elaborate ruse, implicated the Eligor for their own actions, and the remaining human population believed the deception. There was devastation beyond imagining. The remaining records were of little use in vindicating the Eligor from this travesty. It was a masterstroke as it allowed Reaver and those remaining of his Heptagon cult to escape into oblivion."

"Earlier you referred to me as a construct, like the Eligor, like the Ikonian insects. I am a human, not one of them."

"You are a construct, or the progeny of a construct, a genetic creation of the military. Your ancestors were simply weapons, soldiers, just as the

Eligor, just as the Ikonian insects. You would not have been able to gain access to this facility otherwise."

Bishop felt a pang of chagrin at being so casually reduced from the proud inheritor of Old Earth technology to one of the last living descendants of a vanquished army. To be grouped in with the Eligor and the insects was almost too much for him to bear.

"The constructs were not enough. We needed a weapon beyond a mortal human; we needed to build a new human, a new man. The new man would be a mutation, a different biological species, altogether removed from *Homo sapiens* as we know them. I am that ultimate weapon."

"You were human though, yes?"

"Human once, an age ago, but I changed myself, melded my biological essence with the power of the machine. We became one intelligence, an artificial intelligence, a hyper intelligence. But in doing so, I gave up the essence of what it was to be human. I sacrificed my humanity because of the Reaver threat. It was a terrible price to pay, but a necessary one to save humanity."

"Could you not have refused?" Bishop asked.

"There were the Genetic Wars pushing us to desperate action, and he who rides the tiger finds it difficult to dismount. You cannot know the lure of immortality," the Thunderbolt replied cryptically.

"But still the Reavers were not destroyed," Bishop stated, attempting to soothe his damaged ego. His ancestors had failed, but so had the Thunderbolt.

"Like wolves, we flung ourselves upon the enemy and drove the Reavers and their construct armies back and back again. They were poised for destruction when they made good their escape during the Eligor conflict."

"You say 'we.' Were there others of your kind?"

The thunderbolt laughed, a singularly chilling sound to Bishop's ears. "There were the constructs, but they were not like me. Powerful they were, but none had reached the complete melding of machine and body such as I have accomplished."

"You have awaited the return of this Reaver. Why did you not follow them?"

"We of the Old Earth could not duplicate Reaver's time gate device, but we could send one into the future to wait out the centuries and attack at the right time and at the moment of his reemergence."

"Why not several weapons? Why not build several Thunderbolts? One, however powerful, against such odds seems nearly pointless."

"There was nothing left. The wars had devastated the planet. Plague, starvation, and radiation ravaged all life, and the remnants of civilization were quickly falling into savagery. We had just enough left in the way of resources before the final collapse to create this chamber."

"To what end? The wars had destroyed the earth."

"We would see him at last destroyed, at any cost."

So, it was true. Reaver was from the Old Earth, and he had somehow traveled here from the past. "Reaver is free again, has been for some time now. Why have you not come into the world? Why is it that I was needed to call upon you?"

The vision seemed to smile in sardonic mirth. "All of this effort and all of this power lost because of a simple mechanical failure."

"What failure?"

"A power coil."

"A power coil, yes, but this chamber, your abilities ... You seem quite able to me," Bishop said, taking in the monstrous, magically wavering form before him.

"This chamber?" The vision shifted a wide color spectrum. "This chamber is merely a device built to communicate with my mind."

"But all of this power." Bishop swept his arm wide.

"True, the chamber is tied directly to the earth's core, is in fact wrapped about the volcanic vent like the immovable fist of a titan. It sustains my essence and allows me to exist, but outside the chamber, I am nothing without the power coil. My abilities have been muted."

"What abilities, exactly?"

"My exoskeleton is nonactive. Only my mind functions, and even then, only within this chamber."

Bishop stared blankly, not understanding the words.

The vision, seeing Bishop's confusion, spoke again, this time in a simpler fashion. "I can no longer operate beyond this chamber."

Bishop felt a shock run through him. "You cannot leave this chamber? Gods of the Others, what are we to do then?"

"There might be a way. I have had much time to ponder the question."

"What way?"

"There could still be a power coil on this planet; they were not that uncommon. Power coils were installed in many military devices of the time. Surely one can be located even after such a time lapse."

Bishop remembered the Old Earth device he had ridden forth from the cave beyond Ikonia, a beast that might have harbored such a device, but it was gone in the Moeras Kor Depression.

"There was a metal beast, a beast that I rode from a cave. It was an Old Earth thing of immense power," Bishop said.

"Allow me to observe the device."

"Observe it? See it? What do you mean, see it? Do you mean to say you want me to draw it for you?"

A blue ribbon of light flashed and then washed over Bishop. "Think about the metal beast," the Thunderbolt intoned.

The image came to Bishop as clear as if it had happened yesterday. He could not help but think of it, as if it were being pulled to the front of his mind. Then a fearful thing occurred. Before him, materializing in the air, was a small-sized perfect likeness of the Old Earth monster he had ridden. The image turned slowly before the rippling form of the Thunderbolt as if the Thunderbolt were studying a child's toy. Something was picking and digging at Bishop's brain just as Kiel had described the night before; possibly there was a time before the power coil failure when the Thunderbolt could have worked beyond this chamber, extracting information at the cost of the owner's life.

"A Mark Seven. Leviathan. A product of the Ikonian Drive Yards. Yes. The device contains a power coil."

Bishop shook his head. "It is lost."

"You will recover it."

"There is no way; it was lost in the Moeras Kor Depression."

"You will find a way."

Bishop shrugged.

"Listen closely, and remember. You will be provided with a transfer receptacle. After you recover the power coil, you will take it the Ikonian frontier, and there, within sight of their border markers, you will insert the coil into the receptacle. Then I will come to you."

"Border markers—the stone heads that appear to be slumbering?"

The Thunderbolt ignored Bishop's question. "I will implant the instructions within your mind." Then the entity spoke in a sibilant language that Bishop did not understand.

Before Bishop could raise a question, he felt a searing flash of pain as if his mind had been gripped by something seven times colder than ice, a sensation that caused him to drop to his knees.

As quickly as it had come, it was over, and then Bishop knew: the directions for uncoupling the power coil were somehow burned into his mind as if he had been trained in the maintenance of Old Earth apparatuses. He now saw in his mind the Old Earth metal beast, watching the glyphs on its armored side as they melted from "Lëviâthân Modûs VII" to become "Leviathan—Mark VII." He also saw other things in the swirling kaleidoscope of his mind.

Bishop staggered back to his feet as reason returned, rubbing his head and frowning. "By the eight hells! What have you done to me?" His own voice sounded strange and reedy; his body felt momentarily weightless and weak.

"Implanted knowledge into your cerebral cortex. Do not be concerned, it will not cause permanent damage. The process can kill, yet the constructs were designed to survive the method."

Kiel's abortive mission again came to Bishop's mind. Then, it had been a mistake and not an act of violence. "There were those before me, Eligor, who died. You killed them."

"Yes, an act of desperation, it was. I had hoped that some might survive to free me to do what I was built to do, what I must do to save the planet. The death was accidental. It exhausted the last of my reserves. Nevertheless, it would appear that the gamble paid off."

Bishop was still rubbing his head in growing anger. The pain was gone, but not the memory of the pain, which was etched in his mind as surely as the knowledge that came with it. "No permanent damage? Gods of the Others, *I hope not!*"

The vision wavered and flickered but did not respond to Bishop's outburst. "We are finished for now. You will recover the power coil and insert it into the receptacle at the Ikonian border, then I will finally deal with this Reaver."

Before Bishop, there now appeared a shimmering, wavering form on the front of the platform on which he stood. There was a sudden flash. As it faded, there remained, sitting on the floor of the hovering disk he stood upon, two halves of a round grayish ball about the size of a gourd. Bishop gathered up the nearly weightless halves of the receptacle and stuffed them begrudgingly into his pack.

The vision of the Thunderbolt began to fade, and the great vault dimmed. "Recover the power coil and insert it into the receptacle." It was repeated once more, then the Thunderbolt was gone.

"And that's it. No tankard of ale? A sack of gold for my trouble?"

Bishop wheezed, still rubbing his head. But there was no response. The chamber sat cold and still.

Shortly, the catwalk was extended and the door shimmered and lay open. Bishop stood a moment longer, and then, half in frustration, he retraced his footsteps to the surface. At the entrance, the outer door stood open. The heat, the muffled explosions, and the glow of the volcano filtered into the darkened outer tunnel.

After climbing the rope, Bishop again stood with his travel companions on the steaming, ash-covered slopes of Ambrym. "Black gods, human! We thought it was the end for you! I was ready to try chiseling into the door even though I knew it would be hopeless." Kiel barked in undisguised relief. A toothy smile appeared on his sooty scaled face and then was gone.

Bishop half smiled. "Many thanks for caring, my friend," he said as he looked upon the Eligor with new feelings of friendship. He could not easily forget the Thunderbolt's comments concerning these creatures; they had once been allies, before Reaver destroyed that bond of camaraderie.

Kiel, embarrassed about his emotional outburst, looked at the ground. "It's just that you have some very valuable climbing tools. I would have been very distraught if I had lost them. That's all."

"I was worried too," Storm Singer began.

"You cared too?" Bishop said, smiling gratefully.

"I was worried that I would miss dinner," the bird finished, casually smoothing a stray feather.

Bishop's smile flattened. "I should have known it was a food-related worry, you flying rodent."

Storm Singer's ebon eyes glittered in mirth. "What has happened, Bishop? Were you successful? You will forgive my saying so, but you look as if you have seen a ghost."

Bishop smiled then looked at the wolf-bird, who sat on Kiel's shoulder.

"Yes, of a sort. Come on, buzzard, let's get off this demon-haunted mountain and back to the lower camp. I'll tell you all about it there."

Bishop tiredly shambled off toward the trail. A baffled wolf-bird and a confused Eligor trailed after him in silence.

That evening they again sat around a small crackling fire within the tree line of the lower slopes. A gentle orchid-scented wind blew softly through the tree ferns as the red glow of Ambrym weirdly flickered in the eastern sky. Bishop had extracted the two halves of the Old Earth ball and passed them to Kiel.

"I don't know, Bishop. I have seen my share of Old Earth technology, but I am at a loss as to how inserting a smaller ball within these two halves could hope to aid a being hundreds of kilometers away. This is the most advanced technology I have ever heard of. There is no wiring that I can make out. It appears to be a featureless ceramic shell."

"If you had seen what I had within the mountain, you would find it difficult to believe that anything is beyond the Thunderbolt's ability."

Kiel shook his head in disbelief, seemingly fascinated with the device he handled. "The Thunderbolt, a sentient being."

Bishop returned the pieces to his pack. "What choice do we have? Either we recover coil from the Leviathan, the Old Earth beast, or hope that Opal can repel the Ikonian invasion."

Kiel sighed. "No, I think that if we fail, Opal will fall. It's only a matter of time, and time is running out."

Bishop, looking at Kiel as the firelight flickered about his darkened form, set his shoulders in determination. "Then it is settled. We must recover the coil in the Moeras Kor Depression. The only question is how. It would take the two of us a hundred years to dig the thing out. It is enormous; truly, it is as big as a small house, and quite possibly heavier."

"There is a way," Kiel said, setting his shoulders with resolve.

"Well, I'm listening," Bishop remarked.

"The wolf-bird here could fly to Opal and deliver a message to the Grand Union. They know of the bird—I have them believing there is a whole flock of wolf-birds assisting—and they would listen to him. The Union could send a contingent of the army corps of engineers to the site of your ill-fated accident and meet us there."

Storm Singer suddenly looked up from his feather care to stare at Kiel. "Pardon, what was that you just said?"

Bishop looked at Kiel with an equal expression of astonishment. "Are you serious? Even if they could make it past the Ikonian army, they wouldn't have a clue where to even begin looking. And even if they did find it, how are we to find them?"

"The Eligor can use the exit tunnels just as we did. And as for locating your beast, they have their ways. The Moeras Kor Depression has been patrolled for centuries. J'Kra, the Eligor who found you, would know exactly where to look and exactly how to detect the device's presence."

Storm Singer continued to stare, his feathers forgotten. "Fly to Opal?"

"Yes." Kiel became animated as the idea took root. "Deliver a message to the Grand Union and return with a locator."

"A locator?"

"A small device that is very common. We would use it to find the engineers in the great marsh of the Moeras Kor."

Bishop was beginning to nod in agreement. "It just might work. It would save us weeks. And I don't think Opal will last weeks."

"Easy for you to say, but you are not the one doing the flying," Storm Singer stated, still not quite sure he was hearing things correctly.

"Oh, come now, you have been spending most of your time wearing out the shoulder of my shirt. I think a little exercise would do you some good. You seem to have become fat as well."

Storm Singer flared his throat feathers, but before he could respond, Kiel had already extracted a spool of parchment from his pack. Popping the cap, he unfurled a page, produced a hidden quill, and began writing in the unfamiliar spidery script of the Eligor.

Storm Singer glowered at Kiel with a sour look. "The vote has been cast, hasn't it?"

Bishop leaned back onto the warm sandy ground and smiled. "Majority rules, bird. What a relief. I must admit, Kiel, you can certainly think on your feet when you have to. What an amazing idea."

"Yes, a relief," Storm Singer grumbled, trying to find some fault in the scheme. "Where am I to find you, that is, if I am successful? I mean, you would be impossible to find in the forest even for one with my extensive abilities."

"You can leave at first light on the morrow. We will return to the mainland and make camp. That should take us the good part of two days. I would think that you will conclude your business in three or four days at the latest, sooner if you don't dally as you often are wont to do. As soon as you return, we will continue together."

"So, you will be relaxing on the beach while I am risking my life flying across the accursed Eligor Empire, an empire that is swarming with insects too large to make a meal of. Is that it?"

"Something like that, friend bird. You have finally grasped the concept. Pretty good for a feathered rat with a brain the size of a pea." Bishop closed his eyes in mock comfort.

Storm Singer shot daggers as Kiel began to snigger in mirth.

EIGHTEEN

RECOVERY OF THE COIL

> And we all dwell today as children of some second birth after a judgment day.
> —Vena Korela,
> Second Leminkanen Cycle, Runa 78

It had been four days since Storm Singer had returned from his flight to Opal. The wolf-bird had successfully delivered Kiel's message to the Grand Union, and they in turn had provided the bird with an Eligor locator and instructions to set out immediately for the Moeras Kor Depression. The travelers were to link up with the Eligor engineers and attempt to raise the Leviathan from its muddy grave—and all for one purpose: to recover the power coil and attempt to activate the Thunderbolt.

Screaming in rage, flying reptiles followed the little party in their hastily built raft, but before long the trees began to close more thickly over the waterway as they paddled. A mass of swampy forest ahead promised almost complete shelter. Now, in their frustrated fury, a few of the reptiles dared to dive, screeching and cawing at the escaping intruders.

Muttering with growing anger, Bishop swung his sword at a reptile while the rest veered away in angered frustration. They climbed again, disappearing above what was becoming an almost solid roof of greenery.

"So much for that nuisance," Bishop tersely remarked as he again settled himself on the little raft they had constructed. "Hey you, chicken bird, you can come out now."

The wolf-bird cautiously popped his head out from under the packs. "Chicken bird, you say? I killed three before I was overwhelmed, if you will consider," he croaked indignantly. Ruffling his feathers in a regal manner, he strutted out from under the packs and jumped up to Bishop's shoulder.

"I recall that it was you who provoked the attack by getting yourself caught stealing one of their eggs for breakfast. I trust it was worth the effort," Bishop returned sardonically.

Storm Singer began preening indifferently. "Yes, in fact it was delicious. An egg. Can you even imagine? One measly egg is all that I took. Reptiles are funny about things like that."

"I wonder what you would have done if one of those miserable flying reptiles had burgled one of your eggs!" Bishop stated.

The bird closed to within a fraction of a centimeter of Bishop's ear and whispered in a covert tone, "Bishop, I am a male wolf-bird. Male wolf-birds don't lay eggs; females do."

Bishop shook the bird off him and scowled. "I know that, for the love of the Others! You know what I meant."

The bird alighted on Kiel's shoulder. "The human has much to learn. When he finally locates an unlucky mate, my scaly friend, is he in for a surprise."

Kiel showed a toothy grin in response to the bird's prodding.

Bishop's ears burned, but he elected to terminate the conversation, concentrating instead on his paddling.

The channel they had been following split, came together, and then branched again. Kiel, now choosing their way from his position in the stern, seldom hesitated when choosing which branch to take. Walls of interlaced vines brushed them as they glided past. By now the afternoon was far advanced, and the travelers decided to make camp for the evening. After landing the small raft, Kiel collected a pile of wood and built a small smokeless fire to drive away the damp chill of the approaching evening. Bishop retreated to the water's edge and pulled a fishing line from his pack, attaching a small baited hook.

"We will eat no stale rations tonight," he called with no small relief as he lowered the line gently into the water. "I, for one, am sick at the sight of tasteless Eligor oat bread—and rat too."

There were fish aplenty, seeming of the grayling variety, and Bishop was soon cooking several over an open fire. Chewing slowly on a morsel of tender flaky white flesh, he squinted into the firelight, which began to brighten with the fading of day.

"I trust your soldiers have come prepared," Bishop said worriedly through mouthfuls of food, "or this whole excursion will be a gigantic waste of time. The Leviathan is big—big and weighty. Very weighty."

"So you have said on many an occasion," Kiel remarked blandly.

Bishop deftly filleted several neat portions of tender meat from the sharp spiny bones, depositing the fish's skeletal remains in a careful pile. Grabbing a very stale bit of bread, he settled himself down again with his meal. "Better than rat, huh, Kiel?" He looked at the Eligor.

A large fish, its scaly form still twitching with life, its mouth working, its fins spread, was poised in front of Kiel's open mouth. As Bishop watched in morbid fascination, the quivering ichthyoidal morsel disappeared in three bites. Kiel grunted in satisfaction, daintily wiping his face.

"Excellent idea, Bishop. It has been quite some time since I have enjoyed a good thymallus," Kiel purred between mouthfuls.

Bishop swallowed hard, put down his meal, and crossed his arms in disgust. "Graylings. They are graylings. And why do you insist on doing that?"

Kiel finished dabbing at the sides of his mouth and looked up from his dinner in perplexity. "Pardon?"

"Can't you even wait for it to roast on the fire before shoving it down like some sort of ill-mannered heathen?"

Kiel, poised to swallow another fish, stopped the effort and looked at Bishop. "We are on the trail, Bishop. Can't you eat without a set of silver and a twinkling candle? Secondly, I will have you know that there are several higher cultures on this tired old planet that consider raw fish a delicacy. There is an interesting culture across the Western Sea that actually—"

"Yes, yes. We are on the trail. Don't be so finicky about such things," Storm Singer cawed, interrupting Kiel, as he ravenously gobbled the wet, glistening entrails from Bishop's fish cleaning.

Bishop's expression grew sourer as he wolfed his meal down.

Kiel resumed eating. "You need not worry about my soldiers," he said, returning to the previous subject. "The corps of engineers are well trained and know the Moeras Kor Depression well. They will be waiting. They are capable of the task of raising this Old Earth mechanism you have described."

Despite the smacking and slurping sounds around him, Bishop elected to focus on finishing his meal before resuming the conversation, although he made a mental note to forgo any fishing in the future.

"I am sure that the Eligor engineers are capable of many miraculous things, but I don't think you can fathom the size of the device," he explained to Kiel.

Kiel swallowed the last of his meal and scowled. "You have stated that this mission is very important, yes?"

"Yes, I believe that this is the only way to destroy Reaver."

"Then we will raise the beast, and you will extract the power coil, and then we will be done with this whole affair. Now let us not worry about it anymore."

Bishop sighed. "All right, I will not think more on the subject until we are at the site. That is, if we can find the site again."

"Bishop!" Kiel growled.

"Fine, fine, I won't worry about it anymore."

The early morning sky had just begun to lighten in the east when the travelers once again set off in the raft toward the Moeras Kor Depression ahead of them. The small locator Storm Singer had carried from Opal pointed unerringly toward the southwest. Awakening sounds of forest life reached them as they silently glided along. Near afternoon, they passed a mammoth lizard drinking its fill of the water, but the creature gave them no more interest than it would have given a drifting leaf, and soon they had rounded a bend and the monster disappeared from sight. The travelers looked at one another but said nothing. These woods were full of mutations from the Great Change that had occurred after the cataclysm that ended the Fourth Age, but most, though gigantic, were herbivorous and relatively benign. It was the Moeras Kor Depression that was said to harbor the empire's most lethal terrors, a fact that Bishop tried on more than one occasion to mentally dismiss. He had thankfully seen none of these terrors on his first visit and hoped he would be as lucky on his second.

Around midday, the Eligor locator began to point away south from the stream, and the travelers were forced to abandon the raft. "We are very close now," Kiel remarked as the locator began flashing in a steady fashion.

Bishop looked over at Storm Singer, who sat silently on his shoulder. "Find the Eligor and let them know that we are coming."

Without comment, the bird took flight and disappeared among the sun-dappled shadows of the forest.

The trail steadily deteriorated as they closed in on the environs of the Depression. For kilometers now, they had splashed on in silence through the darkened woods, which were spotted with malformed trees that were overgrown with strange luminescent fungi in the places that never saw daylight. Ugly roots and malignant hanging nooses of moss beset them, and now and then a pile of dank stones or a fragment of rotting wall gave a strong hint of some long-past civilization of people who once called these environs home.

The region that Bishop and Kiel were closing in on traditionally was one of evil repute to human and Eligor alike. There were legends of a hidden lake unseen by mortal eyes far out in the swamp in which dwelt huge, formless things with luminous eyes. As the stories went, bat-winged devils flew up out of the lake to feed on mortal flesh at midnight. Even the Eligor, who had long ago claimed the Moeras Kor as part of their empire, had never penetrated its deeper interior, content to hunt and gather from its safer perimeter.

Bishop jerked in alarm as fangs struck into his leg. "Black gods, a snake!"

"No, Bishop, not a snake. It's a leech plant. Watch where you are stepping."

Bishop looked down at a writhing, sucking vine that had attached itself to his leg. He heard a sucking sound as the bladderlike plant expanded and contracted like the lungs of a living animal. He reached down and tore the thing from his leg, holding it for a moment before twisting it apart and hurling the loathsome thing away from him.

"A leech plant, you say? Black gods," Bishop muttered, now paying very close attention to the undergrowth around him. "What other surprises have you elected not to share with me that can be found in your backyard?"

Kiel eyed Bishop, shaking his head but remaining silent.

As the gloom of evening deepened and a misty rain began to fall, the wolf-bird finally returned and settled again on Bishop's shoulder. "I have found them and relayed your message. They are just ahead." The bird pointed a feathered wing off into the growing murk.

"About bloody time, bird. What did you do, stop and build a nest?"

"About bloody time, bird. What did you do, stop and build a nest?" Storm Singer repeated in a near-perfect imitation of Bishop's voice.

Bishop reddened. "You know, that didn't sound like me at all. Why don't you give it up? Face it, you're no good at imitation."

"You know, that didn't sound like me at all. Why don't you give it up? Face it, you're no good at imitation," Storm Singer mimicked again, his ebon eyes twinkling mischievously.

"Do either of you have the slightest inkling as to how dangerous it is here?" Kiel's translator hissed. "Stop bickering and keep your voices down."

"He started it," Bishop growled, jerking a thumb at Storm Singer.

"He started it," Storm Singer mimicked back.

Bishop's eyes widened with rage. "Do you see?"

"Bishop! Storm Singer! *Enough!*" Kiel barked. "Gods of the Others, it's like traveling with two nestlings!"

Storm Singer shrugged and began his feather care as Bishop slogged off in the direction indicated, the bird bobbing in rhythm on his shoulder.

Just as the wolf-bird had said, within the hour, an Eligor soldier intercepted the travelers, silently materializing out of the misty shadows of the primordial marshland forest.

As a specter from a forgotten age, the Eligor soldier stood there in his brass-colored scale armor with his golden eyes glinting in the cold and hazy darkness. Even after such close association with Kiel, Bishop had to suppress an urge to raise his Riika defensively.

First eyeing Bishop, then Storm Singer, the soldier saluted Kiel and spoke. "Ārīs þonan ŷð-geblond up āstīgeð won tō wolcnum þonne wind styreþ lāð gewidru, oðpǽt lyft drysmaþ, roderas rēotað."

"So, you have found the resting place of the Old Earth device?" Kiel immediately questioned.

The Eligor, noticing that Kiel was using his translator, activated his own with a soft whine of power. "Yes, sir. It wasn't too difficult, you know. Its tracks were so large that a blind Eligor could have found them. They led right to a churned-up mud wallow that is currently covering it. I would estimate the device is about two meters under the surface."

"I hope you brought shovels," Bishop said blandly.

The Eligor again eyed Bishop, his eyes narrowing to yellow slits. "You will follow me to the clearing, human."

Bishop looked at Kiel but said nothing. The Eligor were at war, and it was only natural that a human would be looked upon as an unwelcome intruder at the very least.

After another hour or so, the Eligor soldier led them into the work area. Sure enough, as they rounded a dense clump of black, stunted trees, the travelers came upon a detachment of the Eligor Corps of Engineers. They were in the process of cutting down trees. Several that had already been cut lay above the ground, where the Eligor engineers split them and notched the ends, shaping them for the massive iron fittings that would be bound to them. Already, thick rope lay coiled and soaking in oil. This would be fed through metal pulleys, each bearing a large block and tackle. Such force would be necessary for the immense job of resurrecting the sunken monster that was buried somewhere below the muck.

An impeccably dressed corps commander, whose name was Kurus, came walking up to the group and saluted Kiel in the manner of the Eligor.

And dearest to the Eligor heart, Bishop thought darkly, *another uniform—and a becoming one too.* He was painfully aware of his own drab, threadbare, travel-stained clothing.

The Eligor standing before him was arrayed from head to foot in black: a black helmet sporting a silver winged death's-head, black tunic with black buttons, black belt, black breeches, and black boots. The designer had left no detail out to tickle the imagination of the hierarchical-minded Eligor, introducing all sorts of mysterious marks and badges, including red circles, aluminum chevrons, diamond-shaped insignia, and silvered threads. Bishop was sure Kiel had a similarly arrayed uniform that had been left behind at Opal for reasons of efficiency on the trail.

Flummery! Bishop thought.

"The siege of Opal continues," Kurus stated crisply. "It does not go well for us. There have been several attempts by the Ikonians to scale the walls, but so far we have denied them entrance, but only just."

Kiel nodded gravely. "How go your efforts in raising the Old Earth device?"

Kurus turned to take in the work party. "Luckily, we found enough solid ground near your human's unfortunate mud pit to give our equipment the foundation it needs."

"I am not *his* human," Bishop said coldly, stabbing a thumb toward Kiel.

"Whatever pleases you, human," Kurus, very composed, responded to Bishop. Then, returning his attention to Kiel, he said, "We will raise the thing for all the good it will do. But I must be honest, sir: no one is happy about leaving Opal in its darkest hour to come out here in the wood and toy with a rusty bit of Old Earth rubbish. May I remind the commander that Old Earth technology has so far served the Eligor poorly? It is a cruel mistress, and dangerous ex gratia from those who once were."

Kiel nodded in understanding. "Be assured that what we are doing here is the one thing that might save Opal. We will raise the Old Earth device."

Kurus again saluted respectfully, touching the ground and then his forehead. "As you wish, Commander."

"You know, he says *human* like it's a bad thing," Bishop muttered in a quiet tone as they prepared to assist the engineers at their task.

"I am sure it's your imagination, human," Kiel blandly responded.

Storm Singer guffawed as he flew to a low-hanging branch to watch.

Kiel and Bishop took up axes and began helping to dress the trees, while an Eligor blacksmith heated and hammered the metal brackets on a temporary forge. By nightfall the main beams had been raised, then lugged into four trees that hung over the bog, concealing the Old Earth machine.

In the morning, the digging began. Wooden pails were filled with the sticky muck and hauled away while any water that collected was bled off using a hand-operated pump. Sure enough, by midday the upper portion of the Old Earth device lay exposed. Unfortunately, the groundwater running into the exposed pit kept pace with the pumping and bailing. Even attempts at draining the interior were foiled. Apparently the mechanism was not watertight. They would need to raise the device and drain the interior before Bishop could extract the power coil.

Eligor soldiers stripped off their work uniforms and tied rope around their scaled waists. With reluctant expressions, they plunged into the soupy muck and probed about for rope ties. Bishop wondered if the grimacing mouths on the Eligor soldiers gathered on the bank indicated amusement or sympathy at their fellow workers' predicament.

By evening, four ends protruded away from the black pool and sat coiled and ready to attach to the block and tackle. Tomorrow, they would lift the beast.

As evening enveloped the encampment and swirling mists rose from the swamp, the Eligor cooked up a fine meal consisting of spiced venison, a sort of waterfowl, potatoes, dark bread, a green vegetable of some unknown variety, corn cakes, a tangy berry jelly, and thick brown gravy. It was quite simply the best meal Bishop had eaten since leaving the protectorate. The Eligor even seemed to temporarily put aside their distrust in him and made sure he was well-fed. Even Storm Singer was lavished upon and treated like a bird among birds.

"These are fine trail rations," Bishop said, smacking his lips, "better, in fact, than what you have been provided with. Though I am grateful, I am somewhat at a loss to understand it."

Kiel responded, "This day is an Eligor holiday, and the feast is traditional, giving appreciation for a bountiful harvest, friends, and family. We simply call it the Harvest Festival. Its origins are lost to the ages. These soldiers have been hoarding some of these supplies for months for this one occasion."

As Bishop silently ate, he watched the Eligor as they laughed, told stories, sang songs, and joked with one another. Again it struck him how similar these creatures' mannerisms were to those of humans. The Thunderbolt had said the Eligor had been close allies with the humans in the dim days of the Fourth Age. Not for the first time Bishop wondered if they would ever be able to mend the rift created by Reaver's treachery.

At first light, four block and tackle units were threaded and attached to the overhead iron-shod beams, and then cables were connected to a winching system that was bolted to the base of each of the four trees they had chosen to tie them to. Each windlass was ratcheted one turn in unison so as to distribute the weight evenly. The upper beams popped and groaned under the increasing weight, and even the ancient gnarled trees bent beneath the awesome load.

For a time, it seemed that nothing was happening, that the ropes simply could not move the load any farther, but at last Bishop noted water running away from the upper blister of the submerged Leviathan. Slowly, agonizingly, it began to rise.

Even the workers and the soldiers stood in awe of the Old Earth mechanism as more and more of it became visible. Bishop began to sweat as he noted the upper support bending beneath the tremendous weight. The lifting structure was at its limit; it would not hold long.

The winches were ratcheted up one click at a time, until finally the mountain of Old Earth metal was high enough. Eight massive roughhewn squared beams were slipped under its bulk and the winches were reversed, letting the thing down carefully on its wooden cradle.

Collapsing from exhaustion, the Eligor workers stumbled to the ground. Bishop approached the slimy monster, his nose wrinkling in distaste at the stench of the churned-up muck draining away from the Leviathan, and then clambered his way to the top of the great machine. Sure enough, the open interior was awash in black muck and swamp ooze, and though it was slowly escaping through some hidden port at the bottom of the machine, it would take days to drain completely.

"Kiel, time is short; we need to drain this beast out."

Kiel issued orders in the Eligor language. "Ða ne sorga sotora guma! Selre bið ǽghwǽm! Sotora guma!"

Shortly the grumbling and muttering Eligor workers formed a bucket brigade, and little by little the beast was drained and cleaned as best as could be expected. All the while, Bishop paced and waited expectantly.

"That's it, Bishop. It's been drained. Can you complete your job without a shine and polish?" Kiel groused.

Bishop again ascended the bulky side of the monster and squatted above the opening, then, dropping to the still foul-smelling inner enclosure, he walked unerringly to the back and depressed a metal stud labeled "Unstart override" as if it were a routine action, as if he were guided by an unseen force. Cold artificial light blazed forth from the panels above his head, while several smaller lights twinkled to life around him. A cautious murmuring reached his ears from the open hatch.

"Bishop," Kiel called apprehensively. "Is everything all right in there?"

"Yes, yes. Everything is fine," Bishop called back.

Bishop deftly unclipped a metallic service box built into the side of the wall, below the unstart override, and removed a tool. It was strange: he knew what this tool was although he'd never seen it before. It was a ratchet. He handled it adroitly, affixing a "socket" to its tip. He knew what this monster they'd dredged from the bog was; it was etched on the inner hull: "Main Battle Tank—Ikonian Drive Yards."

He also knew every nut, every bolt, every wire, and every indicator within the amazing device. All of what was needed had somehow been fused instantly and directly into Bishop's brain by the Thunderbolt.

Bishop stooped to the floor, placed the ratchet around a recessed bolt, and began turning. Slowly, grudgingly, the bolt began to move, groaning in protest as it was extracted. Then Bishop set about to turning the second and the third. The fourth, however, would not budge. Countless eons of neglect had frozen it solidly in place. Regardless of how hard Bishop strained and tugged, it would not give.

Bishop sat down, sweating. "I'll likely never hear the end of it, but there's no hope for it now." He stared at the stars through the darkened hatch. Then standing, he called out, "Kiel, I'll be needing your help in here."

Moments later, Kiel poked his scaled head down into the beast in something of a state of awe. "So, you will be needing my help again, is it?" Kiel prodded.

Bishop winced. "Yes, well, that's a switch, isn't it?"

"Black gods, Bishop, it's the largest Old Earth device I have ever seen, and it still works."

"Never mind your ogling. Get in here," Bishop returned impatiently.

Kiel gingerly climbed down the metal ladder, all the while taking in the fantastic scene.

He kneeled down, staring at the flooring. "Before you trouble yourself further, Bishop, we need to talk."

Bishop looked up from his work. "About what?"

"The corps commander has raised a valid point. This device, I mean, if it has a fraction of the power that you've stated ... Well, why not just use it against the Ikonians, instead of dismantling it for a dubious weapon that has not proven itself? Time is not on our side, and I fear that we might lose any possible hope of saving Opal if we delay much longer."

Bishop shook his head. He knew better than anyone living how powerful the device was, but he knew of its current weaknesses. "This device was not designed to soak in a mud pit for any length of time, I can assure you of that. I am certain there are any number of subsystems that will no longer operate. Besides, I think you'll have a time finding someone foolish enough to ride this thing into combat."

"Why is that?"

Bishop pointed a thumb to the open hatch above them. "Did you not notice the lid is missing? It could have been blown hundreds of meters in any direction and could have sunk in any number of mudholes around here. Even if we could find it, how are we to reattach it? You might wish to stay here on a hopeless search, but I don't."

Kiel looked at the upper opening and nodded. "Yes, I would guess that the Ikonians would not wait long to trouble the driver with that very obvious opening, but the Eligor are not as helpless as they might seem. It could be possible to construct a makeshift cover."

Bishop thought about this idea. It was improbable that this Old Earth device could do more than generate light, but if there was a chance of speeding this adventure to a conclusion, then it surely was worth considering.

"Very well, Kiel. But if I am right and this beast is inoperative, we will still need to recover the power coil. That should be the first priority. After we extract it successfully, I will reinstall the coil, and then we will find out if there is any hope of activating this beast again. Do you agree?"

Kiel nodded resolutely and set his shoulders. "Agreed. Now, what was it you needed my help for?"

Bishop showed the Eligor how to use the tool and handed it over. "The power coil is under this plate. Try your hand; I can't get it to budge."

Kiel fitted the tool over the bolt and strained. Scaled muscles bulged and veins stood out starkly on his arms. His eyes closed and his neck corded in the effort.

Bishop, hearing a creaking sound, expectantly looked closer. Yes, it had moved—and then a little more. Finally, with a sharp ping, the bolt snapped free, sending both tool and Eligor falling backward.

"Blast it, Kiel! You've broken the head off the bolt!"

Kiel darkened as he gathered himself off the ground. "I see. And it is my fault that the thing broke off, is it now?"

Bishop, ignoring Kiel's anger, looked closer and realized that only a fraction of the metal was still left holding the plate to the floor.

"Wait, I've got an idea."

Returning to the toolbox, Bishop recovered a thin pointed object and slid it under the opposite end of the floor plate. "I'll try to pry it up with this, uh, screwdriver. You see if you can get your fingers under it and lift. Maybe it will be enough."

Kiel eyed the new tool. "The what?"

"The screw ... Forget it."

"And if I break this thing, what then, Bishop? Am I to listen to you to carry on like a nestling that has gone too long without food?"

"Well, don't break it this time."

Bishop slid the screwdriver under the floor plate and pried upward. "Now!" he said, straining.

Kiel grabbed the plate and pulled just as Bishop lost his grip on the screwdriver.

"Black gods, human, you've caught my fingers!" Kiel bellowed in alarm.

"Sorry, sorry," Bishop said, cringing as he hastily inserted the tool again and pried the plate upward.

Kiel added his strength to the effort, and sure enough, the remaining portion of the bolt was slowly drawn through the hole. With a muffled pop, the plate came free.

Kiel set the plate down and eyed his fingers closely. "One, two, three, four, five. All my claws are accounted for, lucky for you."

"Look, I'm not doing this for my health, but I am sorry, Sir Eligor. You'll be knitting again before long, I'm sure of it."

"Knitting …?"

"Never mind."

"I believe that I will wait on the outside of this thing before something worse than a finger pinching happens to me," Kiel stated worriedly as he rubbed his fingers.

"I am sorry," Bishop said again, trying to sound sincere.

Kiel climbed out of the open hatch, leaving Bishop alone once again to conclude his work. Now that the metal floor plate had been removed, he could see a black and yellow striped hexagonal housing with thick cables running away from it on either side. Tiny lights shimmered from the sides in multicolored radiance, each telling its own story. Red script was emblazoned on the surface of the housing, script that Bishop could now understand: WARNING, DO NOT REMOVE REACTOR COVER WHILE IN OPERATION.

Bishop dexterously unlocked four clips and lifted the housing cover. There, resting in a white ceramic depression, sat the power coil. It was about the size of an apple but was a perfect lustrous sphere, the color of hematite. Coming from its center was a bluish glow that suggested immense power, power that would soon activate a weapon that could save the planet from Reaver.

As Bishop lifted the oddly warm sphere from its cradle, all lights within the machine faded and flickered out, leaving him in blackness. The dim glow of the starlight above him marked the exit port. He hastened to the metal ladder.

Bishop had not taken his first step up the ladder when an earsplitting shriek came from outside. Then came the sound of an Eligor yelling and screaming in confused terror.

Bishop scrambled up to the top and looked out just in time to see a shimmering, wavering form moving into the opening surrounding the Leviathan. Several dead Eligor lay shredded, torn, and lifeless behind the wavering attacker. "Kiel!" Bishop screamed, checking the forms anxiously.

"Bishop!" came a cawing sound from the darkened trees.

Storm Singer almost landed on Bishop's head before the bird screamed again. "Something is attacking!" Then he flew off again into the darkness, no doubt attempting to draw the beast's attention away from the Eligor who was fighting the thing in vain.

Bishop stared, frozen momentarily by the horror of the thing. Huge and formless, the monster hovered on skeletal wings over the crumpled body of its latest kill. Luminous eyes, like great disks of yellow fire, surveyed the destruction while the mouth began to feed, sinking fangs into its victim's body, liquefying it and draining it in seconds. Then, in a flash of wing and talon, it moved to the next Eligor with rending, razor-like claws.

The apparition reared and slew with a ferocity that was staggering. Bishop dropped back to the floor and set the power coil down, intent on joining the battle as quickly as possible. But just as he returned to the ladder, he stopped himself.

Wait a minute. What if Kiel is right? What if there's a chance the beast will still operate?

Bishop grabbed the power coil and groped his way back to the exposed housing. Yes, there was the ceramic cradle. He dropped the sphere into the depression, and the lighting instantly flickered back to life.

"I trust the Others built their weapons well," he muttered, hurrying to the front of the beast.

Bishop seated himself and repeated the activation sequence he had stumbled upon back in the cave so many weeks ago it seemed, but this time he did not hesitate as he nimbly attempted to coax the beast to life. "Thank the dark gods of the Others," he cried as the lights began to flicker. If only his luck would hold and it would continue to function!

The sequence of illuminated glyphs appeared as before, glyphs that Bishop now understood.

> Iät uipi Lânnët—Human interface unlocked
> Uipi luotëhët ëtëlât—Fission ignition commencing
> Uipi kâikki ilmân rânnët—Fission ignition now complete
> Tuskissa tulisen synnyn!—Primary weapons charged!
> Riekka! Riekka! Riekka!—Ready! Ready! Ready!

The viewing plates circling his head shimmered and became focused, revealing a scene from hell. More than half the engineering group lay ripped to shreds, while the remaining Eligor were forced back slowly. Kiel was alive. Bishop could make him out in the greenish glow of the vision panels. He was leading the futile assault against the monster, but it wouldn't be long before he joined the bodies that littered the night-shrouded glade. Surely, the beast was exploiting the darkness as it easily avoided the sword thrusts.

Bishop grabbed the handgrips and sighted on the midpoint of the beast. Just as before, the red glowing X centered exactly on the spot between his eyes, which were blazing in hunger. Without hesitation, Bishop squeezed the trigger.

A white-hot bolt of energy leapt out of the beast and slammed into the fiend, accompanied by the sound of a thunderclap. When Bishop's vision returned, there was nothing but a smoldering black smudge where the monster had stood moments before. The remaining Eligor had been thrown several meters from the blast point, but they seemed none the worse for wear as they slowly stood, looking at each other in fearful wonder.

It was then that Bishop noticed the dimming and flickering of the vision screens. The upper lights had also faded and were threatening to wink out. Smelling the acrid odor of hot metal, he turned to find the source. "Blast the Others!" he cursed.

He jumped from his seat and, turning, realized what the problem was with a sinking feeling. His blind haste and desperation to activate the Leviathan must have been strong indeed; he had not taken time to replace the protective housing covering the power coil. A blue ribbon of smoke curled up and escaped through the open lid as an angry glow issued forth from the open floor plate. As he approached, he looked down into the opening, and there, lying in its cradle, was the now white-hot power coil, slowly cooling to a dull orange. Bishop's implanted knowledge did not include the particulars about the coil itself, just information about its function as the primary source of energy for the Old Earth device. Still, he was fearful that the sphere had somehow been damaged because of his carelessness. "There's no help for it now. The deed is done," he murmured.

The fantastic heat the sphere had generated when Bishop called forth its power had, in effect, gravely damaged the surrounding circuitry. The Old Earth beast was finished, but with any luck, the power coil had survived Bishop's mishandling. It didn't look damaged anyway. He would wait for it to cool, then remove it.

"Bishop, what has happened?" came an anxious voice from outside.

Bishop turned and scrambled to the ladder as Kiel's head poked its way in. "Black gods, I thought you were done for!" Bishop exclaimed.

"Bishop, by the Others! What has happened? One minute we were fighting for our lives, and the next—"

Bishop climbed to the opening and wearily sat on its rim. "I activated the Leviathan to save you. It was all I could think of at the time."

Kiel's expression of gratitude was evident even in the flickering and fading light of the beast below them. "Bishop, I know that you believe we should activate the Thunderbolt, but I am forced to ask you to reconsider. The power of this Old Earth machine is quite beyond anything I have ever seen—possibly it is beyond the Thunderbolt itself—and it is here for us to employ now."

A grumbling from the Eligor could be heard below them. "My request does not come from me alone, Bishop," Kiel said earnestly. "They wish to hasten back to the fight at Opal, and I for one cannot blame them." Kiel sniffed. "What's that burnt smell?"

Bishop shook his head. "Kiel."

"There is your ability to operate this weapon, a true gift! I am amazed, Bishop! Truly, I feared you were just too dim-witted to pull it off. We will surely prevail over the Ikonians, and Opal will be forever in your debt!"

"Too dim-witted? what?"

The lights from the beast sputtered one last time and then died, leaving them in darkness.

"I am sure I did not mean that exactly, it's this translator, it doesn't always convey what I intend to impart. What—what has happened?" Kiel questioned in sudden alarm.

"If you must know, I was in a hurry to save your worthless scaled hide when the attack came, and I sort of damaged it."

"Damaged it? The Leviathan? Well then, fix it, Bishop! Surely you know how, don't you?"

"Kiel." Bishop shook his head.

Kiel wearily closed his eyes and rubbed them. "How badly did you damage it?"

"Very badly," Bishop muttered. "I know what you're thinking, lizard, but it wasn't my fault!"

"Is there any hope of repair?"

Another plume of smoke wafted out of the open hatch, causing Bishop to cough. "Not in a thousand—not in a million years."

The sounds of the forest drifted faintly through the trees, accompanied by the rustling and muttering of the remaining Eligor. A soldier below them growled something in its guttural language, and Kiel barked a reply: "Ic þē þā fǣhde feo lēanige eald-gēstreonum swā ic ǣr dyde wundini golde, gyf þӯ on weg cymest maþelode bearn ecgþēowes Biŝoþ."

"Bǣt hē his frēond wrece, þonne hē fela murne Biŝoþ?" the voice called back.

"Acgþēowes Biŝoþ," Kiel muttered.

Chorused groans of despair rose as the words were repeated, their meaning all too clear.

There was a long moment of silence before Kiel spoke again. "I guess you and I are going to the Ikonian frontier after all. You're quite sure?"

"It is quite dead," Bishop stated.

Kiel stared at Bishop with unfocused eyes.

"I'm telling you, dammit, it wasn't my fault!" Bishop growled defensively.

Kiel nodded, rubbing his face. "Yes, fine. Very well then, we will leave at first light."

"It wasn't my fault!"

NINETEEN

THE FIRST COLONY

> I am forsaken and alone. I hear the bestial roar. Every gate is shut but one, and that is disaster's door.
> —Vena Korela,
> Second Ilmarinen Cycle, Runa 1

The eastern sky had just begun to lighten to cobalt when Kiel said farewell to the commander of the Eligor Corps of Engineers, thanking him for his unfailing duty to the Eligor people and the Imperial Intelligence Service.

The corps commander glanced at the Old Earth weapon that many had labored and died for in the past two days. Speaking in the Eligor language, he addressed Kiel, saying, "It pains me to leave this device just lying here after all that we have gone through, but if this, uh, human says it is truly useless, well then, I will just have to trust this, uh, human's word. I guess."

Kiel frowned. "Commander, need I remind you that it was this human who saved us from certain doom last night? I think he deserves better than your misgivings."

The corps commander dipped his head respectfully, sighed, and then looked at Bishop, switching his translator on. "Thank you for your help, human. It was not my intention to treat you discourteously; nevertheless, under the current circumstances, I am sure you can understand my behavior."

Bishop nodded but remained silent. The commander turned to Kiel again. "Go well, Kiel, and good luck. May you feast everlasting with the All-father at the journey's end."

Kiel held up his hand in the traditional Eligor farewell. "Do not despair, Commander. We will prevail somehow." Then he led Bishop and Storm Singer away from the Leviathan and north, toward the Ikonian frontier. There, with any hope, the summoning of the Thunderbolt would at last commence.

The two-day journey through the northern Eligor Empire and to the border of the Ikonian frontier brought with it the usual mix of lurking menaces, unremarkable meals—meals that included some very stale oat bread—and the sheer tedium Bishop had come to associate with this whole ill-begotten adventure. Kiel and Storm Singer had not been very talkative through the journey; Kiel, in particular, seemed preoccupied with worry, while the bird appeared positively morose. Yet, despite all the misgivings and ever-present danger, the travelers finally broke away from the tangle of the Eligor forest and again beheld the borderlands of Ikonia. The line of ancient statues leered down from their age-old positions of vigilance, unmoving and uncaring, marking the boundary between the Eligor Empire and the lands of Ikonia beyond. Bizarre shadows lengthened as the sun sank lower in the western sky, hovering on the horizon like an evil red eye.

Kiel gazed with concern upon the statues that stretched off to the east and west. "I don't like it, Bishop. These Ikonians can detect an Eligor by scent alone, and here I am right at their doorstep, in the middle of a war no less, capering about like a mouse before a baited trap. Perhaps if we were to move back away from these unsettling statues and under the trees and await darkness, we would stand a better chance of not being discovered."

Bishop stared at the Eligor with a smirk.

Kiel darkened. "It's not that I fear them, you clod. It's simply that I would not wish to bring doom down upon us now that we are so close. Surely you can understand my concern?"

Bishop gazed out at the stone monoliths that studded the open expanse before them. It seemed peaceful enough, bees buzzing from flower to flower and birds singing in the open meadow, cottony clouds drifting silently overhead. He had been here twice before, once going into Ikonia, and once when being literally chased back out. Not fond memories.

"Just possibly you are right for once, lizard. Can't say as I blame you for your fretfulness, but this is where we are to summon the Thunderbolt. I was instructed to assemble the sphere within sight of these monoliths, or it would not work."

Kiel stared at Bishop. "I still do not understand. Why here? Why not back in the eighth hell?"

Bishop looked helplessly at Kiel, raising his hands in exasperation. "I'm not making this up. We are to summon the Thunderbolt here, next to one of those eerie, abysmal statues, maybe to save us time. Maybe these statues are made up of something that the device requires to operate. I simply don't know."

Kiel gazed uneasily into the gloom of the forestlands beyond the statues. "Well, let's at least wait until dark before we traipse out there, exposing our backsides. We are so close to our prize now, it would be a pity …"

Kiel let the thought trail as Bishop followed Kiel's gaze into the stygian Ikonian forests to the north. Bishop could identify with the Eligor's anxiety. They were terribly close to success and or catastrophic ruin. It reminded him of his childhood, desperately anticipating midwinter festivals and the expected presents days before the event. Bishop remembered, fervently hoping that if he ever died, it would be some time after the festival so that he would not miss out on the fun. He suppressed a chuckle at the thought of a ten-year-old Kiel capering about in the same selfish manner, although he was sure he never had. "Yes, we are so close. It would be a shame," he responded.

They made their way back into the concealment of the Eligor forest to wait out the remainder of the day. Storm Singer sat high in the trees, quietly watching for movement, but none came.

Finally, after hours of quiet vigilance, the sun began to sink, glowing crimson on the horizon, then disappearing in the deepening purple murk of the approaching evening. Stars winked on one by one, and the ancient, haggard moon rode high over the black mountains to the east, casting a surreal glow over the borderlands of Ikonia.

Kiel lightly shook Bishop, who had been dozing off and on in their concealment. "Wake up. I think we had better get on with it," he whispered.

"Good!" Bishop groused, rubbing sleep from his eyes. "Maybe at the conclusion of the evening you will allow me to return to the protectorate. No offense, friend Eligor, but I am simply getting weary of this adventure of yours."

"Quiet, human!" Kiel hissed, quickly scanning the open glade. "For the love of the empire, you'll wake the dead with that shrill, squeaky human voice of yours!"

Bishop shook his head with annoyance as he looked up into the trees. "Storm Singer, get your fat feathered roast down here."

Kiel glared at Bishop with his yellow eyes widening in frustration.

"Well, what am I supposed to do, use hand signals for the flying rat?"

"You know, human, your species is certainly churlish when you are abruptly wakened from your afternoon naps," Kiel's translator hissed in frustration.

Bishop shrugged and then smiled sheepishly. "I suppose you are right. I am sorry, but I am tired of this trip. It has done nothing to improve my mood."

In a moment, the wolf-bird drifted out of the tree and alighted on Bishop's shoulder. "And what is it that you wish, human? Eggs for breakfast? Slippers for your feet?" he croaked in annoyance.

Kiel bristled. "Black gods and damnation, another loud, grouchy animal. My empire for a bit of silence!"

Storm Singer looked sideways at Kiel and then at Bishop questioningly. "What's got his scaly back up?"

"The lizard is a bit edgy, bird," Bishop whispered. "Scout the perimeter for trouble, keeping those little black raisins of yours peeled for trouble. Now, get!"

The bird ruffled his ebon feathers and, muttering an avian curse involving mites, took to the air and was gone in a flurry of black feathers.

"After you, Sir Eligor," Bishop whispered, bowing floridly.

Kiel rolled his golden eyes and stalked off into the gloaming.

They crept away from the trees and ghosted cautiously into the darkened meadow ahead of them. There, stretching to the horizon both to the east and the west, was a line of stone markers, each carved in the likeness of a slumbering human face with a seven-sided symbol etched in its ancient forehead. If this Old Earth resurrection of the Thunderbolt was to be, then this was the place and the time to make it happen.

Bishop took off his pack and scrounged through it while Kiel crept closer until he was fairly stepping on him. "By the eight hells, I've lost it!" Bishop hissed.

"Bishop! Black gods of chaos!" Kiel choked in fright. "Human!"

"Shh. Quiet. Don't you Eligor ever joke around? I was just jesting. It's right here; don't get so uptight," Bishop half growled, half laughing. "Gods of the Others, man, settle down!"

"Yes, we joke! But by the black gods in hell, this is neither the time nor the place to be making jest, Bishop. Get on with it, will you?" Kiel's translator hissed. He looked about the darkened glade tremulously, wiping his scaled forehead nervously. "By the Others, human, you startled me so badly, I nearly choked up my liver."

Bishop, still silently chortling despite himself, pulled free the two halves of the device he had been given when in the eighth hell and carefully unwrapped the power coil from a bit of canvas, setting everything down around him.

"Well, here it goes," Bishop muttered.

Taking the power coil, he lightly placed it into one of the upturned halves of the receptacle, closed the other half over top of it, and quickly stepped away as if he had lit a skyrocket in celebration of the midsummer's eve.

"Now what?" Kiel asked impatiently.

"I don't rightly know. Just wait a minute."

"Look," Kiel said, pointing excitedly. "Look there!"

"I see it." Bishop cautiously backed a few more paces away from the device, half stumbling over Kiel as he did so.

The sphere seemed to waver a moment. Looking closely, Bishop noted the two halves had fused so that the seam could no longer be detected. Now it was shimmering like rippling water, while around its sides there emerged four bladelike projections that began to turn in unison. Faster and faster they turned until the movement became a blur, like the wings of a hummingbird in flight. Then the thing rose in the air and hovered, whirring silently above them.

"Bishop," Kiel called nervously, backing another step away from the weird contrivance.

"Just wait." Bishop held out his hand.

Now a thin blue needle of light burst silently forth and washed over one of the great stone markers. Then it washed over another, as if the device were attempting to orient itself and familiarize itself with its surroundings. Storm Singer flew down from the dark sky to alight on Kiel's shoulder, drawn, it seemed, by a birdish curiosity. The device noted the movement, for it now cast the sapphire light on Kiel and the bird. As if becoming disinterested in them, the light shone on Bishop, washing him from head to toe in its strange luminescence. The sphere was looking for something, and now it appeared to have found it.

Like a snake uncoiling and striking out, a burst of power came smashing down on Bishop. The shock wave traveled throughout his entire body. At the first impact of the shock wave, he was vaguely aware that he cried out. And then it was over. The device whirred louder, increasing in altitude, and in a burst of speed it disappeared over the treetops to the east, toward the eighth hell, and was gone from sight.

Kiel cautiously approached. "Bishop, are you all right?"

Bishop gazed at Kiel as if he were now invisible.

"Bishop! What has happened? Are you all right?"

"I must go north. The course is clear. You must return to your city. I go to destroy our foe, but where I go you cannot follow," Bishop cryptically droned.

Kiel frowned, looking at Storm Singer in perplexity. "That's it? Just go back to Opal and leave you here to face the Ikonian nation alone?"

"Yes," Bishop responded mechanically.

Storm Singer flew to Bishop's shoulder and stared wonderingly at Bishop and then back at Kiel, shrugging his wings in confusion. "What of me? What am I to do?"

"Kiel will return to his city. You will remain here at the border until my return and report any activity. There is much to do."

True, Kiel wanted more than anything to return to his people and join the battle for Opal. Bishop would travel toward his fate, toward a goal whose progress Kiel could only hinder because of his Eligor heritage, which the Ikonians could so easily detect. The two travelers had assumed as much since leaving the great swamp of Moeras Kor.

"What of the device? Where has it gone?"

"It functions. You should go. It is not safe for you here," Bishop droned.

Storm Singer took flight. "He need not tell me twice," the bird cawed in agitation. "Farewell, Kiel. May the home nest welcome you upon your return."

Kiel stared at the bird as it disappeared. "And that's it?"

Bishop stared vacantly, "You should go."

Kiel sighed, looking around the open glade in confusion. This was not at all what he had expected, though he was not sure what he had expected. Yet what else was he to do? It was clear that something had happened; there was no mistake about that. The device had clearly done something, and Bishop was central to its mysterious purpose. Just what that purpose was, the dark gods of technology only knew. Kiel was resigned to trust that it was necessary in saving the Eligor—and, for that matter, the planet—from the Reaver tyranny. He turned to face Bishop with resolve.

"Very well, go then. And success to you, my friend." Kiel took Bishop in a rough embrace, then turned abruptly. He melted back into the southern wood and was gone.

Bishop awoke with a start, staggering to his feet in confused alarm. The movement came in a burst of fear-borne energy that drained away as quickly as it had come, leaving him tottering and light-headed. He stood swaying in the cheerful sunlight, amid unfamiliar grass and trees, unable to recall how he had come to be there.

Gradually, in bits and pieces, it came back: the activation of the power coil, the burst of light, his crying out. But that had been during the evening, and it was now late afternoon—or might it even be early evening?

With a shock, Bishop noticed that the grass where he had lain remained pressed down, showing the outline of his body. Within the outline the grass had even yellowed, beginning to die from lack of sun.

How many days had he lain there? Within the outline of withered grass, beetles were scurrying to find new shade. But though he had been as motionless as a corpse, apparently no living thing had come closer than the beetles to molesting him. He wondered about Kiel and Storm Singer but vaguely remembered sending them away before he lost all memory.

Bishop's mind clicked another notch closer to full consciousness; with the awakening of his brain came the sense of a presence. He swiveled around, and there, standing as motionless as a mountain, was a technological horror that he knew at once to be the physical embodiment of the Iron Thunderbolt.

The monstrous form stood nearly three meters tall. Armored vent ports along its upper surface steamed in the cool air as if a hellish fire burned somewhere beneath its massive armored shell. Vaguely human in shape, the Thunderbolt seemed to be comprised exclusively of grotesquely misshapen overlapping plates of metal. Two hulking appendages that hung away from either side of the upper body seemed bizarre parodies of massive human arms, each of which terminated in five flexible metallic tentacles that no doubt served as fingers for grasping. The exposed areas that could be seen around the neck, shoulders, and waist were a corded mass of flexible steel cables and wire. The head was, in comparison to the body, a small, nearly featureless shard of armor sporting a thin black slit barely visible under a protective immobile brow.

Twin sparks of greenish hellfire suddenly flamed deep within the slit, locking on Bishop's eyes. In a grating, harsh tone, the Thunderbolt spoke, sounding at one moment like splintering wood, and at another like clashing metal.

"Construct Bishop," rumbled the voice.

It was a statement of fact, not a question.

Bishop backed up a few steps in unconscious prudence. "Yes. I am Standard-Bearer Bishop of the Order of the Protectorate of Merja Soria."

"I am the Thunderbolt."

Bishop had assumed as much; what else could this hellish titan of the Old Earth be? He relaxed as much as one could in the presence of such an entity in possession of untold powers.

Rubbing at his sore muscles, Bishop frowned. "How is it that you have been freed? The last I knew, you were trapped in the eighth hell, and now quick as lightning, here you are standing before me."

"You would not understand. I will attempt to explain."

"Never mind, I'd rather not know," Bishop muttered. "Although I'm perfectly capable of understanding."

The Thunderbolt remained silent.

Bishop rubbed life back into his aching muscles. "Well then, what is it that I am to do?"

"You will accompany me."

"Accompany you? How am I to help with such a grand task as overpowering the Reaver threat?"

"You are a construct," said the Thunderbolt, as if that explained everything. "You will lead me to the Reaver threat."

"Just walk right on up to him and kill him."

"Reaver will die. It is inevitable."

At that response, a strange thought entered Bishop's mind, unbidden: *And, after the Reaver threat is no more, I will take whatever I want. I will destroy those who stand against me. I will maintain fear in all whom I subjugate. That is what I will do.*

Bishop felt a sudden chill run down his spine. Whose thoughts were these? Were they the Thunderbolt's thoughts or his own fears? Who else's memories did he have? Bishop felt a slow horror creep up on him. He had wakened an entity from the Old Earth that seemed capable of snuffing out Reaver like a candle. What would it do after that, shuffle back to the eighth hell and enjoy a long-deserved retirement, maybe take up gardening? But what choice did Bishop have? None. And the deed was done.

"So that's the plan, walk right into Ikonia and kill Reaver?" Bishop said sardonically.

The Thunderbolt made no reply.

Bishop looked at the Thunderbolt briefly and then glanced away toward the north. He lifted his chin with resolve. There was work to do. It was too late for misgivings.

Bishop looked around the glade they inhabited, wondering about Kiel and Storm Singer and then at the setting sun to the west. Noting the position of the sun and the look of the vegetation, Bishop surmised that his companions must be somewhere southeast of the dead city of Terus Kor. "Follow me then," he said, eyeing the metallic giant with suspicion.

There came from deep within the creature an accelerated whining sound. The vent port hissed with near-invisible rippling heat waves. Then, like a ponderous leviathan, the Thunderbolt took a step toward Bishop on oak-tree-sized supporting structures that could only be referred to as legs. Bishop eyed the fantastic sight for a second longer and then, throwing up his arms in resignation, melted into the forest gloom toward Ikonia.

The following day, Bishop knew they were getting close to their goal. The forest was thinning, and the undergrowth had disappeared. A crashing from behind him caused him to cringe. The Thunderbolt might be a tremendous weapon, but its ability to be stealthy was sorely in question. Bishop was about to turn and inform the Thunderbolt of their proximity to the dead city when an Ikonian insect suddenly appeared on the trail in front of them.

Bishop stumbled to a stop, unsheathing his sword, as the Thunderbolt came to rest beside him. Bishop prepared himself for an attack, though the Thunderbolt merely stood motionless. But no attack came; the insect just stared at them as if it did not know quite what to make of the scene before it. The insect's translator hummed to life.

"You are of the colony."

Bishop started. "Of the colony? Thirty-Six, is that you?"

"Yes. Can you not tell?" The translator seemed to convey irritation.

"I … Well, no, actually. I guess I can't. Thirty-Six, what in the eight hells are you doing out here away from your ever-loving colony?"

"This tunneler was expelled after you were freed. Those of the colony will not kill those of the colony, but the Dreamer intended harm, and those of the colony allowed this tunneler to leave unmolested. This tunneler was traveling toward the frontier to die when it sensed your proximity." Thirty-Six seemed to wave its antennae at the Iron Thunderbolt, which was standing behind Bishop.

"There is something there," Thirty-Six cautioned, becoming motionless, the insect's antennae probing the air in the direction where the Thunderbolt stood.

"Ah, you must be referring to my dear friend Sir Thunderbolt," Bishop said sardonically.

Thirty-Six relaxed somewhat. "Your friend has no odor. This tunneler cannot easily sense him. Thirty-Six cannot recognize him."

"He hasn't been on the trail as long as me, I would guess," Bishop said, sniffing at himself. "Sorry."

The insect continued to stare at Bishop with its iridescent compound eyes. "Why have you come back? You are free."

"Yes, well, it wasn't exactly my idea."

Thirty-Six stared.

Bishop rubbed his eyes and then stoically responded to the question. "We have come back to Ikonia to face Reaver, the Dreamer, and defeat him."

"One human and his companion against the Dreamer and the combined forces of the colonies? That is not logical. You will not survive."

"My companion is not altogether human."

Thirty-Six waved its antennae. "Yes, well, then perhaps your goals are achievable." The insect's translator did not relay a sense of confidence.

Bishop shrugged. "Well, Thirty-Six, it's been a wonderful reunion, but we really must be on our way." Bishop's voice became more serious and speculative. "Why don't you hold off on that dying business and help us do something about the Dreamer? Who knows, maybe we will be successful and free your somnambulant nest from his thrall. Would that not be something worth living for? Would that not be something worth dying for?"

Thirty-Six stood motionless for a moment while it pondered the request, its antennae occasionally twitching as it thought. "It seems logical—yes, flawlessly logical. For a few days, Thirty-Six believes that Thirty-Six can manage assisting you. What is it you require of this tunneler?"

"Very well then." Bishop thought. "We need direction, possibly information concerning the layout of your beloved nest." Bishop thumbed toward Terus Kor.

The insect, seeming to understand the directional gesture, spoke again. "You are traveling the wrong route."

Bishop frowned. "I'm a pretty good tracker, Thirty-Six. Terus Kor is right over there, and Reaver is under that great bloody ant nest." He stabbed a finger to the northwest. "Right over there."

"The Dreamer no longer inhabits the Twelfth Colony."

Bishop's finger dropped. "What do you mean, he no longer inhabits the Twelfth Colony? Do you mean he's not under the dead city of Terus Kor?"

"He is not within the Twelfth Colony."

"Well, why in the eight hells didn't you say as much? Where is he then?" Bishop demanded impatiently.

"He has moved his command structure to the First Colony," Thirty-Six's translator said matter-of-factly, as if everyone in the world knew this fact except Bishop.

"The First Colony. Of course." Bishop struggled with the information, but before he could continue, there came from behind him a slight high-pitched hissing sound and then a peculiar smell wafting through the air, like honey.

Thirty-Six stiffened, its antennae waving in the air like grass being blown by a fierce wind.

"I will take you to the First Colony," Thirty-Six intoned. And then without another word, the creature turned and disappeared among the trees.

Bishop looked at the Thunderbolt in surprised confusion.

"I have the capability of communicating with fourteen species of constructs," the Thunderbolt said.

Bishop stared in confusion.

"You will follow the insect."

Bishop shrugged. "Fine. Great, I'll follow the bloody insect for all the good it will do." Following Thirty-Six, he melted into the forest with the Thunderbolt lumbering behind.

Late into the night, Bishop began to stumble and finally sat down to rest, while the Thunderbolt and Thirty-Six looked at him. Bishop frowned. "You fellows might not need to rest, but lest you forget, I am human and need to sleep from time to time, that is, if you don't mind."

"Rest?" Thirty-Six questioned.

"Yes, my power coil needs recharging."

"Power coil?"

"Never mind," Bishop grumbled.

The Thunderbolt's barely noticeable mechanical whine slowed and quieted; a clicking and rumbling from deep within the machine sounded faintly. Bishop was becoming familiar with these unsettling mechanical sounds. "We will wait for you to rest, and then we will continue," the Thunderbolt said.

Bishop's attention shifted from the towering form of the Thunderbolt to the diminutive form of Thirty-Six, which was now standing motionless on the other side of him, staring silently. Then he looked back at the Thunderbolt, who in turn stared mutely. "Well, this is certainly uncomfortable."

"What is it, human?" Thirty-Six asked, perplexed.

"Don't you insects ever sit down?"

"Sit?"

"Yes, sit. Like what I am now doing. Sit. Sit down. Be seated. Rest. Be at rest. Relax."

Thirty-Six looked at Bishop and then nodded in understanding. "We can 'sit.'"

The insect proceeded to fold up into what looked like the most uncomfortable, ghastliest shape Bishop could have ever imagined, resembling an immense dead spider on a gigantic windowsill. "We 'sit' when we are very cold or close to death," Thirty-Six said.

"Great. You can stand up again. Thanks for the demonstration." Bishop realized that he had never before seen so much as one chair in all his dealings with the Ikonians. The idea that there was a species that did not sit down when it was tired or a species that did not even get tired was alien and new to him.

"You are welcome," Thirty-Six responded as the creature again unfolded itself and stood. "In fact, there are several other, quite fascinating stances that are used by those of the nest to customarily show respect. The first is known as the 'introduction stance' which, as you might have guessed, involves the touching of the antennae. This procedure—"

"Fine, great, I'm sure it's fascinating—to other Ikonians. But I need to rest right now," Bishop said, exasperated.

Bishop laid out his tatterdemalion bedroll and crawled into it, closing his eyes in near-exhaustion. Several minutes went by before a nagging sensation began to invade his thoughts. Opening one eye, he first saw Thirty-Six standing there, watching him intently, and then he glanced over at the Thunderbolt. Sure enough, the Old Earth creation was standing there, its two sparks of greenish fire flickering ghostly in the darkness, seeming to be assessing him.

Bishop looked at the two again, shook his head, and got up. "I can't do it. The thought of the both of you leering over me while I sleep is more than I can bear."

Bishop climbed a massive oak and found a wide, flat branch with several smaller branches growing around it like a natural basket. Settling himself on his pack, he called out, "Good night, everyone."

The next day it began to rain. Towering black clouds roiled in from the west and settled over Ikonia, blotting out all traces of sun and sky as they released a torrential downpour. The deluge was interspersed with flashes of branching lightning lacing the clouds with its brilliant light, while deeply rolling thunder reverberated through the forest with earthshaking claps. Bishop cast apprehensive glances at the surrounding gloom. The entire Ikonian army could come instantly upon him and his companions, and they wouldn't know it until it was too late. The two who were traveling with him seemed not to notice the sheets of rain in the slightest. The water beaded and ran off the Thunderbolt's impervious body as if it had been smeared in grease. Thirty-Six acted as if it couldn't even detect the wetness, though its antennae, as if they operated independently of their owner, occasionally shook the water off themselves like a drenched dog.

Attempts to read any trail signs were useless. All tracks were effectively erased in the deluge of rain. "Thirty-Six, are you certain that we are going in the right direction?"

The insect turned to Bishop. "Yes. As stated on thirteen previous occasions, the First Colony is directly ahead. Taking into consideration your rest periods, we should arrive around midday tomorrow."

Bishop looked up at the towering Thunderbolt. "Not to get out of this adventure, but now that you have an Ikonian, why do you need me still?"

The Old Earth monstrosity swiveled its metallic head toward Bishop. "You are a human construct."

"Of course. I forgot about that," Bishop responded. "And that is important because why?"

"The insect has suggested several Old Earth entrances that are keyed to your genetic code, much like the device from which you recovered the power coil. We will use them to gain access to the lower tunnels of the First Colony."

Bishop frowned, stabbing a thumb in the direction of Thirty-Six. "You might be able to communicate with this insect in its own language, but don't forget that I cannot. It would be courteous if you included me in your plans."

"So noted."

Toward evening, the rains lessened and then stopped altogether, the gigantic clouds moving on and leaving a dripping, steaming forest. The sun sank into the deep green mountains to the west and then set, streaking the sky with a violet glow.

It was nearly dark when Thirty-Six suddenly stopped. Its antennae waved and tapped the air around its body. "There are a number of soldiers ahead. I do not believe they have detected us yet, but they soon will."

Bishop looked around in near-panic. "Can we hide?"

"There might be a way to disguise our presence."

The Thunderbolt lumbered forward. "You will take cover behind me. I will terminate the insects."

The whining sound within the Thunderbolt rose in pitch as the monster lumbered to the front of a clearing. A shimmering aura flickered to life around its armored bulk.

Thirty-Six's feelers danced for a moment, and then the insect lowered itself into a muddy depression. Bishop watched Thirty-Six cover its body in the cold muck and quickly followed the insect's actions.

"This will hide our scent."

"I'm sure it does wonders for the skin too," Bishop replied blandly, plastering his forehead.

"Of course, the mud hides our scent. It will protect our epidermal layers."

Bishop gave Thirty-Six a sideways glace but remained silent. He moved to the back of the nearest tree, crouching against it, while Thirty-Six did the same next to an opposing tree. Bishop carefully peeked around the black mossy bole toward the trail in front of him. There, glinting in the gloom, stood the Thunderbolt. Motionless as a statue, the Old Earth monster waited in the middle of the trail, not bothering to conceal itself in the slightest.

Everything was still. Not even a placid breeze blew through the antediluvian forest. The dead air had even stilled the mournful songs of the fall birds. The forest lay in a trance that was broken by no sound but the far-off hammering of a woodpecker, which seemed to render the pervading silence and sense of danger even more profound.

Some time passed with no Ikonians appearing. Bishop was about to question Thirty-Six when the mist parted, revealing a column of about thirty approaching insects of the formidable soldier caste. They at first did not seem to notice the Thunderbolt, but before long the lead insect slowed and began probing the air with its antennae. It seemed confused and did not immediately direct its attention toward the armored hulk in front of it. Like Thirty-Six, this insect was having difficulty identifying the monster as a life-form.

The Thunderbolt, on the other hand, did not seem to have any such difficulties. It raised its massive arm and pointed at the nearest Ikonian. To Bishop, there was a sense of a silent force, imperceptible but awesome, and the lead insect dissolved into a greenish vapor that hung in the air for a moment and then dissipated. The other Ikonians immediately erupted into near-hysteria, wasting no time in encircling the Thunderbolt. Another Ikonian was vaporized in much the same fashion as the first, but still the insects advanced, their feelers dancing frantically in a silent ballet. Within seconds the insects attacked, throwing themselves upon the Thunderbolt en masse, thrusting forward with their spears and arm weapons, yet try as they might, it was impossible for them to so much as scratch the metal plating of the Old Earth creature. Two more Ikonians were reduced to mist, and it seemed that they would soon be destroyed completely, when something went very wrong.

The bluish aura surrounding the Thunderbolt wavered and flickered as if threatening to wink out completely. The metal monster took a faltering step backward and half turned toward Bishop. The high-pitched whine that could be faintly heard within the Old Earth device slowed as the beast seemed to slump in fatigue.

"There is a malfunction. Reset," came a grating voice.

The Thunderbolt teetered, fell to its knees, and then pitched forward onto the sodden ground with an earthshaking thud, spraying mud in all directions. In an instant, the remaining Ikonians tackled the lifeless form and quickly wrapped its mass in thin flexible rope from head to foot. Not a sound did the insects make as they worked, but Bishop could smell a multitude of scents wafting through the air.

Soon the Thunderbolt was dragged away up the trail, leaving a deep groove in the muddy ground as testament to the machine's tremendous weight—testament too to the strength of the Ikonian soldiers.

Bishop looked over at Thirty-Six in maddened perplexity. The insect, still mostly covered with mud, was fully engaged probing the air with animated feelers. It seemed like hours before it detached from the tree and moved quietly toward the trail. "It is now safe."

Bishop joined the insect, scraping the mud away from his skin and clothing. Glowering at the muddy trail leading off into the gloom, he shook his head in exasperation. "Well, that was certainly impressive, wasn't it? The mythical Iron Thunderbolt of legend, terror of the Old Earth, master of the dread technologies of the Others, snuffed out like a candle by a bunch of overgrown cockroaches! Now what in the eight hells am I supposed to do, spit on Reaver?"

"Your companion seemed to tire rather quickly. Possibly he required rest—sleep, as you do," Thirty-Six said in its annoyingly casual manner.

"A fine time to sleep, Thirty-Six. What a waste of time and energy this was!" Bishop slumped, looking back toward the south. "It seems I have little choice left in this matter. I will return to Merja Soria and warn the protectorate. I couldn't hope to get within ten kilometers of Opal. And what good would it do if I could?"

"Does he have a power coil like you do?"

Bishop started. "Power coil? How in the eight hells do you know about the power coil?"

"You once mentioned the need to rest to recharge your power coil. Does his power coil also have a finite wakeful time?"

Bishop's skin prickled at the ray of enlightenment. The power coil. Of course, it was damaged. Bishop himself had damaged it, but it was not irreparable.

"Yes, Thirty-Six, you are most probably right." Bishop sighed wearily as realization crept over him.

"Well, he will be fine when he sleeps."

"It's not that easy, Thirty-Six. His power coil is damaged."

"Oh. Then you will fix it, yes?"

Bishop gave the insect a long look and silently cursed the Others. "It seems I will have to." If only he could restart the Thunderbolt like he had restarted the Old Earth device. Bishop stopped and looked at Thirty-Six, startled by his mental revelation. *That's it! The unstart override!* It simply needed to be reset after the power overload, coupled with the sudden draw upon its energy when Bishop had misused the device. Reset the coil and then it would operate in a predictable fashion. This knowledge was there all along, lying dormant until required. Bishop wondered again at what other nameless knowledge he carried within his own mind, knowledge placed there purposefully by the Thunderbolt.

For a long moment Bishop stared off in the direction of the Thunderbolt's unceremonious exit. He turned to Thirty-Six, who stood silently at his side. "Can you get me close to the Thunderbolt? I mean, without being discovered?"

The insect nodded. "It might be possible. Thirty-Six is a tunnel worker. It knows the passages that lead throughout the First Colony, passages that are now unused and closed up."

Bishop frowned. "How would you know of such things?"

"Thirty-Six is a tunnel worker," the insect repeated, as if the statement was obvious enough. "All our nests are designed according to a master plan; they are identical in form and function. Though you will note the older colonies are much more elaborate, which is necessary to support a larger population—"

"Very well," Bishop interrupted. "Tunneler Thirty-Six, lead on."

All night and part of the following day, the two travelers had breasted the slopes of the northern Ikonian Massif, which ran from east to west across the world like a mighty wall of rock and ice, sundering the northlands of Ikonia from the southern Eligor Empire and the human protectorate much farther to the south.

The sky was a dome of crimson and golden vapors, darkening from the zenith to the eastern horizon with the amethyst of oncoming evening. But the fiery splendor of the dying day still painted the white crests of the mountains with a deceptively warm and rosy radiance. The setting sun threw deep shadows across the frozen surface of a titanic glacier that wound like an icy serpent from the higher peaks, down and down, until it curved in front of the pass and then coiled away again to the left, to dwindle in the foothills and turn and turn again into a rushing torrent of icy, boulder-strewn water. Those who traveled through the pass had to pick their way cautiously past the margin of the glacier, hoping that they would neither fall into one of its hidden crevasses nor be overwhelmed by an avalanche from the higher slopes.

The setting sun turned the snow and ice into a glittering expanse of crimson and gold. The rocky slopes that rose from the glacier were dotted with a smattering of gnarled dwarfish pine trees.

Bishop's lungs strained and burned as he climbed. "I thought I had seen some bad climbing on the eighth hell, but it was a molehill by comparison." He panted "Are you sure there isn't an easier way to the First Colony, Thirty-Six?"

Thirty-Six stopped and eyed Bishop, the insect's iridescent eyes regarding him as if it were peeved. "You have asked that question of me four times. I fear my translator is malfunctioning. This tunneler will repeat itself yet again. The only other route is heavily guarded by those of the First Colony. We would surely be discovered."

"Great. Fine. Just asking." Bishop wheezed as he stooped, placing his hands on his knees in fatigue.

Finally, he joined Thirty-Six. Standing on the icy crest, the two of them looked out over the world. Thirty-Six pointed. "There. The First Colony is there."

The insect's articulated forearm was pointing toward the immense mountain range before them. Bishop followed with his eyes. One towering conical mountain jutted away from the rest, seeming to touch the very sky, hundreds of meters taller than the other mountains in the range.

Bishop returned his attention to the insect. "Which one?"

"The one there."

Bishop looked out again and rubbed his eyes in frustration. "Please tell me it's not the tall one."

"Yes, the one there, the tall one, as you so name it."

Bishop sat down with a groan. "The thing is too tall, Thirty-Six. We'll never make it to the top alive."

"We do not climb to the top. We enter at the tree line."

"But an anthill entrance is always on the top of the—"

Bishop caught the irritated twitching of Thirty-Six's antennae. "Yes, well, I did assume—"

"We are not ants, human."

Bishop again looked across the valley, this time in embarrassment. "Black gods, Thirty-Six, I know that. It's just, ah, let's get this over with."

They scrambled down into a hidden valley and crossed a rushing, stony-sounding river as the sun sank below the western range. The ancient indifferent moon slowly rose as they climbed back up into the pine trees that masked the mountain slopes in a weird half-light, the shadows etched in black. No wind blew through the thinning forest, but a mysterious rustling and whispering was coming, it seemed, from the very ground. They closed on several cliffs. Bishop was somewhat disquieted to note that the elusive moonlight lent the rock faces a subtle appearance he had not noticed before. In the gloaming, they appeared less like natural cliffs and more like the ruins of titan-reared battlements jutting from the mountain slope.

Shaking this allusion off with some difficulty, Bishop came to a plateau and hesitated for a moment before plunging into the brooding shadows of the woods again. A sort of hushed tension hung over the land, like an unseen monster holding its breath lest it frighten away its prey.

Bishop shook off the tension, natural as it was, considering the eeriness of the place, and made his way through the trees, following Thirty-Six. He had a most unpleasant sensation that they were being followed. He froze once, sure that something clammy and unstable had brushed against his face in the darkness. A thin night wind started to blow through the pines with a suggestion of faint unseen pipes whistling an eerie and unfamiliar funeral dirge. The monotony of the sound in this strange setting caused a shiver to run like an icy finger down Bishop's back.

The pair finally broke out into an open glade to behold a frightful scene from a lost civilization. The blasted battlements of a dead city reared from the open meadow, all but invisible from a distance, but now stark in their reality. Only the age-old silence brooded over the mysterious ruins, which were clustered around the lower face of the great mountain. But apprehension was there as Bishop stood catching his breath.

Besides Thirty-Six, Bishop was the one speck of life amid the colossal monuments of desolation and decay. Not even the form of a vulture marred the vast cerulean vault of the sky that the moon glazed with its pale, frosty light. On every side rose the grim relics of a forgotten era: huge pillars thrusting their jagged pinnacles up toward the heavens; long wavering lines of crumbling wall; fallen massive blocks of stone; and shattered images whose horrific features the eroding winds and dust of the ages had half erased. From horizon to horizon, there was no sign of life, only the sheer breathtaking sweep of the wintry mountains, bisected by the wandering line of a rushing, tumbling river course. In the midst of that ruined wasteland, shattered columns stood like the broken fangs of a colossal wolf.

Bishop followed Thirty-Six through a narrow street that was divided by gloomy alleys. The city was a contrast of splendor and decay, where opulent palaces rose among the smoke-stained ruins of buildings of forgotten ages. They came to a newer and more respectable quarter, where latticed windows and overhanging balconies almost touched one another over the street. At the far end of the ghost city, they halted before a cliff face.

Materializing out of the gloom, Bishop noted a tall, dark monolith rearing above the rubble-strewn ground before him. The mountain rose directly behind it, terminating blackly against a scintillating Milky Way that glistened frostily in the sky overhead. The column was octagonal in shape, some ten meters in height and about two meters thick. Anyone could see there was something unnatural about the structure; the sunlight and winds of countless past eons had lashed it as they had the surrounding structures, yet this megalith's ebony surface rose as bright and glistening as if it had been built yesterday—an unnaturalness that was in keeping with the general aura of these devil-haunted ruins. Strange glyphs marched in a spiraling line round and round the shaft to the top. Bishop was reminded of the similar obelisk at the center of Terus Kor. He traced the glyphs with his fingers, and though he suspected they represented no current language used on the face of the earth in modern times, he found that he could read them. They were of the same type as the glyphs within the Leviathan.

"Piti viikkoista pyhyyttä iän kaiken impeyyttä ilman pitkillä pihoilla tasaisilla tantereilla ikävystyi aikojansa ouostui elämätänsä aina yksin ollessansa impenä eläessänsä ilman pitkillä pihoilla avaroilla autioilla ..."

Bishop began translating at about midpoint in the text: "And as they reach to the far-horizon heavens, and in those vast and empty spaces where stars are born, they expanded their sphere of divine dominion beyond the terrestrial ..."

Bishop looked up at the towering mountain beyond the monolith and shook his head. "You know, it's a big rock pile, I'll grant you that. But the stars? I mean, come on now, I don't think you quite made it."

"It was not written by our race. We do not record history thus. It was written by the human followers of the Dreamers who originally inhabited this place in eons past."

"The Reavers? Ah, yes, of course it was." Bishop coughed, realizing his error.

Thirty-Six's translator crackled. "There is an Old Earth portal on the far side of the tower. We will use it to gain access to the lower tunnels."

Bishop gazed over at the mountain face. Other than a slope of weed-choked gravel and scree, there was nothing that looked even remotely movable.

"It will require some digging," Thirty-Six said as it noted Bishop's confusion.

Bishop stared back and then frowned, raising his hands and shrugging his shoulders. "Well, you're the tunnel, ah, thing. Don't look at me!"

Thirty-Six nodded. It approached the grassy pile of gravel and, with a flurry of movement that amazed Bishop, proceeded to burrow into the hillside like a machine, sending a cascade of detritus flying into the air. The insect's four chitin-plated forearms acted like small shovels as they bored into the mound.

Bishop stepped out of the way of the cascading dirt and rock. "Black gods, you weren't joking about digging tunnels, were you?"

"Thirty-Six digs tunnels," came the energetic response.

"You dig tunnels." Bishop nodded. "Natural-born mole if I ever saw one." Looking around fearfully, he added, "We are not going to bring any unwanted attention to our excavation, I trust?"

Thirty-Six, still burrowing into the earth, responded, "The main entrances are in the upper valley, located on the eastern face of this mountain range. We would not inhabit this side because it still contains some of the poisons from the Dreaming time."

"Poisons, are we safe?" Bishop's skin prickled at the revelation.

Thirty-Six stopped digging. "We will not long reside within these ruins. We will be safe as long as we do not dally."

Bishop's eyes widened in horror, and he began gesturing wildly with his hands. "Well, get on with your digging, man! What are you waiting for?"

Thirty-Six stared at Bishop with an expression bordering on confused frustration, then sighed and began digging again.

Soon an Old Earth portal began to emerge, exactly where Thirty-Six had said it would be. Bishop found himself awed at the abilities of these insects to retain information and pass it down through the ages. Certainly, this door had remained hidden under the earth for millennia, until today.

The door was like the one that Bishop had found himself facing on the eighth hell, although it was slightly pitted and stained, and had a peculiar greenish patina. Using a handful of moss, Bishop wiped the dirt away from the portal, revealing a now familiar circle of obsidian-like glass—a genetic keypad, proof that his distant ancestors had been here countless ages ago, long before the current inhabitants took up residence.

Bishop took a deep breath and then hesitantly placed his hand against the glassy black surface. As before, there was a flash of recognizing light. The Old Earth science had not failed even after the passage of fathomless ages.

There was a shudder and the door slid aside. From its depths, the musty, unpleasant stench of things long dead and long unburied welled out. Bishop involuntarily retreated several steps.

"After you, Thirty-Six," Bishop muttered, motioning the insect toward the black hole that gaped before them.

Thirty-Six, without hesitation, proceeded into the musty gloom. "You will follow Thirty-Six."

Bishop, heartily nodded, looked around himself one last time and then fell in behind Thirty-Six, rubbing at his arms as if they were coated with an unseen filth. "I am only too happy to get out of that poisoned ghost city of yours."

Thirty-Six stopped and turned. "It was your city, a human city. It is not ours. Those of the colony live within the—"

"Go, *go, GO!*" Bishop barked in fearful frustration, pushing Thirty-Six into the tunnel.

As they ghosted along, moving ever deeper into the tunnel, Bishop noted other signs of ancient technology besides the door. Small light panels set into the walls at equal intervals lighted the place. His earlier unschooled fascination with the light panels had long vanished, yet the thought of such workmanship surviving through the eons and into the present era still filled him with a sense of awe.

They came to a caved-in section and stopped. Even the Others had not been able to overcome the passing of the ages without an occasional bit of misfortune. Thirty-Six broke off into a more primitive tunnel that glowed eerily from patches of phosphorescing fungus that rippled and flickered with fox fire as they passed.

Bishop, noting the change in the tunnel, questioned Thirty-Six. "This tunnel, it seems different."

"It was built by those who came after the Dreamers, the descendants of the Dreamers who stayed to loot the city above us; they became impervious to the poisons that lurk there."

"Scavengers!" Bishop spit out the word. "Probably nothing worth scavenging in the city, so they left."

"No. They were persuaded to leave by those of the First Colony."

"Well, I'm sure there wasn't any reason for them to stay anyway. I mean, that city was nothing but a rock pile. Scavengers wouldn't have left unless—"

His words were interrupted when Thirty-Six broke into a vaulted chamber that radiated with a new light. Bishop followed, gaping.

The room was filled with riches heaped up in staggering profusion—piles of diamonds, sapphires, rubies, turquoise, opals, and emeralds; ziggurats of jade, jet, and lapis lazuli; pyramids of gold wedges; and teocallis of silver ingots. The floor was strewn with gold nuggets that sparkled and shimmered under the crimson glow of a cold light given off by monstrous phosphorescent toadstools growing about the treasure. Bishop stood in a wonderland of splendor and riches that were quite beyond his ability to fathom. He hurried to catch up with Thirty-Six, who had kept a steady pace, seemingly oblivious to the riches strewn around it.

"So, Thirty-Six, is this the treasure hoard of the Ikonians?"

The insect scanned the vault as if seeing it for the first time, but continued walking. "In the time of the Dreaming, this material served the Dreamers as currency, though of different form and function in those days. After the Dreamers left, it was gathered and hoarded by those humans who came after the cataclysm."

"Scavengers. The foragers left this?"

"Those that came after—foragers, if that is how you wish to refer to them," Thirty-Six stated again.

"But scavengers—they would not have left such a treasure."

"They were not given the option to dispute it. The First Colony grew and enveloped the lands of those that came after." Thirty-Six continued walking. "The foragers were displaced."

Bishop, knowing something of scavenger greed, was shocked at the thought of the force it must have taken to dislodge them from their treasure. Not for the first time he wondered at the wisdom of invading the First Colony.

Bishop's eyes reflected the sparkling hoard. "So, since the scavengers are gone, who owns all this stuff?"

"No one owns this stuff now."

Bishop slowed. "Surely the Ikonians, the First Colony, have laid claim to it?"

"Those of the colony have not."

Bishop stopped. "Why?"

"It is of no use."

"No use? You don't want it?" Bishop turned.

"Why would we want something that is of no use?" Thirty-Six called after him. "It was deposited in the lower tunnels as refuse. It is of no use. Do you understand? It is not food; it does not serve the queen; and it does not tunnel. It is of no use."

"Just like me, right?" A slow, dreamy smile grew on Bishop's face as he quickly retraced his steps. "I think I'm beginning to understand, all right," he purred. "So, Thirty-Six, what—what if I were to just help myself, just a little bit, after I … Ah, what was I saying?" The golden hoard had stripped his mind of reason.

"You have use for such rubbish?"

"Use? What, are you joking? We use this stuff all the time. It's very useful in our culture. Very, ah, useful."

"Then you may take what you require after concluding your task. It is refuse. It is not of the colony. It should not be brought into the colony."

Bishop smiled with a shuddering sigh. "Not of the colony, eh? All right, Thirty-Six, after we, ah, do whatever we, ah, have to do … Just wait here. I really should grab a bit for the road now." Bishop began moving toward the treasure.

"We must hurry. You may retrieve the waste after concluding your task. It will only hinder us now."

"You just said it's useless. I don't see the problem here." Bishop bent to scoop up a pile of gems; they glowed lustrously in the dim light.

"We must hurry!" Thirty-Six insisted.

"What!" Bishop barked, letting the cache run through his fingers in a glorious tinkling waterfall of untold wealth.

"I sense a guardian. Why do you question?"

"A guardian?" The jewels scattered as Bishop jerked around at the mention of his old nemesis.

Thirty-Six picked at Bishop's clothing. "Time is short. You must follow."

Bishop could now hear the distant susurration of a guardian coming from one of the side tunnels, the sound shattering his focus on his otherwise mesmeric avarice. He recalled the feel of the bloodsucking appendages. Suddenly diamonds and gold seemed less important. But still …

"I can handle a guardian," Bishop said finally, raising his Riika.

"No, it is not permitted to kill a guardian. They are of the colony. When you complete your task, Thirty-Six will block off the tunnels that harbor the danger and allow you free access."

"Well, ah, dammit to the eight hells! You and your dratted colony rules! Just don't forget how to get back here, all right?" Bishop grumbled. Thirty-Six continued to drag him away.

"This tunneler will not forget," Thirty-Six said in a somewhat exasperated way, conveyed by the monotone translator.

Bishop's eyes became distant in thought while a thin smile crept across his face. "I can have a barn and horses, and Frayja can have her earrings, a whole drawer full of them."

"We must continue, human," Thirty-Six repeated, all but dragging Bishop from the cave.

The hours passed as the two descended deeper into the mountain, eventually breaking back into the main tunnel. Bishop gave up trying to determine how far under the mountain they were. The tunnel divided, switched back, and continued to slope downward, but Thirty-Six never deviated or hesitated. The floor, walls, and ceiling were now giant blocks of quarried black stone, perhaps a ton apiece. The floor and most of the walls were damp, with the smell of mold accentuating the overall sense of extreme age. Bishop's thoughts began shifting back to the task at hand.

"It might not be the best time to ask this question, but what are we looking for?"

Thirty-Six's translator hummed to life. "We are close. At the bottom of this tunnel is a passage that will lead us to the throne room. It is very likely that the Thunderbolt will be taken there before being dismantled."

"Dismantled? The Thunderbolt won't like that when he wakes up."

Thirty-Six stopped and inspected the blocks with its antennae, probing several of the joints and seams. "This is unusual."

Bishop became alert, raising his Riika. "What? What's unusual?"

Thirty-Six continued the probing. "These seams show an irregularity." The insect examined the floor. "The tiles show a corresponding irregularity."

"An irregularity? In an Ikonian tunnel? Wonder of wonders. Who was asleep that day?"

"We do not sleep. This has been mentioned before. Eight times. Please. Step softly." Thirty-Six tapped the floor with its strange three-toed foot.

"What do you mean?"

"We should walk, not on the circular tiles." The insect moved forward, its tripod-like feet delicately avoiding a complex patchwork of small floor tiles.

"Which ones, Thirty-Six? Bloody Others, your feet are smaller than mine! Which circular tiles?" Bishop studied the mosaic of octagonal, rectangular, and oval-shaped paving stones. "Which ones count as circular? And why does it matter?"

"Circular. Round—circular—tiles must not be stepped on. This was designed by scavengers." Thirty-Six explained this while carefully walking forward.

"Scavengers built this?" Bishop frowned. "But why?"

Suddenly there was a tremor and a groaning sound. "Caution, human! Caution!"

The ground lurched and the ceiling gave. Titanic slabs of rock roared down around them like the waves of the ocean crashing against a sandcastle. Bishop lunged forward, barely avoiding being smashed like a bug. Before the rumbling slowed and stopped, Bishop found he was on the ground, half covered in debris. He choked on the thick swirling dust, disoriented, and quickly looked about him for Thirty-Six.

"Thirty-Six!" he called. Bishop quickly pushed the rocks and dirt from his torso and struggled toward the cave-in, which was now an impenetrable wall of rubble. "Thirty-Six! Where are you! Thirty-Six!" Nothing, not a sound, only an occasional rock settling and the fading rumble of the collapse echoing in the distance.

"What a terrible end, if indeed Thirty-Six has met its end. And my doing, too," he said with a certain sadness. He had come to like Thirty-Six and wished it no harm. He shook his head in despair. "Why didn't you just say there was a booby trap, Thirty-Six?" He slumped, staring morosely at the wall of detritus. "Probably no Ikonian word for booby trap, I would guess."

Bishop spent the better part of an hour trying to dig through the rocks by the light of a patch of luminescent cup-shaped lichen, but the sheer volume of tightly packed tunnel wreckage hampered his efforts. He rejected the idea of using his Riika on the mass, not knowing how precarious the remaining ceiling was. Finally, he was forced to give up. He could only hope that the insect had scrambled to safety on the other side of this cave-in and was not buried beneath it. *An unusual but not wholly unexpected end for a tunneler,* he sadly mused.

Brushing the dust from his clothing, Bishop stood for a long moment before reluctantly turning to continue. He gave into a feeling of angry frustration. "First it was Kiel and Storm Singer, then the Thunderbolt, now Thirty-Six. I have lost all my companions one by one." Then he stopped, not believing his eyes. "Gods of the Others, no."

There before him was a second cave-in, effectively sealing him on both fronts. Bishop leaned against the wall to ponder his fate. "It would appear that I am destined to follow you to the grave, Thirty-Six."

Suddenly a rat scurried under his feet, causing him to stumble backward in alarm. "Blast you to the eighth hell!" he barked in sudden anger.

The rat scampered to the far wall, where it stopped and stared back at him. It seemed to Bishop that the rat, watching just beyond his reach, was eyeing him in sardonic amusement. Bishop took a few steps toward it, frowning, and the rat scampered away to a corner and turned again to eye him. It watched him keenly. He could not help feeling like a fool. Here he was, trapped, alone, and without hope, chasing a stupid rat. Bishop growled as he eyed the beast, which stared back with unwinking shoe-button eyes. The rat squeaked in a parody of laughter as it sat up on its haunches and grinned, its yellow teeth glinting in the deep gloom. That evil grin was just about as much as Bishop could stomach.

"I've got too many worries to put up with your mockery, you little pest. Get back into your rathole." Bishop picked up a rock and held it threateningly. The rat, sensing Bishop's intent, suddenly scuttled aside and disappeared into a little hole in the wall. Its disheveled whiskers protruded cautiously, its nose sniffing once or twice, and then with a final squeak of glee, it was gone.

"Enough of that," Bishop muttered as he bent over to block the hole. *But wait!* Looking closer at the hole, he detected something strange. *What is this?* It was the stone slab just above the rat burrow. A quick glance around its edge confirmed his suspicion. Yes, the slab was apparently movable.

Bishop examined it closely, noticing a depression at its edge, which afforded a handhold. His fingers fit easily into the groove, and he pulled tentatively. The stone moved a trifle and stopped. He pulled harder, and with a sprinkling of dry earth, the slab swung away from the wall as though on hinges.

A black rectangle, shoulder high, gaped in the wall. Phosphorescent fungus grew within the hole just as it had around the treasure.

"The treasure! Lost like everything else!" Bishop groaned. "Well, there's no help for it now. And I can't think of treasure with so many of my friends gone."

Bishop entered the new tunnel, more depressed than ever. He found himself in a narrow tunnel scarcely higher than his head, carved directly through the native rock of the mountain. Thirty-Six had said they were very close to the main throne room. Just possibly this tunnel would take him there.

"Well, thank you, Sir Rat," he said sheepishly, "wherever you are. Next time we meet, I will be more gracious. I most certainly owe you a bit of cheese, and I would be only too happy to share a rock-hard bit of Eligor oat bread, though that would be cruel."

Bishop followed the meandering path of the tunnel as it began to rise steeply away from the lower galleries. The walls of the cave he walked through were various, sometimes black, sometimes veined with pale blue turquoise. Once, they flashed and glittered as though he had come into a sapphire mine. At one dark point in the cave that was heavy with dripping stalactites, Bishop was forced to skirt a still, inky pool of water in which ghostly phosphorescent fish flashed and vanished from sight at his approach.

After several dead ends and endless backtracking, Bishop was finally rewarded for his efforts. At a tunnel junction cut thinly into the wall was a narrow slit that allowed light to stream from the other side. Cautiously, Bishop peered through. The scene below him was fantastic. Despite every danger and obstacle thrown at him, somehow, beyond all hope, he had found what had to be the throne room of the First Colony.

TWENTY

SIEGE OF OPAL

> And that inverted bowl they call the sky, is where,
> beneath it, crawling, cooped, we live and die.
> —Vena Korela,
> Second Ilmarinen Cycle, Runa 28

It had not been a happy homecoming for Kiel. All night the soldiers on the ramparts of Opal had been able to hear the sounds of the enemy as they worked below the city's walls, cutting trees and clearing land. The numbers that had arrived since the initial entrenchment could not be guessed at, but when dawn's dim light crept over the land, it was seen that they had been scarcely overcounted in the inhabitants' fear-spawned speculation. The freshly cleared areas of the outer districts were dark with a vast and busy Ikonian horde, and as far as the eye could see, camps of the invading insects had filled to bursting. And still they came.

As if driven on by some unseen force, the Ikonian soldiers, after settling into siege, had begun feverishly building staging platforms with fresh lumber. Now they poured into the open spaces prepared for them. For days the labor went forward while the Eligor looked on, unable to interfere. As each platform was completed, the insect workers began the construction on tremendous catapults far larger than the ones set upon the ramparts of the city by the Eligor.

At first the Eligor felt secure behind their city walls, which had been designed in ages past to withstand the test of time.

"Impossible!" they muttered. But what of the food supply, which was already far depleted from the human–Eligor conflict a short time previous?

But the Ikonians did not waste their catapult projectiles on the hardened walls of Opal; a mind much more cunning controlled the legions of the insects. As soon as the catapults were loaded, the Ikonians began throwing them in an extreme arc over the black basalt walls and into the city itself. Upon impact, the massive spheres exploded into fire and shrapnel, spreading flame and rending flesh. Soon Eligor were running hither and thither, screaming in madness, as the city seemed poised to erupt in immolating fire.

"Rally to me, good Eligor!" called a booming voice among the tumult. And then Kiel was there, directing fire crews and restoring order.

Upon the walls, Eligor soldiers shook their scaled fists and screamed threats at the pitiless enemy that swarmed before the walls of Opal, but the insects seemed not to take notice, just going about their deadly work as if it were the most mundane of tasks, merely a programmed response to a nameless instinct: *Crush Opal; kill its inhabitants; move on.*

No hours so dark had Kiel known before, not even the days after the Eligor defeat before their attack on the human city of Koth, where it was thought the end had come. But since duty called, he controlled his fear as best he could, as it seemed now that all of Opal was looking to him as their only hope. And so it was that Kiel took command of the last defense of the imperial city of Opal. Wherever he went, Eligor spirits would lift and the shadow of annihilation would pass. Tirelessly he walked from rampart to rampart, from east to west above the walls in his leaf mail, calling to his people.

"Have faith! Be strong! The insects have yet to defeat us! Resist them!" he called, conveying a reassurance that he did not himself feel.

But in his heart, the weight of all the Eligor Empire was upon him, and his thoughts continually drifted to Bishop. What had become of the human? Was it too much to ask now for a miracle, no matter how remote the chance? Always, he thought, *More time. Bishop needs a little more time. We must hold out!* It was the only thing Kiel had left to hold despair at bay.

A young soldier, barely out of the egg, spoke in a defiant tone. "We will resist, Kiel! We will resist! We will drive back the invaders from our beloved city or die in its defense!"

"Of what avail is resistance when the gods themselves have declared themselves against us! Yet I mourn most for the old and infirm, the injured and the very young, those too feeble to fight or fly. But you are right, for me and the brave Eligor around me, we must bare our breasts to the storm and meet it as we may."

On the third night after Kiel's return to Opal, the Ikonian assault was loosed. The vanguard attacked, reckless about any losses as they approached, coming within range of the bows and catapults of Opal. But indeed, there were too few Eligor in relation to their numbers to do them much harm. Slowly, great siege towers rolled closer to the black walls of the city. At other points around the city, the insects closed in on the walls, but it seemed that this was merely a tactic to pull the remaining strength of the Eligor away from the main gate.

Strong though the gate was, being wrought in iron and guarded by two towers of stone, it now became clear that this was to be the main target, as it was against this gate that the Ikonians now threw their heaviest weight. A great engine rolled toward the gate whose carriage held a tremendous ram that must have been hewn from a single tree well over ten meters long and a meter thick. Upon its forward-facing end was an iron cap forged in the likeness of a slumbering human head with a seven-sided glyph etched upon its forehead. Spaced evenly along the entire length of the ram were four great rings of steel attached to the chains that supported its weight.

But the gate still held strong. A hail of arrows rained down upon the insects as they approached, taking a heavy toll. At other points around the city, the siege engines suddenly flamed and broke, lighting the night sky with writhing blazes and ginger-tinged smoke. All around the gate, the area was choked with dead bodies, but then more replaced the fallen, stepping over them as if it were the most natural of things. Then the ram came, ponderously inching forward. It soon became clear that no fire would catch upon its surface, for it was sheathed all about its surface with iron and steel. Before long, it had reached the gate and began to swing. A deep boom sounded as the ram finally struck the great northern gate of Opal, a sound like thunder rolling through the mountains. But the gate, though badly splintered, withstood the first attack. And as the last bit of the luck of Opal would have it, two of the forward chains holding the ram were severed by a chance projectile thrown down by the ramparts of the wall, and its iron-shod head plowed into the ground below. Now it sat still.

A roar of victory went up from the battlements of Opal as all breathed a momentary sigh of relief. The immediate danger had passed, but the Ikonian soldiers swarmed to repair the ram. Kiel wondered again if this short interim would be enough to give Bishop the chance he might need to act—if in fact he was still alive to act at all.

TWENTY-ONE

THE AWAKENING

> The seas burn. The skies descend.
> —Vena Korela,
> Second Ilmarinen Cycle, Runa 45

The great throne room of the First Colony was filled with ranks of Ikonian soldiers that lined the walls in double columns. Other, lesser insects came and went in an endless stream of activity. Bishop's gaze, from where he was hidden, was irresistibly drawn to a jade throne set in the middle of the hall. There, dwarfed by the ponderous splendor around her, a woman reclined. Not Reaver One as he had expected, but a human female! Even at this distance, Bishop could make out that her features were imperious and cold, with a touch of ruthless cruelty about the curve of her mouth—like Reaver. Yes, Bishop thought, there was a similarity to Reaver One. Then it struck him: this could—had to—be one of the Reavers as told in the histories at Opal. Bishop stared, mesmerized. She seemed human enough, yet the knowledge of her suspected identity lent her a supernatural aspect. Sitting on that throne, she seemed a spoiled child engaged in a game of make-believe. Yet, as Bishop soon observed, this woman could become deadly in her game.

Two Ikonian soldiers dragged an Eligor captive toward the throne. The woman leaned forward. In a voice as hard and cold as gray ice, she commanded, "Tell me now, and tell me accurately, what is the remaining troop strength of Opal? What of the alliance with Merja Soria? How is it that—"

"I have no knowledge. I am merely a scout," the Eligor cut in, speaking hysterically.

The sentence was never completed. As the Eligor sputtered, the woman on the throne made a casual gesture with her hand. The soldier's scythe-like forearms flashed out and cut the Eligor nearly in half. A gurgling scream burst from the soldier, red blood spurted into the air, and the corpse fell flatly at the foot of the throne, its scaly heels pattering softly on the polished marble floor.

The Ikonian ranks never wavered. The woman made an indifferent wave of her hand, and the corpse was dragged away by the feet, the dead arms trailing crazily amid the wide smear of blood left by the passage of the body, adding its red streaks to several others, some faint and dark, some not so faint.

"Perhaps the next in line will be more forthcoming," she said indifferently.

Bishop turned from the slit he was watching through and slid to the floor in horror. If this woman did not share Reaver One's genetic make-up, then she surely shared his cruelty. Bishop, recovering, put his eye to the slit once again. As three Ikonians moved to retrieve the next captive, Bishop, following their movements, noticed something else of interest in the great hall: on a slab of raised unadorned granite, bound by steel straps, lay an inert form of ponderous immensity, an Old Earth technological terror.

The Thunderbolt. Bishop had found him.

"Shades of the Others!" he hissed to himself.

The metal monster was close, yet surrounded by so many of the Ikonians that the beast might as well have been on the moon. Did Bishop possess the courage to enter the throne room and attempt to resurrect the monster? He struggled with the question. It seemed desperate, hopeless, suicidal. But perhaps, just perhaps, if he waited, despite all odds, a chance would present itself. Bishop rose and began to case the darkened chamber, looking for a place of entry. He would do what he could in the interim. Securing access to the throne room seemed a good use of his idle time.

Bishop felt along the darkened wall with his fingers. Yes, here at the end of the tunnel was a crack that seemed like a door. There were scrape marks on the floor that suggested the door had been moved in the recent past. *Moved?* Bishop's hackles rose.

Moved by whom?

Suddenly, Bishop heard a slight sound from behind him. A black shadow detached itself from the lesser shadows of the passageway. Bishop swiveled, bringing up his Riika, but it was too late. A crashing blow to his head dropped him, and the arms of oblivion rushed up to take him into a void of unconsciousness.

When Bishop awoke, he dazedly looked around, trying to focus his blurry vision on the brightening scene. Yes, he was now in the throne room, his pack and sword having been removed and now lying in a scattered pile some distance from him.

"Well, that was easier than I thought," he muttered groggily to himself.

Bishop's eyesight sharpened further. Directly across from him, flanked by four Ikonians, lay the Thunderbolt, bound, lifeless, and unmoving. It was closer now, but on the face of it was still well beyond Bishop's reach. And even if he were able to gain unrestricted access, he would never be allowed the time it would take to free the monster from its steel shackles—a tall order in and of itself. Bishop slowly turned his head in the other direction, and as he did so, he was grabbed by chitinous hands and forced to stand in front of the woman he had seen from the hidden portal above him.

The woman gazed down at Bishop from her jade throne, her eyes gray as death. She was as perfect as an alabaster statue, ageless as the oceans, imperious as the sun.

"Who are you?" Bishop groaned, still recovering from the blow to his head.

"The insects know me as a Dreamer, the Eligor called me Madim," she answered haughtily. "Reaver Three to you, Merja Sorian, as if it is of any of your concern, spying dog of this future earth."

"Another Reaver. By the gods of the Others," Bishop swore as he was forced to kneel before the haughty woman.

"Who are you to swear by the Others?" she mocked. "What would you know of the great ones who came before you? You are no more than a degenerate ape by comparison! An evolutionary throwback from a forgotten age of technological enlightenment."

"Remnant from a forgotten age? It appears to me that it is you who are a remnant from a forgotten age, not I!" Bishop growled, becoming angry. "This is my world, not yours!"

The woman's eyes flashed with venom, but her retort was interrupted.

"How charming, a visit from an old friend," came a new but familiar voice from behind the woman who was seated at the throne. "I think you will find escape much more difficult this time."

Bishop looked beyond Reaver Three. With a chill, he saw Reaver One indifferently approaching the throne, followed by yet another human female who looked like the one who was now glaring at him in rage. *Black gods, now there are three of them!*

Bishop remained silent.

Reaver One stood next to the two females and smiled coldly down at Bishop. "Certainly, it is a credit to your cunning that you have found your way unmolested into the First Colony. I believe that will be the first of many questions you will answer."

At a glance from Reaver One, two soldiers advanced ominously and flanked Bishop.

"I won't answer any of your questions," Bishop spat.

Reaver One darkened. "Then I trust pain is something that you enjoy. You will answer my questions."

Something snapped in Bishop, and without thinking, he knocked the two soldiers away from him and sprinted toward the Thunderbolt, the insect horrors at his heels. There was one chance and one alone; if he failed, it would be over for him, for the protectorate, and for the planet. His fumbling hands raced over the dull metal surface as insect hands ripped and tore at him. Bishop was fighting like a wild beast, but as he struggled, he was slowly pulled away from the inert metallic monster. Yes, there was a switch! He groped, attempting to depress the stud, but was dragged inexorably away before his fingers met with success, his blood streaming from a score of wounds. His last reserves gone, he sank back, limp. With much force, the Ikonians once again dragged him and shoved him into a kneeling position before the gloating Reavers. One of the soldiers cuffed him hard on the back of his head. Bishop involuntarily yelped in pain and staggered dizzily, shaking the sweat and blood out of his eyes. Groaning, he strained to look at the Thunderbolt.

Nothing. He had failed.

"There will be no more outbursts and no more escapes," Reaver One said coldly. "Guards, tie this slippery human at once."

Reaver Three raised her hand toward the soldier just as she had done with the Eligor captive. Instead of the blade weapon, the soldier brought forth several thin slivery hooks—their use all too clear. Bishop turned his head, readying himself for the coming torture. He would not answer their questions. He would not be the betrayer of his world.

"I believe I will start the interrogation by asking what you know of the machine yonder." Reaver One stabbed a finger at the Thunderbolt. The two females hungrily licked their lips in anticipation of the coming torment.

Reaver's finger dropped, and a startled expression replaced the arrogant leer that moments ago had painted his ageless face. Bishop strained to follow Reaver's shocked gaze toward the metal monster that lay bound and motionless. Was he hallucinating from the pain and hopelessness of his plight, or had he just seen a movement?

The Reaver females backed away from the throne, their faces now quite intent on the machine that had captivated Reaver One.

It was no hallucination. Bishop perceived the Thunderbolt's massive right hand, showing not even a tremor, moving with deliberate sureness, pulling itself free of its restraint. Had those straps ever been steel that now lay twisted like torn cloth? The Old Earth creation was moving to take hold of the thicker steel band across its chest. The hand found its grip and quivered once. With a ringing snap, the chest band burst, sending a fragment of metal singing like a missile past Bishop's head, ricocheting off a column in a shower of rock, dust, and sparks. Twin embers of emerald fire fixed on Reaver One as the Old Earth creation stood and took in the scene.

Reaver confidently motioned toward the Thunderbolt, and the massed Ikonian soldiers suddenly went wild with rage, attacking their new antagonist in answer to the unspoken command from their master, who held them in thrall.

The Thunderbolt casually tore the great metal bindings that had moments ago restrained him away from the altar and bent them about his fists, forming crude gauntlets. As the Ikonian soldiers rushed at him, he wielded these with terrible effect. For a moment he held them at bay, and then they broke over him in a hellish wave of entomological fury. The Thunderbolt took on an aura of exaltation as Ikonian arm blades stung and smashed against him; he merely laughed and drove his iron fists in straight, with great sledgehammer blows that shattered carapace, muscle, and organ into a hideous greenish pulp.

Bishop, still weak from his own ordeal, watched through bleary eyes as those monstrous iron hands rose and fell. Each time an Ikonian went down, the head shattered and virescent gore splashed as a dark fury swept over the Thunderbolt.

Nightmarish faces swirled about Bishop, their attendant bodies crumpling before the irresistible onslaught as the work of death progressed. Bishop's vision reeled as if the gates of hell had been flung wide open. The Thunderbolt roared in a dark challenge of eager fury. Through the far mists of Bishop's weakened brain, he heard a familiar voice as it rose in imperious command.

"Stay!"

The insects ceased their onslaught almost immediately as if the invisible leash that had held them had gone taut. They stood staring at Reaver One and then back toward the Thunderbolt in confused silence.

The throne room became momentarily hushed yet seemed charged with an electric tension that was almost palpable.

"So, my brother," the Thunderbolt rumbled, breaking the silence, "it has been an age."

Reaver's eyes, meeting that gaze, stood frozen for a long moment. "I wish that I could say that the time has been good to you, traitor," he answered evenly. "But judging by appearances ..." He let his words trail off.

Reaver's arms suddenly shot forward, his fists clenched with forefingers pointing, aimed like some boy's hands holding an imaginary weapon. His waist device glowed white hot as if it were a piece of iron pulled from a blast furnace. Toward the Thunderbolt's looming figure, a soundless scimitar curve of energy flashed as it leaped out of Reaver's arm weapon from across the room, followed by a V-shaped shock wave. The Thunderbolt effortlessly deflected the weapon's discharge, which hit against the far wall, carving out huge scallops of rock and debris. The room heaved and shook with a sound like a thunderclap as raining dust and broken fragments of masonry cascaded down around the macabre scene.

Reaver's face flattened in stupefied astonishment.

The Thunderbolt, unaffected by the attack, casually raised his massive arm and pointed a finger at Reaver. "Did you think I wasted those years in exile foolishly? The circle closes, brother."

Reaver began to turn to flee, horror replacing shock in light of this sudden realization. But it was too late.

The counterblow could not be seen directly, only its effect. To Bishop, watching in a timeless moment of awe, it seemed that Reaver's face stayed where it was, a malignant frozen mask of horror, while behind it, his head and body were sent flying in clods of blood, bone, and gore. Then the face disintegrated into a red mist that hung for a moment, suspended in the air like a cloud dissipating rapidly after a rainstorm, then was gone in a soundless shock wave through the air and earth. Simultaneously, Reaver's two counterparts were flung aside like rags. They smashed against the rock walls and dissolved, leaving a red smudge as testament to their ever having existed. Bishop fell to his knees as a rumbling aftershock ripped through the earth. At that very moment, the once immobile ranks of Ikonians scattered in all directions as if they had been suddenly released from an evil spell.

The Thunderbolt stood silently amid the turmoil, seemingly unscathed from the recent attack except for a reddish glow that remained for a while where Reaver's lightning had been deflected. After a time, even this slight blemish faded and was gone. The Thunderbolt turned its armored head, taking in a scene of pandemonium. Bishop saw too that the chamber was in chaos: broken objects, shattered rock, and frantic Ikonians tearing hither and thither looking for escape. Soldiers came running nearer, then turned and fled, or stood and trembled helplessly as the Thunderbolt's terrible gaze caught and held them. Soon, Bishop was the only living creature within twenty meters of the Thunderbolt's terrible emerald eyes, and now they turned on him.

Bishop felt a chill sweep through him much as had occurred when he was first faced with this technological demon. The burning green coals held his eyes only a moment longer, then moved back to scan the turmoil of the chamber. Suddenly, a terrible voice boomed through the air. "Hear me! I, Levanah, have returned to claim vengeance and put the entire world beneath my armored feet!"

Bishop's skin prickled and his hair stood on end as he rushed to gather his belongings. "Black shades of the Others," he hissed, shakily buckling his sword in haste. Where had he heard that name before?

A noise caught the Thunderbolt's attention, and his armored head swiveled toward it. A massive gate at the far end of the chamber trundled ponderously closed, sealing off the throne room from the outer halls. Apparently the Ikonians were attempting to confine this new threat. The Thunderbolt turned to face the obstacle and leisurely raised his gauntleted hand, palm extended toward this new obstacle.

The deep thrumming sound within the monster rose to an earsplitting scream. The iron teeth of the gate bent and curled like heat-frizzed hair. The gate itself sagged as the great timbers cracked and splintered. Even the massive house-sized blocks of stone that held the hinges slid in their sockets from the irresistible unseen force that pushed against them.

The screaming sound within the Thunderbolt heightened as the monster's open palm glowed white hot like a smithy's furnace. The sound of a thunderclap and its resident shock wave threw Bishop to the floor. In the next instant, the gate exploded, sending shattered timbers the size of whole trees, bounding and spinning with seeming slowness, across the deserted room.

Without further hesitation, the Thunderbolt lumbered off in an apparent search for any remaining Reavers. He would have his revenge, it seemed.

Before Bishop could fully recover and absorb what had just transpired, an Ikonian loomed over him, causing him to recoil in alarm. It didn't have an accelerator. Not an Ikonian soldier, then. The insect stared at him with its feelers probing the air, seemingly perfectly content to simply stand there and contemplate this strange human.

Bishop raised himself to a sitting position and readied his Riika. "I'll smash you if you so much as twitch, insect. Understand?"

A translator hummed to life. "If it twitches, jolts, shudders, convulses? Has this tunneler convulsed in an offensive way?"

Bishop lowered the Riika, his eyes widening in dawning recognition. "Thirty-Six? Is that you?"

"This tunneler's number is thirty-six. Have you already forgotten it?"

"No, but well, you all look ... Oh, never mind. Thirty-Six!"

"Yes, this tunneler's number is thirty-six," the insect repeated. "You should have waited for Thirty-Six, human. It would have been easier for you."

"I was inclined to believe you were dead. How did you get out of the cave-in?"

"Thirty-Six is a tunnel worker. It tunnels." The insect seemed vexed even though the translator carried no emotion.

"You tunnel," Bishop repeated.

They both turned at the sound of another explosion, which rumbled through the mountain. Bishop cocked his ear. "The Thunderbolt is getting his revenge against the Reavers, it seems." Several frantic Ikonians darted across the far end of the throne room, disappearing into a hazy side tunnel as more plaster rained down around them.

Bishop turned to Thirty-Six questioningly.

Thirty-Six moved its feelers a bit more rapidly. "The colony is in chaos, human. The Ikonians are free of the chemical shackles of Reaver One. But there remains the slip gate."

Bishop had heard the term before. "The slip gate? What is a slip gate?"

"It is the device in which the Dreamer was enclosed when he was uncovered and brought forth into our world. The other Dreamers have followed—will follow—him from the Dreamtime."

"Follow, from the past? Through this slip gate?"

"Yes, they have—will—come. And they might have the ability to disable the device you call the Thunderbolt and regain control of the nest."

A chill ran down Bishop's spine as the implications of what Thirty-Six imparted seeped into him. Somehow, a portal to the technological hell of precataclysmic earth now lay open. There would be an endless stream of terror from the Old Earth if the device were allowed to remain in operation.

"Where is this slip gate?" Bishop demanded in growing alarm.

"It is housed in the central pyramid, a place that is forbidden to all Ikonians except the elites, and even they will not enter except on specific days in accordance to our tradition. It is very interesting, human. On the third day of each lunar cycle, and only after chanting the sacred verses for three consecutive mornings—"

"Gods of the Others, Thirty-Six," Bishop barked in exasperation, "let's go. You can tell me all about it on the way."

"As you wish," Thirty-Six curtly responded.

TWENTY-TWO

MIRACLE AT OPAL

> Ring O bells a joyous peal;
> Wave freedom's flag o'er land and sea!
> Above the graves of wrongful slain,
> Let living voices shout again
> In honor of our victory!
>
> —Vena Korela,
> Second Ilmarinen Cycle, Runa 43

The great Ikonian ram had been repaired, and Kiel now braced for the end. Again there came a booming sound from the gate as the iron-shod head smashed repeatedly against its massive frame. As if from some technological blasting device, there was a flash of light and its corresponding thunderous din, then the great gateway split apart, its riven fragments tumbling to the ground. Dust and debris spun through the air as if propelled by a great invisible arm, and the battlements of Opal, which had stood for centuries, shook with a death rattle. The countless combined masses of the Ikonian host began moving toward the splintered wall in ordered fashion, preparing to enter and to eviscerate the city, the last city of the Eligor Empire.

Kiel prepared himself for the end. "I now go to feast with the All-father Everlasting." He tightened his grip on the sword as he took in a deep breath of resolve. There would be no quarter given and no draw.

But the expected rush did not materialize. All around them, the Ikonians stopped. The scene was not to be believed at first, the Ikonians forming into blocks of soldiers, their pennants snapping in the wind. They stood at attention as though on some vast parade ground, frozen as if listening to a whispered command. Like one great superorganism, they suddenly sheathed their weapons and began an orderly retreat toward the northern wood. All was hushed, and then a great roar filled the air as all the inhabitants of the city of Opal roared with victory, if one could truly call it such.

Kiel sagged in fatigue. There was only one answer: Bishop had succeeded. His scaled jaw set with resolve. "I will go to Ikonia and find him, he who is my friend, if it means losing my life to do so, because that is what I now owe Bishop, as does every surviving Eligor within the empire."

TWENTY-THREE

ENDGAME

> Did the madness of yesterday prepare for tomorrow's silence, triumph, or despair?
> —Vena Korela,
> Final Ilmarinen, Runa 2

Thirty-Six led Bishop through a veritable honeycomb of upwardly sloping tunnels and galleries, avoiding its frantic, milling colony-mates by way of uncanny instinct, until they reached a closed portal. Standing in front of this portal, Thirty-Six manipulated a control panel set into the side of the wall and a stone slab slid back, revealing a vast craterlike area nestled between the mountains of the Ikonian Massif, which rose frostily into the starlight around them. Bishop's purposeful trek through the tunnels had taken him such a great distance that the brooding snowcapped peak of the First Colony now rested behind him to the south. A thin, cool pine-scented midnight breeze silently wafted into the tunnel entrance, causing Bishop to shiver.

Thirty-Six pointed. "Behold the apex of the First Colony."

The valley was filled with green pyramidal structures that seemed to be from another age, a true Ikonian insect city residing aboveground. Without hesitation, Thirty-Six led Bishop out into the silent ghost city. Bishop had seen thousands—tens of thousands—of Ikonians below, but here above the colony he observed only deserted silence. Apparently, the insects did not often use the structures aboveground, even though they appeared to be well maintained.

Beautifully constructed jade pyramids, plazas, canals, and boulevards met Bishop's wandering eyes, not the broken ruins of a dead city of the Others like those he had encountered at Terus Kor or Ra. Thirty-Six walked unerringly and reverently toward the center of the city, toward a looming structure that towered above the others. Moonlight shone down upon the alien tour de force, surrounding it in an even more bizarre aura.

Thirty-Six pointed. "The central pyramid."

The central pyramid stood in the middle of the First Colony, enclosed by a square wall of green jade, ornamented on the outer sides with carved images of insects of all forms and types. On each side of the wall, massive gates opened onto the four principal streets of the First Colony. Over each of the gates was the now familiar symbol of the Ikonians, the slumbering visage of a human face, the Dreamer, with the seven-sided glyph etched into his forehead.

"The slip gate is there," Thirty-Six said, pointing at the looming structure ahead of them. "I am forbidden to go further."

Bishop was about to protest when four Ikonian soldiers suddenly slipped out from behind the wall. "Thirty-Six, I will need some help here," he stammered, drawing his sword and flinging the scabbard away from him.

"It is forbidden to kill those of the colony—" Thirty-Six began. Yet before Thirty-Six could complete his response, the soldiers assumed an attack posture and advanced on Bishop.

"Thirty-Six!"

"I have told them you are of the colony."

The soldiers raised their arm blades.

"They're not listening, Thirty-Six! Say it again!"

"They are not listening."

"Good observation, Thirty-Six!"

Bishop raised his sword. He would get one of them before he was overwhelmed anyway. He jerked in astonishment as a twinge of pain came from his right arm. The Riika! Bishop had almost forgotten about it.

For an instant, Bishop thought his brain had shattered. The ground seemed to heave, and the color of the starry heavens overhead sharpened to the point of causing pain. He felt he would explode into a million vibrating fragments, like the bursting of a globe of glass. Like hellfire, the elixir from the Riika raced along his veins, and he became like a giant, a monster, a god.

Bishop faced the four Ikonian soldiers, his sword quivering in expectation as the lead insect rushed at him. Although Bishop was not aware of trying to respond, his blade came up, meeting the enemy's arm blade, turning it aside, and sliding past it in a twisting, lightning-fast stroke that thrust the sword's point through the Ikonian's throat. Both insect and human stared in astonishment at the gleaming metal that joined them. The insect's mouth opened, and a croaking sound emerged. There was a hissing from the Ikonian's accelerator, and the wound shimmered. Bishop consciously tried to pull his blade free, but it would not move; it seemed that his mind was now operating on a superconscious, drug-induced level. Instead, the blade twisted in his hand, ripping through the neck of the creature. Its head lolled and the body fell backward into the next onrushing soldier, causing it to topple with its dead companion. Another insect closed with Bishop, slashing with that same wasplike speed, leaping in without waiting for the attack. After a quick feint, a clang of metal on super-hardened chitin, and a lightning slash, within seconds the second insect's head spun from its shoulders with a buzzing sound, followed by a geyser of greenish blood. The third insect, now free of its dead companion, sprinted forward. As Bishop struck, so did the soldier, with a long forehand sweep that should have cut Bishop in two at the waist. But despite his being human, Bishop moved even faster than the arm blade as it hissed through the air. He dropped to the ground in a crouch so that the blade passed over him. As he squatted in front of his antagonist, he struck at the insect's legs. The blade bit into shell and muscle. As the Ikonian reeled on its wounded leg and swung its blade up for another slash, Bishop sprang up and in, under the lifted arm, and drove his blade to the hilt into the insect's chest. Blue green gore spurted along the creature's waist. The arm blade twisted grotesquely, ripping open the insect's abdomen from head to hip. The insect's accelerator hissed in a useless effort to heal the wound, but as before, the wound was mortal and the Ikonian sank down, dying.

Bishop tore out his blade and whirled, meeting the last of the Ikonian soldiers. Now it was the insect that was on the defensive as its dead brethren lay crumpled around it and as Bishop's sword beat on its arm blades like a hammer on an anvil. The sheer strength and fury of Bishop's strike began to make itself apparent to the soldier as its breath came in gasps and it gave ground. Emerald blood streamed from gashes on its arms, thigh, and neck. Bishop bled too, but there was no slackening in the headlong assault of the Riika possessed sword. The insect backed into the wall and then suddenly sprang aside as Bishop lunged. Thrown off-balance by his wasted thrust, Bishop plunged forward, and his sword point clashed against the stone. In the same instant, the insect slashed at its foe's head with all its waning power.

Bishop raised his sword in defense, meeting the weapon that was now threatening him from above, and instead of snapping, his sword bent and then sprang straight again. The falling arm blade missed Bishop's head by a hair's breadth, scraping along the rock wall in a shower of sparks. Before the insect could recover its balance, Bishop's blade sheared upward through its hip to grate into its back with a sickening clattering sound.

The soldier stiffened, reeled, and fell silently, its entrails spilling out on the floor. Its fingers clawed briefly at the wound, trying to gather its organs, then the body went limp.

Bishop, half blind with blood and sweat, slumped in fatigue as the hellfire of the Riika dissipated. He turned to take in Thirty-Six, who stood silently watching from behind him. "Next time remind me of your aversion to assisting me in fighting those of the colony before I almost get myself killed. Now, come on, let's get on with it."

"This is as far as this tunneler is allowed to go. The inner courtyard and the pyramid are forbidden to all but the elite caste."

Bishop looked back at Thirty-Six in exasperation; the insect would not go any farther. Bishop reluctantly turned and proceeded toward the great pyramid, alone now but for the silent structures that loomed around him.

The mammoth structure at the center of the inner area was a solid square pyramid, constructed like the perimeter wall, out of slabs of finely dressed greenish jade-like rock. Its four sides faced the four cardinal points of the city around it. The central pyramid was again divided into three bodies, or stories, each one receding so as to be of a smaller dimension than the one immediately below it. Bishop crept across the deserted inner field.

The predawn early winter air stood hushed as Bishop looked around him. All the Ikonian soldiers had been dispatched. He had won a free and open route to the great pyramid, which loomed over him in the twilight mist. He moved silently forward and halted again. A darker shadow had detached itself from the inner courtyard and was now moving deliberately toward him. As the darker shadow moved into the moonlight, Bishop took a step back. Here was a type of insect he had never seen before; considerably larger and heavier than the soldiers he had faced.

"Human, you will not pass One," came a crackling voice from its translator.

One? The first Ikonian of the First Colony? "Thirty-Six," Bishop called. But Thirty-Six was now far behind him and out of sight.

Without hesitation, the creature approached. Bishop again felt the sting of the Riika, but this time it was longer and considerably more painful—no, agonizing. He screamed as his mind exploded.

Of that hideous battle, fought in the silence above the First Colony with only the stars to pay witness, Bishop later would recall very little. He remembered tumbling back and forth, locked in a death embrace, the insect's body rasping his flesh as its accelerator-fired eyes shimmered wildly into his. He remembered the taste of hot blood in his mouth, remembered the tang of exaltation in his soul, and recalled the onrushing and upsurging of inhuman strength and fury. Bishop was only half aware that he had cast his sword aside as he now grappled with One in unarmed combat.

What a sight it would have been to the human eye had anyone looked upon that grim field of battle, fought above that alien city, and seen these two wild animals seeking to tear each other to pieces. Bishop remembered the Ikonian's arm breaking like rotten wood in his grip, and then his hand had shot out, faster than sight could follow. Before the insect knew it, it had been grabbed; its neck was crushed like an eggshell between Bishop's steel fingers.

Bishop stood upright, hurling his arms toward the silent stars, a terrible statue of primordial triumph. Down his breast streamed blood from the long lesions left by the Ikonians' frantic talons, shimmering as an eerie phosphorescence flickered across the torn flesh, instantly healing the wounds in a display of curative sorcery, the Riika working its frightful magic.

It could have been centuries that passed as Bishop stood, but he knew it had been mere seconds, before he returned to a semiconscious state and again perceived reality. Ahead of him, unbarred at last, loomed the brooding ziggurat of the central pyramid.

TWENTY-FOUR

THE DUEL

> When the dead of winter comes, iron clouds will pile and stay. In the veiling of the suns, the world will walk in bitter gray.
>
> —Vena Korela,
> Final Ilmarinen, Runa 14

In a few more moments, reality completely returned to Bishop. Looking back once at the diminutive form of Thirty-Six, he passed through the gated inner wall, then approached the central pyramid and began climbing, ascending via a flight of steps built into the outer surface. No more did Ikonian insects spring from shadows and attack. The way was truly clear.

The steps reached to the narrow terrace or platform at the base of the second story and passed around the building. A second stairway brought Bishop to a similar landing at the base of the third.

On reaching the summit, Bishop found an area paved with broad, flat stones. At the far end of this great platform were two elaborately carved stone towers, each of which consisted of three correspondingly smaller levels.

The dais, on which Bishop stood, towered high above all other edifices in the capital, affording one an elevated central view of the fantastic city.

Below Bishop, the metropolis spread out like a map, with its streets and canals intersecting each other at right angles. He could easily trace the symmetrical plan of the city with its principal avenues issuing from the four gates and connecting to the causeways, which formed the grand entrances to the capital. He saw the narrow position of the conurbation, bathed on all sides by the inland lake. Far beyond it stretched a wide expanse of waving fields and dense wood with the burnished walls of other, lesser temples rising high above the trees and crowning the distant hilltops. The view reached in an unbroken line to the very base of a range of jagged mountains farther to the north, whose frosty peaks glittered like fire in the morning sun.

Bishop turned and noted a massive closed door with a now familiar circle of polished black glass upon its surface. Surely, the Reavers had used their hands, just as Bishop was able to do, to open it and gain access to its interior, something the Ikonians could not or would not be capable of. Either the lock was a recent addition, or this city was ancient beyond reckoning.

Bishop laid his hand upon its surface, and as expected, it flashed, causing two ponderous doors to slide silently open, revealing a cathedral-like chamber within.

Bishop cautiously entered the vaulted temple, finding himself in a spacious anteroom, the sides of which were carved with various circular glyphs, perhaps representing the Ikonian calendar. Immediately in front of him stood a colossal stone figure of a slumbering figure. The statue's right hand grasped a bow, and in its left was a cluster of golden arrows, but it was the face that held Bishop's attention. It was the face of the Dreamer—Reaver.

Bishop pulled his eyes away from the immense statue and looked beyond it. Thirty-Six had been correct. Here was the very heart of the mystery. Directly in the center of the cathedral, resting on a stepped dais of polished marble, sat a strange cylinder of Old Earth metal—the slip gate. Bishop shuddered, for here was a device that connected the present world to the technological hell of the past. Lights twinkled on a panel of polished glass like the eyes of a fiendish spider. A hexagonal door built into the side of the device stood open, revealing a ghostly inner chamber, which was shimmering and swirling with a bluish foxfire like some silent otherworldly tornado.

The moment had arrived. Bishop raised his Riika and took aim.

"Stop," a voice rumbled from behind him in the open doorway. "What is your intention, construct?"

Bishop swiveled in alarm. Another Reaver? No. It was the Thunderbolt. The monster must have come from the other side of the pyramid. Apparently, it could be as quiet as a mouse when it so chose.

"Isn't it obvious? I am going to destroy the slip gate so that no other Reavers can come into our time."

"No, I forbid it." The Thunderbolt, lumbering to a point between Bishop and the slip gate, stood still.

Bishop's eyes narrowed. "No? Why would you wish the slip gate to remain open?"

The Thunderbolt stood a moment and then spoke again. "So as to allow my soldiers to enter this future earth. I will control the earth and hold dominion over it. It is my world now. You have given it to me. And for that reason and that reason alone, you still live. You are welcome to participate in the coming order so long as you obey me and my instructions completely."

Bishop stared at the metal beast, at first in disbelief, and then with growing understanding. "You are one of them, aren't you? You're a genetic aberration like the Reavers. You *are* a Reaver!"

The Thunderbolt laughed, a grating metallic sound. "As are you, in your own right."

Bishop's mouth dropped. "What do you mean by that? I'm a normal red-blooded human"—his voice dropped—"construct." He finished the sentence with a whisper, gazing at his Riika and then at the accelerator as if for the first time.

The Thunderbolt nodded. "So, you awaken to understanding, but you awaken too late. But unlike Reavers, constructs were merely tools, designed and created to be used by the Old Ones. Yes, tools you were, and tools you remain."

"Do you mean to say that you and I and the Reavers are related?"

"More closely than your simple wit can ever imagine. But know this: your ancestors, constructs, were merely our programmed soldiers. You, my insignificant human, are merely a remnant of the Genetic Wars of precataclysmic earth. Now, carry out your primary function and serve me as you were meant to do."

Bishop raised his Riika and fired point-blank. The bolt of energy leapt out of the arm weapon and washed over the Thunderbolt as if it were made of impervious diamond. Bishop, realizing the futility of the act, disengaged the Riika before his strength gave out completely.

"Are you convinced now?" The Thunderbolt's eyes sparked with deadly calm. "I tire of this game. Assist as you were meant to, or die."

Bishop glowered at the monster.

"Assist me or die."

With that, the Thunderbolt slowly raised his hand and pointed at Bishop. Bishop calmly looked him in those flaming eyes. "No. I will not assist you, and I will not die."

Bishop again snapped his Riika just above the Thunderbolt's head and, with the last of his strength, fired into one of the massive roof columns. The rock blew apart, and the ceiling sagged and then broke. Tons of rock smashed down upon the Thunderbolt, pinning the Old Earth leviathan beneath its incalculable weight.

Bishop lunged into the anteroom as crashing blocks of granite cascaded down around him. Shortly, the surge of rock settled, the air clearing. Bishop peered into the darkened room. There, pinned under a titanic slab of rock, lay the Thunderbolt, immobile and still.

Bishop stared contemptuously at the iron hulk until a shower of electrical sparks drew his attention away from it. The slip gate had not survived the cave-in either. It lay in ruin, smashed flat by a great block of granite.

Bishop, exhausted, backed away toward the open doorway. The morning light was getting brighter, bringing with it the hope of finally returning to the protectorate. Behind him in the ruined chamber, he heard the rattling sounds of pebbly dirt.

Wearily, Bishop turned. With a thrill of horror, he noticed a movement. The massive blocks of broken basalt moved and shifted. Bishop should have known it would take more than a mere pile of rock to terminate the Thunderbolt. It would only be a matter of time before the thing was loose again.

Bishop helplessly scanned the broken room. The Thunderbolt was lying under the rubble. He crept closer.

What is this?

One of the armored plates had been dented and peeled partially away from the creature's torso. Bishop watched as the Thunderbolt slowly began extricating itself from the rock that had it pinned down. Yes, the plate was loose and hanging by one damaged hinge. It was too late for fear. Bishop grabbed the plate and, with all his might, bent it back, exposing a familiar sight. A black and yellow striped hexagonal housing, an exact copy of the one he had seen inside the battle tank. Yes, the knowledge was returning, knowledge given to him by the very creature that was now pinned before him. Now-familiar red script was emblazoned on the surface of the housing: WARNING, DO NOT REMOVE REACTOR COVER WHILE DEVICE IS IN OPERATION.

"I have little choice."

Bishop unlocked four clips and lifted the housing cover. As the housing was lifted, a white-hot light erupted from the loosened cover, forcing Bishop away from the Thunderbolt. The intense heat prevented him from pulling the cover completely free. Again, the Thunderbolt strained to move, and the massive rock column began to rise. As it did so, the creature shifted. The cover slid farther away and was just hanging now. There, resting in a white ceramic depression, sat the power coil, glowing like the sun with intense heat. The acrid smell of burning metal reached Bishop's nose, and then the voice of the Thunderbolt spoke.

"Human, you are being foolish. Replace the power coil cover before you kill yourself. It is fatal to stand within its sight while it is in operation."

"Suddenly, you seem strangely concerned about my health. When you mean to use someone as a tool, you shouldn't give them such a long handle." Bishop tapped his head with a finger.

The Thunderbolt roared with rage and pushed against the column that had him pinned down. As he did so, the power coil flared with increased radiance, casting the room in a blinding light rimmed in a corona of rippling sapphire. A bluish smoke curled away from the open cover, and the surrounding metal began to glow an angry orange color.

"Why don't you die!" Bishop screamed, covering his eyes and backing away further.

There came from the Thunderbolt a dry, low rumble. Bishop's hair stood on end as he realized the sound was laughter. "You think you have won because you defeated an exoskeleton?" Kaleidoscopic shades of hellfire flickered within the armored eye sockets and then momentarily steadied again, speaking cryptically. "My immaterial essence returns to its prison for now, but prepare yourself, human. The others are awake, that glorious endeavor above the earth! they are coming to free me and let slip the dogs of war!"

"The others, the *Others*! They had their moment of glory but they destroyed themselves and their Old Earth, and we are well rid of them! Bishop screamed. "The slip gate is lying in ruin. Can you not see?" Bishop stabbed a finger toward the wrecked slip gate, whose mass still smoldered and sparked in ruin.

The frightful laughter reached Bishop's ears again.

"Why such glee? You are finished! The circle completes itself!"

No answer came. The whining sound faded into silence, the hellfire within the eye slits slowly died, and the Old Earth device finally lay still.

Bishop let out his breath with a long sigh and breathed deeply once again. The tension drained out of him, leaving his every limb weary. He wiped the cold sweat of terror from his face and combed back the tangle of his disheveled hair with his fingers. The morning sun flamed like a crimson coal, flooding reddish light into the broken chamber as swirling eddies of dust settled to the litter-strewn floor. The scent of dew-kissed mountain pines met Bishop's nose, replacing the acrid stench of the burned-out Thunderbolt and the hellish time gate. It was time to return to the protectorate at last.

Slowly, Bishop retraced his steps to find Thirty-Six waiting beyond the outer courtyard of the great pyramid. "Well, Thirty-Six," he said wearily, "I've killed the Reavers, destroyed the Thunderbolt, and smashed the slip gate. Do you have any other chores for me to do before I retire home to my protectorate?"

The insect turned to face Bishop. "Yes. We would like you to take the others of your kind from our colony. They are not allowed. It is against nest law."

"You are very welcome, Thirty-Six," Bishop grated in sarcastic frustration. "It was no problem whatsoever. Please, no more accolades. No, please, no, you are embarrassing me with your thunderous applause." Then he suddenly sobered. "What others?"

"The others of your kind. You are of the colony; they are not. You will lead them from the First Colony."

"The others? What do you mean, the others? Did you manage to lure other humans to this hellish hive of yours?"

"The others who are like you and not like you."

"Like me and not like me."

"Shaped like you, but large. Not small."

"What?"

"Large. Not small." Thirty-Six hesitated for a moment as if collecting its thoughts. "This tunneler is regretful. The translator is not sufficient. I will try to explain further. There are no threads and no twine on their head tops. They are like you but not like you. They are not of the colony. Please help them leave." It could have been Bishop's imagination, but the insect seemed uncomfortable.

Bishop scratched his head in growing curiosity. "I do not understand you, Thirty-Six. You've left me far behind again. I've just got to see these others you are rambling on about. Why don't you take this diminutive person to wherever these 'large' persons are, and I'll see what I can do for them. Is that acceptable?"

"They are not of the colony. They cannot stay." The insect began to move purposely back to the lower galleries, with Bishop following.

"Yes, I understand the part about removing these large humans. Small, indeed," Bishop muttered as their steps took them lower and lower into the colony. "Do you realize that at the tender age of thirteen I was the ninth largest boy in my class? I hardly think that qualifies as small. Or weak, I might add."

"The large ones cannot stay," Thirty-Six repeated.

"Yes, yes, large, not small. I know, I know. Lead me to these brutish humans, O chitinous one."

The first thing Bishop saw at the bottom of the tunnel was a gathering of distressed-looking insects milling in agitation. Antennae waved in front of an all-too-familiar prison cell, the shimmering energy screen accentuating their troubled features in a macabre fashion.

"Fear not," Bishop growled. "The small one is here."

The insects moved away from the force field as he approached. As Bishop stared into the cell, his mouth dropped open as if it were on a hinge. He turned to face Thirty-Six, shaking his head. "Oh, I mean really, now. I must say, this is too much." Bishop looked back at the energy screen. "This is nothing but a bunch of bedraggled Eligor. They are not humans."

"The large ones cannot stay."

"Large ones! Isn't there an Ikonian word for Eligor? Large ones. These half-starved lizards don't look like they could beat themselves out of a half-rotten burlap sack. Large ones indeed!"

One of the Eligor pushed himself to the front and coughed. "Well," he said, "had I expected you, I would have dressed for dinner and set out the fine silver."

"Kiel?"

"Indeed."

"Why ...? What in the name of ...? Kiel! What happened? I don't remember anything after I activated the power coil. How did you get here? What are you doing in there?"

"It seems that I am staring through a force screen at an ignorant human who is prattling irrelevant questions."

Bishop sobered somewhat. "That's a fine way to talk to someone who, moments ago, was considering helping your scaled hide get out of here."

"My apologies, dear human. Get us out of here. This is humiliating. Please. I promise I will ask precious little else of you from here on out."

Bishop turned to Thirty-Six in mock seriousness. "Are you sure I can't just leave them? They look pretty useful, a bunch of large Eligor like these. You know, lift and tote, lift and tote."

"Bishop, your humor is not appreciated," Kiel grated.

"The large ones cannot stay. They cannot be useful. You cannot leave them, they are not of the nest" Thirty-Six insisted.

"Bishop!"

"Oh, all right, if you insist. Let me take them from their kennel, Thirty-Six, and pray they are housebroken." Bishop smiled merrily at Kiel, who returned the look with dangerous slitted yellow eyes.

Thirty-Six touched a control panel, and the force field flickered, dimmed, then winked out. The Eligor soldiers, looking at the opening hesitantly, soon shuffled out. Kiel brought up the rear, his steps as regal and aloof as ever. "The next time I am of a mind to come and rescue you, I believe I shall rethink the plan."

"Ah, Kiel, my dear Eligor, don't be sour. I do appreciate the thought. And it's the thought that counts, or so I have been told."

Thirty-Six's translator hummed to life, interrupting Bishop's reunion. "The large ones have not consumed their rations. The food is not eaten. That is disruptive to the order of the colony. The rations are not eaten."

Bishop followed Thirty-Six's gaze. There in the corner of the cell was a generously heaped stack of spongy gray fungus disks. A laugh welled up in his throat and burst out like a geyser.

"Kiel," he barked gleefully. "Sit down and eat your dinner, good Eligor. We have a bit of time yet."

Kiel's golden eyes became slits of fire. "I'll only say this once, human. Eligor do not eat mushrooms. They never have and they never will."

Bishop nodded. "Well, we'll just have to rustle you up some fresh rat. How does that sound?"

"That would be acceptable, human." Kiel examined his claws calmly, although his eyes were still mere slits of golden fire. Turning to Thirty-Six, he said, "Now, would you be so kind as to show us the way out of this accursed anthill of yours?"

"The rations are not eaten—still." Thirty-Six looked pleadingly at Bishop.

Bishop leaned close, whispering to the insect: "Thirty-Six. Let's just forget the fungus this one time, let it pass, alright? Don't tell anyone. Just this once."

Thirty-Six pondered silently before the translator crackled in a somewhat exasperated tone. "Very well, human. The food will be redistributed to others of the nest. Please follow."

As Bishop and the Eligor fell in behind Thirty-Six, a squad of Ikonians appeared in the tunnel before them.

"What is it, Thirty-Six? What's going on?" Bishop asked wearily, half raising his Riika.

"Black gods, now what?" Kiel grated, motioning his cellmates to stop.

The idea that the insects had suddenly returned to a benign state was hard to accept at face value. Bishop stood at the ready. A sweet scent permeated the air, and the waving antennae seemed to suggest that something of importance was being communicated to Thirty-Six.

"Thirty-Six, what is it?"

Thirty-Six turned to Bishop. "The queen has summoned you to the royal chamber. She wishes to be acquainted with you and impart her blessings."

"The queen? You mean your mother?" Bishop hesitated. These insects were anything but predictable, and he wished nothing more than to leave Ikonia as quickly as possible. "That's not necessary, Thirty-Six. She can, ah, send me a delicious fungus pie. I really should be leaving."

Thirty-Six stood immobile. "It is a great honor, human. You must receive her blessing. You will then be given custody of the Revered One, and you will escort him safely out of Ikonia."

"The Revered One? An Ikonian will follow us back to the protectorate?"

"The Revered One, the one that is honored, beautiful. The one like you and not like you."

Bishop raised his hand, palm forward. "Don't even start."

Thirty-Six hesitated. "The Revered One."

"A wonderful, beautiful revered Ikonian, not a scruffy, raggedy little human like me, is that it?" Bishop rubbed his eyes and slowly shook his head. "You know, Thirty-Six, if I didn't know you so well, I'd swear you were purposely trying to test my patience."

Thirty-Six seemed to waver uncomfortably but remained silent. Bishop looked over at Kiel and then sighed. "Fine, I'll meet with the queen and escort your 'Revered One' back to the protectorate for all the good it will do. Anything else, pray tell? Take out the trash, scrub the floor?"

"No, thank you."

Kiel stepped forward, still brushing dirt from his worn and soiled uniform. "I would ask if I might take these soldiers to the outer colony and wait for you. I'm sure that you would not wish to be hindered by a mob of scraggly Eligor while you receive your just desserts."

Bishop rolled his eyes but elected not to respond. There would be enough time for apologies on the trail. Thirty-Six communicated Kiel's wishes to the lead Ikonian, and the Eligor were led away from the prison area.

Bishop turned to Thirty-Six. "Well, let's meet your mother and this 'revered' Ikonian of yours. Truly, I have had my fill of your colony and would like nothing more than to take my leave of it."

Bishop, in all his dealings with these insects, had never become used to their peculiar appearance, and now to find himself adrift on an ocean of arthropodal entomology was by no means agreeable. For the briefest of moments, he experienced the overwhelming desire to turn and flee, but there was Thirty-Six at his side, and he took what little comfort he could from the diminutive insect's proximity.

Bishop ascended a great staircase and passed through a series of huge halls, dome-roofed and elaborately decorated, as Thirty-Six pointed out the writhing ideographs of Ikonian history and nest lore. The approach to the queen seemed to have been contrived to give one a vivid impression of her greatness. Each cavern Bishop entered seemed greater and more boldly arched than its predecessor. A thin haze of faintly phosphorescent mist enhanced the effect of progressive size and splendor.

Ranks of Ikonian soldiers stood in perfect order as Bishop passed, forcing him to admit to himself that this impeccable royal host indeed made him feel extremely shabby and unworthy. He was unshaven and unkempt; he had brought along no cut throat for grooming, and so a thick bristle covered his face, hacked at haphazardly at times by his own dull dagger. His ragged clothing was covered with every sort of dirt and grime Ikonia had to offer. There was an unmended tear at the left knee of his trousers that gaped conspicuously when he walked, and the right heel of his boot was loose. He would have given much for something a little more dignified than the rags he wore. After all, he was the emissary of his race. Still, on he went into the vaulted gloom of the grand chamber of the queen of the First Colony, taking solace in the fact that this ill-begotten adventure was nearing its end.

Finally, at the end of the panorama, dimly seen, a flight of steps ascended out of sight. Higher and higher these steps seemed to go as Bishop drew nearer to their base, till at last he came under a huge archway and beheld the summit of this flight of stairs, upon which the queen sat exalted upon her throne.

For a moment Bishop had trouble believing that this queen was real or alive, but she was of the Ikonian type, yet unlike the female he had previously encountered. This one was wingless. Her coloring was not that of a normal Ikonian, but darker, browner, and more mottled. Even the eyes were dark. Bishop, as he approached, wondered if she was blind. There was no insect seated next to her, nor was there an accompanying throne—and Bishop supposed that if there had ever been a "father" of the colony, he was long dead. *How many eons have passed since this creature before me burrowed beneath this mountain to begin the lonely work of the queen, that is, the creation of this First Colony?* he wondered.

Thirty-Six approached the queen very slowly and lowered its head to hers. With great gentleness, they touched their antennae. Thirty-Six then backed away and returned to its place beside Bishop. Bishop was already familiar with the astounding patience of the Ikonians, so he was not surprised at the almost total lack of movement in the silent lines of insects that radiated out from the central platform. Bishop looked at the rows of Ikonians, alert, immobile, and could not to his emotional satisfaction discern the ancientness of the race upon which he gazed.

The queen's antennae wavered, and the chamber fell utterly silent. "Human, you are of the colony. You have our thanks for ridding us of the Dreamers. Though they are our creators and we revere them, they have no place in this time."

Still painfully aware of how bedraggled he must have appeared, Bishop suddenly remembered something of his ambassadorial training and bowed low. "I am honored to help in whatever aspect you might require, Your Highness."

"You will escort the Revered One back to your colony. It would please us greatly."

"I will escort the Revered One, Your Highness," Bishop said, bowing lower.

"Well then, let's get on with it, O tiny-headed one!" came an unexpected croaking voice, sounding alarmingly like Bishop's own.

Bishop jerked his head up in confused alarm.

"Storm Singer?" Storm Singer!

The wolf-bird had appeared, strutting regally from behind the queen, where he had undoubtedly been hiding, enjoying the entire show.

"What in the name of the bloody Others are you doing in here? Gods of the Others, get out of here before you cause a riot!" Bishop hissed. "Gods of the Others, man, birds eat insects!"

"You will escort the Revered One," the queen repeated. Slow, terrible understanding seeped into Bishop's mind.

"No. It can't be ..." Bishop stammered.

"The Revered One," the queen said, directing her antennae toward the bird.

"I ... How in the ..." Bishop choked.

Storm Singer flew onto Bishop's shoulder and began preening as if they had only just recently parted company. "It's rather a long story, really kind of humorous. You see, I was patrolling the border as you instructed when I ran across the queen. She was being evacuated from the Reaver threat and was in need of some assistance, and, well—"

"And, well, you just happened to fall right in with them. Is that it?" Bishop growled.

"Something like that, yes. Our race was apparently quite close to these insects in the distant past, and they seem to have a remarkable memory. There seems to be something about wolf-birds coming from an egg, as do the Ikonians. The egg is sacred to them just as it is, albeit to a lesser degree, to our noble species. As you well know, all higher life shares this common trait. Also, it appears that our creators, the Others, shared a common plan in our makeup that is known to these wonderful and amazing creatures.

"Also, when the queen was being evacuated from the Reaver threat, I shared some of our egg lore with her, also providing a bit of aerial scouting, and told her I was fond of music. Then I sang for her."

"Music?"

"Wolf-bird songs."

"Singing? You *sang* for them? Storm Singer, I hate to break this to you, but you can't sing any better than I can. Worse, in fact!"

Storm Singer cocked an ebon eye. "You are sadly mistaken. I was not granted the name 'Storm Singer' at my first molting for naught." At this the bird croaked, hissed, cawed, and knocked. The gathered multitude of Ikonians, to an insect, waved their erect antennae as if in ecstasy until the bird finished.

Bishop held his ears at the racket. "It's beyond me how any sentient creature could find beauty in something that sounds like a catfight, a squeaky barn door, and a shattering piece of pottery all rolled into one disagreeable cacophony."

"You're being quite disrespectful of my musical abilities, Bishop, and quite disrespectful to the Revered One."

"All right, all right. And after the song and the whole egg thing, you just fell right in with them, is that it?" Bishop growled.

"Something like that, yes. If it at all helps I had you in mind the entire time."

"You will escort the Revered One," the queen repeated once again, interrupting the conversation.

"My apologies." Bishop sighed. "I will escort the Revered One," he grated with no small difficulty.

"This human will suffice, O great queen of the First Colony," Storm Singer intoned. "May you yet produce many blessed eggs, and may those eggs produce many strong Ikonians."

"Don't push it," Bishop hissed.

The queen leaned forward. "Know, O human, that there is no real distinction between us; only in outer appearance does one perceive such a thing."

Bishop nodded, not truly understanding the cryptic sentence.

"Our soldiers will escort you to the frontier. We are forever in your debt."

Bishop, glowering at Storm Singer, bowed forward. Quickly, the bird scrambled to retain his perch. "Always at your service, great queen."

Great stone statues leered down at Bishop from their ageless vigil along the Ikonian border as Thirty-Six said his farewells. Simultaneously, Kiel, followed by the Eligor soldiers, melted into the southern woods, where he would wait. Storm Singer circled overhead, a black speck in the clear blue dome of the early winter sky.

"This tunneler has acquired a gift for you from the First Colony," Thirty-Six intoned.

"What is it, a fungus disk?" Bishop asked blandly.

"Not food. Something you seemed to desire more than food." Thirty-Six tucked his hand into a waist pouch and produced a scintillating object about the size of an apple.

"This waste, I retrieved from the lower tunnels. It was the largest thing this tunneler believed you capable of transporting back to your protectorate."

Bishop had forgotten about the treasure of the scavengers as he dumbly held out his hand.

Thirty-Six handed him the object. With a start, he realized it to be the largest diamond he could have ever conceived of. He numbly held it up to the sunlight; the size and brilliance was spectacular. It had a thousand facets that shown of its own inner light. "Well, I'll be damned," was all he could mutter at first.

"Yes, thank you, Thirty-Six, for remembering. I, ah, don't know what to say."

Thirty-Six stared at Bishop. "You are having trouble with your speech?"

"Something like that." Bishop absently stammered.

"Go well, human of the First Colony."

A smile slowly crept across Bishop's face as he numbly walked away from Thirty-Six and back into the gloom of the Eligor forest. "Go well, Thirty-Six," he said finally, turning, but the insect was gone.

"Yes, go well indeed," Bishop said with a puerile grin as he discreetly tucked the diamond into a safe inner pocket. Yet another mission incident that would have to be left off of his final report to the Order.

The blare of trumpets grew louder, like a deep golden tide surge, like the soft booming of the evening tide as it met the silvery beaches found on the southern shores of the protectorate. The throng shouted; female Eligor flung flowers from the roofs as the rhythmic chiming of iron-shod riding beasts became clearer and the first of the mighty array swung into view in the broad street that curved round the spired Grand Union of Imperial Opal.

First came the trumpeters, slim young Eligor clad in scarlet, marching with a flourish of long and slender golden trumpets. Next were the bowmen, tall Eligor shod in black leather. Behind these were the heavily armed footmen, their broad shields clashing in unison, their long spears swaying in rhythm with their stride. Behind the footmen came what was left of the Imperial Eligor Army. Proudly they marched, looking neither to the right nor to the left. Like bronze statues they were, and never did the forest of spears that reared up above them waver. Then they all stopped, and a hush fell over the city.

High on a parapet at the front of the Grand Union, standing in acceptance of the honors, stood a hooded figure and the first commander of the Imperial Intelligence Service of Opal.

"All things on earth have their term, and at the dizzying height of their vanity and splendor, their strength fails and they sink into the dust. The entire world is but a sepulcher, and there is nothing that lives on its surface that shall not eventually be hidden and entombed beneath it. Streams, tributaries, and rivers move onward to their destination, not one flowing back to its beginning. Rather, they hasten to bury themselves in the deep fathoms of the distant ocean. The things of yesterday are no more, and the things of today shall cease, perhaps on the morrow.

Tombs are filled with the dust of those once quickened by living souls, who occupied thrones, presided over assemblies, marshaled armies, subdued provinces, arrogated to themselves worship, and were deified with vainglorious pomp, power, and empire."

The throng roared in acknowledgment of Kiel's words and then quickly quieted once he began speaking again.

"But these glories have all passed away like the smoke from a dying fire, with no other memorial to their existence than a record on a page of a chronicler. The great, the wise, the valiant, the beautiful. Alas! Where are they now? They are all mingled in the earth. But let that which has befallen them not befall us or those who come after us. Let us take courage, illustrious nobles, true friends, and loyal subjects. Let us aspire to a new day, where all is true and corruption cannot come. Let the dark storms of the past die under the cradle of a new sun, and let the black night of tyranny fade beneath the brilliant light of a hundred myriad stars."

A joyous roar went up throughout Opal. "Kiel, Kiel, Kiel," went the thunderous chant. Kiel, somewhat taken aback by the sounds of elation, glanced back at the members of the Grand Union, only to find that they too had joined in the thundering mantra.

"You are honored above all of Eligor, human," the first commander said.

"Why, that's a comfort," came the bland reply. "Hooded all the while, watching as you receive your just desserts."

Kiel waved a weary claw. "We have been through this before, Bishop. The people would not understand, and besides, the true power—the Grand Union—knows the truth. Furthermore, I did not complain at being left out of the honors at Ikonia."

"Some honor, escorting an empty-headed wolf-bird across the Ikonian border."

As the Eligor army stopped and stood at attention with a clang of arms, they tendered to the two figures the Eligor salute. The crowds roared in appreciation.

Kiel, in response, touched the ground and then his forehead, motioning to Bishop to do the same.

"Gods of the Others!" Bishop growled as he bent. "This is ridiculous."

Kiel stood at attention, waved to the troops, and waved again to the crowd, who again responded riotously. "It is time to meet with the Grand Union."

"And for your service to the Eligor Empire, you are hereby awarded the Order of the Golden Circle of Imperial Eligor."

Seth, the most aged and senior member of the Grand Union, stepped forward and hung the golden medallion around Bishop's neck. Bishop did a double take once he caught a glimpse of a graven cluster of thunderbolts gripped in a gauntleted Eligor hand within the circle.

"From all of Eligor, we thank you and your government for services to our empire that are quite beyond our ability to repay. May our two nations grow to become the strongest of allies, and let the hostility and the misunderstanding of past ages be buried and forgotten on this dawn of a new Grand Cycle of hope and peace."

He then turned and repeated the ceremony with Kiel and finally Storm Singer, although the bird's medal had been hastily customized for his smaller avian frame.

The august assembly of the Grand Union rose from their seats.

Bishop, with difficulty, tearing his attention away from the massive winged skull, symbol of the old Eligor Empire, that decorated the rear wall of the Grand Union, touched the ground and then his forehead as was the Eligor custom. Then, turning, he left.

After the dead were solemnly laid to rest and the broken northern battlements had been repaired and strengthened, the following thirteen days were given up to festivity. The Eligor people, dressed in their gayest apparel and crowned with garlands and chaplets of autumn flowers, thronged in joyous procession to offer up their oblations and thanksgiving in the streets and avenues of Opal. Dances, quadrilles, and games were enthusiastically instituted, emblematic of the regeneration of the world and the beginning of a new Grand Cycle of peace and prosperity. It was an awe-inspiring celebration in honor of the restoration of the old republic and the casting off of the horrors of the days of empire. Few alive had ever witnessed such joy or could hope to expect to see such again.

The days ambled on in a relaxed but expectant way, as the celebration slowly gave way to the harvesting and husking of corn, one of the great staples of the Eligor, which grew freely along the valleys and steep mountain slopes and up to the higher levels of the tableland, and to the filling of granaries in preparation for winter. It was with a general sigh of relief when rat, normally shunned by the fastidious Eligor, was replaced by venison and the first sweet corn cakes after the new harvest.

Though they were good days for the average Eligor, filled with pleasant work, song, food, and drink, Bishop found he was ready to go home, so at last he set out for the borders of his distant homeland with a light foot and a cheery heart, with Storm Singer in the lead and with Kiel as a willing guide, the three of them occasionally singing an old Eligor song of friendship while they walked:

> It is a gentle and affectionate thought
> In the immeasurable heights above us, there,
> That at our first meeting the wreath was wrought
> With sparkling stars of friendship fair.

TWENTY-FIVE

HOMEWARD BOUND

> Home is where I'm free as air.
> The timid forest life is my fare;
> My drink, the morning dew.
> Perched at will on every gate,
> My form is genteel. My plumage is slate,
> And my song is forever new.
> —Song of the Wolf-Bird

The Gondakar Barrier once again loomed above the forest, a gray mass of rock materializing out of the cold autumn mists that for the first time in Bishop's memory spoke to him of home and hearth. Bishop had returned once again to the Protectorate of Merja Soria.

Storm Singer was fairly dancing in anticipation on Bishop's shoulder as they approached. "Hurry, human. Hurry now. Time's a-wasting. The home nest is near."

"You'll be making it back to your mite-infested nest inside my stomach if you don't stop scratching up my shoulders with those crooked, untended claws of yours. No, strike that; you don't even rate that high. You would probably give me a case of the scours."

Storm Singer crowed in glee, and Bishop eyed the corvid in mock anger. The wolf-bird took wing and flew up to the Gondakar Barrier to alert the guards to their homecoming.

Kiel stood at the edge of the clearing, looking up at the ancient structure before settling his gaze on Bishop. "I have returned you safely, human. I will take my leave now."

It was an awkward moment for the two of them. They had been through so much, had in fact evolved from barely tolerating each other to being the best of friends, though neither would openly admit that they had truly become friends.

Bishop muttered back, "Yes, well, I'll be going now."

Kiel looked away into the trees. "Very well, human. Do send word some time, if you would like. I will attempt to do the same—out of professional courtesy, you realize." Kiel glanced at his troops again.

Bishop studied the toes of his boots. "Yes, quite. I'll write you a nice love letter. How would you like that, eh?"

Kiel smiled, baring several fearfully sharp teeth as he held out his scaled hand in the human custom. "That is acceptable, human. I would like that."

Bishop returned Kiel's grin, clasped the Eligor's hand, and then bent and touched the ground and then his forehead in the Eligor fashion. "Go well, O lizard of mine."

"Go well, Sha Tar," Kiel returned.

Bishop's eyes narrowed. "Tell me honestly, what does *Sha Tar* mean? It's doesn't mean 'warrior,' does it?"

Kiel took on an uncomfortable, sheepish look. "Not exactly."

"What does it mean?"

"It is a very old, very ancient word. There isn't a direct human translation."

"What does it mean?!"

Kiel sighed. "Very well. In the subtleties of the Eligor tongue, the words *Sha Tar* mean 'an acquired thing.'"

"Acquired? There's more to it than that, isn't there?"

"Yes, well, acquired, but not necessarily wanted, like a sickness, or a parasite, or an affliction."

Bishop blinked, smiling thinly. "I liked *warrior* much better. What is the word for warrior?"

"*Tar Che*," the translator crackled in response.

At the mention of the word, a few Eligor soldiers chortled, casting mirthful looks at Bishop.

"Tar Che? Are you sure?"

"Oh yes, of course. Tar Che," Kiel returned innocently, followed by a few more suppressed sniggers.

Bishop eyed Kiel suspiciously a moment longer before turning toward the looming wall. Just then, a shrill avian voice called from above them: "Go well, Kiel. May the winds of fortune carry you gently back to your home nest."

Kiel waved as Storm Singer alighted on Bishop's shoulder. Then, motioning to his soldiers, he melted back into the forest and was gone.

Bishop had not advanced very far when the turning angle of the upper hills and forests of the southern Eligor Empire opened beyond the top of the Gondakar Barrier wall onto the lowlands that he called home. With a joyous heart he again took in the picturesque assemblage of water, woodland, and cultivated plains, its shining hamlets and shadowy hills, all spread out like some wonderful quilted panorama before him. In the thin air of the upper slopes, even remote objects took on a brilliancy of color and distinctness that seemed to annihilate distance. Stretching far away below his feet were the noble forests of aspen, alder, and oak, and beyond them, the yellow fields of wheat and corn were intermingled with fruit orchards in a riot of autumn color. Bishop had come home.

After a short stay and debriefing at Gondakar, Bishop and Storm Singer made their way back toward the Anwar Kili Chapter House. Winter had not yet come to the protectorate as it had in the far north; pumpkins sat orange and frosty in the fields. The forests were afire with multicolored leaves, and the nights came crisp and cold. It would be good to settle down next to a crackling fire and relax for a spell, Bishop thought. The Others only knew he had earned it.

"Do you think we will be rewarded for our service to the protectorate?" Storm Singer asked, not for the first time.

Bishop nodded and smiled at the thought. "Probably be a parade, medals, honors …"

Surely, if the Eligor Empire had so lavished a mere human with such fanfare, the protectorate would be much more appreciative.

Two weeks later, Bishop stood at rigid attention in front of Master Bryn within the bowels of the Anwar Kili Chapter House, while a cold sleet fell against the diamond-paned windows and the last of the autumn leaves fell in golden heaps on the outer sill. Bryn's face was creased in a dark frown, marring his smooth-shaven face with a terrible ashen pallor, which together with the deeply sunken cheeks lent a corpse-like appearance to the hulking brute.

"Let me come right to the point, Standard-Bearer Bishop. You have been charged with eight counts of treason and five criminal violations of your original orders."

Bishop's jaw dropped open in disbelief. "Forgive me, a violation of my orders? *A violation of my orders?* I just *saved* the protectorate from an Old Earth terror that is beyond description! How can you, how can any human, say I disobeyed my orders?"

Bryn gripped a fistful of paper and suddenly loomed over Bishop. "You were to gather information and bring it back to the Order for analysis. Is this not your signature stating that you fully understand these simple orders?" He uncrumpled the wad of papers and stabbed a finger several times at one of them.

"Well, yes, but I—we, rather—decided …"

"We, the Order, decide what to do with retrieved information, not a simpleminded standard-bearer. Is that clear?"

Bishop stared in disbelief. "Yes, but—"

"Do you have any idea how close you came to bringing ruin down upon us all because of disobeying your orders and taking this situation into your own hands?"

"I … well—"

Bryn cut him short again with upraised hands. "Yet I understand, better than most, that you were merely doing what you thought correct."

Bishop nodded mutely.

"Therefore, thanks to a personal request on my part, all charges against you have been suspended. Further, you are to retain your current rank of standard-bearer. Understand that you are on probation and are to be taken off active duty for an indeterminate period—time for you to ponder your mistakes and hopefully learn from them. We also need time to determine what all this really means to the protectorate. You simply can't begin to understand the mayhem you have created. The Order is literally in chaos."

Bishop stared in silence as Bryn glared at him in an almost hopeless manner. Apparently, there was not going to be a parade, nor were there going to be medals or honors. It was almost more than Bishop could bear, but he remained silent. There were worse things in the world than being denied a medal. Besides, the Eligor had already given him one, though he had elected not to tell Bryn about it.

"Oh yes, there was also a personal letter of thanks from the fledgling Eligor republic rising from the ashes of the old empire. It went a long way toward exonerating you and keeping you from any disciplinary action. It seems you have made a friend in Opal—no small accomplishment. We must do what we can to endear ourselves to this new government; it could be a chance to put thousands of years of hostility behind us."

Well, that was something at least. Good old Kiel had come through for Bishop.

Bryn looked up from his paperwork with a pitying expression. "In the future, it would do you well to pay closer attention to your orders; they are not fabricated on a whim and usually have everyone's best interests in mind. Do you understand?"

"Yes, sir." Bishop saluted.

"Very well, you are dismissed for now, but you are not yet released from duty and are to stay within the chapter house until further notice. There are others arriving shortly who would like to have a chat with you."

Others? Bishop gulped and turned to leave. "Yes, sir."

"Oh, and I remind you that you are not to discuss your exploits with anyone ranking lower than I. You have caused quite a stir within the Order. It is going to take us some time to make sense of what happened and what it all means for the future of the protectorate. Fail to heed my warning and all the suspended charges will be reinstated—threefold!"

"Yes, sir," Bishop muttered again. He hastily left the office.

Bishop made his way back to the barracks and lay low for the afternoon, considering his plight, while the sleet turned to spitting snow. It seemed he would be standard-bearer within the Order for the foreseeable future, and it was time he accepted the fact. Finally, with resolution, he struck out toward the paymaster's office to gather his back pay. It wasn't much, but he would find a home for it at one of the taverns in town once the Order released him. The closest he'd gotten to female companionship, any female companionship for that matter, in the past several months was when that Ikonian princess had taken a shine to him, he blushed at the thought. Yes, it was time he began living again.

Two frightful weeks of further interrogation had passed. It was with no small relief to Bishop when he was finally released. He hastily made his way to the northern gatehouse of the Anwar Kili Chapter House with a small bag of clinking copper riders. The wintry sky was slate gray with an occasional flake of snow silently drifting to the ground. A gatehouse guard, rubbing his cold hands briskly together, waved Bishop through the gate once it swung open on squeaking hinges. "Heading toward the Tavern Quarter, are we? I surely wish it was me."

"Tonight, I am going to drink myself under the table. I don't care how detestable of an act it is," Bishop returned. "They can't prevent me from doing it anyway."

The guard shook his head and chuckled. "No law that says you can't get slobbered, I would wager."

Bishop stalked off toward the village of Anwar Kili, still muttering angrily to himself. "Taken off active duty! If that isn't the ... Wait a minute." He stopped. "Why am I complaining? It might be years before I am allowed to risk my neck in the service of the Order again. Maybe that's better than a medal after all."

A chance ray of cold sunlight streamed through the leafless trees and down upon the snowy landscape, casting cathedral-like streamers on the sodden ground, as Bishop melted into the somber forest, the dreaded chapter house disappearing from sight. He couldn't get to the alehouse fast enough. The only thing on earth that kept him from lapsing into complete depression was a very carefully hidden fist-sized diamond, given to him by Thirty-six, that he could only consider a sort of retirement investment. And retirement would come as soon as he could effectively arrange it. Bishop smiled, was it honest? No. Was it deserved? Oh hell, yes, it was!

Suddenly, a terrible screech came from above him. "Hoo, Bishop!"

"Gods of the Others, man!" Bishop barked fearfully, ducking and half unsheathing his sword in the process.

Storm Singer, making a knocking laughter-like sound, flitted down through the snow-covered trees and alighted on Bishop's shoulder, absently sharpening his beak on his leather coat.

Bishop rubbed his eyes wearily. "One of these days, buzzard, you are going to end up on the wrong side of an arrow." Then he stopped and stared at the bird. "What in the eight hells is that thing?" Bishop pointed to a small silver medallion hanging around Storm Singer's feathered neck.

Storm Singer puffed his neck feathers out in pride. "Just look what I have been awarded, a medal for bravery and hazard behind the Gondakar Barrier. The Order of the Silver Sky, it is."

Bishop reddened. "They gave *you* a medal?"

"Let me see yours. Surely you have been awarded with a medal for some small effort on your part," Storm Singer said, cocking his head to inspect Bishop's neck.

"Ah, yeah, but I left it at the chapter house. I'll show it to you later," Bishop said blandly. He again began walking toward the distant village, his retirement plans looming ever larger in his mind.

Storm Singer, not stopping to question him further, excitedly told Bishop about his award ceremony in painful detail. Bishop was forced to endure it, nodding and adding a strained "You don't say?" from time to time.

Storm Singer ruffled his feathers again and settled down before remembering something else. "Oh yes, did you hear the news?"

"What news is that?"

"Some bumbling idiot disobeyed his orders while we were away. Could have caused a war. Had the whole lot of them in a lather, they say. I certainly wouldn't want to be in that unlucky human's boots." Storm Singer chortled. "Well, I must be heading back to the home nest. Seems my fellow wolf-birds have planned some merrymaking for me, and I wouldn't want to be late. Maybe we will harass some poor lout while he is at work in the fields."

Storm Singer flew away, leaving a flaming Bishop behind, staring in frustration. "Go well, you motherless pest!" he yelled, stalking off again toward the village, mentally doubling the amount of wine he would consume once he got there.

TWENTY-SIX

THE LETTER

> Then through the leaves came a distant sigh:
> A meteor flashed over the autumn sky.
> Of those that were, the ages murmur still,
> Their voices were in the wood, their footsteps on the hill.
>
> —Vena Korela,
> Toinen Tuleminen, Runa 1

The most important holiday in Merja Soria was the winter solstice, more commonly known as New Winter's Day, the beginning of winter, the last national holiday before deep winter set in.

Since the event was seen as the reversal of the sun's ebbing presence in the sky, concepts of the birth or rebirth of sun gods had been common in ancient times and in cultures using cyclic calendars. The year as reborn was celebrated with regard to life–death–rebirth deities or new beginnings. Some Merja Sorians still practiced these old beliefs.

For most, it was a consolidation of events: the celebration of the birth of the protectorate and the giving of thanks for a bountiful harvest. The festival started when the first of the winter snows began to fall and included feasts and drinking; decorations of gourds and pumpkins, berries and spruce bows; and candles and gifts. It lasted about ten days, culminating in New Winter's Day, the first day of New Winter month.

The weather had turned particularly foul even for the northlands of the protectorate this year. The rains had settled in early and were soon followed by periods of snow—not the crisp cold powder that came later, but a damp slush that seemed always to be half melting, though the snow fell constantly.

For Bishop, whose duties as standard-bearer prevented him from enjoying the season on his family's farm, joining in their traditional anticipatory excitement, the approaching holiday somehow seemed dull and bland. He yearned for the days of his youth and often sighed with regret at his forced entry into the Order. Even the traditional decorations adorning the chapter house and the towns and hamlets of the county of Merja Soria looked decidedly tacky this year. The fir wreaths that festooned every farmhouse with their twinkling candles were somehow not as green and bright as in years gone by. Like the soggy snow, they looked like something being viewed through smudged glass.

Bishop, wrapped tightly in a thick woolen cloak, hurried on through the freezing snow and the silent winter woodland, trying to set his thoughts on the feasts that were, no doubt, laid out in every pub in the country. But happy thoughts were elusive to him in this cold and silent forest. Even the wildlife was hidden and quiet, the silence being interrupted only by the occasional collapse of piled snow from the boughs of the great firs that leered over him in these sodden woods. He sighed again and tried to think happy thoughts, scolding himself for not being more thankful for things that really mattered: health and life, human companionship, good food and drink. He brightened at the thought of the servants scurrying from kitchens to halls bearing smoking roasts; steaming hams; succulent geese; gravies; cheeses; mushrooms—no, strike the mushrooms; aromatic bread fresh from the oven, spread with soft butter; plum tarts; apple pies with clotted sweet cream …

"Ah," he said, breaking the all-pervasive silence of the cold, gray forest, "apple pie and clotted sweet cream. Now there is something to be thankful for."

The tables would be loaded, the fires in the fireplaces would be burning brightly, dozens of candles would fill the halls with their golden light, and the townsfolk would be dressed in their finest clothing, chattering, singing, drinking, and laughing. Bishop had, some days before, decided he would even splurge on a bottle of good red wine, something that was normally too rich for his meager earnings. He would forget this year's trials and tribulations and leave them behind him forever. It was a time of resolution, forgetting the past and looking forward to a bright future.

Yes, he thought, as the first of the town lights came into view through the gloomy trees and wet snow. *I will forget the past, contemplate the future, and enjoy myself.*

Several hours after leaving the chapter house, Bishop was relaxing with a bottle of wine in the Inn of the Seventh Gate, watching a heated game of dice between two initiates. The spitting snow outside had turned into a regular snowstorm, and the sky had become even darker as evening approached. Townsfolk began to fill the halls and, as expected, began to sing holiday songs around a comforting fire.

> Forget me not around your hearth
> When cheerily smiles the ruddy blaze,
> For dear hath been its evening mirth
> To me, my friends, in other days.

Many other songs were sung, accompanied by flute and fife, drum and stringed instruments. It was a joyous group that filled the hall tonight. Bishop joined in with the singing of more than one song.

> Now winter nights are dark.
> The snow, it falls, so hark!
> Let now the chimneys blaze
> And cups overflow with wine
> Let singing words amaze
> With harmony divine.

The trials of the past several months were finally washing out of Bishop as the red wine seeped through his worn body, a feeling accentuated by the warmth of the fire and human companionship. Something bordering on a sensation of relaxed comfort was settling in.

"Taken off active duty," Bishop muttered to himself, still trying to sooth his damaged ego. "It breaks the heart."

Still, it was somewhat worrisome; he had been interrogated and questioned by people at the highest levels of the protectorate, even by the grand master of the Order himself, which was more than a little alarming. He had never even seen His Renowned Holiness before. There was the uneasy feeling of panic just below the surface for everyone he encountered during these discussions. He had even heard whispers to the effect that the fabled Sixth Age was at hand. If this was so, then the Great Houses seemed no closer to uniting than they were before Bishop crossed over into the Eligor Empire so many months ago. The protectorate seemed to be in a quiet state of shock, and the only noticeable difference between now and then was how polite everyone had become since his return. Even Bryn had sobered as more and more details were revealed about Bishop's adventures. The recovery of the key that now rested on Bishop's arm seemed central to the turmoil as there was hardly a meeting that didn't involve a hundred questions as to its function. Persons versed in the dark arts and Old Earth technology had examined the device with meticulous care, but it was in the vein of a rat examining the ordering of the stars and the planets.

Suddenly, a wisp of a shadow caught Bishop's attention.

"So, you've finally come back, I see."

"T-Frayja!" Bishop stuttered.

"You remembered my name. How thoughtful of you," she returned a bit dangerously while absently polishing an ale jack.

Bishop stared in momentary confusion at the frowning green-eyed barmaid. "Oh," he said. "Did we have a—"

"A date? To go for a picnic in the woodland? Meet me here on the twelfth of Yellowleaf? I was here. Where were you, my forgetful standard-bearer?" She tossed her curly ebon hair. "Perhaps I should have asked which *year*." Her eyes flashed in anger. "It's almost midwinter!"

"Frayja, I was called away suddenly. I had no way of contacting you. And besides, that must have been months ago." He dropped his eyes apologetically. "I'm sorry. Really, it's this dratted Order. Curse the day I was forced to join."

"I'm still traumatized, my dear Bishop," Frayja said as she set the ale jack down and absently brushed several crumbs off the serving board.

"Frayja, please, it was as I say: I was called away on a very important assignment. You really have no idea of the trouble I've been through. It was a long way from here, and—"

Frayja frowned, rolling her pretty green eyes. "Spare me and save your strength. I've heard it all before. I've heard it from the best, and I've heard it for the last time! Men, with their promises and their excuses for breaking their promises!"

And why are men driven to such things in the first place? Bishop thought darkly. He shook his head. "No, you don't understand. No. I was really on an assignment."

"For weeks and weeks? Months?!"

"Yes, I ... It ..." Bishop sighed. "Ah, nuts! Look, Frayja, I'm back now and back for good. Why don't you let me make it up to you?"

Frayja's eyes narrowed in suspicion as she played with an offending lock of hair. "How, exactly?"

"Well, speaking of picnics, I know of a secluded meadow in the forest that you would love. There are deer, flowers—"

"Oh, please! Don't insult my intelligence! It's the dead of winter outside. What are we to do, freeze to death in the dark?"

She was about to turn and leave. "Yes, right, well, you do like earrings?" Bishop quickly added, recalling one of the subtler ways to woo a female—bribery.

She stopped and turned as the faintest suggestion of a smile appeared on her young face.

"Yes, earrings," Bishop tumbled on. "And that's not all." A sudden presence drew his attention to the front door.

A courier—an initiate by the looks of him—had entered and was now stamping snow from his boots and scanning the smoke-filled room, his gaze finally settling on Bishop. The courier approached him, saluting smartly. "Sealed document tube from the Anwar Kili Chapter House for you, sir. The gatehouse guard said I would probably find you here." The courier saluted smartly again and stood at attention while melting snow dripped around him.

Sir?

Bishop grabbed the leather document tube and began removing the wax seal. "The Order again? What in the eight hells?" Would he ever be done with them?

"Sir," the courier said as he eyed the suddenly inquisitive Frayja, who was now leaning over the serving board. "Its label indicates that it is for your eyes only."

Bishop moved the tube away from her view, smiling apologetically as Frayja pouted playfully.

"Sign here, Standard-Bearer Bishop," the courier said.

"Sign? Gods of the Others!" Bishop frowned and scratched his name on the required form. The courier saluted again and left, a swirl of snow pouring through the open door before it shut behind him.

Bishop shivered.

"Probably a thank-you from the government for my heroic acts in service of the protectorate," he muttered half-heartedly, breaking the seal open. "Or just possibly it is a promotion. Yes, a promotion to sergeant, knight, or commander. That has to be it." *More like a summons from the camp cook to begin my new career peeling potatoes*, he thought darkly.

Bishop removed a strange document. It wasn't from the Order, nor did it even seem to be from the protectorate. The writing was spidery and stilted, as if the author had just recently learned to write Merja Sorian. Bishop unfolded the parchment and read:

> Friend Bishop,
>
> A strange event has recently occurred in a remote swampy area of our northeastern frontier. At 07:45 on 04, 4008FO, a blazing white orb was seen descending over the forests of the northern woods near the Stony Tunga River. As it plummeted downward, the shock wave leveled trees and partially smashed an Eligor outpost. When it landed—or detonated, rather—a thermal current tore through the area, igniting several forest fires. The destruction was massive, extending away from the site as far as five kilometers in every direction. The surviving observers related that a pillar of fire had climbed above the detonation site for a thousand meters.

The letter continued with descriptions of scientific measurements, theories, and plain old conjecture. Bishop read with growing concern, trying to assign meaning to the complex prose.

"By the Others, why don't you write me in language I can understand?" he mumbled. The letter continued:

> Now all of this could be explained away as a celestial event if it were not for the fact that the four teams sent to the area to find the cause have completely vanished with no explanation. Compounding our alarm, two days ago we lost contact with a large border garrison. A scouting party was sent to investigate and found that it had been totally

> destroyed. Not even the Ikonians could have so completely erased a garrison in a manner such as we found. There are now scattered reports filtering in that suggest whatever it is, it now seems to be on the move, testing our ability to defend ourselves against it before it attacks again. Our worst fears have been awakened as it seems that the very stars are against us.

"The *stars* are against us," Bishop muttered, frowning at the statement. He vaguely recalled the monolith at the entrance to the First Colony. Something about the stars had been inscribed on the ancient column.

He read the sentence again. "Our worst fears have been awakened as it seems the very stars are against us."

"Our worst fears have been awakened." Bishop suddenly broke out in a cold sweat, recalling the last, cryptic words of the Thunderbolt: "The others are awake, and they are coming." The letter shook in Bishop's stricken fingers. The others. The Others?

Bishop, attempting to regain his composure, continued to read the letter:

> The Grand Union of Opal has given me authority to ask for your assistance. Your government has been notified and seems overeager to volunteer your services again. I know of no one better suited for the task. Please come as soon as you are able, and don't forget Storm Singer.
>
> Kindest regards,
>
> Kiel, First Commander, Imperial Security Service of Opal

Bishop's mind spun as he slowly folded the letter, absently slipping it into his pocket. "No," he finally muttered in resolve. "It's an unrelated event. And even if it wasn't, I'm not going through it again, and that's final! Besides, Bryn would never send me after what I did the last time."

Bishop shook his head. "They will just have to get on without me this time! Storm Singer, yes. Bishop, no!"

"It wasn't a promotion?" Frayja asked.

Bishop's eyes refocused on Frayja. "Ah, no, not quite. I'm sure they will be waiting for me to return to active duty before giving me the promotion." Bishop settled down, grabbed the wine bottle, and drained it. "I need another bottle."

Frayja brought another bottle and uncorked it. "Now, what were we talking about?"

"You were promising me another picnic in the woods, but I have not accepted yet seeing that the woods will not likely thaw out for another five months." Frayja wiped absently at the serving board.

"If not a picnic, then how about a play? That's what we will do, all right, Frayja? Yes, a play and a dinner."

Frayja looked at Bishop with calculating eyes. "Well, I don't know."

"Please, I promise I'll be there, predictable as the seasons," Bishop cajoled. "I have also fallen into a bit of prosperity. Why, I'll be able to provide you with anything you want."

The massive diamond that Thirty-Six had given him at their parting was now resting safely five feet under an oak tree, unbeknownst to anyone, including those of the Order. It was real wealth, but Bishop was not yet ready to divulge the true extent of his fortune because he was sure Frayja would claim rights to every copper rider if he were to do so. A ghostly vision of an enormous house filled with earrings and the latest fashions, with the horses and barn still lingering in the distant future like a carrot dangling on a stick in front of a plow horse, filled his mind. He was not being greedy; he was being smart. After all, it was his hard-earned money, and he *was* going to share it, just equally. Women were inconceivably complex and possibly much smarter than he had ever realized, until now. He was, he admitted, a very slow learner by comparison. Wait, were all men this slow-witted by comparison? Possibly. It was a sobering revelation.

Frayja harrumphed, yet her eyes had become meditative. "Prosperity, you say? And if I say yes, what is to keep you from sliding out of it again?"

"You have my solemn promise. I'm not going anywhere for a long time—a long time."

"Well, if you truly promise," Frayja began. "But if you go back on your word again, so help me—"

The fluttering of feathers brought Frayja up short. Bishop, too, turned, just in time to see a black form fly through the open door of the inn and settle on his shoulder, shocking the man who had opened the door as much as it shocked Bishop.

Others in the tavern looked on in startled amazement as the wolf-bird began preening his jet-black feathers nonchalantly.

"Storm Singer! What in the eight hells are you doing here?" Bishop stammered, nearly tumbling off his stool, spilling wine down his front.

Storm Singer looked around the room and hissed softly, "Quick. Quick, human. We have new commands from the Order." The bird ruffled his feathers, causing droplets of cold water to fly all over Bishop's face. "Come along now. Come. We are to leave at once."

Bishop's eyes bulged in disbelief as he dried his face with the sleeve of his shirt. "It's impossible. Bryn nearly flayed me for—" Bishop, remembering that the bird didn't know about his reprimand, stopped himself. "Oh, ah, how is it that you know more than I do about … This wouldn't have anything to do with a letter from up north, would it?" He covertly jerked his thumb in the general direction of the Gondakar Barrier.

"You're leaving again?" Frayja had put the pieces together, and now there was imminent danger in her eyes.

"No, no, no," Bishop stammered. "It's not like that. I, ah, hell, in the name of the accursed Others!"

Storm Singer, taking in Frayja for the first time, interrupted Bishop's stuttering. "Bless me, what a charming creature you have found—and female too. I am surprised, what with your not knowing where eggs come from and all."

Storm Singer hopped onto Frayja's shoulder, and she instantly brightened. "A wolf-bird! What a lovely creature! Why, I've never seen one this close."

"Rare and wonderful, am I not?" Storm Singer gloated in a smug voice that sounded suspiciously like Bishop's as he puffed out his ebon throat feathers and spread his wings proudly.

"Storm Singer, this wouldn't have anything to do with a letter from—" Bishop began again in growing agitation.

"Yes, rare and wonderful," Storm Singer repeated in rapture, as Frayja began scratching his neck.

"*Storm Singer!*" Bishop bellowed.

www.ingramcontent.com/pod-product-compliance
Ingram Content Group UK Ltd.
Pitfield, Milton Keynes, MK11 3LW, UK
UKHW042208200825
7484UKWH00050B/104/J